Selected pr

GLORIA GOLDREICH

Leah's Journey
Winner of the National Jewish Book Award for Fiction

"An absorbing and often moving narrative, written
with sensitivity and compassion."
—*Publishers Weekly*

"Gloria Goldreich is a superb artist. *Leah's Journey*
is exciting reading, a wonderful book that is
hard to put down."
—*Columbus Dispatch*

"A blockbuster."
—*San Diego Evening Tribune*

Dinner with Anna Karenina
"A scintillating and magical visit to great literature
wrapped in the everyday realities of women's lives.
An extraordinary and impeccable keeper."
—*BookPage*

"*Dinner with Anna Karenina* is a mesmerizing book,
beautifully written, and a thoroughly fascinating read
from start to finish…a Perfect 10."
—*Romance Reviews Today*

"Goldreich writes perceptively and unflinchingly
about women and their concerns, large and small….
Those familiar with the authors discussed at the club
meetings will appreciate this book most, but others
should find it satisfying as well."
—*Romantic Times BOOKreviews*

open doors

GLORIA GOLDREICH

ISBN-13: 978-0-7783-2543-7
ISBN-10:   0-7783-2543-1

OPEN DOORS

www.MIRABooks.com

Printed in U.S.A.

For Alon Yoav and Koby Matan,
and for their grandfather, Sheldon Horowitz.

open doors

one

Her cell phone, programmed to the opening bars of Beethoven's "Ode to Joy," rang just as Elaine had reached a crucial moment in the coloring of a glaze and waited for the chemicals to meld. She was thinking, as she often did during the mindless moments when her work was merely technical, of the dinner she would prepare that night, luxuriating in the memory of the brightly hued produce she had carried home from the farmer's market. Thoughts of food always suffused her with an oddly lambent sensuality. She would imagine the shape and color of the vegetables, match them to color, shape and size, envision the pairing of disc-shaped carrots with tubular zucchini, the flash of bright-red bell peppers against slowly browning meat. It was, she supposed, a reaction against the hasty meals of her immigrant parents' home, the food purchased because it was cheap and prepared swiftly because time was money and the kitchen table was needed for the piecework that supplemented a meager income. She had substituted their indifference with her own creative concentration, a checkpoint of her Americanization.

Tonight, she thought, as the phone continued to ring and as she continued to ignore it, she would insert saffron-spiced rice into the scooped-out womb of the pale purple eggplant plucked with much exultation from her own vine. It was a dish that Neil especially liked.

Unlike their friends, other empty nesters who ate out often and filled their calendars with social engagements, she and Neil preferred their quiet dinners in the dinette that overlooked the garden. They reveled in the calm of their quiet home, in their soft exchanges, their easy silences. Their own music filled the book-lined living room during the calm predinner hour as he turned the pages of the newspaper and she caught up with *The New Yorker,* now and again reading an amusing bit aloud, inviting his laughter, his appreciation, as the aroma of the slowly simmering food drifted toward them. Even when their children were young, she would often serve them dinner first and she and Neil would eat their own meal later, savoring their togetherness, the small alcove transformed into an island of intimacy, isolated from the waves of activity that rose and ebbed in the other rooms of the large house.

She might make a soup tonight, she thought, and tried to remember what vegetables she had on hand but the continual ringing of the phone distracted her. She stirred the chemicals, lifted the jar of titanium oxide and briefly considered ignoring the call. Then, with a shrug, she set the jar down on her worktable. It was unlikely but it might be one of her children—perhaps Sarah, who could never clearly calculate the time difference, calling from Jerusalem, or Lisa fitting in a duty call between consultations and the reading of problematic X-rays. She discounted her sons, Peter and Denis. Caught up in their busy careers, they never called during the day.

Sighing, she plucked the phone out of her bag. The caller was probably Mimi Armstrong, the anxious gallery owner who had already phoned twice that morning, concerned about the shipment of tiles especially commissioned for an important client. Elaine had shipped the tiles ten days earlier and she had already given Mimi the tracking number. But she knew that if she did not take the call now, Mimi would surely call again. She wished now she had opted for one of those new phones that displayed the callers' number on the screen. Her son, Peter, who was addicted to technology, had been right. Such a feature would be useful for her as well as for Neil, whose patients often invaded his hard-earned privacy. Next week. She would get new phones for both of them next week, she thought as she pressed the talk button, not bothering to disguise the irritation in her voice.

"Elaine Gordon. And I hope this call is important."

"Elaine." Neil's voice, oddly faint, quivered as he spoke her name. "Elaine, I'm not feeling well. You'll have to pick me up at the office."

She looked at her watch. Eleven o'clock. That hour would be emblazoned on her memory for all the weeks and months to come. She glanced absently at the unfinished glaze, meant to be a deep cobalt, that she would not complete that morning and would never again try to replicate.

"But Neil, don't you have a patient now?"

Later the irrelevance of that question would haunt her but as she asked it, it seemed quite reasonable. In all the years that he had been in practice Neil had never cancelled an analytic hour and his eleven o'clocks were especially in demand. Women patients in the grip of depression, free-floating anxiety, distress, real or imagined (and Neil, sensitive psychoanalyst that he was, considered both equally important) were partial to that hour which, when completed, left them free to have lunch in the village, with hours to spare to think about the session before the onslaught of late-afternoon family life.

"I can't see a patient. I have a headache. A terrible headache." His voice was weaker still.

Responses flooded through her mind. *Take two aspirin. Lie down for a bit. Open the window. Maybe even go for a short walk.* She knew at once that any such suggestion would be foolish, absurd. Neil had never before, throughout their long years of marriage, complained of a headache. He was stoic about discomfort. His hardworking parents had had no time to spare for illness and he had clothed himself in their forbearance. He had never before asked Elaine to drive him home from his office. Always, even on the grimmest winter days, even when his arthritic knee caused him to limp, he had preferred the long walk from the town center to their home. This call, the desperation in his voice, meant that something was wrong, very wrong.

"I'll be there in a couple of minutes," she said, already unbuttoning her smock, surprised that her fingers trembled and that her heart was beating too rapidly. "Hang in there, sweetness, *zieskeit*." But he had hung up. Her endearment lingered in dead air space.

She rushed out of the studio then, pausing only to turn off her kiln and grab her soft oversize leather purse. It was late autumn and although an almost wintry chill tinged the air she did not stop at the house for her coat. She drove down their rural road at a reckless speed and accelerated as she reached the village, screeching to a halt outside the small building where Neil's shingle swayed against the impact of a sudden wind. She had supposed that he would be waiting outside but it was his secretary, pale overweight Lizzie Simmons, who leaned against the front door, the spongy flesh of her face gelled now into a quivering anxious mask.

"Oh, Elaine. Thank God. I wanted to call an ambulance but he wanted to wait for you. I did call the hospital though. Take him straight through to Emergency, they said." Her words tumbled over each other, her voice high-pitched.

"Lizzie, what are you talking about? He told me he had a headache, just a headache." Elaine spat the words out as she raced into the building, furious with this woman who had a flair for the dramatic, a penchant for darkness.

Lizzie lumbered in behind her, breathless, her voice almost a shriek now.

"More than a headache, he said. An explosion, his head was exploding, he said. Call the hospital, he said."

But Elaine was no longer listening. She was in Neil's consulting room, kneeling beside her husband who lay on the leather couch, his hands pressed against his head. His fine-featured face was porcelain white, his agate-blue eyes were bright with pain. Drops of perspiration beaded his high forehead, dampened the irrepressible lick of silver hair that fell across it.

"Neil, Neil, what is it?"

"I'm not sure." That same quiver in his voice, that same faintness as though he could barely give breath to the words that she had heard on the phone. "A terrible pressure, pain at the back of my head. All of a sudden."

"Can you get up? Can you walk?"

"Yes. I think so."

Slowly he brought his hands down, wincing as he used them to bring himself into a seated position and then held them out to her. She took them, pulled him gently to his feet.

"Help us, Lizzie," she said, no longer angry with the woman who loved her husband and feared for him as she herself did.

And Lizzie stood behind him, supported his back and slowly, slowly, thrust him forward. Somehow then, they managed to walk him through the door, down the path. It was Lizzie who settled him into the car, affixed his seat belt with a maternal solicitude and firmly closed the door. Elaine saw her through the rearview mirror as she drove away. Absurdly, Lizzie waved in the manner of mothers who linger after a school bus has departed and even more absurdly, Elaine waved back.

She sped down Cedar Street, past Oak, toward the small village hospital where her two younger children had been born and where her husband's name was affixed to an office door on the small corridor reserved for psychiatric care. She herself had designed the plaque, ivory white, each letter etched in jet. *Dr. Neil Gordon*. But Dr. Neil Gordon sat motionless beside her and Elaine, driving more carefully now, dared not look at him, fearful that he had stopped breathing, that he, whose body had been warm against her own that very morning, was dead.

He was not dead. She heard the labored rhythm of his breath and said his name again and again, willing him into consciousness.

"Neil. Neil. My darling. My *zieskeit*." She did not realize that she was weeping until she braked the car at the emergency room entrance and their friend Jack Newnham, the director of emergency medicine, opened her door and gently wiped her face with his stiff white handkerchief. Swiftly, two orderlies hefted Neil onto a waiting gurney and rushed him into the building.

"Easy, Elaine. He'll be fine," Jack said and she nodded, although she did not believe him. She was a doctor's wife and familiar with such false assurances.

The small emergency room was crowded; the usual midmorning patients filled the molded orange plastic seats. Elaine's eyes skittered from the weeping golden-haired boy who had perhaps fallen from a playground slide and sat on the lap of his Filipino nanny, to the harried young woman holding a bloodied bandage to her finger and then to a muttering old woman in a bathrobe seated beside her elegantly dressed, much annoyed blond daughter. But Neil's gurney had disappeared.

"Where's Neil?" she asked Jack who approached her then and her own voice, shrill with terror, sounded like that of a stranger.

"I've had him taken upstairs. I want to get an MRI before we do anything else. I just need you to fill out the paperwork, Elaine, to sign the release. Just routine red tape. Can you do that?"

Jack placed his hand on her shoulder, an awkward comforter. He and Neil had been classmates at medical school and then had been surprised to rediscover each other on staff at this small northern Westchester hospital. Several times a year the Gordons and the Newnhams had dinner together and Claire Newnham made a point of buying Elaine's ceramics whenever she had to give a wedding gift. Jack and Neil occasionally met for a hurried meal in the hospital cafeteria. Neil was more than a patient or a colleague to Jack. He was a friend. Jack would do everything he could for him. They could rely on Jack. He would keep his friend alive. Elaine seized upon this, newly calmed.

"Of course," she said. Obediently she took the clipboard and, with deft strokes of the pen, gave Neil's date of birth, his allergies, his relatively uncomplicated medical history, listed their insurance carriers and then signed her name on the lines indicating next of kin. She hated the ominous sound of those three words and when she was done, she closed her eyes against them and handed the form back to the nurse.

"Dr. Newnham asked that you wait for him in his office," the nurse said, her voice icy with disapproval. "He has a conference this afternoon," she added accusingly.

Elaine shrugged and followed her down the hall. Nurses, she knew, resented doctors' wives, resented any interference with hospital routine.

"Did he…did Dr. Newnham say how long it would be?" she asked.

"He didn't say. It depends on the radiology schedule but in the case of an emergency…" Her voice trailed off and she blushed as though she had already said too much.

Elaine sank into the chair opposite Jack's desk and glanced at her watch. Only a quarter to twelve. Only three quarters of an hour had passed since Neil's call. Could that be right? She tried to figure out what time it would be in Jerusalem, nine at night or perhaps ten. Sarah's children would be asleep, Sarah herself would be busy at her drawing table or bent over her account books. Her thoughts raced to her other children. It was morning in Santa Fe. Denis would just be leaving for court or for his office. Morning, too, in Encino but Peter, hard-driving ambitious Peter, would already be at his desk, placing calls, taking calls, doing deals. Lisa in Philadelphia would just be leaving her office for her health club. Treadmill and a smoothie sandwiched in between consults—that was Lisa's lunch break. Of course she could reach each of her children if she had to—just as Neil had reached her. This was the age of the cell phone, everyone instantly accessible, lives tethered together without even a wired connection. But there was no need to call them, not yet, not until Jack Newnham returned to report the results of the MRI and tell her what that omnipotent machine had discerned when it trained its magnetic beam on her husband's brain.

She glanced again at her watch. Too soon. Much too soon. Jack would not have any news for at least an hour, perhaps even two. She sighed, picked up a magazine, scanned its pages unseeingly and dropped it onto her lap. Scabs of the white clay she had been working with that morning clung like snowy teardrops to her gray skirt and she scratched at them, allowing the granules to fall to the floor. She used Jack's small private bathroom, tucked her red sweater into the waistband of the skirt and then pulled it out again. What difference did it make how she looked? she thought irritably. Still, almost instinctively, she brushed her thick hair with punishing strokes.

She studied her face in the mirror, frowned at its soft roundness, her too-small nose buried between the rise of cheeks grown too fleshy with age, her mouth too wide, her hazel eyes dulled with worry beneath the thick dark eyebrows. Her hair, unlike Neil's, had barely silvered with age; it fell to her shoulders in a thick mane of irrepressible dark curls. Neil would not let her cut it. He loved her curls, he said. He claimed that he had fallen in love with them, seated behind her in a World Lit. survey course their freshman year at college even before she turned her head and their eyes met for the first time. She did not dispute his claim. She knew that she had fallen in love with him the moment he had smiled that shy tentative smile and told her his name, his voice so soft in that crowded room that she had to strain to hear it.

She washed her face, applied fresh powder and then washed it off. Neil hated her in makeup, hated the scent of cosmetics.

"Oh, Neil." She said his name aloud, looked at her watch. Still too early for Jack to return. She returned to the office and closed her eyes, willing herself to calm.

At last Jack Newnham entered, walking so softly in the rubber-soled shoes that were requisite footwear for peripatetic doctors that she did not hear him approach. She remembered suddenly that Neil often joked that he had chosen psychiatry because it was a sedentary calling and he could wear the elegantly crafted Italian loafers that were his one extravagance. She fought against an inexplicable wave of hysterical laughter. Still, she looked up at Jack, suddenly hopeful. His relatively swift return could only mean good news. There had been no laborious analysis, no repeat imaging. She smiled to indicate her readiness, her gratitude.

He pulled up a chair and sat opposite her, cupping his chin in his very large hands.

"There's no easy way to tell you this, Elaine," he said

slowly. "But the news is not good. Neil has an aneurysm, very near the base of his brain. It's what we call a berry aneurysm, a clustered swelling just where the artery branches out."

She gripped the arms of the chair but kept her voice as measured as his own.

"An aneurysm," she repeated, the word heavy upon her tongue.

It belonged to a lexicon to which she laid no claim. But of course she knew vaguely what an aneurysm was, had absently listened to discussions of surgeries that vanquished the threat. Casual dinner conversations among surgeons, trading OR triumphs and new techniques, exchanging professional war stories over glasses of white wine. Isolated phrases fluttered through mind and memory. *Zapped that damn aneurysm. It was in a tricky spot but we got it… They're using lasers on aneurysms now—interesting stuff.*

"But you can operate. Surely you can operate. Laser surgery." She retrieved the word from the detritus of half-remembered discussions.

She leaned forward, willing him to agree but instead he shook his head and absently scratched at a scarab of blood that had adhered to his white coat.

"No. It's inoperable," he said at last. "The radiologist, Stan Price, agrees. I asked Harv Bernstein from neurology to do a consult but I'm fairly certain Stan and I are right."

Harv. Stan. The old boys' club of nicknames and complacency, the specialists who were summoned from dinner parties and commencement ceremonies for their opinions, bravely and honestly and often irritably offered. They were the dispensers of truth, the oracles of hope or despair. Harv Bernstein had bad breath and his daughter was into drugs. Such knowledge, Elaine thought, would invalidate his judgment. She would not rely on a man whom she did not like. She would insist on another opinion, a neurologist from the city, someone from Columbia or NYU. Someone with sweet breath and well-adjusted kids.

"You'll want to call your children," Jack said miserably. "There's enough time, I think, for all of them to get here."

"Enough time?" she asked witheringly. Did he think that he had the final say, that she would surrender Neil to his death sentence so easily, so unquestioningly? She would fight, of course she would fight. There would be world enough and time. It was Neil they were talking about. Her Neil. Heart of her heart. Her love. Her husband lover. Her *zieskeit*, the endearment inherited from his mother. "He's *mein zieskeit*, my sweetness," the tiny hunched woman had told her. "And mine, too," Elaine had replied and taken his mother's work-worn hand into her own, a tactile promise never broken. She would treasure him and care for him. She would not allow him to go gentle into that evil night. Damn Jack. Damn Stan. Damn their stupid MRI machines rushing his life away. She would turn time into their ally, not their enemy.

"Elaine, an aneurysm can leak at any time. Call your children. Please. That's what Neil would want. That's what they would want." Jack's tone was firm, reasonable. The hardest part of his job was over, the terrible news had been delivered and now damage control could begin.

She sat very still although color rushed to her face and her hands closed into fists. At last she reached into her bag and took out her cell phone.

"I'll call Lisa," she said, not vanquished but compromised. "In Philadelphia."

"Please," he said and pushed his own phone toward her.

She dialed Lisa's number. The phone rang once, twice, three times. Lisa, like Elaine, hated the cell phone, resisted its intrusion and yet, like her mother, she would not let it ring unheeded.

"Dr. Gordon."

How Neil smiled when he heard his daughter say *Dr. Gordon.* "At least have the courtesy to call yourself Dr. Gordon the Second," he had playfully admonished her.

Elaine breathed deeply, spoke quietly.

"Lisa, Dad's not feeling well. I'm here with Jack Newnham. He'll speak to you."

Jack Newnham nodded and took the phone. Calmly, with professional economy, he discussed the technical findings. Elaine heard the words *centimeter, cerebellum, cerebral,* an alliterative confluence. Hemorrhage, he said and colors flooded Elaine's mind. Scarlet, crimson, burgundy. All the varied and terrible shades of blood. She was an artist and she thought in color. She shook her head, banishing the invading images. Jack was listening now.

"Sure," he said. "Absolutely. Wait. I'll put her on. And Lisa. I'm sorry. So sorry, but you know that."

He handed the receiver back to Elaine. Again, her daughter's voice, brisk and confident. She was leaving in a few minutes. There wouldn't be much traffic. She would be at the hospital in two, two-and-a-half hours. Jack had arranged for her to review the MRI. She, too, thought it would be a good idea for Elaine to call Denis and Peter. She would call Sarah in Jerusalem herself.

"But maybe we should wait to call Sarah," Elaine protested although she was secretly glad that Lisa sounded so decisive. "There are other specialists we could call. Other opinions."

"Of course," Lisa said. "We'll do everything. But we have to let the others know. Peter, Denis, Sarah." She repeated her siblings' names as though they formed a mantra.

"Get something to eat, Mom. Take it easy. I'll be there soon, very soon."

She clicked off and Elaine sat holding the receiver as though it were an alien object whose purpose she could not comprehend. Jack Newnham took it from her and gently replaced it.

"I want to see him. I want to see Neil," she said, her voice broken at last.

"He's heavily sedated but I'll take you to him. Of course I will."

He took her hand and led her from the room and down the corridor past the young woman who still cradled her bloodied hand, although now her eyes were closed.

Neil was in a private room on the third floor, the blinds on the large windows so tightly drawn that not even a splinter of light penetrated. He lay beneath a heavy white coverlet, motionless; his long arms, poking through the wings of the blue-and-white hospital gown, were almost rigid. It seemed to Elaine that his face, always narrow, had grown suddenly gaunt as though the pressure of the pain, even in so brief a period, had already diminished him. But his eyes were open and he smiled thinly as she took his hand in her own and bent her head to pass her lips across his upturned palm.

"My wedding ring," he said weakly. "They took it off. I want my wedding ring."

Elaine turned to Jack and wordlessly he took the ring and Neil's watch from his pocket.

"Everything had to be removed for the imaging," he said.

"Yes. Of course."

Elaine held the watch to her ear and then dropped it into her bag. Neil lived by his watch, his days measured out in fifty-minute hours, always punctual, always glancing at the Roman numerals on the face of the time-piece for assurance and reassurance. He had been well trained. His mother, that tiny Yiddish-speaking woman, had always kept her eyes on the clock as she rushed from job to job, sewing seams during the day, cutting patterns at night, every hour another dollar toward her son's tuition, his diploma. His father worked double shifts in a stocking factory, arriving early, leaving late, scavenging minutes to riffle through the Yiddish paper. The watch was his gift to Neil at his medical school graduation, his last gift as it turned out, because two weeks later he died of a massive heart attack and a month later, Neil's mother, too, was dead of a mysterious blood disease. It had occurred to Elaine, who had loved them both, that they had managed, with great effort, to stay alive until their son's future was assured.

Neil would not need the watch until he had recovered and he did not ask for it. She would keep it with her, the sound of its ticking reminiscent of the faint beat of his heart in the stillness of their long-shared nights during their long-shared years. The ring, the wide gold band inscribed in Hebrew with the words from *The Song of Songs,* "I am my beloved's and my beloved is mine," she slipped onto his finger just as she had slipped it on all those years ago as they stood beneath the marriage canopy. The rabbi, the bearded orthodox officiant chosen by Neil's parents, had disapproved of a double-ring ceremony but she had not cared. The ring had slipped on easily and she had whispered the words as she whispered them now in this hospital room. "I am my beloved's and my beloved is mine."

"How do you feel, darling?" she asked, as she gently brushed that silver shock of hair from his forehead.

"Better," he said. "But sleepy. Very sleepy."

"Then go to sleep. I'll be right here."

He closed his eyes, held her hand tightly for a moment, the ring cutting into her flesh, and then released it. His breath was measured, his face relaxed.

"I can stay here, Jack?" she asked, recognizing her new role. She was a supplicant who had to submit to the rules of this small monarchy of healers.

He nodded.

"Of course. Can I send someone up with some coffee, a sandwich, for you?"

She shook her head.

"All right then. I'll be back when Lisa comes."

"Yes. And Jack…"

He paused at the door.

"Elaine?"

"Thank you. You've been very kind."

The initial shock over, she had recovered her persona. She was, as always, a courteous woman, conscious of the kindness of others. Neil slept, she herself dozed off, waking to accept a cup of coffee and a sandwich from a chubby Candy Striper, flushed with the opportunity to do good.

"I hope your husband will be all right," the girl said.

"Oh, he will be, he will be," Elaine assured her.

Her own words comforted her. And Neil, still asleep, did look better. The color had returned to his face and pain no longer contorted his features. She adjusted the coverlet and made a mental note to bring a blanket from home. And pajamas. And his shaving gear. A radio or perhaps his small CD player. Neil needed his music as other men needed food and drink. She rummaged in her bag for a piece of paper, a pen, and made a list. The normalcy of the task calmed her. She was an organized woman, a maker of lists, a completer of projects.

She was still writing, the list having expanded to include books and bedside delicacies, when Lisa entered the room, grave-eyed and unsmiling, tall beautiful Lisa, her shining dark hair helmeting her head, a silk scarf in the russet-and-golden hues of autumn caping the chocolate-brown cashmere sweater that exactly matched the long skirt that fell to the tops of her tan suede boots.

"Mom." Lisa kissed her cheek.

Her daughter's lips were moist against Elaine's dry cheek. Her eyes, the startling blue inherited from her father, were red-rimmed and Elaine knew at once that she had been crying. She drew Lisa toward her in a fierce embrace and held her close.

"Everything will be all right," she murmured, reassuring her daughter, reassuring herself.

Lisa would know what to do, whom to call. Her medical school classmates were in the vanguard of New York's most respected young practitioners, their names appearing regularly in the magazine features Neil had always derided—"The City's Hundred Best Doctors," "Doctors' Doctors," "Physicians in the Know." She needed the best doctor available, a doctor's doctor, a physician in the know and she could rely on her daughter to snare an immediate appointment, an immediate bedside visit. Doctors did that for each other, she knew.

"You look tired, Lisa," she said. "There must have been terrible traffic. It never takes you this long to drive from Philly."

"Actually, I've been at the hospital for a while. I went over the imaging—you know, the MRI—and I met with Stan Price and Dr. Bernstein."

She walked over to her father's bed, lightly touched his hair, passed her finger across his brow.

He stirred but did not waken.

"They're only local doctors," Elaine said. "I want you to call in specialists from New York, maybe one of your colleagues at Penn."

"They're very good doctors," Lisa replied. "Both of them. And I agree with their diagnosis. I wish I didn't but, Mom, the MRI doesn't lie. Dad's condition is serious, very serious."

"No. We'll get another opinion. We'll move him to another medical center. Hopkins. Presbyterian. The Mayo Clinic." Elaine plucked names from memory, a random assortment of medical meccas, and shot them at her daughter, verbal bullets of hope.

"There's no point." Lisa's tone was dead. She did not argue. She stated facts. "There's nothing we can do. I spoke to Sandy—I mean Sarah." The Hebrew name her twin now used still eluded Lisa, even after so many years. "She and Moshe are making arrangements. They should be here sometime late tomorrow. Did you call Peter, Denis?"

"No." Elaine felt guilty, angered by the sudden reversal of their roles. She had been negligent, her daughter conscientious. "I thought I would wait till you got here, until we arranged to get another opinion, until we saw a top specialist."

She would not so easily give up hope. She would be in this, as she was in all things, tenacious. There were things she could do. There were always things that could be done. Passivity was the enemy. She looked at Lisa, willing her to agree but her daughter's face remained frozen into a mask of grief.

"We can get one if it would make you feel better. But there's no point. Honestly, there's no point." Lisa's voice broke and she leaned over to kiss her father's cheek. Her lipstick left a tiny coral crescent on his pallid skin.

"I'll call Peter and Denis," she said and, too swiftly, left the room.

Elaine knew that her daughter did not want her to see that she was weeping. Lisa was the child who had closed the door of her bedroom, shutting them out of her childhood sorrows, her adolescent pain. Always, she had been intensely private and Elaine and Neil, ever tolerant, ever understanding, ever protective of their own privacy, had not invaded those emotional perimeters. Their children had their own way of coping and she and Neil had allowed them that independence. They themselves had lived always in the shadows of their parents' whispered worries, swift to abate fears that could not be articulated. Their own sons and daughters would be free of such burdens.

"Elaine."

Neil was awake and she rushed to his side, lifted his hand, kissed it, smiled at him, grateful that her own eyes were dry.

"Feeling better now?" she asked.

"Sort of. What did they say? What do they think?"

"What do you think?"

He shrugged.

"A brain tumor maybe. Possibly an aneurysm. It will be all right." He winced with pain even as he reassured her. "What did Jack tell you?"

"He spoke to Lisa. She's here now."

"Good. Good. I'm hungry. At least I think I'm hungry. Send Lisa in and see about getting the patient some nourishment." He forced a grin and waved her out of the room.

Lisa stood in the hallway carefully applying powder to mask her swollen eyes, the tear tracks on her cheeks.

"Denis and Peter will be here first thing in the morning," she told her mother and, planting a smile on her face, went in to see her father.

Lisa would not lie to him, Elaine knew. Her daughter never lied. Wearily, she directed her steps to the hospital cafeteria. Neil was partial to their grilled cheese, she knew.

two

Peter, having caught the red-eye from L.A, was at the door with his family at daybreak the next morning. It startled Elaine, bleary-eyed after the long night at the hospital and the few hours of restless sleep at home, that Peter's wife Lauren and his small son and daughter, Renée and Eric, accompanied him. Their presence alarmed and disconcerted her. But, of course, Lisa had described Neil's prognosis with no holds barred. She kissed her blond daughter-in-law's cool cheek and embraced her exhausted grandchildren. She noted that Eric closely resembled Neil; her husband's bright blue eyes stared up at her from the child's face.

An hour later Denis and his partner Andrew arrived. Tall Denis, lean as always, newly returned from a visit to

Andrew's family in Jamaica where the island sun had burnished his very smooth skin and lightened the tangled curls of his chestnut-brown hair, held Elaine in brief embrace. Andrew held out his hand, fumbled for the appropriate words.

"I am so sorry," he said. "This must be so hard for you."

His words, delivered in the lilting accent of his island, were, after all, ill chosen. Elaine withdrew her hand.

"Actually, it's Neil we worry about," she replied and immediately regretted her tone. Andrew, she knew, was uneasy enough with their family, conscious of being a "person of color," as he was described in the short bios offered in the high-end glossy journals that carried his photographs, conscious of being a non-Jew in the heart of a Jewish family, even a family as casual about their Jewishness as the Gordons.

Andrew, for all his talent and grace, would not have been their choice as Denis's lifelong partner, Elaine and Neil had sadly acknowledged, just as it would not have been their choice for Denis to be gay. It pleased them, they assured each other, that Denis was happy with Andrew, and it was incumbent upon them to accept their relationship. And they had, welcoming Denis and Andrew into their home, traveling out to Santa Fe to visit them, always remembering Andrew's birthday as they remembered Lauren's and Moshe's. Their in-law children were swept into the circle of caring and concern, albeit long-distance caring and concern. Denis lived his own life, made his own choices. All that concerned them was his happiness. Their children had full sovereignty over their lives. This they repeated again and again, to others and to themselves. That repetition assuaged the lingering sadness that overtook them in the darkness of the night or, inexplicably, when they stood at their window and stared out at a pale and melancholy wintry sunset.

Their friends admired their attitude, but then Elaine and Neil had long been much admired. It was agreed by friends and acquaintances alike that they had it all. They were successful in their careers, sealed in the cocoon of their insular togetherness, an inseparable, enmeshed couple content with each other and the life they had built so carefully.

"It was good of you to come, Andrew," Elaine added, quick to apologize. She pressed her hand to his cheek, glad to feel the smoothness of his skin against her palm. The night had been long and lonely. She was unused to sleeping without the tenderness of touch.

"Of course I came. How could I not be with Denis at a time like this?"

She averted her eyes. She did not want to think of what he meant by "a time like this."

Lisa flew down the stairs just then and hugged her brothers, smiled at Lauren whom she did not like, held her hand out to Andrew whom she did like and kissed her niece and nephew.

"I have to run. I'm going out to Kennedy to pick up Sarah and Moshe. They caught the last flight out of Ben Gurion last night," she said, pulling on her driving gloves.

"They were able to make arrangements for all those children so quickly?" Lauren asked in surprise. "It would take me hours to get people to do that for Renée and Eric and I'd probably have to beg my friends or pay someone the earth. I can't imagine getting coverage for four children just like that."

"In that community, it's apparently the norm for people to take care of each other," Lisa said coolly. She herself might criticize her twin's community and lifestyle but she resented the disparaging disbelief in Lauren's voice. "The last time I was at Sandy's—Sarah's, I mean—she had three other children staying with her because their mother was sick. And according to her it was no big deal. Anyway, I'm off. We'll see you at the hospital, Mom." She draped an arm briefly and protectively around Elaine's shoulder, kissed her on the cheek, made the requisite funny face at her niece and nephew and dashed out.

Minutes later, Elaine and her sons left for the hospital, Andrew staying behind to help Lauren with the children who had reached the whining stage of fatigue.

Neil was asleep when they entered his hospital room. The shades had been drawn against the sunlight and in the dimness his face was chalk white but his breathing was even, almost rhythmic. Two transparent IV lines dripped clear solutions into his motionless arms. A thin catheter dangled, discreetly concealed by a sheet. She dropped a kiss on his forehead and he seemed to smile but he did not open his eyes.

"Dad." Peter's voice quivered.

"He doesn't hear you, Peter," Elaine said gently. "He's on a morphine drip which induces a very deep sleep."

That much had been explained to her before she left the hospital the previous evening.

"Just routine," Jack Newnham had said and Elaine had decided that Jack was overly fond of the word *routine*.

Denis took his father's hand, stroked his fingers one by one. His eyes grew moist; tears glistened on his sunbronzed cheeks and Elaine fumbled for a tissue and wiped them away as though he were still a small boy rather than the tall lean man whose deep voice resonated through courtrooms.

"He looks so frail," Denis said in bewilderment.

He and Peter looked at each other, their expressions stricken as though betrayed. Their father, that strong wise man who had never been ill, had never complained of even the most minor discomfort, ignoring the slight arthritis of his knee, the very occasional shortness of breath, their father who had raced with them into the surf on seaside vacations and who played tennis still with astounding grace and vigor, was not supposed to look so weak, so pale, so powerless. He was not supposed to die.

"But he'll wake up?" Peter asked. He needed his father to awaken. He needed to hear his calm voice, to see the twinkle of wisdom in the bright blue of his eyes. There were questions he had to ask him, advice that only his father could give. He had thought to phone him for weeks now, to ask those questions, to seek that advice, but the rush of his days, the damn time difference between the two coasts had prevented that. And now this. He buried his head in his hands. Unlike Denis, tears did not come easily to him.

"He'll wake up," Elaine replied, speaking with an assurance she did not really feel.

Denis and Peter sat on either side of their father's bed, Peter, always ready to spring into action sitting erect, Denis's head lowered to the white coverlet. As though sensing his son's presence, Neil's hand rested briefly on Denis's head. Denis had always been his favorite, Elaine knew. He was their last-born, a sensitive child, graceful and athletic with Neil's own gift for solitude and analytic thinking. He was a thoughtful and persuasive arguer and it had not surprised them that he decided on law even after flirting briefly with psychology. Elaine remembered still, Neil's words when Denis had disclosed his homosexuality to them.

"Are you sad?" she had asked her husband, her own heart torn with a grief she would not express. She had turned away so that he would not read the sorrow in her eyes and clasped her hands so that he would not see how her fingers trembled.

"I'm sad that we won't see another small Denis," he had said and he had wept then as his son wept now.

Elaine sighed and went to the window. She lifted the shade and allowed the deceptive harsh sunlight of late autumn to flood the room. Peering down, she saw Jack Newnham's car pull into the parking lot reserved for physicians, taking a spot next to her own car—that was a privilege soon to be surrendered she thought wryly. Doctors' widows could not expect a parking spot. *"Widow,"* she whispered, rolling the word back and forth across her tongue as though tasting it. She saw Jack stop and speak to another doctor—Harv Bernstein, the neurologist who had examined Neil the previous day, who had spoken to her softly, sympathetically but had not met her eyes.

"I wish there was more we could do," he had said.

More? You haven't done a damn thing! She had wanted to scream but she had remained silent, the quiescent wife who now depended on the kindness of doctors and nurses, technicians and aides, the ministrations of strangers.

She pulled a chair up next to Peter, caressed his hand, as though she could somehow pat away his sorrow, and glanced at her watch. It took a quarter of an hour for Jack and Harv Bernstein to tap tentatively on the door and to enter the room, diffident visitors despite the authority vested in them. They shook hands with Denis and with Peter. Harv touched her shoulder, Jack, more daringly, kissed her on the cheek. They both studied Neil's chart.

"No change," Harv said. "Which is all we can hope for at this point. He's resting comfortably."

"How do you know?" she asked harshly and immediately regretted her words.

Jack looked stricken, Harv uncomfortable and Peter turned away in embarrassment. Denis, the skilled mediator, intervened in the conciliating tone cultivated for dealing with recalcitrant clients.

"We know you're doing everything possible," he said.

"And we want to thank you. I wonder if you can give us some idea of what to expect."

The two doctors looked at each other.

"Perhaps we could have this discussion when your sisters get here," Jack Newnham said hesitantly. "Lisa has a very clear understanding of your father's condition. A great deal of her radiology work, in fact, is now focused on the brain. She had an excellent paper published in a journal not long ago which dealt with aneurysms."

"I didn't know that," Elaine said fretfully.

She should have known, she supposed, but her children's professional lives, their accomplishments, had for a long time been shadowy terrain. She and Neil had their own work, their own shared good life. They were not parents who lived vicariously through their children and preened themselves on their successes. They loved their sons and daughters, they were proud of them, and that had always seemed to suffice. Her eyes flitted from Peter to Denis and Denis took her hand in his own and held it tightly.

"Neil knew it. He sent me an offprint," Harv said. "You can be sure that he would rely on Lisa's judgment."

"I am sure of that," Elaine said. "And I want to thank you. I'm just sort of strung out."

"Of course you are." Harv's voice softened and Elaine felt more kindly toward him, remembering his difficulties with his own daughter, knowing that he would never be able to rely on her judgment.

The two doctors, Neil's friends, Neil's colleagues, left

then, again carefully shaking hands with Peter and Denis and smiling sadly, apologetically at Elaine.

A parade of nurses and technicians followed, competent caregivers who nodded at them in sympathy and did their work swiftly and skillfully. The IV drips were monitored and changed, the catheter dealt with, Neil's pulse taken, a droplet of blood drawn from his finger. Peter went down to the cafeteria and returned with coffee which they drank and bagels which they did not eat. They heard the click of high heels on the polished floor, the sound of voices so similar in range and cadence that they could not be distinguished one from the other.

Sarah and Lisa entered the room, talking quietly. The twin sisters did not look alike but they shared the same musical voice, spoke in the same light tone. That identical rise and fall, that sameness of inflection, had once caused their brothers to tease them and now it caused them to smile.

They embraced, the brothers taking in Sarah's full figure, her face sorrowful yet strangely serene, her marriage wig fashioned into the smooth ponytail they remembered from her high school and college days, her years as a cheerleader when the ponytail had bobbed up and down, when it had tumbled out of her cap after a varsity swim meet. But this ponytail was stiff, restrained by a tortoise-shell clip that would never be removed from the synthetic locks. Sarah, who as a girl, then called Sandy, (the name Sarah had been used only at her baby naming and at her bat mitzvah) had favored miniskirts, brightly colored body-hugging tops,

40   GLORIA GOLDREICH

backless loafers in wild jungle colors, now wore a long denim skirt, a heavy, loose white sweater that concealed the curves of her body, the rise of her breasts, sneakers and white socks. But she was beautiful still and her presence brought a new peace into the room.

"How is he?" she asked and approached her father's bed.

"The same," Elaine said wearily. "How was your flight?" She touched her daughter's brow, a gesture borrowed from Neil who could discern fatigue, a raised temperature, the onset of flu, by a touch of his fingertips.

"Like all El Al flights, horrible," Sarah said. "But we landed safely and I'm here, *baruch HaShem*. Blessed be His name."

Her eyes did not leave her father's face and Elaine realized that it had been over a year since Sarah had seen him. She and Neil had talked about going to Jerusalem again, but something had always intervened. She had several commissions to complete—the new terra-cotta formula she was using had sparked a sudden popularity; Neil had been asked to contribute a chapter to an important new medical text. And of course there were their subscriptions—the opera, the symphony, an interesting series of plays at the Roundabout. And so they had put off the trip to Israel, just as they had put off the journeys west to visit Denis and Andrew, Peter and his family, reluctant to leave their work, to surrender their time together, the quiet of their home in the evening hours, the welcoming darkness of their bedroom. And now they would never make those journeys. She would be a solitary traveler, a solitary visitor. Regret tightened about her heart like a vise.

Sarah kissed her father's cheek. Her lips moved in prayer. Neil's eyes opened. He smiled at her.

"All this way? You came all this way?" There was wonderment in his voice. He looked at his children who moved closer to him, at Elaine, who fingered that lick of silver hair, silken to her touch. "You're all here? Peter, Denis, Lisa. All of you. Elaine, isn't that wonderful?"

"Wonderful," she agreed. She marveled that she could bring forth voice. "Of course we're all here. We love you, Neil."

She spoke for all of them because her sons, even Peter, were openly weeping now and Lisa clutched Sarah's hand, her face contorted. But Sarah's expression did not change. Her lips moved in prayer, the softly spoken Hebrew falling in wisps of sound through the silence of their sorrow.

"Neil, how do you feel?" Elaine asked.

"Tired. Very, very tired," he replied.

His eyelids fluttered briefly and then closed. He lay very still.

Lisa lifted his wrist, placed her ear against his heart, lifted the phone and spoke softly into it. A nurse glided into the room and handed Lisa a mirror, a stethoscope. She listened to her father's heart and shook her head. She held the mirror to her father's mouth, his nose, and returned it to the nurse.

"He's gone," she said. "Daddy's gone." Her voice broke and she stepped into Peter's outstretched arms.

"*Baruch dayan emet*, blessed is the true judge," Sarah said softly. She touched her father's head. "*Shma Yisrael*, hear Oh

Israel, the Lord is our God, the Lord is one." She intoned the prayer uttered before death which Neil might or might not have murmured had he been given the time.

Elaine knelt beside the bed. She kissed her husband's lips and slid her hands, one last time, across the smooth familiar flesh of his body.

"Zieskeit," she said. "Oh, my *zieskeit.*"

His eyes were open and she closed them; the lids were soft, soft and quiescent beneath her tender touch. She could not bear that softness. Her grief broke forth then, a cascade of sorrow. She trembled, her heart pounded, her face crumbled.

"Neil!" she screamed. "Neil!"

Her children surrounded her, encircled her and slowly, slowly, led her from the room.

three

They observed *shiva*, the seven days of mourning, together, the house filled from morning till night with visitors, friends and relatives, neighbors, members of the synagogue, all of them carrying offerings, large white bakery boxes tied with thin strips of string, casseroles, fruit platters and baskets filled with gourmet food as though the mourners could eat their way out of their grief. The freezer and the refrigerator were crammed full and cartons of food were driven to the neighborhood food pantry but each day more trays arrived.

Three days after the funeral Andrew flew back to Santa Fe. He had a deadline to meet, a shoot for *National Geographic* of desert wildflowers, but they knew that he felt uneasy as he was introduced again and again as "Andrew, a very good friend"—a convenient but ineffective code. Smiles were too broad, guarded glances too knowing.

Two days later Lauren flew back to L.A. with the children. Eric and Renée could not miss any more school, she told them. There were standardized tests coming up. It was Lisa who noted that Lauren did not look at Peter as she offered her excuse.

Moshe took an early flight back to Israel on the Thursday morning. He wanted to be with his children for Shabbat, he told them regretfully, holding Sarah's hands in his own. They nodded, believing him, because Sarah's red-bearded, soft-voiced husband had never uttered an untruth. He lived by the words he studied, by the prayers he murmured. Tall Moshe (once called Mike) had found his way into the Chassidic world by way of UC Berkeley and a trek through Thailand and, like Sarah, had never looked back. And so on that Sunday morning, on the very last of the prescribed days of mourning, Elaine and her four children were alone in the house they had all called home for so many years, where they had lived as a united family, their bonds as yet unsevered by distances, marriages and conflicting life choices. They sat on the low stools of mourners but at noon, according to custom, they rose and shrugged into their winter jackets. Elaine opened the front door and they felt the welcome breath of the autumn wind on their faces. Slowly then, Elaine walking between her two tall sons, Lisa and Sarah holding hands, they made the ritual circuit around the block, demonstrating that they had rejoined the world, that their family was bereft but intact. A passing car slowed, the woman driver stared out the window, as though bemused by their small procession. Few people walked on this quiet road. Elaine waved and the car sped away. They continued their circuit and then, their pace newly slowed, they returned to the house.

The scent of mourning, of contained sorrow, permeated the living room. The memorial candle, designed to burn for thirty days, emitted the odor of burning wax which co-mingled with the necrotic aroma of withering flowers. The air was heavy with the lingering odors left by the parade of visitors, a confluence of perspiration and perfume, soaps and gels. Elaine thrust open the windows and Sarah and Lisa tossed the dying flowers into a huge black plastic bag. Denis plugged in the vacuum and Peter hauled the kitchen garbage out to the trash cans. The sisters and brothers worked in concert, the distant days of their adolescence when they had argued over such chores, barely remembered.

"Don't bother being too thorough," Elaine protested mildly. "I'll call the cleaning service tomorrow. Right now I want to go to the supermarket. I want to cook us a good dinner tonight."

Resolutely, she knotted a tie around a single trash bag and thrust it aside.

"Mom, the freezer is crammed with food and the re-frigerator, too," Lisa protested.

"I know. But I want to make dinner tonight. I don't think we have to eat sympathy offerings."

She was determined. She wanted to cook for her

children, to fill the house with the remembered scents of their childhoods, chicken slowly roasting in the oven, a fragrant soup simmering on the stove, the sweetness of cinnamon and brown sugar caramelizing on baking apples. After the week of eating meals prepared by others, served on paper plates, and nodding dutifully, appreciatively, at endless expressions of condolence, she wanted her home restored to normalcy. She wanted to sit at her properly set dining room table with her four children, to set their favorite foods before them, to listen to their talk, their laughter, their privacy as a family restored, Neil's very absence a presence.

"All right. Whatever you want," Lisa said wearily.

She looked at her sister, at her brothers. They knew that there was no point in arguing with their mother. They understood that they could not counter her energy, her fierce determination.

"Your mother is not a woman who is easily dissuaded," their father had said wryly more than once.

They watched as she drove away and Sarah went into the kitchen and put up a pot of coffee. Denis set out cheese and brown bread and rummaged through the refrigerator in search of kosher cheese for Sarah and the rolls that came from the only bakery in the area certified kosher by the rabbinate. They all sat around the kitchen table, the brothers and sisters together for the first time in years. It was Peter who commented on it.

"It's funny for it to be just the four of us," he said. "No mates, no children."

"No significant others," Denis added. He was thinking of Andrew but he turned to Lisa.

"You and the guy from Washington still an item?" he asked.

"David. His name is David. Yes. We're still together if you can call my living in Philadelphia and his living in Washington real togetherness. Still, we're okay with it, though. He would have been at the funeral or at least the *shiva* but he's in Europe trailing after some senator."

She looked at her twin. She knew that Sarah, who would not even shake hands with a man other than her brothers or her husband, who concealed her body beneath shapeless garments and went to the ritual bath each month to insure the purity of her marriage, did not approve of her relationship with David. But that was all right. She, after all, did not approve of Sarah's life, of the way she covered her bright hair with that stupid wig, to say nothing of having one child after another. Sarah already had four children and was now in the first trimester of her fifth pregnancy. Lisa contained her anger at the way Sarah submitted to the overwhelming pressure of her family's demands and worked herself into exhaustion at the home-based business she ran so that Moshe could continue to study. Sarah, in turn, in quiet truce, tolerated her relationship with David. And it was only Sarah after all, who knew why Lisa lived as she did. Lisa's secret was safe with her twin.

"I'm sure David was sorry not to be with you," Sarah said, her tone, as always, serene and nonjudgmental.

Lisa smiled gratefully.

She poured the coffee into the brightly colored mugs of Elaine's own design. Their mother had crafted a special mug for each of her children, carefully mixing each glaze and applying it to the clay in different colors and fusions. Peter's was fire-engine red, Denis's a deep blue, Sarah's sunshine yellow and Lisa's a gentle lime. Their father's mug, larger than their own, was chocolate brown and it hung beside Elaine's own smaller coral-colored one on the wrought-iron holder in the breakfast nook.

What would their mother do with that mug? Denis wondered and he realized that he wanted it. He wanted to carry it back to New Mexico as a gift for Andrew. He even thought of what he would say when he held it out to him.

"My mother wanted you to have this."

It would signify Elaine's unqualified acceptance of his relationship with Andrew, as opposed to the controlled tolerance, the requisite political correctness, she and his father had always maintained. But Neil's cup, he knew, would remain in place.

"What will Mom do now?" Peter gave voice to the question that had nagged at each of them during the long week.

"I don't imagine she'll do anything for a while. Nothing dramatic, that is. She has her work. I'm sure she'll go on with that. Her work has always been important to her. Her work and Daddy," Lisa said. "The cornerstones of her life."

Sarah looked sharply at her twin. She wondered if Lisa was even aware of the bitterness in her voice.

"I'm worried about how she'll cope," Sarah spoke hesitantly. "Keeping up the house, dealing with the bills, her day-to-day life." She hesitated and then added, "The loneliness."

"She won't have any financial worries." Denis was in his attorney mode and Peter added sugar to his coffee that he really did not want.

Denis was the executor of their father's will, of course, a choice that had been discussed with Peter. He had agreed with his father that it made sense. Denis, after all, was an attorney who handled wills and estates on a daily basis. He understood the laws, the various shelters available, the changes in inheritance policy from year to year. And he would have the time to deal with anything that might arise while Peter's family was his priority. Neil had discussed the situation with his usual sensitivity. He had been a careful and responsible man and he did not want his other children to resent his choice of Denis. His arguments had been cogent and neither Peter nor his sisters had raised any objection. Denis, Peter knew, would be fair and honest, competent and knowledgeable and yet he could not deny that he had felt a familiar twinge of resentment. He had felt slighted during his father's life because he had always sensed that Denis was his favorite, the last-born child, the son who had inherited Neil's own love of music and athletic grace. He felt that slight anew, in the gathering shadow of his father's death. He had lost any chance of ever being the chosen one, the favored son.

"So Mom is in good shape?" Lisa asked.

"Dad lived carefully, invested wisely. He made separate and equal bequests to each of us, generous bequests, but basically the estate was left to Mom as well as the house and everything else. It's standard practice and I agreed with it," Denis replied. "I'll have my office send each of you the paperwork involved."

"That's all right then," Sarah said. "I think what we're all really worried about is how Mom is going to live her life. She's pretty isolated out here. And she and Dad were so incredibly close, so different from other couples. All they seemed to need these last few years was each other."

"All they ever seemed to need was each other. And their work." Lisa's tone was edged with a thin anger.

Denis went to the window. The leaves of the red maple were slowly falling; wind-tossed, they drifted through the air and formed brittle scarlet hillocks on the tall grass of the lawn. He thought of how Andrew's camera would capture them in midflight and wished himself back in Santa Fe, at a remove from Lisa's petulance, Peter's moody silence and Sarah's piety.

They sat around the table in silence for a few minutes. Lisa was right, they knew. Their parents had always been locked into a passionate togetherness. Their mother's face had burst into brightness when their father entered a room. Their father had spoken her name with tenderness; his hand had rested lightly on her shoulder as they walked down their rural road each evening. Often they had returned from those walks, their faces wreathed in smiles, cradling the first flowers of spring or the glorious foliage of early autumn which they placed in low bowls and tall vases to be set on tables and windowsills, on kitchen counters and bedroom bureaus. They spoke softly as they worked and called to each other as they wandered from room to room.

"Neil."

"Elaine."

"In the living room."

"In the dining room."

Behind closed bedroom doors, pens poised over note-books, their sons and daughters smiled, pleased and embarrassed by their parents' love.

Those loving reassurances of proximity resonated anew in their children's memory, reminding them that now their mother would be alone in this large house on an isolated road, with no one to call to as evening drifted into night.

"She'll feel the emptiness. As soon as we leave to-morrow, she'll feel it," Sarah said and they knew that she was right.

"We'll talk to her. There are things she can do," Lisa said.

Her brief anger had melted. The past, that shadowy era of pleasure and pain, was done with. All scores in the blame game had been settled. She had schooled herself to focus on the future, on days and years to come, on what was yet to be. Her mother would do the same. Lisa did not fear for her, not for that strong determined woman who saw beauty everywhere and created it where she could. Breathlessly, she thrust forth her ideas.

"She might want to rent a small apartment in the city, a kind of pied-à-terre. Near the museums and galleries. And there are all sorts of trips. She and Dad could never really travel because of his patient schedule, but she'll be able to do that now. You know I'm planning to adopt a child from Russia and I'll have to go there. She could come with me."

"And of course she could plan to visit us," Sarah added. "She hasn't been to Israel for a long time. It would be wonderful if she came to us for Pesach."

She did not add that by Passover, her pregnancy, now in its very first weeks, would be advanced. She had not told her mother or her brothers about the new baby. Of course, Lisa, ever the observant physician, watching her twin undress in their girlhood bedroom had scrutinized the barely perceptible thickness of her waist, the dark aureoles of her nipples and had known at once.

"Sandy—Sarah, how wonderful," she had said, but Sarah knew that her sister, so carefully groomed, her body so determinedly toned and slender, did not think it wonderful at all. Pregnancy, with good reason, frightened Lisa although neither of them ever spoke of what had ignited that fear all those years ago. She was unsurprised then, that Lisa chose that moment to tell her that she planned to adopt a child, that she had already begun the process, choosing an agency with Russian connections.

"And David, what does he say about the adoption?" she had asked quietly.

Lisa's long-term, long-distance relationship with David

mystified Sarah. David, a power broker, a partner in a public relations agency that could make or break political candidates, had once visited their Jerusalem home during a pre-election junket. Long divorced, the father of two children, the handsome, graying man, his craggy face softened by an unfamiliar wistfulness, had observed Sarah and Moshe's life, shared a noisy dinner and laughed at their children's antics. Later he had walked alone with Moshe and told him how fortunate he was in his marriage. Lisa, he had said, staring out into the Judean hills, was so different from Sarah, so proud of her independence, her career.

"He would want things to be different for them," Moshe had told her later. "But he doesn't want to pressure her."

Sarah had not doubted her husband's insight nor his wisdom. She had not doubted Moshe from the moment of their first meeting. He would welcome her mother if she came to Jerusalem and it might well be that Lisa and her David would visit as well. The idea comforted her and she folded her hands across the gentle rise of her abdomen.

"Mom's never spent more than two or three days with us." Peter kept his tone casual. He did not want to echo Lisa's resentment. "If she stayed in Encino for a while she'd get to know my kids, get to understand my life."

He did not add that his life had grown uncomfortably complicated. He had, for weeks, thought of talking to his father about those complications. Stupidly, mired in cowardice, he had waited, and now there would be no one to guide him through the emotional maze in which he found himself lost. He was angry with his father for dying, angry with his mother for her long absence from his life and he was angry at himself for the irrationality of that anger.

"They came to Santa Fe together exactly once," Denis said moodily. "Just after Andrew and I built the house. One visit in all those years and it wasn't exactly comfortable. It was easier when Dad came alone, which he did a couple of times, although I'm sure he wasn't too happy about my life."

They looked away. They understood the discomfort, the unease of that lone parental visit, Denis sleeping with Andrew, their mother and father in the neighboring guest room, all of them striving to pretend that the situation was acceptable, normal because, after all, Neil and Elaine were modern, enlightened people. Always they had prided themselves on their nonjudgmental acceptance of their children's lifestyles. Sarah's embrace of an ultra-orthodox lifestyle, Lisa's determination to remain single, Peter's move to California and his early marriage had all been met with the same carefully muted reaction. *If that's what you really want, if you've really thought it through.* The parental mantra that rang hollow, that denied disappointment and attendant sadness.

Denis's situation must have presented greater difficulty, they knew. But neither Peter nor his sisters had discussed their brother's homosexuality with their parents and their own conversations about it had been oblique and evasive.

As long as he's happy, Lisa and Peter had each said guardedly. They were part of contemporary culture, sensitive to changing mores, to political correctness. They had gay friends, gay colleagues. Their brother was part of a large and recognized community.

It makes me sad, Sarah had confided. She did not speak of the constraints of her religious belief, of Torahitic restrictions. She spoke only of what she saw as the emotional deficit in her youngest brother's life. No children to carry on the tradition of their people, no younger generation to inherit Denis's keen mind, his lean visage, the heavy dark brows and thick curling hair so like their mother's. No one to say *Kaddish* for him. She felt similarly about Lisa but perhaps Lisa would eventually marry and if she did not at least there would be the child she was adopting, a child who would be brought up as a Jew. Lisa had assured her of that much. But for Denis, her baby brother, there were no such possibilities.

"We'll talk to Mom tonight, after dinner," Lisa said. She spoke with the authority and certainty she brought to her work, the authority and certainty that had brought venture capital into the radiology labs she had established throughout Philadelphia and that attracted and retained the small army of doctors, nurses and technicians who worked for her.

They nodded. Lisa would find the persuasive words, the firm approach.

Elaine returned and they helped her unload the car. The brown paper sacks overflowed with produce from the farmer's market—huge apples, slender stalks of asparagus which Denis had always favored, full-flowered broccoli for Lisa and Sarah who, as girls, ate the vegetable raw, jicama which Peter had proudly introduced them to. All their favorite foods, they realized, as their mother placed plump Cornish hens and packets of phyllo dough, wild rice and lentils on the kitchen table.

"Now get out of here and let me cook," she said in that impatient tone they remembered from their childhood.

It was Lisa who had observed that Elaine concentrated on her cooking in much the same way that she concentrated on her ceramics, completely absorbed, handling each utensil with respect and skill, regulating the heat of the oven with as much concern as she regulated the heat of her kiln. She focused on each task. Surely, she would focus on reconstructing her life. Her strength invigorated them. The purposefulness and grace of her movements as she reached for cutting board and knives, as she filled a large pot with water, her face flushed, her eyes bright, diluted their fears.

And so they scattered, Lisa and Sarah up the stairs to their bedroom to pack, Peter and Denis out to the backyard where Peter found their old basketball in the garage and they played one-on-one, leaping wildly to drop the ball into the basket that their father had affixed to a tall sheltering oak and which he had never dismantled. Neil had taught his sons to dribble, to shoot with grace and accuracy, skills he himself had acquired late in life. His immigrant father, stooped and weak-eyed from long hours of piecework, had never touched a basketball, in all likelihood had never even seen one.

The brothers played in silence and with great seriousness, each well-aimed shot a tribute of a kind to their father. Just so he had taught them to run, to stretch, to reach. Exhausted at last, they sank into the Adirondack chairs, not yet stored for the winter because Neil and Elaine had often sat outside, even in late autumn, to watch a flock of Canada geese scissor their way through the slowly darkening sky.

"Sarah's right," Denis said. "The next couple of months are going to be really tough on Mom."

"Yup. Loren's dad, Herb, you remember him—he's been in a real depression since Lauren's mom died and it's been almost five years." Peter bent to pluck up a fallen branch. His mother would have to get a couple of maintenance guys in to take care of the property that his father had patrolled with such pride.

"I think women are more resilient than men," Denis replied.

"And how would you know?" Peter asked and immediately regretted his words.

"Oh, guys like me know quite a lot about women," Denis replied easily. "Women trust us more than they do other women, and much more than they trust straight men."

The brothers laughed then and went upstairs to do their packing.

In their girlhood bedroom, Lisa and Sarah sprawled across the twin beds still covered with the spreads in the bright blue Druze design which Sarah had brought back from her first trip to Israel.

"Did I ever tell you that I hated those spreads?" Lisa asked teasingly.

"No. And did I ever tell you that I couldn't stand that Bob Dylan poster you hung over the desk?" Sarah retorted, pointing to the singer's picture, faded within its lucite frame.

"We're even then. Sandy—Sarah—do you really think Mom will be all right?"

Sarah shrugged and went to the window. Always, she had loved that view of their garden. A huge oak grew just below their bedroom, the seasons marked by its out-stretched branches. Barren and sere in winter, they knew that the tender unfurling green leaves meant the onset of spring. Now the heart-shaped leaves fell in showers of gold and russet as summer's greenery surrendered to the chill winds of encroaching fall. Sarah studied the foliage as though she would commit it to memory. Autumn did not come to Jerusalem. The heat of summer plummeted, without easement, into the punishing cold of winter. She loved the life she had chosen but she missed the seasons of her childhood, she missed her sister and brothers, she missed her mother and now, and forever, she would miss her father. Weighted by sadness she opened the window, breathed in the cold fresh air and, very gently, closed it again.

But Lisa was staring at her, waiting for an answer. *Would their mother be all right?* She turned from the window and idly lifted a small glass bird from her bedside table. Once she had collected such miniatures. It startled her that her mother had kept so many of them, but then their girl-hoods, hers and Lisa's, were enshrined in this room with its faded posters and dusty college pennants.

"I don't think it will be easy, but she'll manage. I'm going to try to persuade her to come to Israel. She could teach a master class in ceramics at the Bezalel Art Academy, spend time with the children, help me with my designs."

Sarah sighed at the thought of the pile of orders for the long gowns favored by the women of her community she had left in her Jerusalem workroom. Her fabric designs were popular and the demand for them kept her family economically afloat. Moshe helped, of course, but it had been understood when they married that he was a student, that he would always devote himself to Torah study. It would be wonderful if she and her mother could work together, a childhood dream fulfilled.

"Honestly, Sarah, do you think she'd find it soothing to chase after your kids?" Lisa asked harshly. "Actually, I think she might enjoy coming to Russia with me when my adoption plans are finalized. We could spend some time at The Hermitage, tour St. Petersburg."

Lisa's voice drifted off and the sisters looked at each other and smiled ruefully.

"There we go again," Sarah said. "Back to elementary school. Fighting over Mommy. Will she go to your dance program or my violin recital? Will she take us shopping together and, if not, which one will she take first? Will she come to me in Jerusalem or go with you to Russia? We'll have to talk about it tonight at dinner. Peter and Denis have their own ideas, I'm sure. But Lisa, we're too old to worry about sharing her."

"Well, we were born into it," Lisa said. "We probably fought each other for priority in her womb. Too bad she never even wanted to be shared. It was always Daddy who had exclusive claim to her. She and Daddy locked together in the center of an enchanted circle, the four of us dancing about them. I remember how we kids ate our wonderfully well-balanced meals promptly at six and then watched as she set the table with candles and wineglasses for the not-so-well-balanced dinners she and Dad shared when he came home. Hugs, smiles, kisses and then we were shooed upstairs and they sat and talked, their voices so soft we could hardly hear them even when we sneaked down and stood in the doorway. Is that how it is with you and Moshe?"

"No," Sarah replied gravely. "We always have dinner with the children."

She reached for her sister's hand. She understood how it had felt to stand always on the periphery of their parents' impenetrable intimacy. Fingers clasped, the sisters made their way downstairs and joined their brothers in the dining room.

Elaine had changed for dinner, choosing a soft wool dress of brightest blue, twisting her thick dark hair into a loose bun, her color high, the long silver earrings Neil had bought her in Santa Fe gracefully dangling. The table was set as she had set it each Friday night of their childhoods, the only night when the family had had dinner together. The polished silver glinted, the crystal glassware sparkled, the golden glazed dishes of Elaine's own design were circlets of sun on the woven sky-blue cloth. The siblings smiled at each other. Even in the simple act of setting a table, their mother was an artist, her aesthetic instinct flawless. And the dinner, of course, was delicious, the hens roasted to perfection, the casserole of rice and lentils delicately flavored, the pale green asparagus offset by the bright verdancy of the blanched broccoli. They sat in the seats that had been theirs in childhood, the brothers facing the sisters, Elaine smiling down at them from the head of the table, all their eyes averted from their father's empty chair.

Elaine pointed to the bottle of wine.

"Will you pour, Peter?" she asked. Their father's task, now assigned to his eldest son.

They stared down at their glasses. It had been Neil's habit to offer a toast at such family dinners—wishes for a good Sabbath, words of pride to signify a graduation, a marriage, a celebration of achievement or simply a celebration of their togetherness in this room, at this table. Silence threatened them now and they were relieved when Denis stood and lifted his glass.

"To our family," he said softly.

"To our family."

They spoke in unison, nodded and sipped the golden liquid.

"Terrific wine, Mom," Lisa said.

"Your father's favorite," she replied. "Golan wine. He ordered a case. A case."

Her voice trailed off. A case. Who would drink that case of wine? She imagined herself sitting down to a table set for one, filling a single glass. A woman drinking alone in an empty house. Her fingers trembled as she lifted the wine to her lips and set it down without a single sip.

Her children looked away from her, looked uneasily at each other. Sarah nodded at Lisa who emptied her glass, refilled it and turned to Elaine.

"Mom, I know it's awfully early to talk about this, but have you thought about what you want to do now?"

Elaine stared at her, as though the words had been spoken in a language she could not comprehend.

"Now?" she repeated in the dangerous tone they recognized—hot anger coated with icy calm, the sarcastic whip of maternal disappointment, rare yet painfully familiar. "Now. Now that your father is dead? Now, when his clothes are still hanging in the closet. Now, when we sit down at this table for the first time without him?" Her eyes flashed toward the empty chair, the unset place at the head of the table. "It's a question that might have waited, don't you think?"

"Mom, don't take it like that." Denis, the youngest, the acknowledged favorite, the child who could do no wrong, always gentle, always tender, perhaps too gentle, perhaps too tender, rose from his seat and went to his mother, placed his hand on her shoulder. "We're talking about it now because it's our last night together. We all take off tomorrow and we're worried about you. Except for Lisa, we're all so far away and we want to know how you'll manage. We love you. We want to take care of you."

"I can take care of myself." The harshness of her tone startled her, shocked her children. She saw their faces blanch, their eyes glint, sorrowful and bewildered. But she could not staunch the rush of words, the outpouring of an anger left latent during the week of mourning, the days of loss. "I have my home. I have my work. I have my life. The rest of my life. Don't worry. I won't be a burden to you— not to any of you."

Their voices rose in a flood of protest.

"You misunderstood. How could you think that?" Gentle Sarah, her serenity shaken, gripped her mother's hand. "We want you to be part of our lives. This is the time for you to turn to us, for us to rely on you. We want you to be with us. We understood that you couldn't travel to see us when Dad was bound by his patient schedule but now—now," (bravely she repeated the dangerous word, the word that had so offended and yet could not be substituted for any other), "you have the leisure to spend time with us, to travel to Jerusalem, to California, to Santa Fe."

"Russia. Mom, you could come with me to Russia when I go there to get the baby I'm adopting. We've never traveled together. This would be our chance."

Sarah heard the plea in Lisa's voice and her heart broke for her sister who would be alone with her loss and her grief. As their mother would be alone. Lisa, at least, had colleagues and, of course, her snatched weekends and holidays with David, the lover who appeared and disappeared at will. But her mother's work was solitary and independent. Her heart grew heavy at the thought of Elaine preparing meals to be eaten in solitude, listening alone to the music once shared, wandering through the large empty house that overflowed with memories but was shrouded in silence.

Sarah longed suddenly for the clamor of her Jerusalem home, the giddy laughter and mild quarrels of her children, Moshe's gentle voice, the neighbors rushing in and out, their anger, their laughter, their concerns exploding about her, at once engaging and invigorating. She and Moshe were part of a community, unlike her parents who had cherished a privacy that excluded all others, even, she recognized wearily but without bitterness, their own children.

"How could you imagine that we would think of you as a burden?" Peter asked miserably.

"I'm sorry," Elaine said. "I'm just tired. So tired."

She sat very still and they saw at once that her anger had dissipated into a sorrow that she could not control. They understood that nothing they could say would comfort her but Lisa, courageous, determined Lisa, did not easily surrender.

"You may even find that you'll want to live closer to one of us," she said gently.

"We'll see. It's too early to think about that." Her voice was flat but tears drifted down her cheeks and she lifted the sky-blue linen napkin to her eyes. She had been sad during the week of mourning but this was the first time they had seen her weep.

They sat for a few minutes in uneasy silence and then Sarah went into the kitchen and set the warming baked apples on a serving dish. They ate the cinnamon-flavored dessert, their favorite, their father's favorite, slowly, as though its taste would restore their childhood to them.

"I make this for the kids almost every Shabbat," Sarah said, "but it never tastes as good as yours, Mom."

"Andrew likes it with brown sugar but I stick to the cinnamon," Denis said.

"My kids won't eat anything brown. Not potatoes, not brown rice, not baked apple." Ruefully, Peter helped himself to another serving.

The lives they had so abruptly abandoned in the wake of their father's too swift illness and death, reclaimed them now. Their thoughts centered on their homes in distant cities where the impact of their father's death could be assimilated and where their own grief would not be subsumed by their mother's overwhelming loss. The telephone rang. David calling Lisa. She spoke, softly, briefly and returned to the table, her cheeks flushed.

Elaine smiled.

"The recipe was your grandmother's," she said. "Your father's mother."

They nodded, reassured. The sweetness on their tongues was a legacy, a guarantor of continuity. Their grandmother's recipe now prepared in their own kitchens.

"Remember, Mom, we're always there for you," Denis said.

"I know that. Of course, I know that."

Her anger, inexplicable and unjust, had vanished.

They cleared the table together, carefully dealing with

the leftovers, loading the dishwasher, straightening the chairs and restoring the dining room to an order that they knew would not be disturbed for weeks to come.

There was nothing more to say. Elaine went into the living room and sat in the half darkness. They kissed her good-night, their lips soft against her cheek and went upstairs, willing themselves not to think of their mother staring across the dimly lit room at their father's chair, the mystery novel he had never finished reading still on the small table beside it.

"I can't bear to leave her," Lisa said softly to Sarah, as they undressed. "But I can't bear to be with her."

"I know."

Silently then, the sisters lay down on the narrow beds of their shared girlhood and Lisa listened as Sarah whispered her prayers into the darkness.

The family parted the next morning, in a confusion of hugs and promises, searches for misplaced tickets and last-minute phone calls. Denis and Peter shared a cab to La-Guardia and Lisa drove back to Philadelphia. Elaine insisted on driving Sarah to Kennedy.

"Are you sure you want to make the trip back alone?" Sarah asked worriedly and immediately regretted her words.

But Elaine only smiled.

"I'll have to get used to doing a lot of things alone," she replied and Sarah nodded.

They embraced at the El Al departure gate.

"Mom, please come to Jerusalem soon," Sarah pleaded, struggling against the onset of her tears.

"We'll see," Elaine replied. "We have time."

Time, she realized, as she drove slowly northward on the sun-spangled highway, was something that she would have in excess over the weeks and months to come.

four

Lists. List upon list. Elaine bought a yellow legal pad because she found the light blue lines reassuring and marked each line with a number. Unflinchingly, she specified each day's task, her eyes dry but her heart heavy. Still, her hands did not tremble as she recorded all that had to be done. Each numbered entry, each check of completion meant that she had her life, her new and bewildering life, under control.

"I'm fine," she assured Lisa who called regularly. "I'm getting things organized. There is a lot to do but really, I don't need any help. I can manage."

Lisa did not insist. She would not invade the intimacy of her mother's final leave-taking and she knew that she could not bear to touch her father's things.

The logistics of death, the disposals and cancellations, the forms and formalities, filled Elaine with a helpless fury but her lists gave her ballast. She would do what had to be done. She had not lied to her daughter. She could manage. She would manage. After all, she had no choice.

She wept as she discarded Neil's toothbrush, his straight razor, his comb and brush. She pressed a dollop of his shaving cream onto her hand and then onto her cheek, oddly comforted by the familiar odor. She wiped it off with one of his initialed handkerchiefs, a birthday gift from Lisa, and tucked the linen square into her pocket, removing it now and again so that she might press it to her lips.

Day after day she packed Neil's possessions into cartons, marking each one carefully. His winter clothes for Big Brothers. His tuxedo and dress shirts for the synagogue thrift shop. His shoes, each pair neatly boxed, because he had been a careful man, went to Goodwill along with the contents of his sock drawer. She closed that carton carefully, remembering the beauty of his feet, the curve of the arches, the long tapering toes. She smiled at the memory of how, during the early days of their marriage, she had massaged them gently, an intimate and private prelude to their lovemaking.

Neither of them had known any measure of privacy in their childhoods. She and Neil had grown up in small apartments, sleeping on living room sofas, doing their homework on kitchen tables. They had granted their immigrant parents absolute access to their lives. They had pleased them with their excellent grades, their practical choices. They told them where they were going, when they would return home. Their mothers and fathers had lived with so much uncertainty, so much anxiety, that they, Neil and Elaine, dutiful son, dutiful daughter, spared them any further worry. But they had determined, in that first rush of marital independence, that they would not repeat that intrusive pattern. Their children's lives would be their own. Even now she would not intrude upon her sons and daughters. She would not ask them to help her dispense with the remnants of their father's life. That was her job, her responsibility.

Pajamas and underwear filled black plastic bags which she carried to charity bins in the supermarket parking lot, waiting patiently as each bag shot its way down the chute. That final thud reassured her. She had done her duty and stood sentinel over the last vestige of Neil's most intimate garments. She transported his winter coats and jackets to a homeless shelter in a distant suburb. She would not want to see a vagrant wandering through her own town wearing his camel's hair coat, his red-and-black quilted shirt, his heavy olive drab jacket.

She wrote thank-you notes to the friends and relatives who had attended the funeral, visited during the mourning period and sent messages of condolence. Lisa had urged her to use printed cards.

"That's not my style," Elaine had replied.

She composed each note carefully, struggling to find the graceful phrase, to exercise the control that was so important to her, although too often she sat with her pen poised over the blank sheet of monogrammed stationery.

She cancelled subscriptions, writing polite letters to the various psychoanalytic journals, to the obscure quarterlies and *The Economist,* wondering if it was necessary to tell them that Dr. Neil Gordon had died or if it was enough to simply tell them that they should remove his name from their rosters. She puzzled over their opera and theater schedules, so carefully selected, so eagerly anticipated, and decided, at last, that she would keep those tickets. She would invite friends to accompany her. That, of course, was what women without partners did. They joined forces with other women, established coalitions of the solitary. She wondered, as she fingered the rainbow-colored sets of tickets, who might join her at the Met, who might sit next to her at the Roundabout Theatre. There was Serena Goldstein, a college friend who had been widowed the previous year. Perhaps she could ask Mimi Armstrong, the newly divorced gallery owner with whom she worked. Audrey, a neighbor whose husband was often away on business. They would meet for dinner, attractive, well-dressed women who lived their lives without men.

Elaine sighed, wearied suddenly by the thought of the new relationships she would have to nurture, the new role she would have to play.

"I am a widow," she said aloud and the word hung clumsily on her tongue.

She worked with Lizzie Simmons, Neil's longtime secretary, in his office, clearing up what Lizzie referred to as "his affairs." Lizzie spoke slowly and moved swiftly, her eyes red-rimmed, her lank brown hair pulled into a bun. When

Neil was alive Lizzie had worn it loose and her fleshy face had always been carefully made up, her pale lashes stiffened with mascara, bright scarves at her mottled throat. She had dressed each morning for "her doctor," the man whose day she arranged, whose lunch she ordered, whose phone calls she screened. She had been his office wife and, like Elaine, she, too, was widowed. Elaine wondered if Lizzie, like herself, wakened in the night and wondered if it was true that Neil had died. Did Lizzie come into the office and expect to find "her doctor" seated behind his desk as Elaine expected to find him sleeping beside her in the bed they had shared for so many years?

It startled her that Neil's professional life could be disposed of as swiftly and effortlessly as his toothbrush and his clothing. A young psychiatrist took over the lease of his office and bought the furnishings, the brown leather couch with its matching chair, the mahogany desk, the bookshelves. She and Lizzie packed his books into cartons. Sarah had arranged for them to be shipped to Israel where they would be donated to a private library.

"They'll put a plaque up with Dad's name," Sarah had said. "The Doctor Neil Gordon Library. I'll feel that I have part of Daddy in Jerusalem and they really need the books."

"Fine." Elaine had not hesitated. It was what Neil would have wanted and it pleased her to think that Sarah's children could go to that library and see their grandfather's name, that they might slide their small hands across the leather-bound volumes that he had treasured.

It was Lizzie who had taken care of the final bookkeeping chores and informed patients and former patients of Neil's death. Together, she and Elaine had gone through files and arranged for the storage of records that had to be preserved. They worked, for two weeks, in a companionable silence and when, at last, they had finished, they stood together in the early evening dimness of late autumn and wordlessly acknowledged that their work was done. Neil's presence had vanished from the room that had been his world for so many years.

"Is there anything that you would want, Lizzie?" Elaine asked and she was surprised when Lizzie pointed to the ceramic nameplate of Elaine's own design. She had etched Neil's name in gold upon the earth-toned glaze and it had rested on his desk from his very first day in practice.

An odd choice, Elaine thought, but she nodded and handed it to Lizzie, along with an envelope that contained a generous check. She and Lizzie would not see each other again, she knew. With Neil's death came other small deaths, the withering of friendships, the fading of voices once familiar, phone calls unanswered, invitations unreciprocated.

They placed the office keys on the reception desk and left together. Neither of them wanted to hand them to the young psychiatrist who would sit in Neil's chair and stare through the window at the birch tree that Neil had loved.

They did not embrace but shook hands solemnly, sadly, and it shamed Elaine that tears glistened on Lizzie's cheeks although she herself was dry-eyed. That night she looked at her legal pad and carefully ripped her lists into shreds.

★ ★ ★

"Everything is taken care of," she told Denis when he called. "I'm going back to the studio tomorrow."

"It will be good for you to get back to work," her son said and she heard the relief in his voice. He would call his brother and his sisters and tell them that Mom was fine, that she was adjusting, that she would be okay.

"Yes. I'm looking forward to it." She willed her voice to a lightness she did not feel and remembered to ask him about Andrew whose soft voice she heard in the background.

"He's fine," Denis replied. "Actually, we have some people over…"

"And I have a lot to do," she said quickly.

"Good night, Mom."

She replaced the receiver gently and sat very still in her darkened silent living room and thought of her son, surrounded by laughing and talking friends, in his high-ceilinged Santa Fe home.

She was in her studio at first light the next morning and she surveyed her workplace as though she were a tourist newly arrived at a foreign port. Weeks had passed since she had rushed out in response to Neil's call and in all that time she had never followed the path through her garden to the small stucco building that had been Neil's gift to her on their fifth anniversary. Although she had worked in that large wide-windowed room for four decades, it seemed strangely unfamiliar to her. She opened and closed the door to her kiln, slid her hand across her worktable, encrusted now with dust and droplets of the cobalt glaze she had been mixing when the phone rang, Neil's last and terrible call. She shivered, scraped at the hardened fleck with a finger-nail and tried to remember why she had settled on that color. She glanced at the shelves of chemicals and pig-ments, noted that she needed to replenish her supply of both whites and reds, and tossed styluses and brushes into the sink. Slowly, slowly, she reclaimed the studio, restored it to order, wresting it from the chaos of her loss. Within hours she had swept it clean, washed her implements, sponged the worktable and ordered supplies. Only then did she study the designs for the work she had to complete, pleased that there were so many unfinished projects on hand. She would have to complete the enameled rainbow-colored tiles for a cocktail table commissioned by an interior designer, the insets for a small mural at the local art museum, a series of graceful miniature bowls commis-sioned for Mimi Armstrong's gallery show. Elaine reviewed her sketches of those bowls, womb-shaped and gently rimmed. She had thought to use a celadon glaze for the largest one and gradually to darken it until the fourth and final one was a dark forest green. She would tackle the bowls first, she thought and reached for the clay which would, of course, have to be pounded into a moist softness before it could be properly thrown.

She worked throughout the day, breaking only to eat a quick lunch and hurrying back to the studio, switching on the light as the shadows of early evening darkened the room. She molded the clay, shaped it, refined it, disliked the final shape and pounded it with a mallet so that she might begin again. It pleased her to have such control over her material, to have the power to translate a visual ideal into tactile reality, to reclaim that total immersion in work, blocking out all loss and loneliness. Absorbed and exhausted, she continued to work the clay until her hands weakened and her arms ached. She was startled then to see that night had fallen and reluctantly she retraced her steps across the sere grass of her garden back to her dark and empty house. Still with her coat on, she sat at her kitchen table, covered her face with her hands and rocked back and forth, the keening wail of loss and grief a sound that was alien to her own ears. She did not eat supper that first night but fell into an exhausted sleep on Neil's side of the bed, her head resting on his pillow.

Day after day, she followed the same routine, working from early in the morning until late in the evening. She willed her voice to cheerfulness as she spoke to her children. She was fine, busy, catching up. She asked the right questions.

How was Sarah feeling? Was she getting enough rest?

"Rest?" Sarah's voice was riddled with merry incredulity. "Mom, I have four children and I'm running a business. If you want me to get some rest come to Jerusalem and help me."

"We'll see." The noncommittal reply sufficed. Sarah did not press her. It was, after all, the middle of the night in Jerusalem.

She checked with Lisa on the progress of the adoption.

When would it be finalized? Lisa was vague. International adoptions proceeded slowly, took time. She wanted to come to Westchester but she was busy, involved in opening a new radiology lab in Bala Cynwyd. It was in a beautiful Main Line suburb. Did Elaine want to see it? Why didn't she come to Philadelphia for a weekend.

"Perhaps. Soon. I'll think about it."

Denis and Andrew were building a studio adjacent to Andrew's darkroom.

"A perfect place for you to work, Mom," Denis said wistfully. "I want you to see it."

"Oh, I will," she promised.

Peter sent pictures of his children, Eric smiling, Renée looking sullen. He called from a hotel in Chicago where he had gone for a meeting, from a resort in Arizona where he was scouting out locations for a television show not yet in production. She asked about Lauren and Lauren's widowed father, Herb, whom she and Neil had always liked. She wondered why Peter so seldom mentioned Lauren but feared to ask him.

"Lauren's fine." He hesitated and then too swiftly changed the subject. "I hope you're thinking of coming out to the coast," he said.

"Thinking about it," she agreed pleasantly and he did not press her.

She heard a woman's voice in the background but, of course, he was at work and calling her between meetings.

The conversations with her children wearied her. Too often she ate a cold dinner in the kitchen, standing at the counter as she picked at the food, turning on the television to banish the silence.

The Newnhams invited her to dinner. Two other couples were included and Elaine understood that well-meaning Claire Newnham had struggled over the uneven seating, at last placing Elaine, the single woman, between the two husbands, both of them doctors who had known Neil and spoke gently to his widow. Their solicitude irritated her. She saw the two wives glance at each other and flinched from the pity in their eyes. She drank too much wine and talked too much about her work. She wanted them to understand that she was not defined by her widowhood, her new aloneness. She was glad that she had applied her makeup so carefully and had chosen to wear the gray cashmere dress that Neil had always favored. She told amusing stories that made the men laugh and their laughter caused the women to frown. She supposed, uncharitably, that they feared her; she was an attractive, creative woman, suddenly single again. Their fear was strangely gratifying. Shrugging into her coat, she glanced at herself in the mirror, saw the two men watching her and felt a surge of power.

But when she returned home that night she could not contain a new and unfamiliar melancholy. She wandered through the house, still wearing her long black cape, tears streaking her cheeks, sobbing quietly as she moved through the darkness although there was no one to hear the full volume of the sorrow she could not contain.

"Goddamn it, Neil!" Never in life had she spoken to her husband with the fury she aimed at him in death.

She went to the theater with Mimi Armstrong, meeting her first for dinner at a too brightly lit expensive restaurant. Mimi drank two martinis and talked at length about her unhappy marriage and her even unhappier divorce. Being alone was not that difficult, she told Elaine. She liked her life as it was. She had her gallery, an occasional lover, a circle of friends. Money. She fingered the chunky gold necklace designed by one of the artists she represented, flicked at her streaked hair with a curved bloodred fingernail and when she smiled her teeth were blindingly white. Elaine did not ask her how she coped with the silence of the long nights, with the loneliness that came at daybreak, with the hovering emptiness that haunted even a day crowded with work and appointments.

She had lunch with Serena, whom she had known since college, at whose wedding she had danced. She, too, was widowed, having nursed her husband, clever successful Eliot, through a long and losing battle with cancer. Serena had always been a quiet woman, quiet in her happiness and quiet now in her grief. Her dark hair had turned silver during Eliot's illness and she did not darken it. Her face was thin and fine-featured and she wore no makeup. A cream-colored silk scarf draped her tailored olive-green wool dress. Loss seemed to have drained her of all color and yet when she spoke it was with gentleness and calm.

"How are you coping, Elaine?" she asked and, wisely, did not wait for an answer. "I know, of course I know, how hard it is." She twisted the wedding band that she still wore and Elaine, in turn, glanced down at her own ring.

"I'm managing," she said. "I've taken care of a lot of logistical stuff. Neil's office. His things. The damn thank-you notes."

"Yes. I received mine," Serena said dryly.

Elaine blushed.

"Sorry," she said. "I seem to be drowning in the waters of self-pity."

"Phase one of widowhood. But it passes. Or at least, it gets easier. Work helps." Serena glanced at her watch. She was the librarian at a nearby community college and had a limited time for lunch.

"Yes. I spend a lot of time in the studio. Fortunately, I'm working on some interesting projects." Elaine toyed with her salad, poured herself more wine.

"That means you're spending a lot of time by yourself," Serena observed. "Working alone was okay when there was someone to be with when you left the studio. Without Neil there's an emptiness. The two of you were so focused on each other."

Elaine bit her lips, fought against tears that already seared her eyes. Serena, quiet gentle Serena, had perceived the core of her sadness, the enormity of her loss.

Of course she and Neil had been focused on each other, both of them only-children, solitary strivers, friends before they were lovers, husband and wife when they were barely out of their teens. He was hers and she was his, their hours together a sealed and exclusive expanse of time. Even their children, their wonderful and beloved children, had not penetrated the singular closeness of their shared beginning.

"I'm sorry," Serena said. "I shouldn't have said that."

Elaine shook her head.

"It's all right. You were being honest. Thank you." She dabbed at her eyes, unashamed of her tears, and struggled to invoke a smile. "What else helps? Besides work."

"There are support groups. Bereavement groups. With therapists, without therapists. I've been to both."

"And they work?"

"Elaine, nothing works. You've lost the most important person in your life and what you had can't be restored to you. Nothing is ever going to bring Eliot back to me or Neil back to you. But listening to other people, giving voice to your own feelings helps. For me it meant that I stopped choking on my own loneliness, that I acknowledged my own terror at being alone, that I stopped lying to my children. It was all right to tell them that I missed their father, that I was lonely, that I needed them and that I hoped they needed me. I guess that was what I got out of the support groups, my two meetings with a self-proclaimed grief counselor. I told my children who I was, what I was feeling." Again she glanced at her watch. "I have to get back to the library," she said. "Are you all right? Relatively speaking, of course."

She smiled and Elaine smiled back.

"Relatively all right," she said.

Serena looked hard at her.

"It will get easier, you know," she said gravely.

Elaine nodded. "I hope so."

She went back to her studio and worked late into the

night, Serena's words echoing as she experimented with a glaze, moistened her clay.

The next morning she sifted through her mail, glancing indifferently at her synagogue's monthly bulletin. She was not a regular synagogue attendee and since Neil's death she had not been at a single service.

"Sarah's religious enough for the entire family," she had said jokingly when Denis asked her if she might not find some comfort in a Sabbath service. He himself was deeply involved in what he called a "new-age" synagogue in New Mexico, a revelation which surprised her. But then Denis had always surprised her. She wondered if Andrew joined him when he went to services and if a gay Jamaican man would be welcomed even at a so-called "new-age" congregation, but she dared not ask Denis. She acknowledged then how little she knew about his life, how little she knew about the lives of all her children. She thought, amused at her own honesty, that she had not meant their independence to be quite so complete.

She reread the synagogue bulletin. A small item announced the meeting of a bereavement group later that week. Widows, widowers and divorced members might find it helpful. The text was tactful, the implication clear. Anyone who had lost a spouse would have a forum.

"I won't go," she said aloud but she cut the announcement out and tacked it onto her bulletin board.

It rained on the evening of the meeting and she stared into the darkness, listened to the rhythmic patter and watched the droplets pelt her window. She and Neil had loved rainy evenings. Often they had drawn open the drapes so that they might watch the storm, safe and dry in the warmth of their home, in the islands of lamplight that sheltered them. They had known themselves to be fortune's favored, safe and together. But now Elaine was alone and she knew herself to be vulnerable. A sudden flash of lightning frightened her.

Abruptly, she closed the drapes and, without thinking, she changed from her work clothes into a black pantsuit, a white sweater, appropriate for a widow, she thought bitterly. She applied her makeup, brushed her hair so that the curls framed her face and, seizing her hooded raincoat, drove the few miles to the synagogue.

She and Neil were longtime members of the Woodside Hebrew Center. It was the building's architecture, its clean angular lines and glass brick frontage, that had originally attracted them. It had also pleased them that the congregation's philosophy was basically humanistic, that the various rabbis who had come and gone through the years of their membership had all had an intellectual bent and were both undemanding and accommodating. Their children had all been enrolled in the religious school but little fuss was made over missed attendance or even the indifference with which both Peter and Dennis had approached their bar mitzvah preparations.

"We can't demand more of them than we demand of ourselves," Neil had said reasonably. They both acknowledged that their religion, their Judaism, was peripheral to their lives, observed more in memory of their parents than because of their own inclinations. Why then should they expect more of their children? That was perhaps why Sarah's embrace of orthodox Judaism had so surprised them, why she found it intriguing that Denis attended innovative services in his very innovative community.

The synagogue was dimly lit, the rain lightly hitting the darkened windows and, for a moment, she thought she might have gotten the date wrong. She hesitated at the entry but when a gray-bearded man approached, snapped his umbrella shut and smiled tentatively at her she followed him into the lobby.

"The bereavement group?" he asked, and she nodded. "Downstairs."

She walked behind him down the stairwell into the Hebrew school area and then into the largest classroom where she recalled going to meet with her children's teachers all those years ago. Sandy, she recalled, had been the most troublesome, mischievous in class, disrespectful to the harried rabbinical students who tried to teach the children who had no interest in being taught. She wondered if those despairing teachers would be surprised to learn that the irrepressible Sandy now called herself Sarah and lived in Jerusalem with her husband, a Talmudic scholar. She smiled and looked around the room.

Four women and two men sat in a semicircle at the scarred pale wood desks with attached benches that were too small to accommodate them. Two of the women were determinedly battling their age, their hair expertly colored to nearly identical chestnut shades, loose attractive sweaters almost concealing the resistant bulge of their abdomens. Their pale fleshy faces appeared to have been washed smooth by grief. They were the widows, Elaine decided and touched her own cheeks, pleased that she had remembered to apply makeup.

The other two women, who both wore tailored pastel-colored pantsuits, were thinner, one blond, one dark-haired. The blonde had sharp features, thin lips, narrow green eyes, the pale lashes stiff with mascara. She wore too much jewelry; a necklace and earrings of heavy gold, a matching bracelet that weighted her very slender wrist. The brunette's eyes were large and dark, bright red lipstick accentuating the fullness of her lips, too much rouge dotted high cheekbones. *The divorcees.* Elaine congratulated herself on the accuracy of her perception.

The men were both tall and both wore track suits that hung too loosely. One of them was bald except for a silver fringe of hair, meticulously trimmed. He sat erect, his hands thrust into the pockets of his gray jacket. *Widower.*

The other man was florid-faced, his dark hair thick and matted, his light brown eyes moist. He toyed with his cell phone, placed it in his backpack, removed it and returned it. He coughed, smiled, coughed again. *Divorced man,* Elaine decided.

Newly confident, she slid into a chair beside the gray-bearded man whom she had followed into the classroom.

The thin blond woman coughed, smiled and spoke in a silky, well-trained voice.

"Hi. I'm Judith Weinstein and I'm the facilitator of this

group. Some of you have been here before and some of you are new. Perhaps we can go around the room and introduce ourselves and speak briefly about why we are here."

She smiled expectantly and Elaine cringed. She had been wrong, dead wrong. She saw now that Judith Weinstein wore a wedding band of thick wide gold that matched her other jewelry. She herself was not bereft. She made notes on a pad as each member of the group volunteered a first name and murmured the defining word. *Widowed. Divorced.* Their voices were soft, hesitant. They did not give their last names. It occurred to Elaine that they should be renamed Grievers Anonymous, a support group for the lonely and the newly disoriented.

Pam, the heavy women who sat closest to her, was a divorcee. Lila was a widow. Edna, the dark-haired thin woman, was a widow. Greg, the balding older man, was divorced and Stew, the younger man, was widowed, his wife having died of leukemia only three months earlier. He had, he added, two young children, a three-year-old son and a five-year-old daughter. Mark and Emily. He held his hands out hopelessly as though they might fill his empty palms with suggestions. Elaine thought to take his hands in her own, to invite him to bring his children to her studio, to ask him the name of the young wife who had died, but she said nothing and averted her eyes from his face, now a crumbled mask of grief.

Len, the bearded man, had lost his only son. "Cancer," he said hoarsely. "Thirty-one years old." His wife had not spoken since their son's funeral. "She watches television all day. She goes to the door. Opens it, closes it, and then goes back to the damn TV." He looked around the room as though daring them to match the enormity of his loss, his suffering. His gaze rested on Elaine. She whispered her own name, whispered the word *widow* but could say no more. She sat back as Judith Weinstein asked carefully phrased questions and waited patiently for the painfully phrased answers.

Elaine listened as they spoke. Their pain vested them with honesty. Pam, the divorced woman, had come because she hoped to meet new people, people who would understand how hard it was to be suddenly alone. Her old friends had abandoned her. Married women were afraid of women who were newly single. Elaine thought of Claire Newnham's face, grown suddenly tight, of the glance she had exchanged with the other doctor's wife. Pam was not wrong.

Lila had come because her children had urged her to. She wanted to please them. They saw her participation in the group as her first step toward coping with widowhood.

"They're right," Judith Weinstein said encouragingly.

Lila neither agreed nor disagreed.

Edna had come so that she might hear the sound of other voices.

"It's the silence that I can't bear," she said.

Greg did not know why he had come. It was someplace to go, something to do, he said defensively, removed his hands from his pockets, clasped and unclasped his fingers nervously as he spoke.

Stew and Len remained silent. Their revelations had exhausted them.

"Elaine." Judith Weinstein's voice was soft. She had been well trained.

Elaine stared at her.

"I'm sorry," she said. "I just have nothing to say."

She seized her raincoat and hurried from the room, almost running down the long corridor, mounting the steps two at a time, not bothering to lift her hood against the battering rain as she ran to her car. She drove home too fast and entered the house chilled and shivering.

"I am not like them," she said aloud as she went into the kitchen and filled the kettle. "I am not like them," she repeated, as she sat in the living room sipping her tea. She closed her eyes against the memory of the misery in their voices, the sorrow on their faces, the emptiness in their lives. "I have places to go. I have things to do. I have my children. I will have a life."

She was back at her worktable at first light and she worked with great intensity during the days that followed. She completed the tiles and the insets for the mural. The set of womb-shaped bowls was fired. She called Mimi Armstrong and told her that they would be shipped that week. Politely she declined an invitation to a cocktail party Mimi was giving and a new commission for a ceramic tabletop.

Sarah called at the end of the week, her voice edgy with apprehension. Why was her mother never at home? Why didn't she have a second line installed in the studio? She was worried and Lisa and the boys were concerned.

Elaine imagined her children speaking urgently into the phone, trading anxieties, suggesting plans of action. Their worry filled her with grateful tenderness.

"I've had a big push on to get everything done," Elaine explained. "I think you're right. It's time for me to visit you." Serena's words echoed in her memory. She would not lie to her child. "I want to see you, Sarah. I need to see you."

"Oh, Mom. Oh, that's wonderful."

Elaine heard the relief in her daughter's voice, the welcome in her tone. She was gripped by a sudden eagerness.

"Yes. I think it will be," she said. "I want to call Lisa and your brothers and tell them about it. I'll call when I know exactly when I'll be arriving."

"Oh, Mom, I love you." Sarah's voice was very soft.

"And I love you," Elaine said. It had been such a long time since she had spoken those words. She murmured them again even as she held the silent phone in her hand.

"I love you."

She sat that night opposite Neil's empty chair in a circlet of lamplight and listened to Mahler's Fourth Symphony. It had been Neil's favorite and her own.

five

Sarah Chazani wandered through the rooms of her sun-drenched Jerusalem apartment, pausing to straighten the framed Anna Ticho pen-and-ink drawing of the Judean hills that held a place of pride over their living room sofa. She knew that her mother would immediately notice the misalignment. The paintings that hung in the Westchester home of Sarah's childhood were always perfectly positioned, just as the upholstery was always clean, the bright cushions on the couch carefully plumped, the glossy wood surfaces smooth and free of any clutter. Even during the week of mourning, her mother had maintained that domestic order.

Sarah looked despairingly about her own living room. The children's toys and books, relegated to a corner just that morning, had once again been strewn about the room when they arrived home for lunch. The toddlers, Leah and Yuval, were being cared for, as usual, at Ruth Evenari's home which was the small community's informal day-care center. The older children, Ephraim and his sister Leora had dashed back to school. The brightly colored sweaters they had discarded littered the floor and she gathered them up and tossed them into a closet already so crowded that she could barely close the door. The Talmudic tractate that Moshe was studying lay open on the table. She had thrust the bags of hand-me-down clothing which Ruth had delivered just that morning behind an easy chair, but she saw now that they were instantly visible from the doorway. Wearily, she carried them one by one into the boys' room and concealed them beneath a trundle bed. Her mother would be even more disapproving of a jumble of faded overalls and children's shirts than she would be of a badly hung picture but then of course, her mother had never had to cope with clumsy parcels of much-needed hand-me-down children's clothing. Sarah and Lisa, Peter and Denis had had new wardrobes for each season of the year, the transitions effortlessly accomplished. There had been no overflowing shopping bags or cartons of used clothing in Elaine Gordon's smoothly run, clutter-free household.

Elaine's disapproval would be unarticulated, Sarah knew. Their parents had seldom criticized but Sarah and her siblings had always known when they disappointed. Sarah did not want her mother's visit to begin with that diplomatically contained disappointment and, impulsively, she hurried out to the balcony and gathered in the laundry so that when Elaine looked up, her first glimpse of her daughter's home would not be diapers dancing in the wind.

She folded the newly dried white cotton squares and carried them into the children's room, glancing at her watch. Elaine's plane had landed at Ben Gurion Airport forty-five minutes ago. With any luck she had cleared customs and she and Moshe would now be on their way to Jerusalem. Elaine's smart red-leather luggage would be stowed in Moshe's van which he had cleaned out last night, as carefully as Sarah had cleaned the house, gestures of welcome, bids for approval.

Sarah imagined her mother and her husband sitting side by side as Moshe drove south to Jerusalem, struggling to make conversation, Moshe pointing out landmarks, Elaine asking questions about the children, about Sarah's home-based business. Her husband would, as always, be uneasy with Elaine and her mother, in turn, would try too hard to relate to him.

"She's really a wonderful woman," Sarah had told Moshe that morning. She wanted him to appreciate Elaine's talent, her energy, her independence of spirit.

"It's not that I don't like your mother," Moshe had replied. "It's that I hardly know her."

Although Sarah and Moshe had been married for ten years they had seldom spent time with either her family or Moshe's parents who lived in an upscale Cleveland suburb. Moshe's father, a prominent attorney, and his mother, an interior designer, were bewildered by their son's embrace of orthodoxy. How had Mike Singer, the clean-shaven captain of the Berkeley rowing team, a student who had aced his MCAT exams, and happily trekked through the far east now with one girlfriend, now with another, morphed into Moshe Chazani, the bearded Talmudic scholar? How could they, his parents (who loved him still, who, of course, would always love him) deal with his lifestyle, so alien to their own? Harriet Singer, his mother, gaunt with disappointment, had asked Neil that question as they sat together at their children's wedding. Her voice had been bitter, her eyes glazed and Neil, who had similar questions about his own daughter, had offered an uneasy response, a throwaway professional platitude. Sarah and Moshe (as they now called themselves) were mature young adults, capable of deciding their own destinies, he had assured her.

He had not told her that he and Elaine had also been unhappy with Sarah's decision. Unhappy but accepting. Their children were independent adults. Sandy (he had always had difficulty thinking of her as Sarah) had the right to live the life she had chosen.

Still, Neil and Elaine had visited Jerusalem only twice since the wedding, once when Leora was born and once to see the small apartment on Ramat Chessed that they had agreed to help purchase for the growing family. It had not surprised Sarah that her parents had not come more often. She understood that they led busy lives, that her father's schedule prohibited long journeys and that her mother would not leave him for any length of time. As always, they prioritized the time they spent together. She knew that they had no real understanding of the life that she and Moshe had chosen.

She remembered their shocked reaction on her return from her junior year at the Hebrew University when she told them that she had decided to embrace orthodox Judaism and that she was determined to return to Jerusalem and study at a woman's yeshiva.

Her father had been conciliatory. Ever the skilled analyst, he had probed her reasoning, asked subtle and not so subtle questions. Was she fearful of growing up, of assuming the responsibilities of adulthood? Was she retreating into the protective cocoon of an insular religious community because she could not cope with the demands of real life? Perhaps she wanted to see a therapist who might help her work through her decision. He had, as always, been gentle and when he saw that she would not be swayed, he said no more. He had, at last, set one condition. She was to complete her senior year and then, if she still wanted to, she could return to Jerusalem.

Her mother, however, had been more persistent.

"But why? Tell me why you are so attracted to this community, these ultra-orthodox people. You are our Sandy. Why should you become their Sarah? What do you have in common with them? What can they possibly offer you?"

And Sarah had struggled to explain. She had tried to speak to her mother of that autumn afternoon, her very first month in Jerusalem when she had agreed to accompany her roommate, Tina, to the Western Wall of the temple on a Friday afternoon.

"It's supposed to be really spiritual," Tina said.

Tina was a tall, thin Californian who wore her light brown hair in a long lank braid and played mournful tunes on her recorder. She had taped a huge colored poster of Buddha over her bed and, at odd intervals, she dimmed the lights of their room and lit fragrant candles.

"I don't even know what that means. I've never thought about being spiritual," Sarah, then still called Sandy, had protested but in the end she had agreed to go and had even worn the requisite costume, a long denim skirt and an Indian shirt whose sleeves fell to her elbows.

The approach to the Western Wall was crowded, as it always was, on the eve of the Sabbath. Sandy and Tina were caught up in a throng of jostling Chassidic men draped in prayer shawls and religious women, their heads covered with scarves of a gossamer weave or crowned with scalp-hugging wigs. Small boys in huge skullcaps, their curling earlocks damp from their visit to the ritual bath, ran past them, twirling the fringes that dangled from their oversize white shirts. In front of the Wall, members of religious Zionist youth groups organized graceful circle dances, the boys on the men's side of the plaza and the girls on the women's side. Sandy stared at them, moved by their faces so bright with joy, each dance step a prayer in motion, their eyes lifted now and again to the slowly darkening sky. She watched as women stepped forward to place carefully folded bits of paper in the crevices between the ancient stones.

"What are they doing?" she asked Tina.

"They've written out prayers that they want answered," Tina replied indifferently. Her eyes raked the crowd and she waved suddenly to a tall blond bearded youth whose corn-yellow hair was twisted into a very tight ponytail. Sandy recognized him. He was Craig, a British student in her philosophy class who asked irrelevant, sardonic questions and was rumored to have access to very good pot.

"Do you have a prayer you want answered?" Tina asked as Craig approached them.

Sandy did not answer although she knew what she would pray for. She would pray for a belief that would give her the same ardent joy that illuminated the faces of the dancing girls. Ignoring Tina and Craig, she moved forward and suddenly, surprisingly, she was directly in front of the Wall. She lifted her fingers to it, surprised by its smoothness, even more surprised to see the outcroppings of greenery between the stones, nature's tenacity affirmed. Impulsively she pressed her lips lightly to the cold stone. She wished for a prayer but having none, she returned to where Tina and Craig stood.

"Hey, we're going to a café in the Old City," Tina said. "Want to come with?"

Sandy shook her head. "You're through with being spiritual?" she asked wryly.

"We just want to get some coffee. Can you get back on your own?"

"Sure."

Tina and Craig left then and she stood alone in the plaza that was slowly emptying as the worshippers and dancers hurried toward their Sabbath dinners.

"Are you alone?"

She veered around. A tall bearded man wearing a long black coat, a black hat perched on his very large head, smiled at her.

"Yes," she said.

"May I invite you to have Shabbat dinner with my family? We live not far from here and my wife, Rachel, is an excellent cook."

His voice was soft, his eyes gentle. She hesitated.

"If you agree you will be granting me a great privilege, that of welcoming a Sabbath guest into my home. My name is Nachum Cohen."

He smiled at her and she smiled back. Her own acquiescence surprised her but wordlessly, she walked beside him, down the narrow streets of the Jewish Quarter and into an old stone house. She followed him through a small book-lined library into the candlelit room where crystal and silver and china shimmered on a long table covered with a snow-white cloth. Faces, like those of the swirling dancers, bright with joy, wreathed in smiles of welcome, turned toward her.

"Shabbat shalom," they said in unison.

"Shabbat shalom," she replied shyly.

That, of course, had been the beginning.

She had spent that evening with the Cohen family and

their guests, young people like herself, two American boys who were students at a nearby yeshiva, an Australian girl who was studying nursing at Hadassah Hospital where Rachel Cohen was an emergency-room physician. The five Cohen children were exuberant youngsters who dominated the dinner table conversation, talking as rapidly as they ate, jumping up now and again to help their mother bring serving platters piled high with roast chicken, potato puddings and sweet carrots in from the kitchen. The two elder boys, talkative twins, challenged their father on an interpretation of the Torah portion. Their sisters registered their opinions in high sweet voices. Even the youngest girl, Nurit, who could not have been older than seven partici- pated in the discussion.

"My teacher says that Sarah was very wrong to send Hagar into the desert," she asserted, nodding so vigorously that her dark braid swept from side to side. "It was cruel."

"Let's talk about that," Nachum Cohen said and they did, for over an hour, guests and the host family alike, offering opinions, listening attentively as Nachum offered one explanation and then another.

Fascinated, Sandy listened. The biblical personalities were alive in this dining room, vibrant guests at this table where conversation soared and laughter erupted with startling suddenness. Then the meal was over and the singing began. She did not know the songs but she understood the joy and happiness of the melodies that filled the room. In unison, led by the two elder boys, they sang the grace after meals and she found herself humming along as Nurit placed a small hand on her own, a gentle gesture of welcome and inclusion.

"Will you come again?" Rachel asked when she left.

"Perhaps," she said awkwardly and then turned swiftly back. "Yes," she amended. "I would love to."

She walked back to the university that night and thought of Friday-night dinners at her family's Westchester home. Sometimes her mother remembered to light the Sabbath candles and sometimes she didn't. They rarely had guests because her parents were always exhausted by the end of the week. Their dinner table conversations were quiet, almost careful. Laughter sometimes but never song, never prayer. Their father might talk about some political issue, their mother might ask about a school assignment but never would they discuss a Torah portion. They would not even know what portion was being read on a given week. They listened patiently when their children spoke but their interest was dispassionate. The family scattered after dinner but always Neil and Elaine retreated into the living room and sat across from each other in the lamplight, books in hand, chamber music softly playing.

It occurred to Sandy, on that long walk back to the dormitory, that in her parents' home she sometimes felt like a guest, while in the Cohen home she had felt like a member of an extended and welcoming family. The thought seemed disloyal and to atone for it she wrote a long letter home that night, describing her courses, her new friends, the beauty of Jerusalem. She had been right, after all, she wrote to her parents, not to join Lisa who had opted to spend her own junior year abroad in Rome. After all, she and Lisa, companions from birth, deserved a vacation from each other. She decorated the letter with a pattern of interlaced stars and flowers so that they would know she had not forgotten her interest in design, would see that she was nurturing her talent.

She did not write home about her visit to the Cohens, nor did she discuss it with Tina who had given up spiritualism for socialism and was now spending weekends at a left-wing kibbutz. But she continued to spend Friday evenings at the Cohens' and, within a few weeks she was spending all of Shabbat there. By the time she went to visit Lisa in Rome on winter break she was keeping kosher, an undertaking that amused her twin.

"But why?" Lisa had asked.

"It reminds me of who I am." Sandy had fumbled for a reply and the one that she offered seemed inadequate.

Lisa was gay during that visit, in love with Rome, in love with Bert, her lab partner, in love with the winding streets of the city, in love with the way the sun rose so slowly over the slope of the Palatine hills. She and Bert watched it rise and watched it set, she told her sister proudly. She was in love with her own body and during Sandy's visit she walked about her apartment in her underwear and studied the rhomboids of golden Roman light that danced across her very smooth skin. She knew who she was and Bert, wonderful Bert, knew who she was, too. She had no need to search for answers at a Sabbath table in a distant city.

"So who are you?"

"I'm not sure. I'm trying to find out," Sandy said and envied her sister who was so free of self-doubt.

Her answer had been painfully honest and back in Jerusalem she determined to pursue a certainty that would match Lisa's. She enrolled in classes in bible and Jewish philosophy at a woman's institute that Rachel Cohen recommended. She worked hard at her Hebrew and volunteered to teach an art class at Nurit's school.

She returned to the States knowing that Judaism was at the core of her being, that she was happiest studying Jewish texts and sitting at the Cohens' Friday night dinner and that she wanted to live in Jerusalem for the rest of her life.

"So who are you?" her twin asked teasingly, almost maliciously that first week home as they packed to return to Penn. She lit a cigarette and snuffed it out before Sandy could answer.

Lisa had lost her gaiety and Sandy understood the pain that had caused that loss and the resultant bitterness that hardened her sister's voice and shadowed her eyes.

"Actually, I'm Sarah now," she had replied then, concealing her hurt at her sister's flippancy. The name by which she would be called from that day on defined her, told her who she was.

She kept the bargain she had made with her father, completed her education and then returned to Jerusalem. Weeks after her arrival, Michael Singer, newly arrived in Israel from a trek through Thailand, sat opposite her at the

Cohens' Shabbat table. Sarah immediately sensed that tall, grave-eyed Michael, who spoke softly and listened carefully, was different from the other young people whom Nachum often invited home—the potheads who would briefly replace dope with Torah study, the world-weary hippies who had not heard that the sixties were over, the dropouts in search of themselves. Michael was serious, his questions—and he had many—laced with depth. He wanted to study. He wanted to find an intellectual and spiritual discipline that would give his life a sense of purpose. He had not found it during his brief stint as a medical student nor had he found it during his wanderings in the far east. He enrolled in a yeshiva and was completely engrossed in his studies. Torah and Talmud fascinated him. A life lived within the parameters of Jewish law intrigued him, offering as it did purpose and commitment, discipline and faith. He confided all this to Sarah and it seemed to her that his words gave voice to the secrets of her heart. He articulated the answers she should have offered to her sister, her brothers, her parents who saw her return to Jerusalem, her embrace of orthodoxy, as betrayal and desertion.

Six months later, she wrote her parents that she and Michael, who now called himself Moshe, planned to marry. Neil and Elaine had protested mildly, Michael's parents vociferously. In the end they had all come to the wedding as had Michael's brother and Sarah's siblings, uneasy guests at a celebration they could not call their own.

Sarah knew that she and Moshe mystified their families.

Her pregnancies had been a source of concern rather than joy.

"How will you manage?" her mother had asked worriedly.

"I have my little business and I love it. Moshe teaches. We don't need very much," Sarah had replied patiently.

She was proud of the work she did at home, designing the fabrics and creating the patterns for the long dressing gowns that were popular among orthodox women. She contracted out the manufacture of the garments to other women in the community who were grateful for a new source of income.

Her mother's question had irritated Sarah, ignited a resentment she would not reveal.

"I'm doing exactly what you did," she added.

She was, in fact, emulating her mother. Elaine had always spent long hours in her studio, creating her ceramics, maintaining contact with galleries and clients without neglecting her family.

Elaine did not remind her daughter that their situations were totally different. The Gordons had not depended on her work for sheer economic survival nor had it intruded on the needs of the household. Elaine's studio was apart from the house and she skillfully juggled her time so that her professional life did not interfere with either Neil's needs or the needs of her children. A succession of au pairs, pleasant smiling girls from the UK and Scandinavia, helped of course but Elaine herself, ever calm and organized, was responsible for their orderly home, for the well-balanced meals served at appropriate hours, for a kitchen sink, that unlike Sarah's, never overflowed with dirty dishes and cutlery, for beds, also unlike Sarah's, that were never covered with unsorted laundry.

Still, Sarah did manage both her business and her growing family. Her days were exhausting but that exhaustion was threaded with gladness. She wakened each morning, looked out at the Jerusalem hills, listened to Moshe's rhythmic breathing, the sweet, sleep-bound voice of a child, and thought herself blessed to be living this life in this city at this time. It saddened her that her father, her gentle, generous father, had never come to terms with the life she had chosen. His visits to Jerusalem had been too brief, his judgment too clinical. He had offered her acceptance but not the approval she had craved.

But her mother's stay in Jerusalem would span enough time so that, at last, she might experience the rhythms of Sarah's life, and come to know and understand Moshe, to respect his quiet kindness, his intellectual acumen, his devotion to her and the children.

Sarah passed her hands over the gentle rise of her abdomen. This new pregnancy could no longer be concealed. Lisa, sharp-eyed and sharp-tongued, had warned her that their mother, always worried about the sheer physical demands on Sarah, would not welcome the arrival of yet another baby.

"Do you really want this baby?" Lisa had asked then.

"Of course I do."

Her reply was swift and certain. She thought it wonderful that a new life would so swiftly follow her father's death.

Lisa's question annoyed but did not anger. She and her twin, ever emotionally enmeshed, had always been best friends. The disparate paths that they had taken had not altered that. She acknowledged that she herself had difficulty accepting Lisa's single life, her professional ambitions, her relationship with David that seemed to preclude any thought of marriage. She did, with a wrenching sadness, understand why Lisa wanted to adopt a child but, by tacit agreement, the sisters did not discuss it. They had pledged themselves to a complicity of silence that distant evening, when the chilly winds of an early Roman winter had shaken the last of the autumn leaves from the trees. Lisa had wept that night and shivered and Sarah had brought her tea, covered her with light blankets and whispered words of comfort that she knew to be lies even as she uttered them.

She shrugged away the memory and wondered, as she glanced again at the clock, if she should tell her mother that she and Moshe had already decided to name the new baby after Neil. Would such a revelation bring comfort or sorrow? It saddened her that she could not predict her mother's reaction, but then they had lived apart for so many years. This visit, this very long visit, would surely bring them closer together.

The child within her stirred and she felt a surge of joy. She walked to the window and saw Moshe's van pull up, saw her mother shade her eyes with a gloved hand and stare up at the window. Excitedly she waved and Elaine, seeing her, blew her a kiss that seemed to flutter through the soft Jerusalem air.

Dinner that first evening was exciting, the children clamoring for their grandmother's attention, Ephraim and Leora proudly practicing their English and, even more proudly offering to teach Elaine Hebrew. Golden-haired Leah gave Elaine the finger painting she had carried home from day care and chubby Yuval, the baby, scrambled onto her lap and fingered her heavy silver earrings.

"*Savta*," he said happily.

"That means 'grandma,'" Leora explained importantly. "Say 'Grandma,' Yuval."

"*Savta*," the child repeated and they all laughed.

Moshe was solicitous, refilling Elaine's wineglass, insisting that she try the pomegranate jam.

"Sarah makes it herself," he said proudly. "From the fruit of our own tree." He pointed to the tall tree that grew in the courtyard, its heavy red fruit shimmering in the half darkness, its fragrance wafting sweetly through the room.

Elaine tasted it and smiled her appreciation as she had smiled her appreciation from the moment of her arrival. She had accompanied Sarah on a tour of the house, admired the brightly colored cushions of Bedouin weave scattered across the shabby beige sofa, the lamp bases of intricately patterned Armenian ceramic, the table carved of golden olive wood. She had protested mildly when Sarah told her that she and Moshe would sleep in the living room during her visit so that she might have the privacy of their bedroom.

"Moshe insists," Sarah had told her. "He's scoring

mitzvah points—honoring a mother. It's the most harmless of his good deeds," she had added wryly.

She did not speak to her mother of the wandering, wasted American kids Moshe occasionally brought home, of the amounts of money he distributed to the beggars whose pathetic appeals he could not resist, of the time he had given his good winter coat to an aged scholar.

"It's not easy being married to a saint," she would jokingly scold him but they both knew that she would not want him to be otherwise.

Elaine had agreed reluctantly to the sleeping arrangements. She had smiled at the bunk beds in the children's rooms, piled high with the stuffed animals that arrived routinely from the States, birthday and Chanukah gifts from the aunts and uncles, the cousins and grandparents, who found it easier to mail packages than to board planes.

"You've done wonders with the space," she said as Sarah showed her the wooden cabinets Moshe himself had built in the bedrooms.

Sarah cringed at the criticism inherent in the compliment. The space, Sarah's space, was too small. In her mother's eyes it would always be too small.

"But what about the new baby? Where will you put the crib, the changing table?" she asked as she fingered the gay blue bedspread with its sprinting bright green frogs and smiling yellow butterflies. It was her first reference to Sarah's pregnancy.

"We'll manage," Sarah said curtly, her heart heavy with disappointment.

She remembered how Rachel Cohen had greeted her news with an affectionate *mazal tov,* a swift embrace. Foolishly, she had expected as much from her own mother.

"Of course you'll manage." Elaine's tone was calm, reassuring. "I love this fabric. Your design?"

Sarah nodded. That had always been the maternal pattern, she remembered. Implied criticism and then a palliative compliment. Positive reinforcement, her father had called it, his professional vocabulary spilling over into the life of his family. The memory of her father singed her with sadness and she was relieved when the children burst into the house, when the dinner evolved into a time of easy talk and laughter. The tension was broken. She would have to stop overreacting to her mother's every comment, she told herself. She would have to keep the mysterious hormones of pregnancy under control.

"The jam is delicious." Elaine lathered it across a slice of apple. "I've never even tried to make jam."

"I'll teach you," Sarah said.

"I'll help," Leora volunteered happily.

"We'll all do it together," Elaine agreed. Together. It occurred to her that it was the first time she had uttered that word since Neil's death. Suddenly, despite the fatigue of jet lag, she was suffused with a contentment, too long unfamiliar. She had been right to make this journey. She reached across the table and took her daughter's hand in her own as Moshe began to softly sing the grace after meals.

six

Elaine sat on Sarah's kitchen balcony the next morning, Yuval peacefully asleep on her lap, and, like a dispassionate theater patron, she observed the daily life of Ramat Chessed. Bewigged women in faded long-sleeved cotton house dresses hurried down the street carrying plastic baskets laden with vegetables and fruits, packages of laundry wrapped in brown paper, gallons of milk in clear plastic bags. They called to each other in Yiddish and in Hebrew, exchanged morning greetings. *Boker tov. Gut morgen.* They did not stop to chat. The milk might spoil, the beds were still unmade, impatient husbands waited for a breakfast grapefruit. Elaine recognized them. They were women not unlike her mother and mother-in-law, women whose lives were governed by work, who did not know how to walk slowly, who would not pause to look up at the sun-streaked sky. She marveled, still, that she had escaped their lives and was bewildered, still, that her daughter, talented and educated Sarah, destined for a golden future, had chosen to recreate her grandmothers' arduous existence. She sighed and bent her cheek so that it brushed her grandson's feathery hair.

She watched the young mothers, colorful scarves covering their hair, gauzy pastel skirts dancing about their ankles, who wheeled strollers and held the hands of toddlers. They too walked swiftly and chatted animatedly with each other. Like Sarah, they had to shop for large families, prepare noontime meals for schoolchildren and scholar husbands. As Sarah had done earlier that morning, they would bring their children to Ruth's pink stucco house, the neighborhood day-care center, and then hurry to their own jobs.

A group of yeshiva boys, almost bent double over the load of heavy books they clutched to their chests, walked four abreast down the road, their heads, covered by oversize large knitted skullcaps, bobbing up and down as they engaged in earnest discussion. Elaine smiled at the thought that a Talmudic question might have infiltrated their dreams and was now being clarified in the light of early morning. The boys were followed by a gaggle of laughing girls in the requisite orthodox uniform: long denim skirts and long-sleeved white blouses, brightly colored ribbons threaded through their hair. Drivers honked their horns impatiently or skirted around the groups of students; the occasional angry shout was greeted with indifferent laughter.

On the corner, bearded men waited for the buses that would carry them to offices in Jerusalem or along the Modiin–Tel Aviv corridor. Like Moshe, they wore long black frockcoats and snow-white shirts but unlike him they carried laptops and briefcases. Moshe's own life was dedicated to Torah study and teaching at the yeshiva, although Sarah had assured Elaine that he helped her with the business when he could.

"I would hope so," Elaine had replied dryly and immediately regretted her words. She had not come to Jerusalem to judge and criticize, she reminded herself. She had come to observe and understand, to decide if, in some as yet undetermined way, she might meld her own life with theirs.

She shifted position so that Yuval's head rested on her shoulder. She thought of how different this busy street was from her own quiet suburban road where pedestrians were rarely seen and even traffic was sparse. Her neighbors' children were ferried to school in carpools, their faces hidden behind tinted windows. Their mothers sprinted in and out of their SUVs, their pursuits solitary, their movements swift. There was no laughter beyond her windows, no voices raised in greeting when she entered and left her home. She lived in a sealed chrysalis of suburban silence. She had, now and again during the months after Neil's death, stood outside the house after working for long hours in her studio. She yearned then for the sounds of life, for the assurance that the dense quietude that surrounded her was penetrable. Inevitably, she had retreated indoors, hugging the shadow of her aloneness and too swiftly turned on the television, filling the empty house with meaningless sound and movement. In contrast, Ramat Chessed pulsated with activity, a confluence of life and sound and color.

"Mom, is Yuval still sleeping? I'm almost finished," Sarah called to her from the kitchen.

Sarah had been bent over her drawing board when Elaine awakened, Yuval perched on her knee. She did her best work in the morning, she explained, after Moshe had taken Ephraim and Leora to school and dropped Leah and Yuval at Ruth's. She had begun work especially early that day because she wanted to complete a new fabric design before going into Jerusalem with her mother. Yuval had been a little cranky so she had kept him home.

Elaine had taken the baby from her and watched as Sarah's pen moved swiftly across the sheet of white paper, creating a garden of fanciful flowers.

"Fabrics with flowers are very popular with my customers," Sarah explained. "I'm forever looking through botany books in search of new ones."

"This is where you always work?" Elaine asked. She thought of her own studio with its long-scrubbed worktable and carefully designed cabinets, the drawers for tools and pigments, the files and work sheets spread on easily accessible shelves.

"It's not bad." Sarah had shrugged. "The drawing board

is collapsible and I simply store it under the kitchen table when I'm not working. And this box holds everything—colors, rulers, shears. We're going to add another room now that Denis has transferred the money." She had blushed and fallen silent. The money, of course, was the small inheritance Neil had left each of his children. It pained Sarah that her father's death would make her new ease possible.

Elaine had wanted to reassure her that it was all right to speak of Neil's legacy. It would have pleased him to know that it was being put to good use. She wanted to tell Sarah that she would be glad to make additional funds available, but she said nothing. This was, after all, her first day in Jerusalem. It was too soon to rush in with offers and suggestions that might not be welcome. She was a guest in her daughter's world. She would have to tread carefully.

Sarah came out to the balcony and pressed her lips to Yuval's forehead.

"He's cool enough," she said. "I thought he felt a little warm this morning. He catches cold so easily."

"I've read that children in day care seem to catch colds from each other," Elaine said and immediately regretted her words.

Sarah's color rose.

"Mom. Please."

Elaine recognized the edge in her daughter's voice. Lisa, of course, would have been less restrained.

"Sorry."

She smiled apologetically and Sarah put her hand on her shoulder in forgiveness.

★ ★ ★

Elaine and Sarah went into the city that afternoon, leaving Yuval at Ruth's. Sarah was relieved to note that her mother approved of plump, florid-faced Ruth, whose bright head kerchief was always askew and who spoke in gentle, musical tones, cuddling first one child and then another as she moved briskly from one miniature play station to another. Her garden was littered with battered playground equipment, and the children scurried up and down the faded red plastic slides and dashed in and out of a frog-shaped sandbox. Leah waved happily to them but did not leave the small table where she was concentrating on a puzzle, and Yuval gurgled happily when Michal, Ruth's eldest daughter, carried him into the house for lunch.

"Leah's small motor skills are definitely improving. Look at how well she's doing with that puzzle," Ruth said and her cultivated British accent surprised Elaine. "Where are you and your mum off to?"

"I want her to see Machane Yehuda. Mom's a gourmet cook and I wanted her to pick out the fruits and vegetables. She makes the most terrific soups."

"I hope you'll come for dinner and taste them," Elaine said.

It occurred to her that she had not cooked a soup since before Neil had died. Recipes flooded her mind. Potato and leek. Zucchini and pepper. Too sophisticated for Sarah's children? Perhaps just a simple vegetable and noodle soup to begin with. Newly invigorated, she smiled at Ruth.

"I even know how to make a trifle," she said and Ruth laughed and bent to comfort a crying toddler.

"I'll be delighted to sample your soup and your trifle," she said.

"Was Ruth born in England?" Elaine asked Sarah as they boarded the intercity bus, automatically taking seats near the rear exit. It was safest, Sarah had explained casually, as she paid their fare and Elaine had asked no questions. Suicide bombings on buses had grown rarer but they had not ceased.

"Born and raised in England. Her father's an Anglican minister in the Midlands. You don't get more English than that. Her mother, I think, was born in Germany. Ruth— actually she was called Juliet then, Ruth is the name that's often given to a convert—came to Israel on a jaunt when she finished her doctorate in early childhood education in Bristol and just never went back," Sarah replied.

"I suppose some well-meaning Hasidic man approached her at the Western Wall, invited her home for a Sabbath meal and sealed her fate," Elaine said dryly.

"Actually it was Ruth who became interested in Judaism on her own," Sarah replied, struggling to keep her irritation under control. "She volunteered to work on a religious kibbutz. She told me once that she felt that because she was part German, she had an obligation to do something for the Jewish people. But, of course, it went beyond that. She was impressed by the orthodox lifestyle. She began to read on her own and then she took some courses. Eventually, she came to Jerusalem and enrolled in a seminar."

"And then she met a handsome religious man and decided to convert," Elaine guessed. She stared out the bus window, moved anew by the gentle hills of Jerusalem, the olive trees that crouched low to the ground and the cypresses that arched skyward. She felt her own spirit soar and understood her daughter's love for the beautiful city she called home.

"No." Sarah smiled, oddly pleased that Elaine had guessed wrongly. "Ruth decided to convert before she ever met Avi. The rabbis actually tried to dissuade her. They refused her request three times. That's in accordance with tradition. The rabbis want to be assured of the potential convert's conviction and so they reject the petition again and again. Ruth was able to give them that assurance and she passed every test they gave her. I think she knows more about Judaism than I do. In any case she met Avi two years after her conversion— she organized an educational program for children with cancer at Hadassah Hospital and Avi, who had been wounded in Lebanon, was doing rehab there and they met in the cafeteria. He wasn't even religious but that changed when he met Ruth. Anyway, they've been married for years, they have a great family and our community is lucky to have them. I can't imagine my life without Ruth's day-care center."

"And her father, the reverend…the minister, and her mother, they accepted her decision?" Elaine asked.

"No. They were hurt, angry. They're still hurt and angry. But they're honest about it. They don't pretend that they approve." Sarah spoke slowly, softly, but she stared straight ahead, evading her mother's eyes.

"How fortunate for Ruth," Elaine said bitterly.

"This is our stop." Sarah rose and touched her mother's arm, a mute gesture of apology. The words she had spoken were sour in her mouth.

The bus lumbered to a halt on a narrow street lined with shops and outside stalls. Sarah and Elaine made their way into the market and joined the throng of shoppers who hurried from stand to stand, filling their string bags with shimmering produce. Young mothers wheeled overflowing shopping carts with one hand and balanced strollers with the other as they called to each other in a mélange of languages and gestured warningly to their laughing children. Bareheaded university students examined fruits and vegetables and stuffed their purchases into backpacks already laden with books. Small boys, earlocks curling about thin pale faces, trailed after their parents; men in the heavy black caftans reminiscent of medieval Polish aristocracy, broad-brimmed Borsalinos perched on their heads, hurried past. Bewigged women whose long skirts fell to their ankles haggled with vendors, ignoring young women in miniskirts. Girls dashed past them, clutching the hands of smaller brothers and sisters, hugging plastic sacks of milk and bundles of sesame-encrusted rolls wrapped in white paper. Twin girls, dressed alike in long-sleeved gingham dresses and white stockings, their dark curly hair held in place with white plastic headbands, linked hands and trailed their very pregnant mother who wore a dress fashioned from the very same gingham.

Elaine was reminded of Sarah and Lisa as small girls. She

had, on principle, never dressed them alike but she remembered that they had both fallen in love with the same pink sweater although Lisa had chosen to wear it with a pleated navy skirt and Sarah had worn it only with jeans, her luxuriant chestnut-colored ponytail caught up in a matching pink ribbon. She wondered if Sarah ever thought of the girl she had been, if she remembered that pink sweater, if she ever yearned for the life that might have been hers. But Sarah, walking with the graceful gait unique to pregnant women, smiled as she waved to one friend and then another. She lifted her face to the sun's brightness and delicately inhaled the scent of the thyme that blossomed on the hillsides of Judea and permeated the cool air.

She's happy, Elaine thought in wonderment and her heart soared.

She watched the antics of a group of high school youngsters, happily munching *pittot* stuffed with *felafel,* who incurred the wrath of stall keepers as they plucked olives and pickles from tall barrels and then ran away. Jolted from her mood and newly energized, she paused to study the mounds of produce, the pyramids of lemons and oranges, the snow-white cauliflowers and the varicolored mushrooms in huge straw baskets.

The colors delighted her.

"I wish I had thought to bring my sketch pad," she told Sarah who immediately plunged into her oversize burlap purse and handed her a drawing pencil and a pad.

"I always get ideas for fabric designs here," she said and they smiled at each other in mutual recognition.

They shared the artist's eye, the appreciation of shape and color, the urge to capture elusive impressions on paper and canvas, on clay and tile. Sarah remembered suddenly that the happiest hours of her girlhood had been spent in Elaine's studio when she had created her designs with quiet absorption as her mother shaped her ceramics and mixed her glazes. Those were times of precious togetherness, of an intimacy that excluded the rest of the family. She had felt then that a special bond had been forged between them and she wondered wistfully if that sadly frayed bond could be fortified during her mother's visit to Jerusalem.

She glanced down at the stiff white page of her sketch pad which Elaine had so swiftly covered and was pleased to see a dancing pattern of small ovoid eggplants interspersed with long thin stalks of celery.

Smiling, she filled a plastic bag with the gleaming purple and pale-white eggplants and added two bunches of celery, selecting those of the brightest green and the thickest crowns of leaves.

"Your drawing is perfect for the new line of aprons I'm planning," she told her mother. "We can work on the colors and then turn the vegetables into a ratatouille. We'll be creative and economical. And gastronomical, too. Is there such a word?"

Elaine's responsive laughter was sweet and full-throated. It was, she realized, the first time she had laughed since Neil's death. She stood very still, her pencil poised in midair, her heart newly lightened.

"Gastronomical will be our word," she told Sarah as they walked on, wandering from stand to stand. They filled their string bags with ruby-red tomatoes, shimmering orange-and-yellow peppers, bright green cucumbers and tender spinach leaves that floated through their fingers like the wings of butterflies as they scooped them out of the huge crates still damp with morning dew.

At last they exited the market and turned onto Jaffa Road where they settled into a small café for a quick lunch.

"I like your market," Elaine said.

"I love shopping there," Sarah agreed. "There's so much excitement, so much color. I love picking up an orange that still has a leaf clinging to the stem, or a clump of beets with soil on the roots. It's as though everything I touch connects me to the land." *And to God,* she thought but did not utter the words.

"As opposed to the sterile supermarkets of Westchester," Elaine said. "I apologize for your deprived childhood."

"Mom, I wasn't making comparisons," Sarah protested.

"Of course, I know that. I suppose I'm just trying to understand, Sarah."

"Understand what?" Sarah added honey to her mint tea and stared moodily into the cup.

"Understand the way you live, the way you think."

"And the way I believe."

"That, too," Elaine said and she reached across the table and touched her daughter's hand as the sounds of a flute played by a street musician trilled through the small café.

She reached into her purse and dropped a few coins into the cup he held out to her.

Sarah smiled and added coins of her own.

"Our beliefs aren't that different, Mom," she said. "We both believe in acts of loving kindness."

"Loving kindness." Elaine spoke the words softly, suffused with a new calm, a new contentment.

seven

Elaine's days in Jerusalem fell into a set routine. She cooked. She made soups and casseroles. She created stews and taught seven-year-old Leora how to shape the dough for the mini rolls Sarah loved. Quiet Leora, with her large dark eyes and the thick curling chestnut-colored hair that she had inherited from her mother, delighted her. She asked about Elaine's work and laughed when Elaine shaped the dough as she might shape a malleable chunk of clay. In charmingly accented English, Leora peppered her grandmother with questions about life in the States, about Sarah's childhood, about the grandfather she had hardly known. She would lay claim to her mother's past.

"Tell me about Aunt Lisa. *Ima* was so lucky to have a

twin. There are two girls in my class who are twins—Noga and Nurit. I wish I had a twin."

"Was *Saba* Neil handsome? I think my *abba* is handsome."

"Tell me about Uncle Peter and Uncle Denis. Did they tease their sisters the way Ephraim teases me?"

Elaine found herself making up stories, charming Leora with tales of trips that had never been taken, a tree house that had never been built, melding them effortlessly with actual memories of the family's life in their sprawling Westchester home. She chided herself for those untruths, for those fanciful embellishments, but it pleased her that she was pleasing Leora.

Yes, she told her granddaughter, Neil had been handsome but more important than that he had been good. Memories of his goodness, of the goodness of their vanished life together, choked her and she turned away so that Leora would not be frightened by her gathering tears.

She was swept up in the frenetic activity of Sarah's home. Women dashed in and out to deliver completed garments, to pick up additional fabric, to borrow a cup of sugar, to deliver a freshly baked cake or return a saucepan. Small children were left for an hour, two hours, sometimes for an afternoon that stretched into evening because of some emergency. The phone rang with news of births and deaths, weddings and funerals. Sarah prepared meals for families in mourning, desserts for engagement celebrations, dashing from stove to drawing board, stirring a soup while taking an order on the phone.

"Your sister is a whirling dervish," Elaine told Lisa who called regularly. "Me? I'm fine. Really."

She knew that her children worried about her. She overheard Sarah's late-night conversations with Peter and Denis, her murmured reassurances.

"Mom's doing great," she told her brothers. "I think she really needed this change. And she's helping me a lot."

Elaine worked with Sarah on fabric designs, urged her to use more complex patterns, more challenging shapes. She listened as Sarah explained the mysteries of silk-screening, of how she cut her patterns so that the folds of the robe did not obscure the design. Elaine wakened in the night and made quick sketches. A pouch of a solid fabric could be attached to a sash. Pockets could be fashioned as flaps. The ceramicist's tricks, layered dimensions, could be translated onto fabrics. She would fall back into a light sleep. Her nights were restless but her days passed in a frenetic pace that was at once soothing and exhausting. Loss clung to her like a shadow but there was no time for grief.

She moved easily through Ramat Chessed, learned the names of Sarah's neighbors, the ages of their children. She was greeted on her walks with pleasant smiles. She was a guest in their community and they accepted the fact that she did not cover her hair, that often the sleeves of her shirts did not entirely cover her arms. She understood that for now that was acceptable. And she, in turn, made small compromises. She did not wear slacks, she was careful not to extend her hand in greeting when she was introduced to a religious man.

She acknowledged that Sarah's serene adherence to the mores of the community, the strict separation of men and women in the synagogue, of boys and girls in the schools, mystified her. She and Neil had fled the orthodox synagogues of their childhood, the small crowded rooms that stank of the sweat of the worshippers and the mildewed pages of their prayer books, reverberant with the atonal cacophony of mumbled prayers and droning Torah readings.

They understood that their immigrant parents had clung to the practices of their past, that they had derived comfort from prayers intoned in familiar accents, but they themselves had opted for the bright and airy suburban synagogue where families sat together in comfortable cushioned pews crafted of pale wood. They had attended only infrequently but it pleased them that their children were exposed to an aesthetic ambience, to a dignified service presided over by a rabbi who spoke with a Boston accent and a cantor who occasionally gave operatic performances. Sarah, Lisa and their brothers had attended religious school in wide-windowed rooms and celebrated their bar and bat mitzvahs with a tasteful service followed by a joyous party. How was it then that Sarah, who had read so beautifully from the Torah at her bat mitzvah, was content to attend services in the Ramat Chessed synagogue where she sat behind a curtain in the stifling women's section and passively listened to a prayer service in which only the voices of men could be heard?

Elaine dared not ask. She simply avoided the synagogue. It was good to sleep late and awaken to an empty house. There was little enough privacy during the week.

She wakened early each morning, dressed swiftly and set a pot of water on the stove even before she brewed her tea. Vegetables for that evening's meal were simmering by the time Moshe returned from the predawn prayer quorum. She watched as he lifted his fingers reverently to the mezuzah affixed to the doorpost, as he carefully replaced the royal blue velvet bag that contained his prayer shawl and phylacterics in the drawer, as he washed his hands and murmured a prayer, and then poured himself coffee and came to sit beside her on the small enclosed balcony that overlooked the garden. He spoke softly to her then with the quiet intensity of a man who was not afraid to share his thoughts and feelings. In that, he was not unlike Neil, Elaine realized, a similarity that was unsurprising. Hadn't Neil, accomplished analyst that he was, often observed that women tended to marry men like their fathers? Sarah had not proven him wrong.

She listened sympathetically as Moshe spoke of his worries about the children. Leora was too quiet, Ephraim too mischievous, Yuval caught cold so easily and Leah was an exhausting bundle of energy. Elaine offered patent reassurances. Children change, they develop, they grow. *And sometimes they grow into strangers.* The thought came unbidden. She hugged it to herself as her son-in-law refilled his cup.

Moshe told her how grateful he was that she was helping Sarah. His wife worked too hard. There was her business, the children, her devotion to the needs of the community. It would be wonderful if Elaine could spend more time with them, even more wonderful if she could see herself living in Jerusalem for even part of the year. The parents of many of their friends had done just that and their presence made a difference.

"It's not an easy life that we have chosen," he said, but there was no regret in his voice.

"Why did you choose it?" Elaine asked.

He considered, then answered carefully.

"It gives me everything I did not have before. All through college, then in medical school and when I traveled, I felt a kind of emptiness. I wanted my life to mean something beyond myself and I wanted to feel myself part of a caring community. I found all that in the yeshiva world. There's a spiritual and intellectual complexity in the sacred texts that engage me in a way that my secular education never did. I love studying and I love teaching. And it comforts me to know that there is meaning in every small action of my life, acknowledged meaning. Everything is sanctified—the washing of hands, the sight of a rainbow, the rising of the sun. I wish I knew a blessing for Sarah's smile. She's wonderful, your daughter, my wife."

"Yes, she is." Elaine smiled at him in agreement as the household stirred into wakefulness and another busy day began.

Each morning Moshe loaded the van, some days with the bolts of fabrics which he would distribute to Sarah's small army of seamstresses and on other days with the cartons of finished garments to be delivered to customers in distant enclaves. The rest of his day would be spent at the yeshiva where his time would be divided between teaching and studying.

Elaine helped Sarah dress the children and give them breakfast. There was the inevitable search for a vanished shoe, the dash to prepare lunches, spats between Ephraim and Leora.

"Stop teasing me."

"I wasn't."

"You were."

"Baby."

And then both children were running down the road to school turning to wave goodbye to Sarah and Elaine who stood on the balcony and waved them on.

Together, they walked Yuval and Leah to Ruth's house, already in chaotic disarray as toddlers scampered through the garden, cradled stuffed animals, laughed and sobbed. Ruth moved calmly through her small kingdom, her cell phone tucked into the pocket of her bright red apron, a diaper always in readiness on her shoulder. Now and again, she would respond to a buzz on the intercom and rush upstairs, leaving her daughter Michal in charge.

"Avi probably needs her," Sarah explained to Elaine the first time Ruth dashed away in midsentence.

Avi worked at home. He was a theoretical physicist whose research had attracted international attention. His work was accomplished on a specially designed computer. He was blind. Sarah had told her in that calm, accepting tone that Elaine found both admirable and infuriating. A grenade had exploded in his face as he guarded a school in a Gaza border settlement while he was on duty there.

Occasionally, if Sarah had errands to run, Elaine remained at Ruth's. She showed the toddlers how to shape clay, amused them by creating small animals with scraps of plasticene, intricate shapes with pipe cleaners. She watched as Ruth rushed from one child to another, dispensing hugs, smiling reprovingly at two small girls who quarreled over a stuffed animal.

"You're wonderful with children," she said.

"It's my joy," Ruth replied. "It's my way of giving back."

"Giving back?" Elaine asked.

Ruth hesitated, looked hard at Elaine but before she could speak, Avi, tall and lean, his hair and beard the color of the ochre desert where he had been born, approached them, tapping his way carefully across the garden with his white-tipped cane. He smiled pleasantly at them and lifted his face to the sun.

"It's good to feel the warmth beginning. You will see how beautiful our country is in the springtime," he told Elaine. "You can feel the heat even in the evening sun."

She marveled at how he had adjusted to the loss of his sight, of his ability to see the changing colors of his country as its meadows burst into blossom, how he could speak with such pleasure of the evening sun whose light was forever lost to him.

It surprised her then when some days later Avi had himself talked about Gaza in his calm, gravelly voice, during a Shabbat dinner.

"Gaza, *Gush Katif,* was beautiful," he said, in the wistful voice of a man who would never again be able to focus his gaze on beauty. "But the price the State paid for it was too high."

"If you had it to do over again, would you serve in on the border, *Abba?*" It was Ruth and Avi's lovely teenaged daughter, Michal, who asked the question. Michal, Elaine knew, would begin her army service within months. Unlike many orthodox girls, she had elected to be inducted into the regular army. Elaine wondered if Michal was suddenly questioning her own decision.

"I would," Avi replied, twisting the handle of his white cane. "You know, Michal, I found my way to orthodoxy only after I was wounded. I began to ask questions about why it was that I had been sent to that settlement, why it was that I was standing in that exact place at that exact moment and I came to understand that it was the hand of God that sent me there. That grenade could have hit the school, could have hit children. And if I had not been wounded, I would not have been sent to Hadassah Hospital and I would not have met your mother. Again, God's hand." He smiled and moved closer to Ruth, pressed her fingers to his lips.

"But why didn't the hand of God prevent that grenade from being thrown at all?" Elaine asked, struggling against a sudden anger. *And why didn't the hand of God prevent that clot, that berry-shaped cluster of blood from exploding in Neil's brain?* She choked the thought into silence. Her hand trembled and drops of wine from the glass she held spilled out onto the snow-white cloth. Tear-shaped scarlet drops.

Her question, each word etched with anger, ricocheted against their wall of silence. She demanded reason. They could only offer faith. Too swiftly, Sarah began to clear the table. The remaining flames of the Sabbath candles sputtered and burned out. The older children slipped away from the table, as though sensing the new uneasiness. It was Moshe who spoke at last.

"The sages teach us that we cannot always understand the ways of the Lord. Avi speaks of the hand of God and we understand that it is a hand that often moves in mysterious ways," he said gently.

Elaine did not reply. She looked around the table. Moshe, his eyes closed, had already begun to chant the grace after meals. Dov, one of his students, lightly tapped the table as he lifted his voice in prayer. She envied them their faith, their certitude. She did not open her own prayer book but sat in silence, smiling only when Leora, who sat beside her, rested her head on her shoulder.

Later that evening, as she sat on the balcony, Sarah, wearing a long gauzy robe of her own design, came and sat beside her.

"I want to thank you for trying to understand, Mom," she said. "I know it's hard for you to accept our life, our belief."

Elaine nodded. "I've tried. But I think of the difference between your life and Lisa's. I don't agree with all the choices she's made but her path is easier. She used her talents. She has a profession, a comfortable life. She lives in familiar territory."

"Familiar to you. Alien to me. And not everything about Lisa's life was a choice." Immediately, she regretted her words. Lisa's secret was her own. Sarah was not free to share it with their mother. "And I am using my talents. I'm still involved with my art. You know that. We've been working together, you and I, haven't we?" She willed Elaine to acknowledge their shared efforts of the weeks past. "And I'm using my talents as a mother, a Jewish mother."

"As I didn't?" Elaine asked.

"I didn't say that. But for you and Dad, being Jewish was just part of who you were. It wasn't central to your lives. You belonged to a synagogue the way you belonged to a political party. You sent us to Hebrew school the way you gave us piano lessons. Bar and bat mitzvahs were more like social occasions than religious observances. It worked for you and Dad because I think in a way you were each other's spiritual life, but I always felt a kind of emptiness. I don't feel that anymore."

Sarah fell silent and leaned forward, studying the small Sabbath eve parade that progressed past the balcony. She loved the peace of this hour, the communal pattern repeating itself week after week. Couples returning from Sabbath dinners strolled homeward at an unhurried pace. A sweet stillness blanketed the neighborhood. There was no traffic on the road, no sound of radios or television, only the distant hum of Sabbath songs. A group of boys looked up and waved at her as they passed. A small family walked down the quiet street, the father carrying a sleeping child, his black fur-trimmed hat pushed back, his eyes lifted skyward. He sang softly, perhaps a prayer, perhaps a lullaby. She rested her hand on the gentle rise of her abdomen. Was it possible that her unborn child could hear that prayer, that lullaby? She leaned closer to her mother who spoke so softly that she had to strain to hear her.

"We both grew up in orthodox homes, your father and I," Elaine said. "Immigrant homes. Our parents—your grandparents' lives had been poisoned by all that had happened to them in Russia. All they kept were the rituals. Joyless. Life-stifling. And the fear. They went to the synagogue to weep. We wanted our lives, your lives, to be different. We didn't want your childhoods to be darkened as ours had been. We had Friday night dinners, the holidays, and it seemed enough. None of you ever asked for more."

"I didn't know what it was I was missing until I came to Jerusalem, until I spent Shabbat with the Cohens. And then I realized what I had been missing and what I wanted. I tried to talk about it with you but I kind of felt an emotional shutdown. Dad put all sorts of psychological slants on what I was saying and you just listened, argued briefly and accepted it—the way you accepted Denis's homosexuality and Peter's decision to marry Lauren and Lisa's decision not to marry at all. So I stopped trying."

"Then I stand guilty of the sin of acceptance?" Elaine asked harshly. "What would you have had me do, what would you have had me say? Was it so bad to accept my children's decisions, to accept the lives they had chosen for themselves?"

She stared at her daughter, flushed with anger. She and Neil had prided themselves on being unlike friends who had descended into depressions when a child dropped out of college to trek through the far east, or another couple who had disowned their son when he married an Asian doctor. Even Serena, her college roommate, had been estranged for many years from her daughter when she revealed that she was gay. But the Gordon children had always been free to make their own decisions. And now, it seemed that it was that very freedom that Sarah—and perhaps the others—had resented. She waited tensely for Sarah's answer.

"Not bad. Just not enough." Sarah's voice trembled with sadness. She would not tell her mother that it was Lisa who claimed that their parents' calm acceptance came easily because they simply did not care that deeply.

"They are central to each other's lives," Lisa had said bitterly. *"We're just appendages. You and me. Denis and Peter. Oh sure, they love us, but we're not their focus. All we have to do is not rock their boat, not interrupt their gourmet dinners for two, their quiet evenings alone, their precious work."*

"What would have made it enough?" Elaine asked.

"We would have wanted you to understand why we made the choices we did, to be part of our lives. To do what you're doing now, sharing and caring."

Elaine touched her daughter's hand. It was very cold. She encased it in both her own and they sat together for a few more minutes in the velvet darkness and then went inside, wearied and unconsoled.

★ ★ ★

Some days later Moshe suggested that Elaine accompany him on one of his longer journeys to deliver completed orders of Sarah's robes to customers north of Jerusalem.

"We want you to see Israel. Jerusalem is wonderful but the rest of the country is beautiful. I'll be driving along the coast and through orchard country. And now both the citrus trees and the almond trees are in blossom. Sarah, can you spare your mother for a short while?"

"Of course," Sarah agreed. "And Moshe is a great guide, Mom."

"Can I go?" Leora asked wistfully.

"You have your school trip, Leora. You don't want to miss going north with your class. And Michal will be going along to help the teacher," Moshe said.

"All right then," Leora said, no longer disappointed. She adored Michal and always contrived to sit next to her when the Evenarises came to dinner. Perhaps she could sit next to her on the bus. She kissed her grandmother, as though to apologize for being so easily dissuaded and dashed off to find the bright yellow sun hat Elaine had brought from America. She wanted to wear it on the trip.

"So what do you say?" Moshe looked expectantly at Elaine.

"Well, if Sarah can manage."

She glanced at her daughter, who nodded. It occurred to Elaine that perhaps they were mutually relieved to have some time apart. There had been a subtle tension between them since their conversation on the balcony. They had said too much, or perhaps not enough. She was certain only of

one thing. She would no longer be content with a coun-
terfeit acquiescence. Sarah had demanded sharing and
caring, an abandonment of superficial acceptance. She
would follow that dictate. Hazardous as it might be, she
would speak her mind.

"You'll have a great time, Mom," Sarah said.

"Yes. I think I will. It sounds like fun."

She saw Sarah and Moshe exchange a glance of amusement. *Fun* was not a word they had expected her to use.

She packed a small bag, aglow with the anticipation she
had always felt at the onset of even the briefest journey.
She dreamed that night that she and Neil, hand in hand,
were hiking a shaded mountain pass. Suddenly she was
alone but unafraid. She walked on and crossed a mysterious border that descended into a valley. As she approached
it, sunlight streaked down the incline and she stood within
its folds, draped in radiance. She awakened eager to
continue a journey that had already begun.

They set out at dawn, as the melancholy pastel rays of
the early spring sun ribbed the sky, spreading toward the
slowly vanishing moon. Sarah, wrapped in a shawl, shivered
as she gave Moshe last-minute instructions.

"Don't leave anything with Levenson at Gan Yair unless
he pays you for the last shipment. Make sure Malka at
Shoshanim counts everything while you're there. Last time
she said that we had shorted her two robes although I'm
sure we didn't. I credited her but I'm not going to do it
again. And give my mother some time to see Caesarea.
She'll love the view," she said.

"I will take excellent care of your mother. And of Levenson. And of Malka," Moshe assured her good-naturedly. "And I want you to promise that you'll take very good care of yourself. And our treasures." He glanced up at the bedroom windows where the children slept, his farewell kisses still damp upon their foreheads.

Elaine marveled at the tenderness of his tone. Each day she grew fonder of her tall, bearded son-in-law, the brilliant scholar, the devoted husband, the gentle father.

"And Moshe—be careful," Sarah said. "You're sure you don't want to take your rifle?"

"I will be very careful," he promised and placed his hand on the gentle rise of his wife's abdomen as though his touch might protect the unborn child sheltered there.

"You should take a weapon," she murmured.

"No." His voice was firm. "I have all the protection I need."

He opened his jacket and pointed to the pocket where he had placed the leather-bound book of Psalms that had been Sarah's wedding gift to him.

"And don't take any side roads." Sarah lifted her hands to his face and looked at him, her eyes narrowed with worry.

"Only the main highway," he promised.

"All right." Defeated, Sarah embraced him and then kissed her mother.

"Have a great time, Mom."

"I will," Elaine said.

She settled herself comfortably on the front seat of the

van, her sketch pad on her lap, her colored drawing pencils in easy reach. She worked as Moshe drove, their silence companionable. She wanted to capture the shapes and shades of the terrain as the hills of Judea descended into the plains and flowering citrus and almond trees replaced the tall cypresses that stood guard over the ancient city. She envisioned a series of enamel tiles, each one discrete—a tree, an outcropping of rock, a vineyard trellis—together forming a tactile portrait of the lovely landscape she was slowly beginning to understand.

Sarah had introduced her to Galit, a ceramicist, who had offered her access to her studio. Elaine felt a new eagerness to work in her own medium, to create her own glazes, to feel the heat of the kiln against her face, to inhale the scent of the damp clay and the acrid chemicals. After Neil's death, she had completed works already in progress but now, for the first time, she felt the urge to create something new. The tiles could actually be formed into a mural, perhaps a memorial to Neil. It could be placed on a wall of the hospital or perhaps in the synagogue. She imagined the plaque, etched in flowing script. *In Memory of Dr. Neil Gordon, Healer of Souls.* The thought pleased and soothed her. Neil would remain a presence in the lives of others. His name would not be forgotten.

She worked easily throughout the trip north, now pausing to contemplate a new view or simply to close her eyes against the sun's fierce brightness. She accompanied Moshe as he delivered the cartons and took new orders. He introduced her to his customers, bearded shopkeepers, bewigged women who sold the robes to their neighbors, young couples who **ran boutiq**ues. Sarah's designs were attracting buyers outside of the orthodox community.

"My wife's mother," he said to each of them. "She, too, is an artist."

Elaine was moved by his pride in Sarah, his pride in her. She was amused when he addressed Levenson who owned a shop in Netanya.

"My mother-in-law is keeping our books now," he said slyly. "And she is upset that we seem not to have received a payment for our last delivery. Myself, I don't care but my American mother-in-law…" He shrugged and Levenson stared at her through narrowed eyes and wrote a check.

"I understand, Rav Chazani," he said. "I, too, have a mother-in-law."

At Malka's market stall in Binyamina, he insisted that she count the robes in the carton.

"It's my mother-in-law's idea," he explained. "That seems to be how they do business in America."

Sullenly, Malka complied.

"And could you sign the receipt?" Elaine asked sternly.

"Moshe, I didn't know you had it in you," she laughed as they sped northward.

"Remember, I used to be Mike Singer and Mike Singer took a selling job every summer vacation," he said.

"It's interesting to see Moshe Chazani morph into Mike Singer," she said and thought that it would be even more interesting if Sarah Chazani occasionally morphed into Sandy Gordon. It was not an idea she would share with her daughter.

They went as far north as Caesarea. Elaine followed Moshe as he explained how the ancient Roman city had been so carefully excavated. They stood atop a cliff and looked down at the clear blue-green expanse of the Mediterranean Sea and the waves that gathered momentum as they rushed to their foam-rimmed death against the dark rocks of the sea wall.

"Magnificent," she said.

"God's gift," he replied and murmured a prayer.

They stayed at the home of an orthodox couple who ran a small bed-and-breakfast. It pleased Elaine that the woman wore a robe of Sarah's design.

Moshe spoke to Sarah on his cell phone, summarized their adventures, asked about the children.

"Of course I'm being careful," he said. "We'll be home tomorrow before dinner."

"Mom, make sure you leave early," Sarah said worriedly when Moshe passed the phone to her. "There have been a couple of incidents."

Incidents, Elaine knew, was Israeli shorthand for terrorist attacks.

"We'll give ourselves plenty of time," she assured her daughter.

Sarah did not answer. Instead she spoke of Leora's excitement over her class trip.

"She looked like a little sunflower in that yellow hat."

They did set out early, making only one stop and then once again they headed southward. Refreshed, Elaine once again took up her pad.

Her pencils flew as she worked swiftly to capture the passing scene, settling for outlines she could later fill in from memory. She was so absorbed in her work that she barely noticed the motorcycle that sped by as though to pass the school bus just ahead of them. Her pad slipped from her lap and she was jerked forward, restrained only by her seat belt, as Moshe suddenly accelerated. He bore down on the gas pedal, his hands gripping the wheel, his lips clenched.

"Moshe, be careful," she shouted but relentlessly he drew abreast of the motorcyclist and he turned the wheel sharply.

"Moshe!" she screamed as the motorcycle swerved and careened, the rider's head swiveling, his eyes wide with fear.

Again Moshe pressed toward him, this time crashing hard against the front wheel so that the cyclist was thrown from his seat into a culvert and the cycle itself toppled over on its side like a wounded animal.

The bus ahead stopped and Elaine saw the faces of bewildered children pressed against the window. She gasped at the sight of a small girl in a bright yellow sun hat.

"Leora," she thought. "Our Leora."

But Moshe was already out of the car, running toward the fallen cyclist. The bus driver, pistol in hand, and two other men were following him. She, too, raced after them, pausing when Moshe waved them away as he bent over the inert body. The rider had fallen on his back. Blood trickled from his mouth and his eyes were closed although his hand twitched. Moshe kicked his hand away and snapped open his black leather jacket. Strapped about the youth's waist was a leather belt laden with cartridges that glinted in the sunlight. Two wires, one blue and one orange ran from the belt into the sleeve of the jacket. An attached detonator lay on the ground.

"Elaine—the shears—in the back of the van," Moshe shouted.

She hurried to the van, found the shears and ran back. The bus driver, his face very pale, perspiration beading his brow, handed them to Moshe. Carefully, his lips moving in silent prayer, Moshe hefted them, held them at one angle, corrected it and then, with a single lightning-swift movement, he clipped the wire.

The driver wiped his brow. One of the security guards turned away and vomited into the culvert. Moshe stood and although he still held the shears, Elaine saw that his hands were trembling.

"Move the bus," he instructed the driver. "All the way down the road. Elaine, go with him."

Elaine hesitated and then remembered her glimpse of the yellow sun hat. She hurried after the driver, gripping a rail as he moved the vehicle swiftly down the road and then looked at the children. The small girl who wore the yellow sun hat was blond and tears streaked her cheeks. Elaine took the child, who was not her granddaughter, Leora, into her arms, and rocked her gently, spoke to her soothingly even as her own heart beat too rapidly and her hands trembled.

Sirens sounded. An ambulance pulled up, two police cars, then an army truck. Traffic backed up as uniformed men and women filled the roadway. Moshe spoke to one officer and then another. He pointed to the belt. Delicate as surgeons, soldiers from the demolition squad cut it away from the inert body, placed it into a receptacle and sped away. A white-jacketed doctor bent over the cyclist who was then moved onto a stretcher and into the ambulance. Lights flashing, it sped down the road. A police tow truck arrived. Moshe watched as the damaged motorcycle was carted away.

An army officer boarded the bus. He spoke to the driver and the security guards in Hebrew, checked their licenses and registrations, carefully recorded their statements. Then he turned to Elaine and spoke to her in English.

"Your son-in-law is a very brave man, Mrs. Gordon," he said. "He saved the lives of all these children. He knew exactly what he was doing."

He patted the golden curls of the child still nestled on her lap.

"I have a daughter just her age," he said.

"My granddaughter—she has a yellow sun hat," Elaine confided haltingly.

Unspoken words, fragile as a spider's web, trembled between them. They understood that all the children in their lives, all those they loved, were vulnerable to acts of insane violence, to the impact of exploding cartridges that would sever golden-curled heads from slender bodies and send yellow sun hats skittering across highways slick with blood. Elaine trembled and gently placed the child on a seat beside a window. She shook hands with the officer and walked with him back to the van where Moshe sat, the leather-bound book of Psalms in his hand. She waited patiently until he finished reading, waited again as he replaced the book in his jacket pocket and called Sarah.

"There was an incident," he said, his voice, very calm. "But it's over and we're on our way home. Is Leora home? Good. Did she have a good time? Good."

"How did you know—how could you have known that he was a suicide bomber?" Elaine asked as he drove, very slowly now, toward Jerusalem.

"His jacket was bulky—too bulky. And although he moved rapidly, he had poor control and kept zigzagging. I just knew he was heading for the school bus. Instinct, I suppose. Luckily, I was right."

"And how did you know what to do about the wires?"

"In the army I worked in the demolition squad. I still work with them when I do reserve duty. Sarah never told you that?"

"No." She wondered what else Sarah had neglected to tell her about her husband, about her life, about the perils of her days and the fears of her nights, all sustained by the faith that Elaine struggled still to comprehend.

She sat back and closed her eyes. The danger was over, they were safe, Leora was home, that school trip, at least, uneventful, and yet, inexplicably, she began to cry. She made no move to hide her tears from her daughter's husband, the gentle bearded man who recited Psalms, analyzed the most difficult Talmudic tractates, spoke gently to his children and, with calm and skill, disarmed a belt loaded with explosives.

eight

The pace of life in the Chazani household accelerated as Passover drew near. In addition to the frenzied house-cleaning, the ritual emptying and reordering of every drawer and cabinet, the washing and polishing of Passover dishes and silverware, there was the press of Sarah's business. She and her seamstresses worked furiously to complete the orders on hand. Each day there were calls from shopkeepers and boutique owners in distant parts of the country, seeking to increase their inventory.

"It's a gift-giving season," Sarah said wearily as she reluctantly agreed to add fifteen robes to the order of a widow who sold them from her home in Cfar Saba.

"She needs the money," she explained to Elaine. "And you should be flattered. She especially wanted your fabric design."

"All right. I'm flattered. But you're doing too much," Elaine said worriedly. "You should rest more. For the baby's sake, for your sake."

She looked impatiently around her daughter's kitchen. Every surface was covered—the table with the remnants of the children's breakfasts, the counters with cans from the pantry which Sarah was readying for Passover purchases, the worktable with tissue-paper patterns and fabric scraps.

Sarah cleared the table, thrust the dirty dishes into a pan of soapy water and turned away from her mother.

"I'm fine, Mom. Really. Aren't you working at Galit's studio today?"

Elaine recognized the edge in her daughter's voice. Sarah, like herself, craved time alone, time to quietly wrench order from domestic chaos, free of the voices and needs of others. She, of course, had always been able to escape to her studio, but Sarah's crowded home offered no such refuge.

And, Elaine acknowledged guiltily, she did want to spend the morning in Galit's studio, engrossed in her own work. She had completed the first enamel tile for the mosaic mural, Neil's name etched in strokes of silver and gold dancing skyward, and she hoped to fire it that day.

"I'll be off then," she told her daughter. "And I'll pick up the cake for Michal's farewell dinner tonight. My treat."

Michal would be inducted into the army early the next morning and Ruth had invited the Chazanis and other friends to a festive meal to mark her leave-taking.

"It's a rite of passage for Israeli kids—the beginning of

their army service," Ruth had explained to Elaine. "And it's particularly important for Michal. Most of the Ramat Chessed girls opt for national service rather than the army. That's usually the pattern for orthodox girls. But Michal always said that she wanted to be an officer. Maybe because of Avi..." Her voice had drifted into a worried whisper.

"I would think it would be just the opposite," Elaine had countered. A girl whose father had been blinded in a military action, who understood the danger, might be deterred, especially if army service was not the norm in her community.

"She wants her courage to match her father's," Ruth replied quietly. "And like Avi, like all of us, she relies on the protection of God."

"And perhaps the protection of Gideon," Elaine added, smiling.

Handsome Gideon, himself an officer in an elite tank squad, had long been Michal's boyfriend, an unusual coupling in a community which frowned on any physical intimacy between unmarried young men and women, even imposing prohibitions on their being alone together— prohibitions which Michal and her Gideon ignored.

"Perhaps." Ruth had smiled. She approved of Gideon and she approved of Michal and Gideon together. It pleased her that he would be at the dinner that night. He brought a glow to her beautiful daughter's face that delighted her.

At Galit's studio, Elaine shrugged into her bright-red smock, tied her hair back and made small corrections on the completed tile before sliding it into the kiln. It was not as sophisticated as her own but Galit, an accomplished ceramicist, was skilled at regulating the heat. Flushed and excited she began work on the second tile. The design, a crouching olive tree canopied by graceful silver leaves, some shaped like stars and others like teardrops, pleased her. The colors were somber grays and greens which would contrast dramatically with the brilliant golds and blues she envisioned for her depiction of the Jerusalem skyline.

She worked quickly, her color high, trading one stylus for another, sanding away an error and patiently correcting it. She relished her total absorption in the complex composition. She wanted to capture the gently sloping hills of the city, the skyline of spires and rooftop clotheslines, the symbols of a city consecrated to prayer and pledged to life, the city that Neil had loved. She watched her design take shape, indifferent to the passing hours, unaware of Galit's movements from drafting table to drawing board. She was cocooned in her work, free of thought and worry, of loss and loneliness.

She did not even look up when the phone rang. Galit touched her on the shoulder.

"That was Sarah. She said to make sure the cake had a chocolate mousse icing. That's Michal's favorite."

Elaine glanced at her watch.

"I had no idea it was so late," she said.

She moved swiftly then, placing a damp cloth over the still unfinished etching, spraying fixative on the newly fired tile.

Galit looked at it approvingly.

"The glaze is exactly right," she said. "It's wonderful when that happens."

"Yes, it is," Elaine agreed.

The long months of grief, the bewilderment of sorrow, had blocked that wonder, but now it had been regained. She looked around the spacious studio, flooded with the sunshine of late afternoon. Galit had spoken to her about sharing the space. With a few renovations, this work place would suit her, Elaine thought. She could work here easily if she should decide to stay in Jerusalem for longer periods, if she could find a small house or an apartment. She would not choose to live in Ramat Chessed, of course; it was too confining, too religious, but possibly she could find something not too far away. She smiled at the idea, loosened her hair, tried briefly and unsuccessfully to brush the tangle of dark silver-edged curls into smoothness and hurried to the bakery.

She bought the cake with chocolate mousse icing for Michal and held the white box carefully on the crowded bus that carried her back to Ramat Chessed.

Order had been restored to Sarah's kitchen. Ephraim and Moshe sat together at the dining room table, Moshe patiently helping his son with his arithmetic homework. Leora played on the floor with Leah and Yuval, the baby, slept peacefully in his carriage. Sarah proudly showed her a pile of brightly patterned robes, newly pressed and ready to be delivered. Elaine smiled.

"Your work is beautiful," she said softly and fingered first one garment and then another.

It was not, after all, such an improbable life that her daughter had chosen. There was peace and purpose in this home. Love canopied the family. Work and study were accomplished. She took Sarah's hand and felt the loving pressure of her daughter's fingers interlaced with her own. Wordlessly, they acknowledged that a line had been crossed, a new recognition achieved.

Michal's farewell dinner was festive. Ruth had reclaimed her house and transformed it from a day-care center into a home, toys and play tables banished to the balconies, high chairs lined up in the garden. Pots of early blooming red anemones, still fresh with the dew of the Galilee, blazed on every table and the fragrance of lamb stew simmering in a marinade of thyme and wine mingled with the aroma of freshly baked *pitta* breads. Each new arrival brought a covered dish, each dish tasting of vanished kitchens in distant lands. Hungarian goulash, a tagine of steamed chicken and eggplant, chopped salads of tomato and cucumber blanketed with glittering sprigs of parsley.

Beautiful Michal, her rose-gold hair the color of the tendrils that escaped from Ruth's ritual head covering floating about her shoulders, wore a linen dress of the palest blue. She drifted through the room trailed by her younger siblings, with handsome Gideon, proud and impressive in his officer's uniform, never far from her side. Elaine had been introduced to his own kibbutznik parents and to his grandparents, a diminutive white-haired couple, their faces gaunt, their bodies stooped.

"They are holocaust survivors," Sarah had whispered to her.

Elaine had thought of Ruth's mother, the German woman who had married the English minister. Here then, in this Jerusalem living room, history had come full circle and, perhaps, recompense of a kind was realized. Could this be what Ruth had meant when she spoke of giving back? The question teased but she knew she would find no answer to it.

Elaine looked at Avi, carefully maneuvering his way from group to group, the affable host pausing at each table, smiling, always smiling, holding his cane too lightly, his unseeing eyes concealed by the dark glasses he always wore. She supposed that he, and perhaps Moshe and Sarah as well, would call it the hand of God. Neil would probably have thought of it as a kind of psycho-historical transference. She herself simply thought that Michal and Gideon were a wonderful young couple whose beauty and strength radiated throughout this room filled with friends and relatives who had gathered to wish them well.

"I love you, Michal," small Leora said.

"I love you too, Leora," Michal replied gravely. She had worked in her mother's day-care center long enough to learn that the words of small children must be accepted with great seriousness.

Leora turned to Elaine.

"And I love you too, *Savta*. Will you stay with us forever and ever?"

Sarah, watching them, cradled Yuval with one arm and

rested the other on the rise of her pregnancy. The child she carried, the child she would name for her father, kicked gently as she looked first at her daughter and then at her mother. Moshe touched her shoulder. They waited for Elaine's answer to the question they themselves had not dared to ask.

"Forever is a very long time, Leora," Elaine said at last. "But we'll see."

And then they all turned their attention to Avi and Ruth who stood together in the center of the room, their glasses held high.

"We wish our daughter, Michal, great happiness in this brave new adventure," Avi said. "*L'Chaim*. To life."

"*L'Chaim,*" Ruth repeated and the single word resonated throughout the room.

Elaine too lifted her glass to her lips. The wine was too sweet and too warm but she drank it with pleasure and then bent to kiss Leora's forehead.

The night before the Passover seder Sarah's home was at last in readiness. The windows sparkled, the ceramic floors were spotless, every surface had been cleared and dusted. Moshe had emptied his large library and had shaken every book to dislodge any lurking crumbs and handed them one by one to Leora and Ephraim who carefully wiped each volume before returning it to newly polished shelves. Elaine had helped Sarah carry the carpets and draperies outside where they were beaten and spread out to air in the sharp cleansing light of the Judean sun. All that week the balconies of Ramat Chessed had been a riot of color as bedspreads fluttered in the gentle breeze and brightly colored pillows, newly washed and still damp, formed small islands on lawns of tender young grass. The Passover silverware had been polished, the holiday dishes placed on the shelves, and the food and groceries neatly stacked in cabinet and refrigerator.

Once, during that week, Elaine had escaped the frenetic activity of the household and taken the bus into Jerusalem. Seated in the crowded café of the Anna Ticho Museum, nursing a cup of coffee which she really did not want, she was approached by a well-dressed American woman who asked diffidently if she might share the table. She had nodded her assent. The woman set her tray down and removed her designer sunglasses. Her eyes were red-rimmed, her face very pale. She was from Oregon, she told Elaine, on a visit to her son and daughter-in-law who lived on Har Nof, an extremely orthodox Jerusalem neighborhood. She had planned to spend Passover with them but she had decided to leave before the holiday.

"I can't bear their life," she had said. "I don't speak their language. I hate their narrowness. My son is a stranger to me. How did my Joey, the boy whose field hockey uniform I washed and ironed, whose college applications I drove to the post office at midnight become a bearded man who calls himself Yosef, who mumbles prayers when he washes his hands, when he eats a piece of bread, when he sips a glass of wine? He went to Brown, my Joey. He played the guitar. He got into Harvard Law and now he sits all day and studies in a yeshiva. I feel, God help me, as though I have buried my only child. My husband was right not to come with me."

Tears had streaked her face. She clenched her fists, her well-manicured nails cutting into the soft flesh of her palms.

"Perhaps if you tried to understand him, if you tried to understand the life he has chosen it would be easier for you," Elaine had said gently as she rose to leave.

She had no words to assuage the woman's grief, to compensate her for a loss that was, after all, real and enduring. She had wondered, as she traveled back to Ramat Chessed on the bus, why she had not told the mother whose son Joey had become Yosef, about her daughter Sandy who now called herself Sarah. She thrust the thought from her mind and stopped at Ruth's house to pick up Leah and Yuval. Sarah was busy enough.

As the holiday drew nearer the women of the community rushed from household tasks to food markets, their faces flushed, their arms always laden, often juggling a string bag overflowing with fruits and vegetables and a sleeping infant. The men sped away in their cars and returned with cases of eggs and cartons bloodied by meat and chicken which were swiftly carried into kitchens and emptied into refrigerators that had been scrubbed clean, each shelf newly lined. Schoolchildren raced importantly up and down the streets in earnest pursuit of forgotten ingredients for a cake, an elusive spice for a soup. They popped in and out of Sarah's kitchen. "My mother wants to know if you have nutmeg." "Sage." "Dill." And Sarah had turned away from her worktable to rummage in her cabinets and sent the small messengers home clutching the fragrant packets.

The seamstresses had dashed in to deliver the completed robes and they waited shyly as Sarah examined each one before handing them the money due them. Their faces brightened with relief as they counted the notes. Their earnings, Elaine knew, would be spent on new holiday clothing and shoes for their children. Sarah's enterprise sustained many families besides her own.

Moshe and Sarah placed the completed robes, each one wrapped in tissue paper, in a large carton which he would deliver the next day to waiting customers in the north. The widow in Cfar Saba had called several times and Sarah had repeatedly calmed her and assured her that the robes would arrive early in the afternoon on the day of the seder. She did not remind her that she had only accepted the last-minute order as a favor.

"Why make her feel bad?" she had asked her mother.

"I didn't know that I had given birth to a saint," Elaine had retorted and, seeing the color rise in Sarah's cheeks she had immediately regretted her words. "But isn't Moshe cutting it rather close—driving north to make the deliveries and then rushing back to be in time for the seder?" she asked, her concern an apology of sorts.

"No. I'll leave before dawn," Moshe said. "I'll be in Cfar Saba by lunch and home well before evening. That's one of the advantages of living in a small country."

"You'll be careful, Moshe?" Sarah's voice trembled.

There had been a suicide bombing in a Tel Aviv café days earlier and a drive-by shooting only hours later.

"I'll be careful. I'll take the tunnel road. And Ruth asked me to pick up Michal and Gideon. Michal's base is just kilometers away from Cfar Saba and she has leave for the holiday. So I'll be well protected by two soldiers of Israel."

He laughed and Sarah smiled. It was odd to think that Michal, whom she had known from babyhood, whose hair she had plaited, was now a soldier who carried a rifle as casually as she herself had once carried a book bag.

"All right. I'll get the children and we'll do the search for *chametz*."

Elaine and Neil, who had always hosted a seder, even using special dishes and cutlery, had never observed the pre-scribed ritual of searching for any remaining crumb of leavened bread but Sarah and Moshe, of course, would not ignore it. Elaine had watched Moshe conceal a crust of bread in a bit of newspaper and place it behind counters and into corners. She watched now as Leora and Ephraim followed their father while Leah toddled after them on her chubby little legs. Sarah carried Yuval, resting him on the shelf of her pregnant abdomen. She was pale with exhaus-tion and yet her eyes were soft and when Moshe lit a candle her face glowed in its gentle radiance. Holding a feather and a wooden spoon, he made his way through the house, brushing the feather into corners and across surfaces and feigning surprise at the discovery of crumbs. He brushed them onto his spoon and, chanting the ancient Aramaic prayer, he used the candle to set them aflame, then tossed the scorched remnants from the kitchen balcony into the cool night air. Smiling, he turned to his family.

"We are blessed," he said. "Our home is now holy and ready for the holiday, *Baruch HaShem,* blessed be God."

"Baruch HaShem," they responded solemnly.

Elaine remained silent. Suffused with an inexplicable melancholy she took Leora's hand in her own.

"Shall I read to you before you go to sleep, Leora?" she asked and the child nodded sleepily.

"A busy day tomorrow," Sarah warned. "Still a lot of cooking to be done."

"Yes," Elaine said. "I know."

She knew, too, as she lay awake that night, that the web of silken sadness in which she was suddenly entangled was woven of loss and denial. It had been beautiful to watch the children trail after their father, enchanted by the glow of his candle, the devotion of his prayer, but she herself had been a spectator, rather than a participant. She had felt herself at an emotional remove. She acknowledged the beauty of Sarah's world but she could not lay claim to it. Not yet. Perhaps not ever. *Perhaps.* The word lingered, its very uncertainty encouraging. Possibilities abounded. Smiling, she fell asleep.

Moshe was already gone when she awakened. He had left hours earlier, Sarah told her, crawling out of bed before dawn and driving northward into the darkness. She herself had already begun the cooking for the festive seder meal

and Elaine rushed to help her. Together they cut up vegetables to be plunged into the huge pot of boiling water
where a chicken was already simmering. Sarah whipped
egg whites and Elaine shaped matzoh balls, sculpting them
as carefully as she shaped the damp clumps of clay in her
studio. Leora dashed in and begged to be allowed to help.
Sarah showed her how to chop the walnuts and apples for
the seder plate. Elaine looked at her daughter and granddaughter, their faces flushed, their brows damp. She herself
hurried to the oven, removed a golden potato pudding,
thrust in a squash casserole. All sadness left her. This was
a gift, she thought. Three generations cooking together in
a kitchen flooded with sunlight.

This could be my world, she thought exultingly. *I could make
it my world.* There was a range of possibilities. Her nocturnal thoughts asserted themselves in the radiant light of day.

The phone rang. Lisa calling to wish them a happy
holiday.

"How are you doing, Mom?" Lisa asked.

"Fine. Great." Elaine calculated the time difference. It
was the middle of the night in Philadelphia but Lisa's voice
was determinedly upbeat. She and David were going to
friends for the seder. She had planned to spend the holiday
with Peter and his family in California but Lauren had
seemed hesitant and Lisa herself was wildly busy oversee-
ing a new clinic.

"What do you mean—Lauren seemed hesitant?" Elaine
asked.

"I can't say exactly. You know how she is. Her moods."

"Yes. I know how she is, her moods."

They were all uneasy with Lauren, the cool distant girl to whom Peter had become engaged during his senior year at UCLA. Elaine and Neil had thought him too young to make such a decision. They had found Lauren difficult to talk to, too status-conscious, too particular about the labels in her clothing, the size of her engagement ring. Elaine had crafted a pendant for her as a gift but Lauren had returned it.

"It's not my style," she had said and her words had wounded.

Neil had spoken to Peter about postponing the wedding.

"Neither of you have really lived yet," he had said calmly, reasonably. "You're both very young."

But Peter would not be dissuaded and in the end Elaine and Neil had simply accepted the marriage, repeating to each other the familiar mantra—their children's lives were their own. Peter was an adult and free to make his own decision.

They saw Peter and Lauren infrequently, visiting California when their grandchildren were born and now and again to celebrate a birthday. Peter's own visits east were hasty and Lauren seldom accompanied him.

Disconcerted by Lisa's call, Elaine called Peter later that day at his office. He was busy, he said. Lots of deals going down. Everything was fine. But when was she coming home from Israel?

"You have a couple of other kids, you know," he said teasingly but she discerned an unfamiliar edge in his voice.

"Have you spoken to Peter?" she asked Denis who called just before sundown as Sarah put the finishing touches to the beautifully set seder table, arranging a bowl of yellow roses at either end.

"He's fine," Denis said and hesitated. "Really fine," he added. "But I get the feeling that he's a little tense, too much going on. The business. The kids. Lauren. You know."

She did not know but there was no time to ask questions. Denis had to rush home. He and Andrew were hosting a seder, he explained. She did not ask him who their guests would be.

"Have a good holiday," she said and hung up, although she kept her hand on the receiver.

The optimism she had felt earlier had evaporated, leaving her vaguely dispirited. The conversations with her children in America exhausted and disconcerted her. Wearily, she braided Leora's hair, tied Ephraim's shoelaces. Sarah, dressed for the seder in a pale blue, wide-sleeved dress that flowed in graceful folds over the rise of her pregnancy, her hair covered with a matching kerchief, wandered out to the balcony and peered down the street.

"Moshe should have been home by now," she said worriedly.

She tried his cell phone. There was no answer. She went to another window and again looked out at the road. It was all but empty of traffic at the preholiday hour. The purr of a single car could be heard in the distance but it faded into silence. Elaine shivered, picked Yuval up as though the warmth of the toddler's body might vanquish the chill of her sudden fear.

"Wait for *Abba* outside," Sarah told Leora and Ephraim who scurried out the door.

"I'll see him first."

"No, I'll see him first."

Sarah shook her head at their amiable bickering and turned the radio on. The program of Passover music was interrupted by the sonorous voice of the newscaster. Elaine did not understand the Hebrew but she recognized the sorrow in his voice and she held Yuval even closer. Sarah stood very still, all color drained from her face, her hands clasped.

"What is he saying?" Elaine asked.

"There's been a terrorist attack on the tunnel road," Sarah said, the words falling heavily from her lips.

"That's the road…" Elaine did not complete the sentence but Sarah nodded.

"Yes. That's the road that Moshe would be traveling on."

"Oh, Sarah."

Elaine moved toward her daughter but Sarah shook her head. She stood very straight, her hands resting on her abdomen, as though the life she carried offered protection against the incursion of death.

"Please. It's the holiday. I have to bless candles." Her voice was faint but steady.

Elaine watched as Sarah held a match to the wicks of the tall white candles set in the brass candlesticks that had belonged to Neil's mother. The flames leapt up and she

passed her hands over them and then lifted her warm
fingers to her eyes as she whispered the benediction. She
spread her arms out, as though to embrace the flickering
lights themselves, and murmured the supplementary prayer
for the holiday. Elaine's voice joined her daughter's in those
gentle words of gratitude.

"Blessed art Thou O Lord our God who has granted us
life and sustenance and permitted us to reach this season."

"He'll be all right," Sarah said softly but her face was
ashen and her hands trembled.

Elaine seized her daughter's shoulders and gripped her
in a fierce embrace. She willed her own strength into her
daughter's quivering body, pressed the warmth of her lips
to forehead and cheeks grown cold with fear.

"Of course, he'll be all right." Her voice resonated with
maternal authority.

Sarah nodded and breathed deeply. Color returned to
her face. She tucked stray tendrils of chestnut-colored hair
beneath her kerchief and bathed her wrists in cold water.

Elaine was grateful that Leora and Ephraim dashed into
the room just then and even more grateful that the children
seemed unperturbed by their father's absence.

"God's going to be mad at *Abba* if he's late for the
seder," Ephraim said cheerfully.

"Oh, I think God will forgive him," Sarah said calmly.
She was still pale but her hands did not tremble as she filled
the wineglasses and carried out the seder plate.

Their guests arrived. Two of Moshe's students, tall young
men with soft curling beards who greeted Elaine in Ox-

bridge accents and presented Sarah with a bouquet of roses. A Russian family newly arrived in Ramat Chessed, the parents gold-toothed and chubby, the children wide-eyed and silent. The Evenarises, the younger children darting in first, followed by Ruth who carried a covered casserole and Avi whose cane clicked rhythmically across the tiled floor.

"Michal," Ruth called out gaily. "Where's my soldier daughter? I've made that lamb dish you love."

She paused and looked around the room.

"They're not here yet," Sarah said and Ruth stared at her.

"Has Moshe called?" she asked.

Sarah shook her head.

"Were they traveling on the tunnel road?" Avi asked. "There was a report—"

"That was Moshe's plan," Sarah said. "And yes. I heard the report."

They would not repeat the words of the newscaster. They spoke the cryptic language of adults intent on protecting children from a dark and threatening reality. Words were dangerous. Silence was safer than the revelation of that which had not yet been ascertained.

"Let's begin the seder," Sarah said softly.

Her cell phone was tucked into the pocket of her dress and she touched it as she might touch a talisman. As long as it did not ring they were safe.

They took their places at the table, opened their *haggaddot*. Elaine wondered how they would manage to sing the songs, to read the story, to celebrate the tale of freedom, enchained as they were in their own fear and apprehension but the children asked the four questions in a sweet chorus and Avi's strong voice began the chant of response.

"We were slaves unto Pharaoh in Egypt," he intoned but before he could go further the door opened.

Moshe stood in the doorway, flanked by Michal and Gideon.

Sarah rose from her seat, her cell phone clattering to the floor. She hurried to her husband, whispered his name, lifted her wide blue sleeves and fell, like a wounded bird, into his outstretched arms.

The room was electric with relief and excitement. Their contained grief exploded into joy. They waited for Moshe to wash the grime of the journey from his face. Michal changed out of her uniform into the bright green linen dress Ruth had brought for her. Elaine looked at her, startled by a marked change. Michal had lost the glow of casual innocence. Her face was newly serious, her gaze uneasy. She saw that Ruth, too, stared at her daughter with concern and moved closer to cover Michal's hand with her own. But Michal did not lift her eyes from the *hagaddah* as the reading of the ancient tale continued. They chanted and sang and read the text swiftly and seriously, filling and refilling their wineglasses at the prescribed times, dipping the parsley in salt water, grimacing at the taste of the bitter herb and creating matzoh sandwiches with the *charoset*.

At last the meal began and it was only when the soup was served that Avi asked the question that had haunted them even as they completed the reading and focused on the ceremony.

"What happened, Moshe? Did you see the attack?"

Michal's spoon clattered to the table. She hurried from the room and Gideon followed her.

"Our car was one of those attacked," Moshe replied.

Sarah pointed to the children and lifted a finger to her lips.

"No," he said. "It's good that they know what happened. You can't protect your children but you can prepare them. There is a lesson in what happened to us for them."

"Then tell us, *Abba,*" Leora insisted.

"There were several snipers, positioned in the overhang near Modiin. They all fired at once, each aiming at a different car. The van in front of us went out of control briefly and then sped away. The driver of the car behind us was wounded. I could see his face in my rearview mirror—a student I think, very young, red-haired. The bullet must have broken his cheekbone because I could see the blood running freely."

"And your car?" Ruth asked.

"I rolled up the windows as soon as I heard the disturbance. Gideon, of course, is experienced. He pushed Michal onto the floor—she was frightened, so frightened. He released the bolt of his rifle although, of course, it would have been impossible for him to see his target. I accelerated even as he took aim, but before he could shoot a bullet came through the window. A silver bullet that I knew was zipping straight toward my heart and I knew too that I could do nothing to avoid it. To stop the car would have been suicide. It was impossible to slow down or back up. I said the *Sh'ma* and continued driving, pressing down as hard as I could on the gas pedal. I wondered why I felt no pain. I wondered why there was no blood. The bullet could not have missed me. For a wild moment I thought that I might even be dead, that I was living in a nightmare, driving in a dream."

"But you weren't, *Abba*." Leora climbed onto her father's lap, pressed her small hand to his lips as though to feel his breath, lay her head against his heart so that she might hear its beat.

"No. Of course I wasn't," he said and stroked her hair, threaded her braid through his fingers.

He placed his hand on his jacket and they saw now that a jagged hole had torn through the fabric. He unbuttoned it and removed a small leather-covered book from the inside pocket. Lodged in the soft leather, penetrating through to the pages of the book, was a silver bullet.

"Your Book of Psalms," Sarah said and reached over to take it from him. She passed her fingers across the leather worn smooth by constant use, touched the bullet that might have claimed her husband's life and, with sudden force, she pulled it loose.

"It was your marriage gift that saved me," Moshe said.

"It was God who saved you," Sarah replied.

"*Baruch HaShem*. Blessed be God." Their voices rose in unison.

Elaine's heart beat too rapidly. Her palms were damp, her face afire with a fury she could neither comprehend nor control. She stared in bewilderment at her daughter, at her grandchildren, at Ruth and her family, at the devout young men who had abandoned their lives in England to chase after the blessing of this elusive God whose name they endlessly blessed. Didn't they realize that their faith was flawed, their gratitude, their unquestioning gratitude, unreciprocated with compassion, that their loving kindness was too often met with inexplicable cruelty? She stood, trembling, overwhelmed with grief and fear. She would rescue her daughter, her daughter's family. She would pelt them with the truths they could not, would not see. Like Moshe, she, too, had the parental mandate to protect and to prepare. Her words came in a rush, her voice rising, her throat dry. Her lips parched.

"But what about the red-haired young man in the car behind you—the student—or perhaps he was a young father—surely he was someone's son—is his family saying *Baruch HaShem?*"

They looked at her and she read the surprise and sadness in their eyes. They pitied her because she could not believe as they did, because she refused the comfort of faith. She stared defiantly back at them and then left the room. In the kitchen she clutched the counter so tightly that her knuckles whitened.

"Mom. Mama."

Sarah's voice was very soft but Elaine did not turn. She washed her face and went into the bedroom. She brushed her hair, wrestling with the tangle of dark curls tinged with silver. She stood at the window and looked across at the houses opposite. Candles burned in every window. Tables were covered with white cloth, and silver goblets over-flowed with scarlet wine. She saw women with flushed faces carrying in serving platters and bearded men rising to pass around plates laden with the thin round matzoh that had been carefully watched as they baked. She was an outsider, an alien, an observer of a life to which she could never lay claim. There was no perhaps. Possibilities did not abound. She had her truths and they had theirs. What might have been would not be, but the very heat of her anger had cleansed her, offered her new and realistic hope. Other doors would open; there would be new tomor-rows.

At last, she returned to the table and took her place. When Yuval cried, she went to the nursery and took the baby into her arms, cradling him throughout the rest of the seder, soothed by the sweet warmth of his breath against her skin. No mention was made of her outburst, no protest offered to her words.

Three days later Peter called from California. Lauren was scheduled for surgery at the end of the month. Elective surgery but still worrisome. Would it be possible for Elaine to come out to the coast and help with the children? Elaine heard his unspoken words. *It's my turn, Mom. I want my turn.*

"Of course, I'll come," she said. "I'll leave right after Passover."

"Your brother needs me," she explained to Sarah who watched her pack.

"I understand," Sarah said sadly.

She knew that it was more than Peter's need that

impelled her mother to leave Jerusalem but she asked no
questions, offered no arguments. She would not jeopardize
the new closeness that had grown between them. They had
spoken truth to each other. Strength had flowed from
heart to heart. She watched as Elaine spread bubble paper
to encase the tiles that would crown the mosaic.

"They're beautiful," she said. Her fingers traced her
father's name, silver letters that soared to the evening sun
so tenderly etched onto the enamel. "Look, Leora. See
what *Savta* has made."

The small girl gravely studied the tiles. She touched her
grandmother's hand.

"You'll come back, won't you, *Savta?*" she asked.

"Of course I'll come back."

Elaine smiled at her daughter, at her granddaughter, and
turned away so that they would not see the tears that
streaked unbidden down her cheeks.

nine

The Mylar balloon was a bright pink, exactly matching Renée's T-shirt and only a shade paler than the bouquet of roses she would carry in her other hand. Peter Gordon had asked the vendor to stencil the word *Eureka* in silver across its surface, followed by *Welcome Grandma!* but he saw now that he should have chosen a darker color so that his mother would be able to read it even from a distance as she made her way toward them in the LAX baggage area. Troubled, because such details were important to him, as members of his production teams quickly discovered, he carefully outlined each letter with a black magic marker.

"What does 'eureka' mean, Daddy?" Renée asked, turning from the guest room window where she had been watching Jose, the Mexican pool boy, desultorily skimming leaves from the sun-streaked water.

"It's the motto of the State of California. And it means 'I have found it,'" Peter said, smiling as he etched in the final letter.

He remembered still how that single word, inscribed on a Hilgard Avenue bench, had impacted on him when it was explained by the student guide who escorted his group of incoming freshmen across the bridge and onto the UCLA campus all those years ago. That mandatory tour had taken place in early autumn, a Los Angeles autumn which was, really, hardly different from a Los Angeles summer. Back home in Westchester the leaves were already turning and his father had surely lit the first fire of the season to ward off the evening chill. Peter, a continent away, had imagined his parents sitting before it, wearing their matching sweaters and sipping their glasses of wine, a violin concerto blocking out the sound of the wind that rattled the brittle branches of the maple tree. His mother would have murmured something about seeing to the storm windows, his father might speak of snow tires, of winterizing the basement. They would smile at each other, content that they would be insulated against the chill of encroaching autumn, the cold of winter, and turn back to their books, their music.

But in Los Angeles, the sun burned with a golden brightness that caused him to shield his eyes from its radiance. Bougainvillea in brilliant shades of fuchsia and subtle tones of purple grew along the grassy paths that led from one terra-cotta walled building to another. He had watched a tiny hummingbird sip nectar from the scarlet bristles of a bottlebush tree and looked up at the blue-misted Santa Monica Mountains in the distance and thought to himself, "Yes. Yes. I have found it! Eureka!"

The student guide's words, so carelessly tossed out, had become a mantra of a kind, a validation that he had found, in this sun-drenched state, the light and freedom to be himself, to live by his own lights. He had known, even then, that he never wanted to leave California, that he never wanted to return to that large sprawling home of his child-hood where he had always felt himself oddly excluded. Perhaps it was because he felt himself to be sandwiched between his older twin sisters—Sandy who shared his mother's artistic talent, Lisa who had always known she wanted to follow their father into medicine—and Denis who shared their parents' love for music, their penchant for solitude, and whose melancholy troubled and absorbed them.

Peter had felt himself the perennial outsider, always hovering at the edge of the family, isolated from their interests and concerns. From childhood on, he had been the producer of his own life, crafting his own scenario. Lauren, who was lethargically pursuing a graduate degree in psychology, advised him, in the supercilious tone she used when discussing anything professional, that he suffered from what she called a "middle child" syndrome and he had not argued with her.

He had, however, never told his wife how Elaine and Neil had been surprised when he decided to attend UCLA

and even more surprised when he told them that he
wanted to study finance and film production.

"Finance?" his father had asked, pronouncing the word
slowly, as though it were plucked from a foreign lexicon.

"Film production will be interesting," Elaine had said but
he had discerned the doubt in her voice.

Still, they had not objected to his choice. They were,
as always, accepting parents, who respected their children's
decisions, practiced at withholding judgment and granting
reasonable consent. They acknowledged that Peter was
the child whose interests were so alien to their own. Finance. Film production. They shook their heads in
amused bewilderment but raised no objections. Were
they actually relieved, Peter, wondered later, that he had
chosen a profession so distant from their lives, that he
would live on another coast and not impinge on the
solitude they clearly craved?

It was another thought he had not shared with Lauren.
He did not want to add fuel to the smoldering fires of her
resentment of his family.

Eureka, he had written to his parents in his first letter
home but they had never asked him what the word meant.
He wondered if his mother, seeing it scrawled across that
welcoming pink balloon would ask about it now.

"Hold the balloons, hold the flowers," he instructed
Renée, thrusting them into her reluctant hands and turning
her toward him.

"Hey, you're only meeting your mother at the airport,
Peter. You're not choreographing a scene for a film."

Lauren stood in the doorway watching them, her lips curled into a derisive smile, her hazel eyes narrowed. She had just returned from her morning run, and the pale blue tank top that hugged her breasts was sweat-darkened. Her fine blond hair, tied back into a lank ponytail, glistened damply and she dabbed at her narrow-featured face with a sodden neckerchief.

"You don't have to practice holding those props, sweetie," she told her daughter and Renée immediately set them down and dashed out of the room.

"That was a stupid thing to say," Peter said, struggling to keep his tone neutral.

He did not want to have a scene with Lauren, not with his mother arriving that day and her father invited for a family dinner in the evening. He was concentrated on avoiding any unpleasantness at all. Too much was at stake.

"Was it? I think it was pretty accurate. You've been preparing for this visit the way you prepare for a major production. You redecorated the guest room as though it were a film set," Lauren retorted dryly.

She glanced around the room and he followed her gaze.

He had, he admitted to himself, opted for the autumnal colors that he knew his mother favored. Unlike the pastel hues that dominated the rest of their house—the California palette, their decorator, an expensive Rodeo Drive innovator, had called it—he had chosen a russet carpet, draperies and a bedspread in graduating shades of gold and amber, and placed Elaine's own ceramics on the rosewood bureau and bedside table. He had resurrected the enamel box she had crafted for them as an engagement gift, an offering which Lauren had never liked and never displayed, and set it next to the radio, already tuned to the UCLA classical music station he knew she would seek out. The bookends of a dark cobalt glaze that she had made for his college room were in place on the desk.

He smiled wryly. Lauren was not wrong. He was adhering to the pattern of his childhood, setting the stage, even rehearsing a mental script. He was, as always, the producer of his own life.

"All right. I want things to be nice for her. I want her to be comfortable. It's been tough for her since my dad died."

He adjusted the photograph of his family that he had placed on a low table. The group photo had been taken in Jerusalem when they had all assembled for Moshe and Sandy's wedding. (He could not, even after all these years, think of his sister as Sarah.) Flanked by the bride and groom, his parents were seated, their fingers linked, looking at each other, their shoulders touching. Lisa and Denis knelt at their feet. He tried to remember if Andrew had been at the wedding. Yes, of course he had been there. But circumspect as always, his brother's partner had remained at a remove from the family portrait and probably no one had thought to include him. He and Lauren, she newly pregnant with Eric, stood just behind them, Renée, a pig-tailed toothless toddler then, held close in his arms. Lauren had been radiant in the glow of her pregnancy, her blond hair floating to her shoulders, smiling, her eyes soft, her head resting on his shoulder. It had been a long time since she had rested her head on his shoulder, a long time since she had flashed that soft-eyed smile.

"You know how close she and my dad were," he added. "So it's especially tough on her."

"Not as tough as it is for a lot of people who've been widowed," Lauren retorted and he cringed at the harshness of her voice.

She was thinking of her own father, he knew. Lauren's mother had died three years earlier and her father, gentle Herb Glasser, was still mired in the depression of loss.

"She has her work. She has her children. She has resources," Lauren continued. "Everyone seems to be making time for her. Not that she ever really made time for you and Denis or for your sisters. You know yourself that it was always your father and her work that came first," Lauren said bitterly.

"That's unfair. She was a terrific mother. My friends in high school envied our family, our home. Dinner always on the table, everything organized. But her work was important to her so there wasn't a lot of time. Lisa used to say that she rationed out the hours of her day. The studio, the house, the time she and my father spent together. They had something really close, really special."

"Really exclusive." Lauren shook her head wearily and stared out the window. Jose had finished at the pool and was now raking the pale yellow palm fronds that littered the bright green expanse of lawn.

"You never really liked her, did you?" Peter asked, his

own question, dormant all these years, startling him. But, of course, he seemed to be facing a lot of new truths these days, too many, perhaps.

"It's hard to like someone who has never liked you. Maybe even harder than loving someone who probably never really loved you." Lauren's voice was edged with bitterness and she turned away so that he could not see her face.

He clenched and unclenched his fists. They would have to talk very soon. But not yet. Not yet. After her surgery. After his mother's visit.

He took the balloon, twirled the string and released it. It soared to the ceiling and bobbed gently about. *Eureka! Welcome Grandma.* The words were clearly visible. His mother would surely see them. His spirits lifted. This visit would be different. She would have time for him, time that he needed. His sister Lisa had confided, during a late-night phone call, that Elaine no longer had to be miserly with her minutes. "We get Dad's share," his sister had said, her voice so muffled that he wondered if she had been weeping.

He turned to his wife.

"Lauren," he said, annoyed by the plea in his voice, the words unsaid.

She shrugged.

"Don't worry. I'll be nice. I'll be great. It's just that I'm so edgy. The surgery. And everything else."

"Yeah. I know. You'll be fine. You always are."

He flashed her a grateful smile, touched her shoulder

lightly. He was the producer, offering positive reinforcement. He did not mention the "everything else." There was
no point. It had no relevance to the scenes so soon to be
played out.

"Renée," he called. "Let's go!"

He grabbed the balloon and the flowers, brushed
Lauren's damp cheek with his lips as he rushed past her.
With Renée's hand in his, they hurried out. The freeway
might be jammed and he wanted to be on time to meet
his mother's plane. He was a man who was never late. Like
all good producers he knew the penalties for lateness.

LAX was, as always, a frenzy of activity. Elaine waited at
the baggage carousel and watched the bags and parcels
being disgorged from the New York flight whirl around
and around. Surfboards poked their way through cardboard containers and were impatiently plucked up by
muscular young men who hugged them to their chests.
Matching Gucci suitcases tumbled over each other, claimed
by one young woman and counterclaimed by another,
their voices rising shrilly as they leaned forward to examine
tags and were finally forced to surrender the luggage to yet
a third woman, a blonde whose mink coat was draped over
bare shoulders and whose eyelids were painted so heavily
with blue shadow that Elaine marveled at her ability to read
her own name.

Girls in diaphanous pastel-colored sundresses floated by
and young men in business suits loosened their ties and
clutched their PalmPilots as they rushed past.

Bilingual signs flashed throughout the cavernous room. Ground transportation counters and car rental agencies advertised their locales in Spanish and English, in Japanese and Arabic, the neon letters reflected in dancing lights across a floor scuffed by the wheels of suitcases and trolleys. Skyhops and taxi drivers shouted at each other and at their passengers, elbowing their way past an army of limo drivers who waved signs. MR. AND MRS. LIFSHITZ. MR. YAKIMOTO. KELLY AND BRIAN. There were squeals of pleasure as reunions were realized and a child's plaintive cry, "Mommy, Daddy," was an eerie wail amid the cacophony of jangling cell phones and warnings about the dangers of leaving luggage unattended. A disembodied voice announced flight delays and flight arrivals, advised passengers, who all seemed to be named Scott or Nicki, that their parties were waiting for them at the information desk, at the Avis counter, at Gate Eleven.

It was with relief that Elaine retrieved her own bag from the carousel and gasped with pleasure at the sight of the pink Mylar balloon that Renée held high.

"Peter!" she called, wheeling her bag past a Japanese family caught in a massive embrace which they interrupted to bow courteously to her.

Peter rushed toward her and Renée thrust the bouquet of pink roses into her arms and hugged her.

"Hey, Grandma."

Elaine breathed in the citrus scent of her granddaughter's skin, smoothed her silken blond hair, and looked into her eyes. Renée had Neil's eyes, deep blue flecked with gray, and long-lashed.

"Sweetie," Elaine said and returned her granddaughter's embrace, lightly traced a pale eyebrow, silken soft as Neil's had been.

She turned to Peter, surprised as always by his height, the thickness of his hair, the brightness of his skin, the easy grace with which he moved toward her through the frenetic airport crowds. He wore the California uniform— light blue cotton shirt and carefully pressed khaki chinos and his bare feet, as narrow as Neil's own, were encased in wide-strapped leather sandals.

He was no longer the boy who had left their home all those years ago to find his own way in the coastal city across the continent. He had transformed himself into a Los Angelino, not unlike Sandy's emergence as Sarah, the orthodox Jerusalemite. Their children, after all, had created their own persona. She wondered whether this should be a source of pride or of disappointment.

"How's my Californian?" she asked.

"Glad as always not to be a New Yorker," he replied, smiling.

Elaine held Renée's hand as they followed Peter out to the parking lot, shedding her sweater and scarf. As always, she had forgotten the ferocity of the midday heat of Los Angeles. She was grateful when Peter turned up the air-conditioning as they began the drive out of the airport. He grinned at his mother, the teasing grin of his boyhood. But when he spoke there was a sharp edge to his voice.

"I thought you'd be accustomed to the heat after spending so much time in Israel."

"It's a different kind of heat," she said. "I did stay longer than I had planned to but Sarah really needed me."

She recognized, with some surprise, the note of apology in her words. Why should she apologize to Peter for her visit to Jerusalem, for her long stay with Sarah's family? Perhaps because she had discerned the accusative tone in his voice.

Peter did not take his eyes off the road as he nodded.

"I know. Someone has always needed you more than I did. The girls. Denis. Dad. A gallery owner on Madison Avenue. A decorator in Connecticut." He spoke the words lightly, but they were laced with a bitterness he immediately regretted. *Damn it. Two minutes into the visit and he was already playing the neglected middle child. Lauren would be proud of him.*

"Peter!" His name, spoken sharply, was a protest and he countered it by placing his hand on her head.

"Sorry, Mom. Just joking. Don't take me seriously. Your dad's a big joker, isn't he, Renée?"

But Renée, still clutching the balloon, had fallen asleep on the backseat. The fragrance of the pink roses, already wilting, drifted sadly through the speeding car.

As they moved past the gleaming new buildings that rose like concrete canyons to surround the airport and then past strip malls and shopping complexes until they reached the freeway, Elaine asked about his work, about Eric, about Lauren.

He was working hard, he told her, cursing briefly as traffic slowed to a halt and drivers in every lane honked their horns imperiously. One new project after another. A pilot sitcom had just been bought by a cable television company. He had produced a series of industrial films for a Japanese electronics firm. And he was negotiating a contract for animated commercials with an ad agency.

"The animation thing is really big now," he said, skillfully changing lanes to avoid yet another jam. "But what I'm really excited about is a documentary on the Russian Jewish experience. We're going to start shooting soon."

"We?" Elaine asked.

"I'm co-producing with the writer. Her script is brilliant."

Deftly then, he changed the topic and spoke glowingly of his son, his voice resonant with pride.

Eric was doing great in school. Terrific grades. He even seemed to like Hebrew school. The only reason he had not come to the airport was because he was being tutored for the entrance exam to a prestigious private school and Lauren hadn't wanted him to miss a session. He was a great athlete. Soccer, swimming, tennis. He was actually being coached by a former pro.

"It sounds like a pretty packed schedule for a little boy," Elaine said carefully. Eric was nine, only a year older than Leora, his Jerusalem cousin who played neither soccer nor tennis but who laughed easily, daydreamed over books and drawing pads and skipped rope with her friends in the sun-spangled gardens of Ramat Chessed. When did a child who rushed from school to tennis lessons to tutoring sessions have time to daydream? she wondered.

"Well, Lauren thinks all this stuff is really important. All our friends' kids have the same sort of schedules."

Peter avoided an off-ramp and swerved intrepidly past an interchange that swept onto a concrete parabola and Elaine stared out the window at the coastal road, at the shimmering expanse of the Pacific Ocean bathed in the pale subtropical light of southern California.

"And how is Lauren?" she asked as they veered eastward toward the Santa Monica mountains.

His face tightened. He glanced back at Renée as though to make sure that his daughter was still asleep before he replied to his mother's question, but when he spoke his tone was flat and his eyes were riveted to the freeway.

"She's a little stressed out. She only takes one psych course a semester for her graduate degree but she's on a million committees. PTA. Fund-raising. Country club beautification. Synagogue dinner dance. Benefits for the Disease of the Month. And of course she's constantly chauffeuring Renée and Eric to lessons and playdates and juggling our social calendar—that's what she calls it. She hardly has time to pick up takeout meals for the kids on the days when Maria, our housekeeper, is off. We're both so busy that sometimes it seems that the only time we're together is at some dinner party or a fund-raiser."

"Sounds a little stressful for both of you," Elaine said.

"Well, that's the way we live. A lot different from the way you and Dad lived, I know. But maybe not that different. You were both always busy, caught up in your work, Dad with the hospital and his patients, you with the studio and your shows."

"Yes. I suppose we were," she admitted but she wondered how he could compare his family's frenetic life with the calm and serenity she and Neil had created in their home, where dinners were always served on time, soft music played and their cars remained in the driveway from early evening until morning. Still, she would not challenge him, not on this first day of her visit.

"And how is Lauren feeling?" she asked. "You said this surgery was elective."

"Yeah. It's apparently no big deal. She has some uterine fibroids and her gynecologist thinks they should come out sooner rather than later. Routine surgery."

"Yes. Of course."

Elaine did not remind him that she was a doctor's widow and she had listened often enough to Neil's colleagues' discussions of operating room dilemmas to know that no surgery was really routine.

"Are we almost home, Daddy?" Renée asked in a sleepy voice.

"Almost there, baby," Peter said. "We're just passing Ventura. Another couple of miles and we'll be in Encino Hills."

"Great. Grandma, I can't wait to show you my room. Mommy did it over for my birthday. It's all pink and purple with silver stars on the ceiling."

"It sounds beautiful," Elaine said and glanced at Peter who grimaced slightly.

"I did tell Lauren that there were enough stars in the skies. We really didn't need to have them in the house. But you know Lauren."

Elaine nodded. But the truth was that she did not really know her son's wife, that through all the years of Peter's marriage she and Lauren had never spoken with any intimacy nor had they ever quarreled. Theirs was the peace of the uninvolved, devoid of intensity, informed only by their relationship to Peter. Elaine was his mother, Lauren his wife. They were not bonded by an affection independently forged. They had simply accepted each other because there had been no other choice.

Elaine remembered still how startled she and Neil had been when Peter wrote them, during the spring semester of his senior year, that he was engaged to Lauren Glasser and that they planned to be married in the autumn.

"Married?" Neil had sputtered as he handed her the letter with trembling hands. Neil who seldom lost his calm, who prided himself on withholding judgment, had been pale with anger. "He's twenty-one, he's a kid, he hasn't lived yet."

"We were very young when we married," she had protested mildly.

"That was different. We were different. You were different. You weren't a blond sorority princess driving a sky-blue convertible and charging sweater sets at I. Magnin."

They had looked at each other then, acknowledging that it was not Peter's decision to marry at so young an age that disturbed them. It was his decision to marry Lauren.

He had brought the very slender, large-eyed blond girl home to Westchester during winter break, an awkward visit that they remembered with little pleasure. Lauren had changed her clothes twice a day, looked at herself in every mirror she passed, said little and laughed nervously. When she spoke about her family she was careful to specify their professions, their schools, their addresses. Her uncle Robert, *a dermatologist*. Her cousin Lloyd, *a senior at Yale*. Her parents' friends, the Rosens who lived next door to them in Beverly Hills, *attorneys. Corporate attorneys,* she had added, her whispery voice rising slightly. Peter had bought theater tickets, opting for orchestra seats "because that was what Lauren was used to." He had taken her to dinner at the Tavern on the Green and, twice during that visit, he had accompanied her on shopping trips to New York and they returned to Westchester with overflowing shopping bags, intent on displaying their purchases to Lisa and Sandy who examined the cashmere sweater sets and designer jackets with little interest.

"Pete's valley girl," Lisa had called Lauren dismissively, annoyed at the amount of time she spent in the bathroom, applying makeup and brushing her hair, which she washed once in the morning and once in the afternoon, using a lemon-scented shampoo that Lisa knew sold for twenty-five dollars a bottle.

Elaine and Neil had flown to Los Angeles days after receiving Peter's letter. Ostensibly, the purpose of the trip was to meet Lauren's parents and discuss the wedding. They did meet the Glassers, a pleasant couple who were delighted with the engagement, delighted with Peter. Lauren was an only child. An older son had died of leukemia. Gertrude Glasser had wept when she told them that, and Herb, her husband, took her hand in his own and stroked it comfortingly although his own face was briefly frozen into a mask of sadness. It was that loss, that terrible loss, that had caused them to cherish Lauren. To coddle and spoil her.

"She has always been our princess," Herb Glasser had said. They had smiled apologetically. "Whatever she wanted we gave her."

But she was such a good daughter, really. A swift emendation, because they had seen the look Neil and Elaine exchanged. She had never caused them any difficulty, any disappointment. Implicit in their words was the assurance that she would never cause Peter and his family any difficulty, that she would never disappoint them. If their daughter wanted this marriage, then they wanted it for her. Many couples married right out of college. Why not?

"But they've had so little experience," Elaine had murmured.

"So they'll find experience together." Gertrude Glasser's voice had been soft but her tone had been firm, her meaning clear. If this marriage was what her daughter wanted, then her daughter would have it.

Elaine and Neil had dinner alone with Peter. They had presented him with all their carefully rehearsed arguments. He was so young. He had never traveled. Unlike his sisters, he had never even studied abroad. So much lay ahead of him.

"What's your hurry?" Neil had asked in the gentle, reasonable voice that calmed his patients, caused them to contemplate new vistas, different options.

Peter's answer had shocked and wounded them.

"I want a family," he had said sullenly.

"You have a family." Elaine had spoken swiftly, harshly, because she had seen the hurt and bewilderment in Neil's eyes. "We are your family."

"Look," he had said, "I love Lauren. I think about her when I wake up in the morning. I think about her when I go to sleep at night. And she loves me. I'm the most important person in her life. Just like Mom's the most important person in your life, Dad. And you're the most important person in hers. So you can understand that. I want what you have. I need what you have. And Lauren gives it to me."

He had looked at Neil, looked at Elaine, as though inviting them to challenge him, but they had remained silent. Peter's words had struck a vein of truth which they could not deny. Sadly, they recognized that he had felt himself locked out of their lives. However inadvertently, their very closeness had caused him to feel isolated and alone.

"She gives him what he needs," Neil had said sadly that night. "It will be all right."

In tacit agreement then, they had raised no other objections to the marriage but smilingly, they had agreed with the Glassers that Lauren and Peter made a beautiful couple and they would surely be happy.

And that prediction had seemed to hold over the years. Lauren remained a stranger to them, their relationship correct although devoid of intimacy, but the marriage seemed to be a happy one. The children, Eric and Renée, were bright and attractive and, during their brief visits to L.A., Neil and Elaine saw that Lauren was an involved and devoted mother. Peter was successful in the career that his parents still had difficulty understanding and he and Lauren moved from one home to another. They abandoned the stucco bungalow with its red-tile roof that had been the Glassers' generous wedding gift to them, for the larger house, a comfortable ranch encircled by patios, when Renée was born. They had moved to an even larger home with a small pool when Eric was four months old until at last they had settled in the huge sprawling Encino Hills white wedding cake of a house on Canyon Drive with its tennis court, a kidney-shaped pool and a garden replete with persimmon, avocado and citrus trees.

"Their last stop?" Neil had asked wryly, after their visit to Canyon Drive, but by that time he and Elaine had understood that their elder son had been assimilated into an L.A. culture wedded to mobility and constant change.

The constant moves, they knew, were a California pattern but still it bewildered Neil and Elaine who had lived in their Westchester home for so many years. They had blamed Lauren for the restiveness, for the steady climb upward. She was, they thought, socially ambitious, materialistic, but they had masked their disapproval and visited infrequently, although Peter constantly urged them to spend more time in California. They offered excuses and knew them to be feeble. Neil had his obligations to his patients, they explained and Elaine had her commissions to complete.

"You haven't seen the house since we had it redecorated, have you, Mom?" Peter asked as he swerved off the freeway and onto the residential avenues. His cell phone rang and he glanced at its screen but made no move to answer it. "The office," he explained. "Some deal I'm working on. It can wait."

"You remember that your father and I had planned to come last year but something always came up. A conference, patients' schedules, my deadlines. And then…" Her voice trailed off. The sentence would have to end with *and then he died* and she could not bring herself to say the words. "And then there was no time," she said at last, staring out the window at the huge pseudo-Spanish mansions, white columned and red roofed, at the palm trees that shaded verandas studded with wrought-iron chairs on which no one sat.

"No time," he repeated. "I was going to come east last year, you know. I wanted to talk to Dad. To get his advice. We had even made a tentative date and then…"

Now it was Peter who was silent and she touched his arm gently. How was she to comfort this son who had sprinted so swiftly into manhood, who lived in a world she did not understand?

"What did you want to talk to him about?" she asked.

Something was troubling Peter. She had sensed it even

when he was in New York. She had heard the tension in his voice during their phone conversations, taken note of the new worry lines etched around his eyes when he embraced her at the airport. "Is everything all right?"

"Everything's great," he said and flashed her a smile, a smoothly rehearsed California smile that never reached his eyes. "We're here," he said, pulling into the circular driveway, its pink flagstone ribbed with sunlight. He helped Elaine out of the car and called to his son.

"Hey, Eric, come say hello to your grandma."

The small boy hurtled down the broad redbrick steps and hurled himself into Elaine's outstretched arms. She held him close, kissed his bright freckled face and looked beyond him, at Lauren, elegant in a tailored pale-blue pantsuit. Her daughter-in-law leaned against the wrought-iron rail, her fair hair caping her shoulders, staring sadly out at them. And then, catching Elaine's glance, she forced a smile and hurried toward her, brushing her mother-in-law's cheek with lips that were too cool, her hand reaching out to smooth Eric's hair into place even as she called softly to Renée who emerged from the car, cringing against the sun's fierce brightness. It was only Peter whom she ignored and who, in turn, only nodded as he walked past her, carrying his mother's bags up to the guest room.

Dinner that night was carefully choreographed. Herb Glasser arrived early and he and Elaine sat on the patio, sipping their white wine. She had always liked Lauren's soft-spoken, silver-haired father. He was a self-made man who, years ago, had understood Los Angeles and anticipated its expansion. He had quietly acquired plots of land, predicting that the chapparal-studded fields and wild meadowlands would be valuable acreage as the development of the city accelerated. He belonged to the new group of Jewish entrepreneurs, the builders and developers who had replaced the movie moguls of another era. He was unsurprised by his success but he had never flaunted it. It was important to him only because it enabled him to offer his family a comfortable life. But there were other things that were more important, much more important, he had told Elaine and Neil all those years ago and they had known that he was thinking of the boy who had died, Lauren's unknown brother. Donny had been his name and his passing had cast a long and impenetrable shadow across their lives. Herb Glasser was not a man who reconciled himself easily to loss. And now he had lost both his son and his wife. Lauren's family, Lauren's happiness, was his only comfort.

Elaine had seen him rarely since Gertrude Glasser's funeral and she was saddened to see how much he had changed. He was too thin, his eyes deeply sunk into a face that seemed beveled with sorrow, his light linen suit hanging too loosely on his much diminished body. He found it difficult to eat alone, he said and he stared without appetite at microwaved meals and filled his supermarket cart with frozen dinners that would remain in the freezer well past their due date. He had, he confessed with typical self-deprecation, only learned how to turn the oven on after his wife's death.

"And you, Elaine," he asked gently, as they watched the pink evening primroses blossom for their brief journey into life. "How are you coping?"

Unexpectedly, her eyes filled with tears.

"It's hard," she said and it occurred to her that she was weeping for his loss as well as her own.

"I know."

They were not unlike two invalids, slowly recuperating from the devastating effects of the same disease.

They sat quietly then, cocooned by their sadness, and breathed in the scent of the citrus trees that bordered the pool, the lemons and oranges glistening amid the dark green leaves.

"But the children, my Lauren, your Peter, they are happy," he said and she nodded.

"I think so," she said and wondered why his voice rose slightly, as though he were asking a question rather than making a statement.

Still, the dinner was pleasant, the table beautifully set with sparkling crystal and highly polished silver, the earth-colored ceramic dishes splashed with blue, a glaze that Elaine studied and admired.

"They're new," Renée reported proudly. "Mommy thought that you would like them. She bought them especially for you."

Elaine smiled at her daughter-in-law, touched that Lauren had thought to please her, touched that she was so welcome in this house. Perhaps during this visit she would learn to understand her son's wife. She looked at her grand-children, their hair damp from the quick showers they had taken after their afternoon swims, their skin golden, their faces shining with happiness and health, delighted to be allowed to stay up so late, to have dinner with their parents and their grandparents. And Peter, circling the table, filling their wineglasses, exuded proprietary pride in his home, his family, his success so evident, his life so clearly enviable.

Elaine felt a surge of contentment. It was good to be with Peter's family, to listen to her grandchildren's soft voices, their sweet and sudden laughter.

"I bet this is different from dinnertime at Sandy's—oops—Sarah's," Peter said.

His words surprised Elaine and she did not reply.

He smiled at Lauren as he tasted her delicious cassoulet and lifted his glass.

"I want to toast my wife who is responsible for this won-derful dinner," he said. "And my mother who traveled so far to get here."

The children glowed. Elaine and Herb Glasser clicked their glasses and Elaine saw that Lauren had blushed with pleasure at Peter's words. A wave of relief washed over her. Her premonitions were misplaced. She was just tired, her perceptions shadowed by her own grief, her own uncer-tainty. Everything would be all right. Swiftly, she corrected herself. Everything was all right.

ten

Within days, Elaine grew accustomed to the rhythms of her son's household. The mornings were a flurry of activity. Because she'd slept badly during those first days in California she heard the jangle of phones that rang before daybreak and listened as Peter spoke to a scout searching for a location in Japan, a banker in England, a disconsolate actress in New York. He paced nervously up and down the hallway, juggling the phone and his razor, lowering his voice as he passed the guest room.

"Why can't they call you at the office?" Lauren's irritable protest was repeated daily as she passed him and before she knocked at the children's doors. She had already completed her morning jog and she hurried authoritatively through the house in her very white sneakers, her shorts and T-shirts damp with sweat.

"Renée! Eric! You'll be late. Very late."

The children scurried from bedroom to bathroom, quarreled briefly, searched for missing sneakers, wept because homework assignments were misplaced, struggled with elaborate monogrammed backpacks that did not zip properly.

Maria, the Mexican maid, padded her way into the kitchen to start breakfast. She glided across the terrazzo floor, singing softly to herself in Spanish as she poured orange juice into the pitcher, reached for milk and eggs, the yogurt that Lauren bought at the Gelson's dairy counter that sold only organic products. The refrigerator door opened and closed with the eerie silence peculiar to expensive appliances. Elaine watched as Maria plucked cereal boxes from pantry shelves that slid soundlessly open, and flicked on the coffeemaker precisely as a car sped up the circular driveway and the daily newspapers landed at the door with a heavy thud. The *Los Angeles Times,* the *Wall Street Journal, Variety,* the *New York Times.* The small mountain of print stood precariously beside Peter's coffee mug at the breakfast table. Elaine noted with odd satisfaction that he always read the *New York Times* first, the east coast of his birth taking precedence over his adopted city, so precariously balanced at the edge of the Pacific Ocean.

On alternate days a team of Japanese gardeners arrived, small-boned men in bright blue jumpsuits who scurried across the property with shining implements, trowels and rakes, hoes and scythes scraped clean, ready to plant and weed, to control the luxuriant foliage and replace any languishing shrubbery. The air vibrated with the clack of pruning shears as the bougainvillea was clipped back. Sprinklers hissed as sprays were trained on the apricot and peach saplings, their dark leaves already interspersed with pink-and-white blossoms. Often, Lauren rose from the breakfast table, coffee mug in hand, and hurried to the gardeners to discuss the quality of the mulch used in the herb garden, the need to uproot one or another of the dwarf trees and replace it with topiary she had admired at someone's home.

"My wife missed her calling," Peter said wryly one morning, looking up from the newspaper. "She should have been a horticulturist."

"It's wonderful that she enjoys the garden," Elaine said carefully.

"I don't know what she enjoys anymore," he replied curtly and he listened without interest as Lauren returned to the table and explained an idea she had for a herb garden. Tarragon. Rosemary. Sage. A lot of her friends were growing their own herbs.

"Marjoram and thyme grow wild in Sarah's garden," Elaine contributed and Peter glanced at her sharply.

"I don't think you can compare Sarah's garden to ours," he said and that familiar edge in his voice surprised Elaine. It was puzzling, that Peter saw himself competing with his sister whose life and aspirations were so different from his own. Neil, astute analyst that he was, would comprehend the hidden meaning of Peter's words—sibling rivalry perhaps, a struggle for position, a need for validation. She imagined his soft voice weighing the choices and then realized, with resurgent sorrow, that Neil was dead and she could not share her puzzlement about their elder son with him.

"Middle child syndrome," Lauren murmured. "Still competing with his big sister."

She smiled but Peter flushed angrily. Lauren shrugged and searched for her car keys as the children shouldered their backpacks.

Lauren drove Renée and Eric to school each morning in the huge cream-colored SUV that joined the caravan of other oversize cars, driven by the young mothers whose children stared glumly through car windows sealed against the encroaching heat. They too had left homes where maids cleared away breakfast dishes and pool boys busied themselves checking filters and skimming leaves. All the young women drove with the ease of those for whom cars have always been an extension of their lives, mindlessly braking and accelerating, waving to each other, now talking on their cell phones, now swiveling their heads to talk to a child sulking in the rear seat. They moved steadily down the broad avenue lined with date palms that led to the Redwood Academy. It was, Lauren had told Elaine proudly, the best private school in the area.

"Expensive but worth it," she had added. "It feeds into the most prestigious high schools, most of their grads going Ivy."

"Renée is only ten years old," Elaine had said mildly and immediately regretted her words as Lauren's face tightened.

"There's nothing wrong with planning ahead," she had retorted. "These kids are going to face a very competitive world and it matters a lot where they go to school."

Elaine had swiftly nodded, signifying an agreement she did not feel.

Peter left for work each day, lowering himself into his own small red sports car, his laptop and cell phone on the seat beside him. When traffic slowed to a halt on the freeway, as it so often did, he caught up on phone calls and e-mails, he explained to his mother. He was a Los Angelino and knew the hazards of time wasted, of deals left undone because a message had been left too long unanswered, a call had been unreturned.

"A Porsche," he told Elaine when she admired the car. "It's great for weaving in and out of freeway traffic when you're in a hurry."

"And are you always in a hurry?" she asked.

"Hey, this is California. Everyone's in a hurry. That's why we have these freeways. We're the happening state, Mom."

His office was on Sepuvelda Boulevard, close to the action, he explained. That was what his business was all about—the action. To be an independent producer he had to be everywhere at once. It was, he said, a twenty-four-seven deal.

His schedule dizzied Elaine. There were evening meetings, business conducted over dinner and drinks, all-nighters when a film had to be viewed, edited and then reviewed and reedited. There were unexpected flights to distant locales to deal with unexpected problems. Phone calls of explanation to Lauren. He would not be home at all. He would be home late. He would try to make it home the next night. Three times during that first week of Elaine's stay, he made such calls.

Lauren pursed her lips, checked a calendar crowded with notes and reminders. Her voice rose plaintively.

"Don't forget, we have the dinner at the club."

"You'll miss Renée's dance recital."

"But you promised to be at that committee meeting."

She and Elaine had dinner with the children, pizzas ordered in, Maria's overly spiced fried chicken, macaroni and cheese. Comfort food that did little to comfort, eaten with the television on, Eric and Renée staring at the screen, Lauren on the phone scheduling visits to the dentist, the dermatologist, the hairdresser.

Lauren's own days were chiseled into carefully measured segments, every minute and hour accounted for. She spoke worriedly of carving out time for her surgery which had been postponed for a week or more. "Thank goodness," she had said, when the doctor's secretary called. "I hardly have time to breathe this week."

"But don't you want to get the surgery over with?" Elaine had asked.

"It's elective surgery. Routine. No biggie." Lauren had shrugged, crossed out one date on her calendar and penned in another. But Elaine had noticed that her hand trembled as she wrote and when she had finished she had set the pen down and closed her eyes, her head turned upward to the warmth of the blazing sun.

Mornings Lauren played tennis at the Hillcrest Country Club, her regular doubles game followed by meetings of the various committees on which she served. Often she stayed for lunch at the club and then worked on plans for the spring gala which she was chairing. She typed up the minutes of the Canyon Drive Civic Association, all the while fielding phone calls, scheduling and rescheduling playdates, talking to a contractor who would be renovating the kitchen and a designer who had some interesting ideas for the upstairs bathrooms. In the afternoons she was once again behind the wheel of the SUV. Renée and Eric had to be driven to Hebrew school, to music lessons, to dance class, to soccer practice, to tutoring sessions—math for Renée, reading for Eric—to playdates in Balboa Park, in Van Nuys. There was food shopping and clothing shopping and invitations to reply to and invitations to be extended. She belonged to a book club, attended a yoga class, volunteered in the guidance department of an inner-city school. She was trying to complete her graduate work in psychology but given her obligations she could manage only one course a semester. If Peter's schedule dizzied Elaine, Lauren's exhausted her.

"It's such a frenetic life," she told Herb Glasser with whom she had lunch at the club while Lauren played a doubles match. "Peter and Lauren. Always rushing madly about, always on the go."

They sat at a shaded table on the patio, at a remove from the golden-limbed, shiny-haired young women in pastel-colored tennis outfits who picked carefully through green salads dotted with alfalfa sprouts, avoiding croutons in which an excess calorie might lurk. Elaine, wearing a loose dress in a geometric pattern of Sarah's design, her curling dark hair now silver-streaked and tucked into a loose bun, felt herself an aging trespasser among the young on this isle of ease and unending sunlight. Ponce de Leon, she decided, should have gone west to California rather than south to Florida in his search for the fountain of youth. She noticed that Herb concentrated on his half-eaten sandwich and barely raised his eyes. She would have thought that his long residency in California would have exempted him from the unease she felt.

"Too much on the go," he agreed. "And it's not a life they live together."

She looked at him sharply. He, too, had sensed the unease in the marriage, the miasma of discontent that lingered in the Canyon Drive home.

"We lived very differently, Neil and I," she said.

"We, too. Quiet, maybe too quiet, but always with each other. Especially after our Donny died. All that was important to us was each other and, of course, Lauren. We didn't want her to be unhappy ever, not even for a minute. She wanted horseback riding lessons so there were horseback riding lessons. A trip to Europe right after high school. So there was a trip to Europe. Marriage right after college—a big wedding, a new house. When she told us she wanted to get married we thought she was too young, we thought they should wait a year, two years, but we didn't say anything so there was the wedding, the house. And then Gertrude and I were alone. Together but alone." Herb Glasser looked beyond her toward the Santa Monica mountains.

Elaine leaned forward and touched his hand. She was surprised to find his fingers cold to her touch although the day was warm.

"I know," she said. "I understand how it was with you and Gertrude. Just as it was with Neil and myself. We each had our own work, of course. Neil in his office, me in my studio. But even when we were apart we were a presence in each other's life. Sometimes I would call him in the middle of the day because I knew he was between patients and I just wanted to hear his voice. Sometimes when he had a cancellation, he would drive home for lunch and surprise me. I always thought such an hour of sharing a sandwich and sipping coffee was a gift. Now—now there are no more surprises, no gifts. Alone is alone. The phone doesn't ring. The door doesn't open." Elaine spoke with a muted sadness.

He nodded. He spoke very softly.

"Gertrude and I spent maybe ten nights apart, through all the years of our marriage. Maybe when she had the babies and had to be in the hospital two or three nights, once or twice when I had to go east for business. And dinners we always ate together, at home, at a restaurant but always across the table from each other. I'll tell you a secret,

Elaine. Even now, if I'm eating alone at home, I set a place for her across the table, everything, silverware, a plate, a napkin, a glass of water. I fill the glass to the top, the way she liked it. If I go to eat in a restaurant and the table is set for two, I tell them to leave the extra place setting, I ask the waiter to fill both water glasses. And then I don't feel so alone. And then I can eat. Not much, but something. Do you think that's crazy?" He flushed, as though shamed by his own revelation.

"No. I don't think that's crazy," she replied. "I understand about dinners. I think maybe that's what I miss the most— the dinners we shared when the day's work was done but it wasn't yet night. We'd sit at a small table in the half darkness, a table so small that if we reached our hands across it our fingers touched. We would talk very quietly then and if the phone rang we didn't answer it. Sometimes, at that hour I forget that Neil is dead and I talk to him. Quietly, very quietly. I wonder what he would say about something that happened during the day, if he'll be able to explain something I didn't understand. And then I realize that he's gone and I can't ask him, not for his opinion, not for his explanation. Not ever again."

Her eyes filled and she wondered anew why the finality of death still overwhelmed her. Her grandmother, whom she had loved dearly, had died when she was a small girl, six years old or perhaps seven, and she had trailed after her mother, her grieving mother, stupid child that she had been, asking over and over again when the old woman was coming back. But now she was a grown woman, not a small girl; she had attended countless funerals, mourned her parents and her husband, and she still found the very concept of death incomprehensible. Surely, those who had gone would return. How could it be that breath was stilled, that beloved faces drifted through dreams and gentle voices lingered only in memory? It was no wonder that the faces of mourners were masks of misery and disbelief. How could they conceive of the terrible finality to which they were asked to bear witness? She knew that Herb Glasser, who had buried a son who had never grown to manhood, and a wife whose place he still set for dinner, shared her bewilderment. She moved her chair closer to his so that they sat together in an arc of sunlight.

"Lauren and Peter, they don't often have dinner together," Herb Glasser said sadly.

"I know. Their crazy schedules. Peter works late, travels. And of course Lauren has her class, meetings," Elaine countered.

She was fair. She distributed the blame equally. Lauren and Peter were both overloaded, prisoners of their own affluence. He worked long hours but his work, his income, made their lifestyle possible. The house, the cars, the tuitions, the memberships in clubs and synagogue, dinner parties and gardeners and maids and pool boys, all demanded a payout at the end of the day. They had to keep running just to stay in place—Peter earning, Lauren spending, the symbols of their success essential to both of them.

"Peter doesn't call Lauren during the day. Just to hear

her voice." Herb looked up, waved to his daughter who walked toward them, swinging her tennis racket, a smile frozen on her lips, her eyes concealed by oversize sunglasses.

"And Lauren wouldn't be home if he did," Elaine added defensively.

"Theirs is not marriage as we knew it, you and I," he said and they fell silent as Lauren approached.

He rose from his seat to kiss his daughter, to take her tennis racket and pull out her chair, filling her water glass to the brim because she was her mother's daughter and he knew that was how she liked it. He looked at Elaine, inviting her into a complicity of silence, and she nodded. What could they do, she and Lauren's father? Their children were adults, childish adults playing a dangerous game. Elaine was grateful to Herb Glasser who shared her apprehensions, who acknowledged his powerlessness and her own.

What was it Moshe had said—"you can't protect your children but you can prepare them." In Jerusalem, she had thought his words wise, even profound, but now they sounded naive, perhaps even foolish. She and Neil had cautioned Peter against marrying when he was so young, but they could not have prepared him for the hectic pace of the life he himself had chosen, for the recognition that the girl he loved might change over the years into a woman he might not even like. And how could Herb Glasser have prepared Lauren for empty evenings, for meals too often eaten alone and too many nights without touch and tenderness? It was Neil's mother, that wise old Yiddish-speaking woman, who had said, "When children are little they sit on your lap, when children are older they sit on your heart." Elaine sitting opposite her daughter-in-law on the club terrace, felt the heaviness of her son's sadness on her heart. Herb looked at her and Elaine turned away from the worry in his eyes.

Mimi Armstrong called from New York that night, exultant because all of Elaine's ceramic pieces had sold at her last gallery show.

"Even those womb-shaped ashtrays I wasn't so crazy about," she reported. "Some young couple bought them for their second home, or maybe their third home. You're hot, Elaine, but hot goes cold pretty quickly in the art world."

Elaine smiled. Mimi was coarse, hardened by her messy and expensive divorce, but she was an honest and shrewd businesswoman.

"That's good news, Mimi. I'm glad you were able to sell everything," Elaine said carefully, ignoring the gallery owner's sly warning.

But Mimi, as always, was persistent.

"You'll have to get some new work together for display soon. Maybe even a small show. Boutiques are the thing now. Lots of ceramicists are doing boutique exhibits. The magazines love them. *House and Garden, Real Simple,* even *Vogue.* But I can't promote your work if I don't have a damn thing for a photo op."

"Mimi, I'm at my son's house in L.A. You know that. I

don't have access to a studio or a kiln. No equipment. And frankly, not too many ideas."

"You'll get ideas. As for studio space and a kiln, I spoke to my friend, Renee Evers. She has a gallery on Rodeo Drive and another one in Santa Monica. Real big-time. She knows all about studio space, kiln shares—she shows the work of a couple of ceramicists who work together, communal studios, communal kilns. That could work for you while you're on the coast. And she wants to meet you. She's a big fan of your work. She has one of your tile tables in her home—she lives in some big spread up in Sherman Oaks. *Très* posh. You'd be working with someone who's cutting edge." Mimi was talking breathlessly now, racing against possible protests.

"Everyone in L.A. has a big spread," Elaine managed to say. "And everyone is cutting edge," she added.

She moved to the window. Lauren, in white slacks and a white sweater, walked beside the pool. Peter was home, the door to his office closed. A citrus-scented breeze cooled the air but Lauren remained alone in the gathering darkness. Elaine's heart turned.

"Okay. Whatever," Mimi continued. "But it's fantastic that a dealer of Renee's stature is interested in your work. I gave her your son's number. She's going to call you, to have lunch, to talk and I want you to meet her, to hear her out. Will you do that, Elaine?"

"I don't know."

"Remember, Elaine, you owe me." Mimi's voice hardened.

She was right, Elaine knew. She did owe her. It was Mimi who had mounted her first show and kept the commissions coming in so that Elaine could work quietly at home. It was because of Mimi that she had never had to dash around Soho networking, carrying photos and samples of her work in and out of galleries and interior decorator shops as so many other artists and craftspeople did. She could remain in her studio, always available when Neil called, when he popped in for an unexpected lunch.

And Mimi had been kind after Neil's death. She had invited Elaine to have dinner with her, accompanied her to the theater, to concerts, urged her to stay over in the city and avoid the vast island of the double bed, one side of which would now forever be undisturbed. For all her brashness, Mimi understood the dangers nighttime held for the newly alone. Mimi was right. Elaine did owe her. If she worked out a deal with Renee Evers, Mimi would probably get a slice of the commission.

"All right. I'll meet her," Elaine agreed.

Renee Evers called the next morning and Elaine agreed to meet her for lunch at a French restaurant in Santa Monica.

Elaine was relieved to spend the day on her own, away from the unease in her son's home, and she sensed that Lauren, too, welcomed the time apart.

"I was going to ask if you wanted to sit in on my psych seminar, but a day in Santa Monica will be a lot more fun," she said.

Elaine nodded, touched that Lauren had worried about

her. As the days passed she found herself growing fonder of the daughter-in-law she had never really liked. She thought it touching that Lauren called her father daily, that he had an open invitation to dinner on Canyon Drive.

"He and my mother were so close," she explained to Elaine. "I hate to think of him being alone." And then she had blushed, remembering that Elaine who had been so close to Neil was also alone.

"My dad's coming for dinner tonight," she added, as she rummaged for the keys to the car Elaine would drive. "I did tell you that Peter and I are having some friends over, didn't I?"

"Yes. You did," Elaine assured her.

Twice that morning Lauren had reminded Peter to be home by eight. Twice she had told Maria to give the children an early dinner, to set the table for ten. Twice she had asked the Japanese gardener to bring bouquets of yellow roses into the kitchen. Lauren's unease puzzled Elaine but Peter's indifference to his wife's anxiety angered her.

She had watched as the family left the house, Renée and Eric darting too quickly into the SUV, Lauren tight-lipped and pale. Peter, dressed in full L.A. uniform—a mustard-colored shirt with a polka-dotted ascot tucked jauntily into its monogrammed pocket, a navy blue knit tie that exactly matched his lightweight blazer—talked on his cell phone even as he lowered himself into the small red Porsche. He and Lauren did not wave to each other. They did not say goodbye. Elaine watched the two cars speed

down the circular driveway and remembered that Neil
had never left the house without kissing her goodbye, on
the lips, on the cheek. He had sought her out in the
kitchen, in her studio, in her bath, each small leave-taking
an affectionate exchange. Didn't Peter remember that?
What, after all, had his parents' marriage taught him?

She shook her head wearily and dressed for her meeting
with Renee Evers, remembering to tuck Mimi's last catalog
and some photos of her recent work into her bag. She felt
a new optimism, a gathering enthusiasm. It would be good
to discuss her work, to perhaps contemplate new projects,
to give voice to the ideas that had teased her in Jerusalem.
She wanted to continue work on the mosaic. She had
some completed sketches and itched to begin work on new
tiles. She hoped that Renee Evers had a sympathetic ear.

It was still midmorning when she arrived in Santa
Monica, enough time to wander about before the
luncheon meeting. Like a tourist on holiday she strolled
down the pier, delighting in the clarity of the air, washed
free of the ashen smog by the seaborne Pacific wind. She
had entered a vast playland where men threw softballs at
weighted bottles and grown women wore necklaces of
paper flowers. She smiled at the children on the carousel,
their pudgy sunburned arms outstretched to grasp at the
dangling golden rings. They were small apprentices, early
initiates into the California way; they too, she supposed,
would strive after the elusive gold of success and accom-
plishment, the bigger house, the deeper pool, the A-list
friends—all life's golden rings scavenged and held too close,

all of them tarnished when looked at too carefully. Peter's merry-go-round, Elaine thought sadly. The whirling ride no longer enticed, but he could not afford to abandon it.

She shaded her eyes and stared at the swimmers who allowed the gentle wavelets to propel them farther and farther from shore and then floated on their backs, their faces shimmering with the brightness of sunlight beaming on water. Surfers rode the waves, soaring as they crested and disappearing behind the scrim of falling water. She walked past the huge waterfront hotels on Ocean Avenue, their sparkling glass frontage reflecting the foam-fringed breakers. There was a new lightness to her step and she smiled as two couples on Rollerblades glided toward her, dropping their linked hands so that she might pass. Their verve and ease energized her. She could, she told herself, despite all her reservations about the materialism and the pace of life, grow used to the verve of California life, its warmth and excitement. Like Herb Glasser, she could revel in the nearness of her grandchildren, her loneliness obviated by Renée's sweetness, Eric's energy, their swift embraces and joyous laughter. It would be wonderful to be a constant presence in their lives, at least for part of the year or perhaps for longer than that. She had, after all, the rest of her life to consider.

She would not miss the chilly winds of winter or the long days and nights of falling snow that streaked the windows of her silent house and left ice patches on her rural road. Her life could be divided up, she thought and imagined herself spending the winter months in a bright sunlit studio high in the California hills. Here, there would be no irreconcilable ideological divide. She thought, with renewed sadness, but without regret, of her outburst on the night of the seder and promised herself that she would call Sarah as soon as she returned to Canyon Drive.

On impulse, she darted into a shop and bought a turquoise skirt of a gauzy fabric that fell to her knees. It was too expensive, she told herself, and besides, she had nowhere to wear it, but she watched happily as the smiling young Asian saleswoman wrapped it in bright pink tissue paper and placed it in an oversize stiff black shopping bag. It was, she realized, the first new piece of clothing she had bought since Neil's death. Like a convalescent charting her own recovery, she counted this as a good sign. She would wear it to Lauren's dinner party that very evening.

Swinging her shopping bag, she entered La Grenouille, the small French restaurant Renee Evers had selected, which was almost obscured by a hibiscus bush heavy with pink blossoms.

"Ms. Gordon? Ms. Evers is waiting for you."

The suave, smiling maître d' led her to a table.

Renee Evers was a tall woman whose thick blond hair was fashionably unkempt. The ubiquitous California chic harlequin-framed sunglasses were perched on her forehead and heavy ceramic bracelets slid up and down her freckled arms. She toyed with her silver pendant, tracing its sharp geometric design and finally tucking it beneath the high stiff polished-cotton collar of her burgundy linen dress. Idly then, she removed her dangling silver earrings, studied them, replaced them and rummaged in her huge straw purse. She was a woman whose hands had to be constantly moving, Elaine realized, and she imagined her moving through her gallery, rearranging objects, moving a vase from one plinth to another, placing one bowl in a window and setting a sculpture at an odd angle.

Her voice was deep and pleasant, her accent distinctly New England. She was pleased to meet Elaine.

"I bought some of your pieces from Mimi," she said. "Some I kept. Some I sold. My clients love innovative designs, especially new arrivals to California."

"Why newcomers in particular?" Elaine asked.

"I guess it's because almost every new Angelino is yearning to be transformed. L.A. isn't just a different city, it's a new life. Instant rebirth. A chance to reinvent themselves, their surroundings. I know I felt that way when I first came out here from Boston. Straight out of college. Back east I felt that I'd been a failure, maybe beginning in kindergarten. I couldn't live up to my parents' expectations and I couldn't escape their judgment. I wanted to be far enough away so that they wouldn't be able to see what I was doing, so I could build a new life on my own terms. I chose L.A. because the Pacific Ocean is really pretty far from Boston harbor. And I think that holds true for a lot of my clients, especially relocated easterners. They want homes that don't remind them of houses left behind, decorative objects that are different from any they owned before. It's a funny thing but do you know what I sell the most? Bookends. They're off the shelves as soon as I set them out. I think that it's because the books my clients place between them celebrate the new lives they've chosen, announce their identities, their new interests—art books, photography books, books of poetry, printed pages on display, advertising choices, defining lifestyle. You don't happen to have any ideas for ceramic bookends, do you?"

Elaine smiled.

"Actually, I do," she said. She reached into her bag and showed Renee the photos of some of her recent work including several sets of bookends in varying shapes, crescents and ovoids, turrets and globes, smoothly glazed or dappled.

She wondered, as Renee studied the photos, if Peter, too, had chosen to study in L.A. and then to live there, because the west coast city was, in fact, so distant, at such a far remove from Neil and herself, from an acceptance which he might have mistaken for indifference. Elaine recalled how Sarah had perceived that calm quiescence to be dishonest although dishonest was not the word Sarah had used.

But Renee Evers's words rang true. Once settled on the Pacific coast, from his student years on, Peter had reinvented himself, abandoned the boy he had been and created a new persona and furnished himself with a new set, new props, new costumes just as he created new sets, new props, new costumes for the films and commercials he produced.

The troubling thought lingered as she and Renee studied the menu and gave the very pretty waitress their order.

"Another refugee from the east. An actress waiting to be discovered," Elaine guessed as the girl walked away.

"And some of our kids are fleeing to the east." Renee shrugged. "Go figure. My own daughter is living in Connecticut and my son is in Rhode Island. Since my husband died they keep after me to live closer to them, even live with them but I keep telling them that my life is still my own. I've been widowed, not crippled. I can't imagine being dependent on my kids although they're great—loving supportive etcetera, etcetera. But to have my life entangled with theirs would be like writing a letter of resignation and I'll be damned if I'm ready to resign from my own life as I've always lived it. Do you know what I mean? But I assume you do. Mimi told me that you were recently widowed."

"I do know what you mean," Elaine said. "But I was thinking only today of juggling time—of working out here a couple of months a year if I could arrange studio space."

"Oh, I can help you with that easily," Renee said. "Would you excuse me for a second, I have to call the gallery and naturally I forgot to bring my phone."

"Of course."

Alone at the table, Elaine glanced about the restaurant.

The long, silver-walled room was dimly lit, as though offering a penumbral refuge from the broad Santa Monica Boulevard, so bright with sunlight. The tables, covered with paisley cloths, each with a basket of fresh flowers at the center, were placed far apart and those in the rear were set into small alcoves. Elaine had not even noticed them when she entered. But now she saw that even the table at the very rear of the room was occupied. She could not see the faces of the man and woman because their heads were bent close but she noted that their fingers were inter-twined. The young woman's auburn hair brushed her companion's forehead. He bent his head even lower and kissed her hand. Lovers, Elaine thought with a tinge of envy. She remembered Neil's fingers threading their way through hers, the touch of his smooth skin against her own hands calloused and hardened as they were by tinctures and chemicals. She watched the couple greedily as though their noontime intimacy might magically dilute her own solitude.

As she watched, the man stood briefly to remove his navy blue blazer. She saw then that his shirt was mustard-colored and when he turned briefly to talk to the waitress, she saw his face clearly. Her heart stopped. Peter. It was Peter. She watched as he spoke to his companion, perhaps discussing a choice of dessert, of wine and then he turned again to the waitress. She saw the smile that played on his lips, the softness of desire in his eyes, as he pointed to the menu. The waitress glided away and once again they inclined their heads toward each other but now his hand rested on her outstretched arm.

Elaine looked away, smiled at Renee who had returned to the table, at the waitress who was setting her salad down and again stared across the room. She was not mistaken. It was her son. Her breath came in harsh gasps, her hand trembled. She nibbled at her food and set her fork down.

"Are you all right, Elaine?" Renee asked.

"Actually, I'm afraid I have a migraine coming on," she lied. "I hate to run but—"

"No. It's fine. I understand about migraines. I get them myself. Look, don't feel you have to stay. We'll talk on the phone about the studio space you'll need. You are interested, aren't you?" Renee was solicitous, concerned.

"Yes. Yes, I am. I'm glad we had a chance to meet."

Elaine spoke truthfully. She liked Renee Evers. She was a nice woman, an understanding sister in the sorority of the bereaved. Their meeting, however brief, had been reassuring. Studio space could be arranged. There would be a market for her ceramics. She could escape with ease into her work, resume the design of the mosaic, her energies diverted from the tensions of her son's home, so newly threatening.

Hurriedly then, she rose. It was important that she leave the restaurant before Peter saw her.

"We'll talk," Renee said. "Feel better."

"Yes. I will. Of course I will. And thank you."

She was halfway down the street when she heard running footsteps. Peter, she thought. Peter had seen her and was pursuing her. *Oh, what will I say to him?* She hesitated and slowly turned. It was the pretty waitress, flushed and breathless, who held out her shiny black shopping bag.

"You forgot this," she said.

"Oh, yes. Thank you."

Clutching it, she hurried on. The bag was heavy in her

grasp and she wondered why she had bought a garment in so vivid a color. Had she fallen victim to the Los Angeles contagion—was she too trying to reinvent herself?

eleven

Elaine was surprised to find Lauren at home when she returned from Santa Monica.

"Didn't you go to your class?" she asked in surprise.

Lauren shrugged.

"I was halfway there and suddenly I just felt exhausted. And I began to think of everything I had to do for tonight. So I just got off the freeway, turned and came home."

Her tone was flat and she sat quite still, staring through the glass patio door at the violet-and-blue tubular flowers on the newly blooming jacaranda tree. Sensual flowers, Elaine thought, but then all the flora of California, the pepper trees laden with red berries, the thickly blossomed fruit trees, the red and magenta bougainvillea, burgeoned in a riot of brightness, of effortless reproduction, exuding the teasing fragrance that hung heavy in the air.

"You're probably just a little tense about the surgery," Elaine said.

"I suppose." Again Lauren spoke without affect and still she remained motionless, ignoring Maria who padded into the room, hesitated and left. The phone rang but Lauren did not answer it.

"The machine will get it," she said dismissively when Elaine reached for it.

"Lauren, is everything all right?" Elaine asked daringly. She and her daughter-in-law had never had a conversation of any intimacy, observing careful parameters.

Lauren nodded.

"Everything's fine," she said. "Why wouldn't it be? I'm just awfully tired. I've arranged for the kids to be picked up so I think I'll just grab a nap."

She went upstairs then and Elaine knew instinctively that Lauren would not nap. She would lie on her bed, her eyes wide open, blanketed by a misery she would not acknowledge.

It was clear to Elaine that Lauren knew that there was something very wrong with her marriage, that she was conscious of Peter's too frequent absences, his odd irritability. But did she know any more than that? Elaine wondered. Did she herself, in fact, know any more than that? It might well be that the young woman with flame-colored hair was a casual friend of Peter's, perhaps even a colleague, that the lunch in the dimly lit restaurant at the ocean's edge was in fact a business meeting grown suddenly intense. But even as she struggled to create a plausible scenario, she knew herself to be wrong. She had, in those isolated moments, witnessed a deeply sexual intimacy. She had seen Peter's face clearly, discerned the desire in his eyes. He was, she knew with sudden certainty, having an affair. He was skating perilously on the very thin ice of infidelity.

Anxiety gripped her and she hurried to her own room, where like Lauren, she lay across the bed and struggled to organize her thoughts. She had never thought about the sex lives of her adult children. It had been bewildering enough to watch their infant bodies mature, to see the small limbs that had entwined themselves so trustingly about her neck and shoulders, the tender pink flesh whose sweet softness she had soaped, morph into strong and healthy boys and girls. Her sons' voices deepened, her daughters' waists narrowed, their laughter was bold, vested with eagerness and anticipation. Bathroom doors were locked, bedroom doors closed, physical privacy observed. Her children grew and grew, racing through the years into complex pubescence, sprinting into adulthood, marrying, taking lovers. Her babies were now men and women, themselves parents of growing children. They had crossed into emotional and physical territory into which she could not and would not trespass. Their sexuality was mysterious to her. It had not occurred to her ever to conjure up a mental picture of Sarah and Moshe in their marriage bed, of Peter and Lauren or Lisa and David engaged in the act of love. Oddly, it was Denis and Andrew who triggered her imaginings. She had asked Neil once how he dealt with the mental image of their younger son and his partner entangled in sexual intimacy. *"I don't." Neil had smiled. "I'm a psychoanalyst trained at suppression."*

It seemed impossible then, to think of Peter involved with a woman who was not his wife, to imagine him lying beside a woman whose flame-colored hair tumbled over his bare shoulders, a women whose face Elaine had seen only for the briefest of moments.

She thrust the thought aside. Eric and Renée arrived home and she went downstairs to caution them to be quiet because their mother was very tired and they must not waken her from her nap. She was having guests for dinner and needed the rest, she told them. The children nodded indifferently. Midweek dinner guests were not a rarity for them and they were, after all, used to eating alone while staring at a video on nights when their parents had company.

Elaine dressed quickly, pleased that her long silver earrings went so well with her new turquoise skirt. She swept her dark hair back, frowning at the silver strands that wove their way through its thickness. Her own vanity amused her. For whom was she dressing with such care? For Lauren, she decided. The dinner party was important to her and Elaine felt a new urgency to please this daughter-in-law who had so suddenly and unexpectedly engaged her sympathy. *Poor Lauren,* she thought and her voice was troubled when she spoke to Lisa who phoned just as she went downstairs to help Maria arrange the flowers.

"Are you okay, Mom? Is everything all right?" Lisa asked.

"Fine. Everything's fine," she assured her daughter. "Lauren and Peter are great. And the kids are marvelous." That last, at least, was true, she thought as she listened absently to Lisa's description of a weekend with David in Washington and her optimism about the progress of her adoption application. The little girl was beautiful in the photos the adoption agency had sent but the Russians were, of course, being total shits, asking for more and more documentation, demanding additional fees for minor adjustments.

"Adoption's not only stressful, it's expensive," Lisa complained. "But it's worth it. I really want this child, Mom." Her voice, usually so confident and authoritative, was strangely plaintive.

"It will all work out," Elaine said reassuringly.

Lisa's yearning perplexed her. Why, she wondered, had her daughter opted for adoption rather than marriage and motherhood or even motherhood without marriage? But Lisa's reasons were concealed behind a veil of silence and Elaine and Neil had agreed to respect that self-imposed and puzzling privacy. "She'll speak to us when she's ready," Neil had said, ever the patient professional, prepared to wait for a breakthrough. But Neil had died and the questions that had haunted them remained unasked and thus unanswered.

"Yes, I suppose so." Lisa's response was flat and without conviction.

Elaine, guiltily, was relieved when the doorbell sounded.

"I have to get the door," she told her daughter. "I'll call you at the end of the week. Please, Lisa, don't worry."

"I'm fine, Mom."

Of course she was fine, Elaine thought. Lisa was self-sufficient, motivated, the excellent student who became an excellent physician and, surprising them all, a brilliant businesswoman. There was no need to worry about her, she assured herself, as she opened the door to Herb Glasser.

His thick silver hair was neatly brushed, his blue-and-white striped seersucker suit immaculately pressed. He was a handsome man, Elaine thought and when he bent to kiss her cheek, she recognized the fragrance of his aftershave lotion. It was the brand Neil had favored. Herb could not have known that, of course, yet she was oddly grateful to him for wearing it. It did not surprise her that he was the first to arrive. He had, she suspected, waited impatiently to set out for Canyon Drive, looking too frequently at his watch, anxious to escape the emptiness of his own home, the solitude of yet another long evening alone.

Lauren, elegant in black satin harem pants and a sheer, wide-sleeved white shirt through which her skin glowed golden, hurried into the room. She kissed her father and glanced worriedly at her watch.

"Peter promised that he would be early," she said plaintively.

"Probably he got delayed. Very bad delays on the freeway." Herb smiled reassuringly at his daughter.

"He knew that it was important to me that he be here early."

Lauren went to the window, looked out at the gathering darkness.

"So he'll be a little late. Nobody else is here yet. I'll make the drinks. Don't worry." He spoke in the calming rhythmic tone of a parent trying to soothe an unhappy child. He glanced at Elaine, a mute plea for assistance.

"He'll be here any minute, Lauren," Elaine said. "He would have called if he was going to be really late."

"I suppose you're right." Reluctantly, Lauren allowed herself to be comforted.

But Peter had still not arrived by the time the other guests swept in, three attractive young couples, exuding excitement because of a school budget that had passed and a country club fundraiser had succeeded beyond expectations. They toasted their success with champagne spritzers and plucked canapés from the silver tray Maria carried through the room.

"Ooh, yummy."

"Ooh, delicious. Did you get the endives at the green market?"

"I love the green market."

The women, all determinedly slender, wore linen dresses in pastel colors, halter topped or scoop necked, their sun-streaked hair floating about their shoulders, their voices musical, their laughter easy. Their husbands, in chinos and soft cotton shirts, smiled at them, spoke to each other with great seriousness. They were men whose separate worlds converged, California style. Their wives were friends, their children went to the same schools. They did deals together, belonged to the same club, the same synagogue, which they referred to jokingly as the VBS.

"The religious school at VBS is really great and they do marvelous bar mitzvahs," the man called Carl told Elaine.

"Valley Beth Shalom," Herb Glasser explained to her, his tone dry. "They like to call it the 'very big shul' which, of course, it is."

Elaine smiled, refilled one young woman's wineglass, answered her question about her work. Ceramics was not her hobby, she explained. It was her profession.

"Yeah. Well, I might take a course. A workshop. See if I like it," Carl's wife, Suzanne said. "If I have the time, that is. Between carpools and committees and stuff. Carl is always traveling so I'm stuck with the nitty-gritty. I can't imagine where you found the time, Elaine."

She thought to tell them how different child-rearing had been for her. Strenuous, yes, but not frenetic. Music teachers came to the house. There were no tutors, no frantic academic competition. The children rode their bicycles down quiet suburban streets to Hebrew school, to ball fields and playgrounds, to their friend's homes. "Our kids are pretty independent," she and Neil had told their friends proudly. Their lives had been structured to nurture that independence. Her studio just outside her back door, Neil's office a few miles away. She had not been imprisoned behind the wheel of her car, checking her watch, tearing from one after-school activity to another. She had been at her potter's wheel or setting her kiln, taking pleasure in the work of her hands, excited by a new glaze that captured the colors of an autumnal sunset, a trivet that she had molded to the shape of a banyan leaf, fielding phone calls from customers and galleries.

"Peter says that his mother's work was always her priority," Lauren said smoothly.

Elaine stared at her daughter-in-law. Was that how Peter had perceived her? Was that really how he had described her to Lauren? She thought to murmur a protest but Lauren had glided into the kitchen and Suzanne looked at her expectantly.

"I think there were fewer pressures when our kids were growing up, certainly less driving and, I think, less striving. My work was important to me but not as important as my family." She disliked the defensive tone that had crept into her voice and she was relieved when Lauren invited them into the dining room.

"Peter must have gotten really hung up," she said apologetically. "We might as well begin."

"The freeway," Carl said.

"Two accidents on the 405."

"Maybe three. I heard three."

"This damn city."

They all shook their heads and smiled forgivingly. They were fortune's favorites, basking in sunlight, aglow with prosperity. Los Angelinos all, by birth or by choice, they loved the damn city of their discontent, reveled in its spaciousness of sky and nearness of sea. It was, at once, their

own Riviera, their Alps, their Sahara. They loved its brightness, its excitement, the big cars they drove along its
freeways, the beautiful homes with white stucco walls and
red-tiled roofs they glimpsed from behind their oversize
sunglasses, the lives they had invented for themselves amidst
its radiant landscape. They loved sitting down to dinner in
Lauren and Peter's beautiful dining room, eating the salad
made from avocados plucked that very morning from a tree
whose swaying branches were in easy view of the table.
They squeezed lemons, newly picked, the rinds still warm
from the afternoon sun, into their tall glasses of sparkling
water.

Their conversation flew from topic to topic. New books
were discussed and new films and books that had been
optioned for films and films that were being turned into
books. They laughed at the absurdity of it all and pulled
out small notepads to record the names of the books, the
films. They bemoaned the proliferation of shopping malls.
The real money, Carl said, was in the record thing. No, the
music thing. No, the film thing. Suzanne was insistent.
After all, weren't they sitting in Peter's house, eating his
avocados and he, after all, was deep into the film thing. They
all laughed and Lauren smiled and glanced at her watch.

Maria served the main course, wild salmon with ju-
lienned vegetables—all organic, Lauren assured them,
bought at the organic produce counter at Gelson's that very
morning. Peter arrived as she rose to pass the vinaigrette,
slamming the front door, smiling his apologies, kissing
Lauren lightly on the forehead.

"A late meeting…a call from the east coast…those idiots can't get the time zones right and then of course—"

"The freeway," they screamed in chorus.

"The damn freeway," he agreed, accepted their sympathy and hurried upstairs to change. His mustard-yellow shirt was badly rumpled; a grease stain shimmered on the mono-grammed pocket, the polka-dot ascot was gone.

He rejoined them, wearing a pale green cotton sweater, a gift from Denis, Elaine recalled irrelevantly, as the con-versation switched to summer plans for the children. There was a baseball camp at Pepperdine University. Carl and Suzanne had already registered their sons. A new day camp was enthusiastically endorsed. It offered horseback riding and go-carts.

"And computers?" Lauren asked anxiously. "I want to get Renée interested in computers."

"Definitely computers."

"What I would like," Herb Glasser said, "would be to take my grandchildren to Israel this summer."

They all looked at him in amazement, as though he had suggested taking Renée and Eric to another planet.

"Maybe another year." Peter reached for a roll. "They're too young and it's too dangerous right now."

"Not too dangerous for your sister and her family," Elaine snapped and the harshness of her tone surprised her.

"Sandy—Sarah—and I live very differently," he said shortly.

"Obviously."

She stared down at her plate, no longer hungry, relieved

when the conversation shifted back to safer areas—a new restaurant in Little Tokyo, a café in the Fairfax district that was hosting play and poetry readings, the selection of a committee to work with Lauren on an autumn gala.

The guests left after coffee and dessert. It was, after all, a weekday night, a great night for a dinner party because weekends were so jammed with screenings and performances and recitals, but still they couldn't stay too late. They would awaken early to take business calls from different time zones, hit the freeway before the rush hour began. The young mothers had to drive their kids to school, and finish jogging before the sun rose too high and the produce markets got too crowded.

"Great dinner, Lauren."

"Thanks, Peter."

Herb kissed his daughter good-night.

"Are you all right?" he asked.

"Just a little tired, Dad," she said.

"You go to sleep. I'll help Maria with the cleanup." Peter was conciliatory, his hand light on her head. He smiled conspiratorially at his father-in-law. They knew how to pamper their princess.

"All right." She offered no argument. "Tell Maria not to put the wineglasses in the dishwasher. Are you coming up, Elaine?"

"In a few minutes," Elaine said. "I think I'll have another cup of coffee."

Herb watched Lauren walk upstairs, his forehead creased with worry. He held his hand out to Peter, to Elaine, murmured his own thanks and left, walking too slowly down the pathway.

Elaine went into the sunroom and Peter followed her a few minutes later, carrying two cups of coffee.

"Warm milk and one sugar in yours," he said. "Just the way you like it."

She took a sip.

"It's very good," she said. "As good as the coffee at La Grenouille."

He set his own cup down and looked at her sharply.

"I was there for lunch today," she said. "I saw you. Who is she, Peter?"

He covered his face with his hands, his long fingers covering his eyes, crystal teardrops sliding down the backs of his hands.

"Sorry," he said and his voice was muffled.

"Peter."

Once, when he was a small boy, she had found him seated in his room, weeping. Even then, shamed by his tears, he had covered his face with his hands. She could not recall now if his misery had been triggered by the failure of an examination or his rejection by a school team but she did remember that she had gently removed his hands and cradled his head against her shoulders, smoothing his hair, murmuring his name, assuring him that it would be all right, everything would surely be all right. Now again, she moved toward him, took his hands in her own and smoothed his hair but she could not assure him that everything would be all right.

"I'm sorry, Mom," he said again. "I've just been so miserable for so long that everything welled up and I lost control."

"It happens," she said. "Your father thought that it was a sign of strength for a man to cry."

"And did he ever cry?"

"Now and again."

With his hands pressed to his eyes, tears leaking through the long graceful fingers Peter had inherited, Neil had wept when Denis told them that he was gay, when Sandy told them of her decision to move to Jerusalem. But she would not share those memories with her son whose tears sprang from a different source.

Peter regained his composure, took up their cups and went into the kitchen to refill them.

"Her name is Karina," he said as he once again sat opposite her. "She's a writer. I met her when I was putting together a nature program for some kids' channel and she came in to doctor the script. We were on the same wavelength, sort of making fun of the project but treating it responsibly. We were shooting on Catalina Island which meant we had to stay over a couple of nights and we ended up spending a lot of time together. We talked a lot, compared our lives, our families. She was born in Russia, came to this country when she was twelve and she won a full scholarship to USC and did an MFA at Berkeley. She's serious about her writing—what she calls her real work. She's had two stories published in good literary quarterlies and she's written a film script about her family. Half fiction, half autobiographical. It's going to make a great documentary. Actually I'm already working on it with her. It's fresh cinematic territory. Nothing's been done about the integration of the Russians and her family is the perfect prototype. The odyssey from the austerity of Moscow to the overwhelming plenty of L.A. The juxtaposition of values. I'm thinking black-and-white for flashbacks and color for the contemporary scenes—cutting-edge stuff. I finished scouting out locations and we're all set to begin shooting. It's a big investment but it's something I really want to do and I think it will work."

"I know that you've always been interested in producing documentaries," Elaine said carefully.

"Interested? Actually, I thought working on documentaries, on serious teaching films would be my life. It was what really grabbed me when I started working in cinema. But it didn't work out like that. I needed to zero in on work that would pay the bills—commercials, made-for-TV films, sitcom pilots, even instructional films for the big corporations—and it turned out that I'm really good at all that crap. I make money, a lot of money, but the more I make the more we seem to need. The house, the kids, vacations, memberships. Those meaningful documentaries I was supposed to be making get put on hold while I keep balancing the checkbook. That was one of the things I talked to Karina about. I told her how frustrated I felt, how the things that I really wanted to do kept drifting further and further away from me. That's why I'm so excited about doing the film about Karina's family and why I'm so grateful to her for pushing me to get started on it."

He took a long sip of coffee which Elaine knew had to be tepid by now.

"You didn't talk to Lauren about it?" Elaine asked. "About how you felt your career was getting sidetracked?"

"Lauren and I don't talk," he said shortly. "We make logistical arrangements. We schedule things. When I'll be home, when she'll be home. Who to have over for dinner when. Whose invitation to accept for this party, that screening. We discuss problems with the house. The landscaping. Should we resurface the pool? We race around with the kids on the weekends, getting them to birthday parties, soccer games, T-ball. Her focus is on things—getting this—getting rid of that—keeping up with her friends. Oh yes, and making her father happy and making the kids happy or at least trying to keep them from a state of terminal whining. I can't remember the last time we had a real conversation of any substance."

"She doesn't care about making you happy?"

"She doesn't understand what would make me happy, which is strange because when we met I thought that I had finally found someone who was entirely vested in me. We were at the center of each other's lives then. We told each other everything. I try to figure out what happened to that feeling, how it got lost. It's as though we've forgotten the secret language that once made us laugh and cry and hold each other tight. Sometimes I think that

we're two strangers who happened to get trapped on the
same treadmill, running in place but never arriving
anywhere. It's different with Karina. She understands.
She knows what the pressures of the rat race are like
because she's always supported herself, paid her own way.
Lauren was her parents' little princess. They bought her
anything she wanted. She grew up flashing credit cards
as though they were magic wands. And the scenario didn't
change when she married me. Karina keeps herself to a
budget. When she has to she takes a hack job but she
sticks to what she calls her real writing. And she knows
how to listen. I can talk to her about my ideas, the kind
of films I want to make and I know that she's focused,
that she's interested and that she honestly understands
where I'm coming from and what I want to do. Mom, I
just love being with her, being alone with her." He looked
at Elaine and her heart turned when she saw the pain in
his eyes. "It's been a long time since Lauren and I spent
any time alone."

"You and Lauren have children, responsibilities. It's hard
to find time to separate yourself out when you're raising
a family," she reminded him.

"But you and Dad managed to do it." He laughed
harshly. "Your quiet dinners. Your quiet talks. I remember
how I would look out of my bedroom window and see
you walking together in the garden, hand in hand. You
were so wrapped up in each other that it didn't matter that
Sandy and Lisa were upstairs dying their hair magenta and
Denis and I were beating the shit out of each other in the

basement. Denis once said that we could run away from home and it would take hours before you and Dad noticed that we were gone. Lisa called you 'the cult of two.'"

Elaine looked at him, surprised by the bitterness that tinged his words, shocked by the anger that darkened his eyes.

"Sorry," she said and wondered why she was moved to apologize. Those quiet hours with Neil were her treasured memories. She found it bewildering that Peter, like Sarah, had resented them, and resented them still. But then, she had found so many things bewildering in the months since Neil's death. She and her children had emerged from the chrysalis of their grief into the clarity of a wounding honesty.

They sat for a few moments in silence, listening to the sad nocturnal serenade of the nightingale that lived in the lemon tree.

"Are you sleeping with Karina?" Elaine asked at last.

He stared at her, his face contorted in misery but he did not answer.

"Does Lauren know about her?"

"Lauren knows that something is really wrong between us. She knows that I'm away more than I have to be and that I'm tuned out, that I'm irritable. She's said that. But she hasn't asked any questions and I think that's because she's afraid of an honest answer," he replied, his voice flat.

"I think she knows more than that." Elaine thought of Lauren's face locked into sadness, her worried gaze, the odd inertia that paralyzed her without warning. "It's not fair to her, Peter."

"I wanted to wait until this surgery is over. I know it's a simple procedure but it's something that has both of us on edge. I don't want to hurt Lauren. And I don't want to hurt my kids. They're the heart of my life, Renée and Eric. They mean more to me than anything else in the world. Sometimes when I look at them I wonder how I got so lucky. I watch Renée at ballet, Eric sprinting across the softball field and I think I'll explode with joy. I can't lose them. They're too important," he said and he stared sadly into his empty coffee cup as though he would read his future in the remaining dregs.

"More important than Karina?" she asked.

He did not answer.

Again his hands flew to his face. Again he crouched over in despair but no tears flowed.

"What am I going to do, Mom?" he asked. "What the hell am I going to do?"

"I don't know," she said quietly. "But it's not a question that has to be answered tonight."

Together then they rose and moved about the room, flicking off lamps, drawing the drapes closed. Elaine took her son's hand and they walked through the dark house and up the stairs, tiptoeing because they did not want to disturb Lauren or waken the sleeping children.

twelve

Lauren's doctor called the next morning. Lauren's surgery was scheduled for the following week. She would have to enter the hospital a day earlier for pre-op procedures.

"Okay. That's fine." Lauren's phone voice was calm as she reached for her calendar and circled the date, penciled in the time she had to arrive but Elaine saw that she was very pale and her hand trembled as she set the phone down.

"It's just routine surgery," she said. "Prophylactic really. Just fibroids. But the doctor thinks they should come out and they do cause some discomfort."

"The doctor's right, Lauren," Elaine assured her. "And I know it's routine. I know a lot of women who have dealt with it. Do you know what we should do today—we should

go into town, have ourselves a really good lunch and go
shopping. I want to buy you a really fancy negligee. No
woman should go to the hospital without a new nightgown."

"That's what my mother always said. She bought me a
pink peignoir when I gave birth to Renée and a blue silk
nightgown when Eric was born." Lauren smiled at the
memory. "Thanks, Elaine. Let's do that."

"Great."

Elaine felt a shaft of shame. She had not thought of
Lauren as a young woman in need of maternal nurturing.
She had never, until that very morning, felt at all motherly
toward her son's wife.

Lauren and Elaine spent the morning strolling up and
down Rodeo Drive, stopping at boutiques where they
knew they would not buy anything for the sheer joy of
marveling at the designs, at the bright colors and tasteful
displays. They reveled in the touch of the delicate fabrics
and laughed at the absurdity of the prices. They peered
into the shining glass windows of larger stores and stared
at the shoppers, marveling at the trendy outfits, the high
boots and short hemlines, jaunty capes of geometric
designs tossed carelessly over T-shirts, women in saris and
young girls in very short shorts who whizzed past them
on Rollerblades. They exchanged knowing looks when
they stood on a corner behind a very tall blond woman
dressed in a black satin pantsuit, cradling a tiny white
poodle whose diamond-encrusted collar matched her own
dangling earrings and double-stranded necklace.

"Los Angeles," Lauren said laughingly. "Don't you love it?"

"Actually, I'm beginning to," Elaine replied.

It was in Little Tokyo, at a shop that sold exquisite silks, that they found a kimono of rich blue lined in a delicate yellow satin which Lauren pronounced to be perfect.

"Just what I wanted," she said. "And I never would have had the nerve to buy it for myself."

"It's beautiful. And it looks beautiful on you," Elaine agreed. "Peter will love it," she added daringly.

The joy faded from Lauren's face and she bit her lips.

"Will he?" she asked wistfully.

They ate lunch in a small Japanese restaurant. Colorful paper lanterns that swayed gracefully over the black lacquered tables lit the narrow dark room. It was, Elaine realized, the first time that she and Lauren had ever been alone in an ambience of intimacy.

"My parents loved this restaurant," Lauren said. "We used to come here a lot when I was in high school. And Peter and I had dinner here almost every weekend when we were at UCLA. We used to think of it as 'our restaurant.' We had a special booth—that one over in the corner."

She stared across the room into the shadowed recess of that nook where once she and Peter had spoken softly to each other in the secret language of lovers, had smiled and reached across the table to touch each other's hands.

"And now?" Elaine asked gently.

"We haven't been here in years. It kind of disappeared from our radar. We just don't have special places, special days, anymore," she said sadly.

"Why is that, Lauren?"

Their meals arrived before Lauren could answer and they studied the beautifully arranged plates of shimmering sashimi, carefully avoiding each other's eyes. Lauren plucked up a piece of tuna in her chopsticks and set it down again.

"Sometimes I think it's simply because we have such crazy schedules," she said at last. "Peter's so caught up in his work and I'm so busy with the kids, running the house, my own obligations, my dad, that there never seems to be time just for the two of us, Peter and me. No time to come here and just sit in our old booth and talk and laugh."

"Maybe you could let some of your involvements go," Elaine suggested. "Make more time to be together, just the two of you."

Lauren laughed bitterly.

"I wish I knew how. I wouldn't know what to cut out. Most of what I do, I do for the kids or for my father or for Peter. It's part of my pattern. I always thought that it was my job to make everyone around me happy. When my brother died I decided that it was up to me to give my parents pleasure, to compensate them for their loss so I was the good and pretty daughter who never caused them any sadness, any difficulty. I went to school in L.A. so that I'd be near them. And then when I met Peter I kind of did the same thing. He was so lonely when we first met and he talked about how he'd always felt that he was an outsider in his own family and so I made sure that he didn't feel that loneliness, that he always knew that he was at the very center of my life, always a part of me because he had never really felt a part of your life. I probably shouldn't be telling you all this, and I don't want to hurt you, but I want you to understand how it all began for us, for Peter and me. We were both lost kids and we got lucky and found each other. And we loved each other. I wonder if he remembers now how much we loved each other, how we couldn't stand to be apart. We kept each other's course schedules and waited outside classroom doors just so that we could walk together from one lecture hall to another, every minute that we shared was sweet and precious."

Lauren smiled at the memory and looked across the room at the shadowed booth they had once laid claim to, as though the ghosts of Peter and herself as young lovers lingered there still. She sighed and turned back to Elaine.

"Peter told me how happy I made him and I kept on trying to make him happy," she continued. "I'd had a lot of practice doing as much for my parents after Donny died. I made plans that would please him, booked tickets for shows he would like, fixed up a home that would make him proud. It was important to him that you and his dad see how well we lived, how well he had done. He always felt that he had to work harder than his sisters, harder than Denis, to carve out a place in your family, to get you to notice him."

Elaine stared at Lauren as though she were speaking an unfamiliar language.

"How could he have felt like that?" she protested. "We loved him. We valued him. I guess we didn't make him aware of how much we cared. We just assumed he would know. Or maybe it was because his father and I were so enmeshed. We adored our children but in truth, we lived for each other. Like you and Peter, we were at the center of each other's life."

Her eyes filled. The husband for whom she had lived was dead and she was alone, harvesting the bitter crop of her children's festering resentments, the hurts that neither she nor Neil had ever suspected.

"Peter understood that," Lauren said. "Intellectually, he accepted that. But he couldn't help the feeling that he was always on the periphery. Just as you and his dad lived for each other, he wanted someone to live for him. And I did that. I knew how to do it. I had practiced for years with my parents. Peter's happiness became my happiness. When we moved to the hills, I got involved in loads of social stuff because when Peter started his production company he needed the kind of contacts he made at the club, at the synagogue, even in the PTA. I was doing my job because if he was successful, he'd feel good about himself. He'd be happy. *Happy.* The magic word. And that's what I wanted for him, what I still want for him. It's what I want for Renée and Eric. For my father. For everyone I love. I'm the happiness fairy. That's why I make sure my kids don't miss anything. That's why I'm driving them here and I'm driving them there. That's why I call my father every day and why I play tennis at the club so my dad can watch me and have lunch with me. So I'm constantly on the run and so is Peter. His business is expanding, he gets busier and busier and we see each other less and less. Sometimes I feel as though I'm living with a stranger. Sometimes I think that Peter has a whole other life that I don't know anything about. I know his work is overwhelming and I know that we need the money but I can't help feeling that something is happening. I feel the distance between us and worse than that, I feel so alone. I want to know what's going on, in his head, in his life, but I'm afraid to ask him. What am I going to do, Elaine? Can I do anything at all?"

Her question was a plea, a sad echo of Peter's own words.

"It will all work out, Lauren," Elaine said and she shivered at the falsity of her answer.

She wanted to be truthful with this daughter-in-law, whom she had never loved, whom she had just begun to understand. She had not credited Lauren with the insight and compassion so newly revealed, nor had she understood the love and need that had thrust Lauren and Peter into marriage when they were both so very young. She saw the pain in Lauren's eyes but she could offer neither honesty nor comfort. Her loyalty to her son constrained her.

Impulsively, she reached across the table and took Lauren's hand in her own. They sat in silence, the lights of the colored lanterns dancing across their linked fingers.

thirteen

Peter drove Lauren to the hospital.

"Pre-op stuff," he told Elaine when he returned. "I'm really glad you're here, Mom. Lauren explained everything to Renée and Eric but they're still a little freaked out. They hear hospital and they think about Lauren's mom. They think about Dad. Renée actually asked Lauren if she was sure she would be coming home because her grandma didn't and her grandpa didn't. Lauren explained everything to them but Renée just kept crying and Eric held tight to her arm the way he used to when he was a baby."

"Lauren's a wonderful mother, Peter," Elaine said.

"I know that. Goddamn it, I know that." Fury spiked his tone but she did not flinch.

"You should think of all the good things in your life

together. What you shared in the past. What you'll share in the future." She hated the preachy sound of her own voice, the hurtful clichés she spewed forth, but they were words that she needed to say. Passivity was abandoned. She would fight for her son and his family.

"And do you think I haven't thought about them?" he asked bitterly.

He slammed out of the room and she shivered in the aftermath of his anger. Walking down the hall moments later, she passed his den. The door was open and she heard him speaking softly, too softly into the phone.

"It will be all right," he said. "I understand. Don't worry."

She thought with relief that he had called Lauren at the hospital, that the gentleness of tone was meant to reassure his frightened wife. Her words had made a difference. She paused for a moment and knew at once that she was wrong.

"I have the production script ready," he continued. "Your revisions were right on target. I have to check out some of the cinematography segues when we go from color to black-and-white. But I have it under control."

Elaine heard the impatient tap of his foot as he waited for a response but his voice, when he spoke again, was calm and reassuring. "Tonight's no good. I have to be with my kids. You understand that. But I'll try for tomorrow night. No, I'll do more than try. I'll be there. I promise."

He was talking to Karina, of course. She hurried to her own room and closed the door behind her, heavy with disappointment, hot with anger. But she knew that she would say nothing more. Not now. She had, perhaps, said too much already.

Eventually she went downstairs and watched him check his attaché case.

"I have two meetings this morning," he said, not meeting her eyes. "But I'm going to try to get to see Lauren as soon as I'm done."

"She'll appreciate that," Elaine said. "And I'll stop by the hospital to see her before I pick the children up from school."

"You know their schedules?"

She glanced down at the list Lauren had printed out with such care. Eric had soccer practice. Renée had a ballet lesson. Each of them had playdates afterward. Lauren had attached MapQuest directions with their friends' addresses, phone numbers, the mother's name.

"Lauren printed everything out," she said.

"Yes. Of course she would." Elaine could not tell if his words were edged with admiration or annoyance.

Still, she was relieved, when she went to the hospital that afternoon, to find Peter sitting beside Lauren in the patients' lounge. Lauren wore the blue kimono that matched her eyes. Her blonde hair fell about her shoulders. Pale without her makeup, she seemed oddly vulnerable, almost childlike. And Peter looked at her, his face a mask of regret and tenderness.

"We've been talking, Peter and I," Lauren told Elaine. "Strange, isn't it, that I had to go to the hospital so that we could find some quiet time just to talk."

"That's the way it is when you both lead such busy lives," Elaine said.

"Yes. Peter's life, especially, has been extremely busy." There was no sarcastic tinge to Lauren's words, only an accepting sadness.

What had he told her? Elaine thought angrily. And why at such a time when she's frightened enough?

"I explained to Lauren how involved I am in this documentary," he said, as though reading his mother's thoughts and fending off her unarticulated accusation. "I told you about it, Mom. About how I'm working with this talented young Russian writer. The one I told you about?"

"Yes. I remember." Elaine stared hard at her son and turned away. She did not want to be complicit in his deception.

"She sounds very interesting," Lauren said. "You said that she was called Karina."

"Karina," he repeated and the name, spoken so slowly, hung uneasily between them.

Later, speeding down the freeway to pick up the children at school, Elaine reflected on the oddness of that exchange. It was strange, too, she thought, that Peter and Lauren, for all their sadness, had seemed, for the first time since her arrival, at ease with each other. It was as though they had been released from a strangling tension and could breathe freely again.

Denis, Sarah and Lisa all called that evening to speak with Peter, to express their concern, to offer their support.

"It's wonderful that your children are so close," Herb

Glasser said, looking up from the game of chess he was playing with Eric.

"Maybe it's because they live so far apart," Elaine replied jokingly although she recognized the grain of truth in her words. Arguments and anger, resentment and irritation, were neutralized by the span of thousands of miles and the confusion of changing time zones.

She turned back to her sketch pad. She was designing another tile for the mosaic and Renée sat beside her, listening gravely to her explanation of how her work progressed, how each tile would capture an aspect of Neil's life.

"If Mommy dies I'll make a mosaic for her," the child said.

"Mommy's not going to die," Elaine replied calmly but she averted her gaze from the sorrow in Herb's eyes and showed Renée how her drawing could be scaled down to the size of a tile.

"It's wonderful for the children that you're here," Lauren's father said when Renée and Eric went up to bed. "Do you think of maybe living in California for at least part of the year? You would have family nearby."

"It would be less lonely," she admitted, filling in the words he had left unsaid. "And I have thought about it."

He nodded and rose to leave.

"Would it be all right if I came here in the morning?" he asked hesitantly.

"Of course."

She understood that he did not want to be alone during

his daughter's surgery, that he did not want to wait for news in the hospital where first his son and then his wife had died. She herself took a circuitous route from her home into town to avoid even the sight of the hospital where Neil had drifted into death.

Peter went into his den and closed the door firmly behind him. Elaine understood that he wanted no additional words of advice, no maternal platitudes. She called Lisa then, asked the questions which had already been answered and listened to her doctor daughter's impatient reassurance.

"It's just a routine procedure. In-and-out stuff. No danger. Lauren's a strong and healthy young woman. A no-risk candidate for that kind of surgery," Lisa said brusquely. "And, Mom, the adoption agency called. I'm going to go to Russia fairly soon. They sent more photos of my little girl. She's just beautiful."

"I'm sure she is," Elaine said. "Is David going to Russia with you?"

"He's got a ton of projects going in Washington just then," Lisa said. "But I'll manage on my own. I always have, haven't I?"

Bitterness edged the question that did not require an answer. Both of them knew that Lisa had always managed on her own, that she had prided herself on that independence. But this was different. Elaine hesitated, struggled to find the right words in which to phrase an offer that might not be welcome.

"Lisa, do you want me to go to Russia with you?" she asked at last, her tone tentative, uneasy.

"I want you to do what you want to do."

The sudden coldness of her daughter's reply was unnerving.

"Let's talk about it again soon," Elaine countered.

There were so many things she had to talk about with her children, so many things to be clarified, so many discontents to be aired. Her visits to Sarah and Peter had taught her that much.

"Don't worry about Lauren, Mom." The caution was Lisa's apology, compensation offered for words that could not be unsaid.

It was late but she turned back to the drawing she had begun with Renée. This series of tiles would portray Neil, the father. She drew only his hands, those long tapering fingers, resting gently on a child's head. But which child? she wondered as her pencil flew. She held it tight and fought to contain the inexplicable sorrow which threatened to engulf her.

The surgery was scheduled for eight in the morning and Peter, grim-faced and tense, left for the hospital at six-thirty.

"Damn freeway," he said. "I don't want to get caught in a traffic jam. I'll call you when she's in recovery."

"She'll be fine," Elaine assured him. "Lisa said—"

"I don't care what Lisa said," he snapped. "I'm sorry, Mom." His voice softened. "I'm just so damn on edge. About so many things."

"I know," she said and thought that if he was still a small boy she could soothe him with a hug, run her fingers through his hair, murmur words of reassurance. But he was a grown man, a father himself. She could offer him neither advice nor comfort. Adult children, she remembered with wry bitterness, sit on your heart, not on your lap.

She busied herself preparing the children for school, assuming a casual carefree attitude as she drove them there, so that they would not be infected by her own anxiety. Back on Canyon Drive she asked Maria to brew a pot of fresh coffee and she was relieved when Herb Glasser rang the bell. She, too, did not want to be alone.

They sat together in the sunroom and watched Jose pass his net across the clear blue water of the pool. His graceful rhythmic movements were strangely comforting and they followed his progress as though he were a dancer gliding across a stage.

"When I was a boy," Herb said, "I took two buses and then a train to swim at the beach in Coney Island. For twenty cents I got a locker on the boardwalk where I could change clothes and take a shower. A towel was five cents more so we brought the towel from home. I wanted more for my children. I wanted them to have everything, to grow up in a fairyland, to walk through their own garden to a swimming pool. That was why we came to California when they were little, Gertrude and I. Here my business could grow. Here I could give them everything. And I did. The house, the pool, the wonderful schools. But what I couldn't give them was health. First my Donny. A strong boy, a laughing boy. The smartest in his class. The best on every team. To look at him was to smile. And then one day he's tired, very tired. Tests. Doctors. Hospitals.

Leukemia, the doctor said, like he was apologizing that a boy like Donny should have such a disease. And Donny was gone. And now Lauren. In the same hospital where Donny died, where Gertrude died. That's why I couldn't go to that hospital this morning. I couldn't sit again in that waiting room where I waited only for bad news. 'We're sorry about your son, Mr. Glasser.' 'We're sorry about your wife, Mr. Glasser.'"

"This is different, Herb," Elaine said, struggling to keep her own voice free of tension. "It's just a routine procedure. I spoke to my daughter, Lisa, last night. That's what she said. A routine procedure."

"When my Gertrude went into the hospital it was also for a routine procedure. A small cyst. A nothing. Routine. But she died during the routine procedure. 'We're sorry about your wife, Mr. Glasser.'"

He set his coffee cup down and looked past her at the expanse of lawn. Jose, having finished at the pool was pruning the rosebushes, carefully avoiding the full-grown yellow blossoms which, Elaine remembered suddenly and irrelevantly, Lauren favored.

"She'll be all right, Herb," she said.

"She's all I have." His voice broke. "Her and the children. I'm alone. Alone in that big house I built for my family. Quiet in the morning, quiet in the evening. I choke on the silence. I pinch myself to make sure that I'm alive, that I'm feeling something. I call information for a phone number so I can hear a voice. And then the phone rings and it's my Lauren. Come watch me play tennis, Dad.

Come for dinner, Dad. Come to Eric's baseball game, to Renée's recital. It's my Lauren inviting me back into life. It's different for you, Elaine. You lost your Neil and that was a terrible thing. But you have four children, grand-children. Your work. And your friends. Women have friends. They meet for dinner. Go to the theater. They shop and have lunch. I see the widows, all around me. They talk, they laugh, they're together. Men alone—we close the doors to our houses and turn on the television set but we don't listen, we don't watch."

"I have four children, all scattered," Elaine said. "But I don't get invited to dinner, to ball games, to dance recitals. I'm too far away. Too much removed from their lives, actually from the way they live their lives."

She thought of Sarah and Moshe and their murmurs of blessing. She could not fit herself into the circle of their belief. She shook her head, banishing the memory of her fierce anger at the seder table.

She glanced around the sunroom with its white wicker furnishings, pastel pillows and sand-colored sisal carpet, an ambience of studied brightness, keyed to pleasure. In her loose gray cotton dress, wearing the jet ceramic pendant of her own design, her mass of thick black hair, she was an alien presence in this life that her son had chosen. Unlike Renee Evers, unlike Peter himself and perhaps Herb Glasser, she could not reinvent herself and become a Cali-fornian. Peter, like Sarah, had drifted into a precinct that was foreign to her just as she and Neil created a life that was very different from that of their immigrant parents. A generational divide was inevitable, she supposed. Life moved on. Children created their own lives, went their own ways. Renee Evers had fled to the west, her children had returned to New England.

"Besides I have my work, my studio," she continued. "Neil had it built so that my window faces our wonderful maple tree."

The tree would be fully leafed now, she thought, its branches casting dancing shadows across the carpet of wildflowers with which they seeded their back lawn. Sometimes, molding a piece of clay, she had willed her fingers to follow the dance of the branches.

"There are studios in California. I rent to artists," he said and she understood that he was not only urging her to live closer to family, he was extending an invitation into his own life, extending the intimacy of their shared grandparenthood. He would have her be his companion, his partner in their shared battle against the silence of empty rooms, the starkness of a table set for one.

"A gallery owner made me such an offer," she said.

Her own words surprised her. She recognized that she had not immediately rejected his suggestion but was actually placing it in the range of consideration.

"What did you say?"

"I said that I'd think about it. When everything calms down."

"Yes. This is not a good time to make decisions. We will talk about it more. When the surgery is over. When other things are settled."

She looked at him sharply but she did not ask him what he meant. He was a father with an acute sensitivity to his daughter. He would, of course, have guessed that something was wrong, that Lauren's life was newly and dangerously unsettled. He looked at his watch, looked at the clock, looked at the phone.

They both jerked forward when it rang. Fearfully, they stared at it, allowed it to ring again and then Elaine answered it.

Peter's voice, calm, relaxed.

"The surgery went well," he said. "No complications. She's fine."

"Of course. Of course. She's fine." Her own words tumbled over each other in an explosion of relief. She turned, beaming, smiling to Herb who seized the phone.

"Good. Wonderful. She's awake? I'll come. Soon. I'll come."

Color returned to his face, light to his eyes. He set the receiver down and he and Elaine embraced. She relaxed into the strength of his arms, listened, with her head pressed against his chest, to the slowing of his heartbeat as the fear that had haunted him eased. He touched her hair, and, oddly, tenderly, traced the arc of her eyebrow with his finger. Her heart turned and she drew away, fearful that it might break.

He left then, eager to see Lauren, and she took up her sketch pad. She concentrated again on the drawing of Neil's hand, of those graceful fingers that had so often passed across her face, resting now on her lips, now on her eyelids and, yes, tracing the arc of her eyebrow.

★ ★ ★

She picked up the children at the end of their school day but she did not follow Lauren's carefully prepared schedule.

"We're celebrating," she told them happily. "Mommy's fine. We're going out for ice cream."

"But where's Daddy?" Renée was a child who would always be in need of reassurance. She did not take good news at face value but required witnesses, reiteration. As a small girl, she would ask, at the conclusion of a fairy tale, "But how do we know they really lived happily ever after?" If Elaine was reading she turned to Neil, if Neil was reading she turned to Elaine. Two adults were needed to testify to the truth. Neil had called her a cautious child. Elaine thought it more likely that she was a frightened child. And her fear today was not misplaced. She had been old enough to register the deaths of two grandparents. She understood that hospitals were ominous venues.

"Daddy will be home for dinner," Elaine assured her. "He wants to be with Mommy this afternoon."

Peter did come home for dinner, arriving with Herb and carrying a pizza which immediately turned the evening meal into a celebration party. Elaine found paper plates and cups left over from a birthday party with a *Lion King* theme.

"My party," Eric said proudly. "Mommy makes the best birthday parties. My whole class says so."

"Mommy wanted you to have pizza tonight," Peter told

the children. "And she says we can have pizza again when she comes home."

"When will she come home?" Renée asked.

"The day after tomorrow," Peter said.

"Is that when she's coming home, Grandpa?" Renée asked, ever in need of corroboration.

"Definitely," Herb said and placed another slice on Renée's plate.

Peter immediately cut away the crust that Renée disliked. He was, Elaine thought, a very good father.

She watched him, noting the creases of fatigue about his eyes, the pallor of exhaustion that blanched his face. His cell phone rang and he carried it into another room. It was a long conversation and when he returned to the table he shoved his plate aside and turned to the children.

"Listen guys," he said apologetically, "I'm sorry but there are problems on one of my shoots. I have to drive down to the desert so I'm going to take off now. I'll see you tomorrow."

"You mean you're not going to sleep here tonight?" Eric asked and his voice quivered.

"Hey, Eric, you know sometimes that happens with my work. It's happened before." Peter tousled his son's hair but he did not look at either his mother or his father-in-law.

"Yeah, but Mommy was always home."

"Well, Grandma's here."

"I like it when you and Mommy are both home together," Renée said. "Besides, it's dark. You can't have a shoot in the dark."

"That's why we have lights, Renée. Remember, I showed them to you when your class came down to the location in Palm Springs. Anyway, I have to get some things and start moving. It's a long drive."

They stared down at their plates, the party atmosphere evaporated. The uneaten pizza slices lay in cold and congealed triangles on the soggy paper plates. Elaine brought out chocolate pudding. They stared at it indifferently and then ate it very slowly. They did not look up when Peter returned, minutes later, carrying a flight bag and his laptop. Renée twitched impatiently when he kissed her forehead and Eric turned away. Herb Glasser nodded his farewell. Elaine walked Peter out to his car.

"This is the wrong night to be away," she said quietly. "The children are still nervous about Lauren."

"She's fine. I told them that."

"They really need you to be with them," she insisted.

"And I need to do what I'm doing," he replied curtly.

"Peter, your highest priority must be your children."

"And were your children always your highest priority? Were we Dad's highest priority?" he shot back and then bit his lip, reached out and touched her shoulder.

"Sorry," he said.

"I'm not the one you should be apologizing to."

He flinched at the hardness of her tone and shook his head wearily.

"They'll be all right. I'll call," he said and he revved the motor of the small red sports car and drove too quickly down the circular driveway and onto Canyon Drive.

★ ★ ★

The phone rang early the next morning but it was not Peter. It was Sarah calling from Israel, the children chattering in the background. It was late afternoon in Jerusalem. Sarah's kitchen counter would be covered with vegetables for the evening meal, her table buried beneath the children's homework and fabric samples.

"Lauren is fine," Elaine assured her before Sarah even had time to ask.

"Yes. I know. Lisa called last night and told me. Actually, I'm calling about Lisa. Although I don't want her to know that I spoke to you."

"Is everything all right?" Elaine asked.

"The adoption agency wants her to travel to Russia to meet Genia. That's the child's name. Lisa had thought that David might go with her but it seems that he's too busy with work and I think she's really uneasy about traveling there alone."

"I did offer to go with her," Elaine said. "I want to go with her. But she insisted that she'd be fine on her own."

She remembered now the sudden chill in Lisa's voice when she had made that tentative offer, her own words hesitant because Lisa had always been so resistant to her advice and suggestions.

"Lisa is not as independent as she would have us think," Sarah said. "She's careful about revealing her feelings."

"To me? I'm her mother, Sarah."

Sarah did not reply and in that long-distance silence Elaine imagined the words unsaid. *Especially to you.* It would seem, she thought bitterly, that her daughters knew and understood each other better than she understood either of them.

"Of course I'll go to Russia with her," Elaine said. "I'll insist on going."

She remembered Lisa's reply to that initial offer. *I want you to do what you want to do.* She understood suddenly that Lisa wanted to claim her heartfelt involvement, her unconditional commitment to both the journey and the adoption.

"That would be great, Mom. Lisa's not as strong as everyone thinks she is."

"I'm glad you called, Sarah," Elaine said. In the background she heard Moshe talking softly to the children, heard the baby Yuval chortle and Ephraim's voice chanting a Torah lesson. Leora took the phone from her mother, breathless with the exciting knowledge that her voice was traveling thousands of miles from Jerusalem to Los Angeles.

"We miss you, *Savta,*" she said. "Are you working on the tiles for Grandpa's mural?"

"I am," Elaine assured her. "And I miss you, too."

She and Sarah said their goodbyes then. Elaine heard the relief in her daughter's voice and thought of how protective the twins had always been of each other. When they were smaller she had sensed that they vied with each other for her attention, for Neil's notice, but as they grew older, although their life choices were very different, their closeness intensified. They were best friends, lending each other

support and, Elaine supposed, sharing secrets. There had
been a special bond between them since their junior years
abroad, the year Sarah (Sandy then. Sandy who wore miniskirts that showed her slender legs and sleeveless blouses that
revealed arms now covered to the wrists) spent in Jerusalem and Lisa in Italy. Lisa had had a boyfriend that year but
she had never told Elaine how and why that relationship had
ended.

Elaine sighed. She had not, before, thought that her
children concealed the truths of their lives from her or
from Neil, nor had she suspected that they harbored resentments.

"Our kids know that they don't have to hide anything
from us," she had more than once assured friends who discussed their own problems with their children. "Of course
we respect their privacy."

Peter, and Sarah, too, had disabused her of that complacency.

She went into the kitchen and, following Lauren's me-
ticulous printed instructions, told Maria to prepare lamb
chops and broccoli for dinner that night. The Mexican
woman nodded.

"I am glad that Señora Gordon is all right," she said. "I
do not like hospitals. They are bad places."

Elaine smiled.

"I think so, too," she said. "But the señora is fine. No
need to worry."

fourteen

Elaine spent the rest of the morning completing yet another tile that she envisioned as part of a triptych, a circle of children holding hands. It would represent their children, their grandchildren, the generational validation of their shared life, enduring beyond Neil's death. Her drawing pencil flew and she thought that she would need larger templates, a strong stylus for the initial etching.

She reached for the phone, intending to call Renee Evers but even as she touched it, it rang.

A man's voice, so muffled by sorrow that it was unrecognizable to her, said her name, Peter's name, Lauren's name. She struggled to understand the words that he spoke, struggled to determine who it was whose voice faded into a bleat of misery and realized that it was Herb Glasser.

"Herb, what is it? What's happened?"

"Lauren. It's Lauren. Find Peter."

"You must tell me what happened." She spoke with calm authority, Neil's legacy to her, the tone he used to coax calm from an agitated patient, to reason with a distraught child. But now she herself was talking to a father, to her daughter-in-law's father, agitated and distraught.

Still, the formula worked. His answer was terse, coherent.

"Lauren suddenly started hemorrhaging. They don't know why. She's lost a lot of blood. It's dangerous, they say. Find Peter. Elaine. Find Peter. I'm afraid for Lauren. My Lauren." His voice broke again and he hung up.

Her hand trembling, she called Peter's office. He was out. His secretary did not know where he was. A location meeting, she thought.

"Try his cell phone," she suggested helpfully and even more helpfully she gave Elaine the number.

Her fingers trembling, her heart pounding, Elaine punched the numbers in. She heard one ring, then another and yet another. At last a woman's voice, edged with laughter, answered.

"Peter Gordon is unable to come to the phone just now," she said playfully.

"This is Peter Gordon's mother. Give the phone to him immediately," Elaine said harshly.

Peter's voice was tense, exuding uneasiness.

"Mom, what's going on? Oh God, I know I said I'd call in the morning but I got hung up here. Are the kids very upset?"

"I'm not calling about Renée and Eric, Peter. I'm calling because you have to **get over** to the hospital right now."

Curtly then she repeated Herb's words, heard Peter's gasp of disbelief, his protest of denial.

"She was fine yesterday. She was great."

"This is today, Peter, and she's not fine, she's not great. The doctors think her condition is grave. I'll meet you at the hospital. How long will it take you to get there?"

"A half hour. If the freeway isn't tied up. I'm on my way."

A half hour. Then he wasn't in Palm Springs seeing to a problem on a shoot. But of course, she had known that all along. He was with Karina who had answered his phone with flirtatious laughter, with the sexual arrogance of a lover fully aware of her power. Driving to the hospital, Elaine seethed with anger at her son who had submitted so easily to the careless demand of the woman with flame-colored hair, who had kept a promise tarnished from its inception. *"I'll try for tomorrow night,"* she had heard him say the night before Lauren had been admitted to the hospital. *"No, I'll do more than try. I'll be there. I promise."* He had had no right to make such a promise.

She raced through the hospital corridors to Lauren's room and wordlessly drew up a chair so that she might sit beside Herb whose gaze was fixed on his daughter's face, her fair skin blanched of all color. Her eyes were closed, her brow damp with sweat.

"You reached Peter?" he asked.

She nodded, still flushed with fury at her son.

But her anger melted when Peter entered Lauren's room. His shirt was misbuttoned, his tie hung loose. He was pale, his features contorted with misery, his eyes dull. He nodded to Herb who turned sorrowfully away. Licking his parched lips, he approached the bed. Lauren was in a deep sleep, large patches of snow-white gauze affixed to her frail arms.

"The bandages are because of the blood transfusions," Elaine told Peter, as though this knowledge might somehow reassure him.

His eyes remained fixed on Lauren. He knelt beside the bed, took her hand in his own and pressed it to his lips. He kissed her fingers one by one. She did not stir.

"Lauren." He whispered her name. "Lauren." His voice was louder. "Lauren!" Louder still. He would shout her into wakefulness, into health.

He rose only when a young doctor approached the bed to monitor Lauren's breathing, to press a stethoscope to her heart, to lift her eyelids and train a light on her eyes which immediately fluttered shut, her expression unchanged. The resident glanced at the IV tube with its steady trickle of shimmering fluid and adjusted it slightly.

"Should she be sleeping like that?" Peter asked.

"She's in a light coma. Probably a reaction to the trauma of the hemorrhage. It could have been induced by the anesthesia. That happens sometimes," the doctor replied gravely.

He made an entry on the chart that hung at the foot of the bed.

"But she'll be all right?" Peter was insistent.

"It's too early to make any predictions."

The reply was perfunctory. The doctor was already moving to the door, impatient to complete his rounds. He was too young, Elaine thought, too inexperienced. He did not yet know that it did no harm to offer hope, to address anxiety with gentleness. She had often heard Neil speak to the families of patients on the phone, addressing their concerns with calm and patience, always allowing the candle of optimism to flicker bravely.

"When will it not be too early?" It was Herb who asked the question and perhaps because his voice broke and his eyes were red-rimmed, the young doctor spoke more softly.

"A few hours. Perhaps a day. Perhaps longer. I'm sorry, sir. I can't be more specific than that."

"I understand."

Herb stood beside his daughter's bed, smoothed the fair hair.

"She had braids when she was a little girl. Long golden braids that fell to her waist. Did you know that, Peter?"

"No. I didn't."

"What else don't you know about Lauren, Peter?"

The two men looked at each other, Herb's eyes heavy with disappointment, Peter's glazed with shame. Elaine pitied both of them. She stared sadly at Lauren who lay motionless on the high hospital bed, her head resting on a pillow covered, improbably, with a pillowcase patterned with pink primroses. This, after all, was California, she thought bitterly, where flowers blossomed even on hospital linen.

Peter's cell phone rang but he glanced at the caller's number and did not answer it. *Karina,* Elaine guessed. She glanced at her son who stood at the window, looking down at the graceful palm trees that lined the path to the hospital. Sunbeams danced on the fronds that swayed in the desert wind.

"Our kids were born in this hospital," he said softly. "Renée and Eric both. What am I going to say to them? Oh God, Mom, what am I going to say to them?"

"Nothing yet," she replied with a calm she did not feel. "We don't know anything so there's nothing to say. I'm going to pick them up from school and today we'll follow the schedule that Lauren gave me. We're going to act as though everything is normal. But Peter, come home for dinner. You, too, Herb. Renée and Eric will need you. They'll need both of you."

The two men nodded and then, to her surprise, Herb put his hand on Peter's shoulder and together, father and husband took seats beside Lauren's bed.

Elaine was relieved that Renée and Eric seemed relaxed as they climbed into the car after school. They quarreled briefly about who would sit in the front seat. Renée prevailed, and they chattered happily about student council elections, about an improv group that had performed in assembly that day as Elaine maneuvered the car into a slow lane. Why, she wondered, did Los Angelinos drive so fast? Was everyone in the city in a hurry?

"Those actors were really cool," Eric said.

"Cool and weird," Renée agreed. "Grandma, when is Mom coming home from the hospital?"

"Soon, I think," Elaine replied vaguely, her heart pounding although she kept her voice neutral. "Your dad and Grandpa will be home for dinner. What kind of dessert should I get?"

An ordinary question for an ordinary day, designed to divert them, and immediately successful.

"Apple pie," Renée said.

"Peach," Eric countered.

She drove them to the temple for their religious school classes, went to the bakery and picked up a pie, half apple, half peach, and returned to Canyon Drive where she called Peter at the hospital.

"No change," he said, speaking so softly she could barely hear him. "How were the kids?"

"Fine. I told them you'd be home for dinner."

"And I will be."

She called Lisa and described Lauren's condition.

"It's unusual," her daughter said carefully. "But it happens. Bleeds like that sometimes occur after surgery because of a weakness in a blood vessel. But the transfusions should have taken care of that. The doctor is right that the coma is the result of the physical trauma. That or the anesthesia. He's right on target. I think Lauren will be fine, Mom."

"I hope so. And Lisa, when all of this is over, let's talk about your trip to Russia. I want to go with you."

"You're sure?" Lisa asked.

"I'm sure. You know your grandparents came from Russia. Dad was born there and came to the States when he was really young. He had only very vague memories but it would be interesting to visit their village while we're over there. I might get some ideas maybe for the memorial mural I'm working on. I did tell you about the mural, didn't I?"

"That would be interesting," Lisa agreed. "And I assume you also want to meet your new granddaughter," she added dryly.

Elaine flinched at the coldness in her daughter's voice. Another maternal sin, she thought. This one of omission. Her children's emotional ledgers grew more crowded by the day. The debit column overwhelmed. The words she had said and the words she had not said. Their perceived exclusion from the circle of parental intimacy. And now her mention of the village of Neil's birth when Lisa's thoughts were concentrated on the child she would take into her heart, into her home. Elaine sighed. The circle was unending. She was guilty before her sons and daughters as they, in turn, would be guilty before their own children. There was no foolproof formula, neither for life nor for parenting. She and Neil had made their mistakes. Their sons and daughters would make their own. Carefully, struggling against the surge of her own irritation, she answered Lisa.

"Of course I'm excited about meeting your daughter, my granddaughter. And Lisa, I'm glad her name is Genia. That was my mother's name."

"Oh, Mom, you'll love her. Her picture is so cute." Lisa was appeased. "Keep me informed about Lauren. I'm sure she'll be out of danger very soon."

"I will. Of course I will," Elaine assured her but she was uneasy when she hung up. Lisa's very reassurance implied that Lauren was, after all, in danger.

She hurried to pick up the children and thought of the frenetic pace of Lauren's life, the role of the freeway mother endlessly changing lanes as she sped from one activity to another.

Peter and Herb arrived for dinner, dutifully ate the lamb chops and broccoli although they had little appetite. They pecked at the pie but Maria carried full plates back to the kitchen. Peter helped Eric with his homework, played Junior Scrabble with Renée, patiently answered their questions. Their mother would be home soon. She couldn't talk to them on the phone because she needed a lot of rest.

"That's what Ellen said." Renée nodded wisely. "She sits next to me and she told me that her mother slept a lot after her operation. But she's fine now. She's the class mother. Do you think Mom can be our class mother next term?"

"Maybe," Peter said even as he and Herb looked sadly at each other.

The phone rang. Peter answered it, frowned and carried the phone into the next room but still his voice was audible.

"I told you I'd call when I could. I can't talk now. I'll try to call later. Try. I can't say for sure."

He spoke curtly. The caller had to be Karina, Elaine

knew, but on this night he would not be seduced into making promises that he could not keep.

He and Herb returned to the hospital, the children went up to bed and Elaine took up her sketch pad. She worked steadily and then called Renee Evers.

"I'd be interested in arranging for some studio space," she said. "If things work out." *If my daughter-in-law regains consciousness, if she does not die.* She banished the thought and continued. "I could do some bookends for you and I want to do some tiles for a mural. My own project."

"Just let me know when," Renee said and Elaine hung up, pleased that she had made the call, that she could perhaps anticipate the onset of normalcy, of a return to the world of her work, the stylus tight between her fingers, the breath of the open kiln hot upon her face.

The phone rang yet again and she answered it. *Let it be Peter telling me that everything is all right.* The wish, unspoken, was her silent prayer.

But it was a woman who spoke softly into the phone.

"This is Karina Mendelowitz. Is Peter there?" That remembered voice, breathless now, untinged by laughter, hesitant.

"He's at the hospital. With his wife. I'm Elaine Gordon, his mother." Her words were calculated to wound.

"I've tried to reach him on his cell phone. He's not picking up."

"No. He wouldn't." She offered no quarter.

"I spoke to him earlier. When he was at home. But it's urgent that I speak with him again."

"Hospitals are strict about the usage of cell phones."

"Will you tell him I called?" It was more plea than question.

Elaine glanced at her watch. Peter would not be home for hours. The children were asleep. They could be left with Maria.

"Karina, Ms. Mendelowitz, where are you now?"

Karina hesitated. The question surprised her, Elaine knew. She herself was surprised by her own daring in asking it.

"At Jason's, a coffee shop on Balboa. Not far from Canyon Drive. Why?"

"Actually, I know where it is. I'd like to meet you, to talk to you," Elaine said. "I could be there in fifteen minutes."

Again, a moment of hesitation. Elaine waited.

"All right." A whispered assent threaded with uncertainty.

Elaine told Maria that she would be going out for an hour and drove, too swiftly, to Balboa. Speeding down the broad boulevard, she reflected that Neil would not have approved of her action. Always, he had insisted, in his calm and careful manner, that parents had no right to interfere in the lives of their adult children. She had acquiesced, deferred to his professional insight, unwilling to quarrel with him. She had contained her anger at his oh so sensible edict, restrained her impulse to intervene, to protect one child or another from a dangerous decision. But she would restrain herself no longer. There was too much at stake. She knew what she had to do.

She remembered suddenly that during their courtship she and Neil had quarreled bitterly. They had parted in anger and did not speak for days. She had been certain that they would never speak again. Plunged into despair, she cut classes, lay on her bed and turned her face to the wall. She did not eat and although her parents asked no questions their faces were pale with misery and from behind her closed door she heard their worried murmurs. He had phoned at last, his own voice husky with sadness and fear. Later, much later, she had asked him why he had called. "Because your mother phoned me. She told me how miserable you were. I wasn't supposed to tell you that," he had confessed and she had understood that it was her mother's interference that had led to their reconciliation, to the life they had built together.

"Would you have called me if she hadn't phoned?" she had asked and he had not replied.

She had never reminded Neil of that. Neil, the trained and accomplished psychoanalyst would perhaps not have approved of the long-forgotten interference of her immigrant mother who saw only her daughter's misery and acted instinctively. As she herself had done when she spoke with Karina.

But did she have her mother's certainty, her clarity? Her mother had thought only of protecting her daughter and had taken the only path open to her. She had known exactly what she wanted to say to Neil. But what, after all, would Elaine say to her son's lover? Would she issue a plea, utter words of castigation? She did not know. She was trespassing on treacherous emotional territory. She gripped the steering wheel with sweat-dampened palms and drove recklessly through a red light.

But I must do something. She spoke the words aloud as she parked and entered the dimly lit café. That, she understood, must have been how her own mother had felt. A parental mandate, maternal intuition. A child's happiness must be protected no matter the risk. And she was bent on protecting not only Peter and Lauren but the children, Renée and Eric, who tossed restlessly in their sleep, fearful for their mother, unaware of the jeopardy that threatened their magical world.

Karina was seated at a small table in the rear. The copper-colored hair that framed her narrow fine-featured face, caped the high collar of her black linen jacket. With her high cheekbones and almond-shaped hazel eyes, she had a Modigliani beauty. She sat very erect, unsmiling, her gaze guarded, as Elaine approached.

"Karina?" Elaine held out her hand and Karina extended her own. Their palms brushed in acknowledgment of an uneasy truce.

"Elaine. May I call you Elaine?" Karina asked, her slightly accented voice flat and without affect.

"Yes. Of course."

Elaine took the chair opposite her and waved the approaching waitress away although her mouth was dry, her tongue tufted with anxiety. Karina stared down at her half-eaten sandwich, toyed with a crust of bread and crumbled it between her fingers.

"How is Peter's wife?"

"Lauren. Her name is Lauren. But you must know that. She's very ill. She's in a coma. Peter is with her. Which is why he hasn't returned your calls." She spoke very slowly, each word a bullet on a steady emotional trajectory. She wanted to wound this woman, to pierce her carapace of calm.

"I know. I have a friend who's a nurse at the hospital. She told me."

"Then why have you kept calling?"

"I'm worried about Peter."

"He's coping."

"Is he?" She smiled bitterly. "Then I suppose I shall have to do the same. But then I'm very good at coping."

"I'm sorry. I know that your life hasn't been an easy one."

"I'm not looking for your pity. I don't need anyone's pity. Actually, you could say that I've been fortunate. I was still young enough when we emigrated from Russia to be educated here, to develop my talent. I'm a writer, a very good writer, I think."

"I know that. Peter told me that he admires your work."

"I have had some success. And that is very important to me. My writing is my passion. It is more important to me than anything in the world. It absorbs me totally. I know you will understand that because Peter has told me how you were deeply involved in your own work, that you spent hours and hours in your studio."

She leaned closer toward Elaine, as though inviting her complicity. Elaine stared at her in surprise.

"But my work was never at the center of my life," she protested. "My husband. My children were always more important to me than my studio life." *My husband.* She recognized, with sudden insight that she had placed Neil first. She had not said, as she might have, *My family.* And yes, it was true. Neil had always come first in her life. She had loved her work, cherished her children but for better or for worse, her husband had been her passion. She would not apologize for that. Not to herself, not to others.

"And now there is this documentary I am working on with Peter," Karina continued as though Elaine had not spoken. "It has absorbed both of us, Peter and myself, for so many months now. It is the kind of work Peter always wanted to do and for me it is more important than anything else I have done. It brings to a focus my family's situation and by extension the situation of many Russian Jews—the disorientation, the loneliness. The challenge of building a new life, of rescuing a vanished culture. I wrote my heart into it. And Peter was so involved that he would call me sometimes in the middle of the night to suggest a change, to introduce a new idea. We have everything scheduled, Peter and I, everything coordinated. Interviews, reminiscences. Locations. Staff. This is the week we begin shooting so that we will be ready to edit and screen for distributors well before the Cannes festival. The camera crew is ready to begin earlier than we thought. Perhaps even tomorrow. Which is why I must speak to Peter."

"He can't deal with this until Lauren is stabilized. He needs all his energy for her and for his children. He has to be there for Renée and Eric. You must know that they are the center of his life," Elaine said.

"And Lauren, his wife, their mother, is she, too, the center of his life?" Karina asked caustically, her question a challenge. She, after all, had been his lover. She had slept beside him on nights when his wife had slept alone. She wanted his mother to recognize that, to understand that. "I am important to him. That much I know. He and I can do wonderful things together. But first we must complete this project. He must meet with the camera crew tonight, tomorrow morning at the latest."

"I see. You say that you are important to him, Karina. And that may well be. But I know that he is very important to you for different reasons. You need him so that you can make your film, make your mark."

"I care about him." Karina blushed hotly. Her hand trembled, causing her spoon to rattle against the thick coffee cup.

"If you care about him, you will let him concentrate on his family now," Elaine replied coldly. "I would not want him to know that while his wife was fighting for her life, you were worried about your documentary."

"Are you blackmailing me, Elaine?" Karina asked defiantly.

"I am thinking about my son and his family," she replied.

"You didn't answer my question." Karina stared at her.

"That's right. I didn't. Probably you know the answer."

She left then but glanced back when she reached the doorway. Karina stared after her, gripping her cell phone, her finger nervously twirling a tendril of fiery hair.

Elaine drove back to Canyon Drive feeling strangely calm. She had done what she could for her son, for Lauren and for her grandchildren. She had been surprised by Karina. She had thought to meet a softer woman but she understood that it was that very ambition, that determination that had attracted Peter to her. And it was that same ambition, that same determination that would, in the end, ruin his life. She knew this with an intuitive certainty. Like her mother, she had an obligation to intervene on behalf of her child.

Peter knocked at her bedroom door when he came home and she followed him downstairs and brewed tea for both of them.

"No change," he said as he cradled the cup. "But they say there is a change in her respiratory pattern. Which is good. They're going to give it a couple of more hours and then do a CAT scan, whatever the hell that is. If she doesn't wake up."

"I think she will," Elaine said. "Lisa thinks she will."

"You know what I was remembering, sitting by her bed this afternoon, tonight?" Peter asked. "I was remembering how we met, Lauren and I. She sat in front of me in a humanities lecture and when she leaned back her hair brushed my hand. I'll never forget the feel of it, like a piece of silk against my skin. Then she turned around and I thought that I was looking at an angel. We talked after class and from that first minute, that first conversation, I felt as though all the loneliness of my life had drifted away. It was as though I had found my other half. We couldn't stand being apart after that first week together. We'd wait for each other between classes, have lunch together, dinner, phone calls every night before we went to sleep. Her voice was the last sound I heard, her face lighting up my dreams. I remembered, tonight, how we'd go down to Little Tokyo on weekend nights, always to the same restaurant, always sitting in the same booth, our hands across the table…" His voice drifted off.

"We went to that restaurant, Lauren and I. She showed me that booth," Elaine said.

"She remembered." Sadness and regret rimmed his voice.

"She remembered. How could she forget?"

"I did. Or I thought I did. So much drifted away from me, from us. I thought that we had lost each other, Lauren and I, that we'd been ambushed by carpools and schedules, by a calendar so crowded with what we were doing that we had no time for being what we were. Until today. When everything came rushing back to me and I thought that I would drown. Wave after wave of memories washing over me, bringing me back to how she was, how I was, how we were together. I looked at Lauren today and I remembered her face when Renée was born, when Eric was born. Did I ever tell you that both our babies were born at daybreak? Beautiful sunrises on both those days. I held her hand and we looked at them, at those perfect little beings, those beautiful tiny lives arrived in the world because we loved each other. And then we both looked through the window at the same time and watched the sun begin to climb, watched that honey-colored light of dawn brush the fronds of the palm trees, those same fronds that shivered in the wind today. Pale as she was today, Lauren's face glowed on those miracle mornings and I thought then that we were both bathed not in sunlight but in joy. We were blessed. She told me, the morning that Eric was born, that I was her life. And I told her that she was mine." His voice broke. "That's what I remembered when I sat beside her and watched her sleep and sleep and sleep."

Tears slid down his cheeks but he did not wipe them away.

"She'll wake up," Elaine said very softly.

Her own voice broke. She was moved by her son's eloquence, by the depth of his feeling.

"But what if she doesn't? What if she doesn't wake up because she doesn't want to? Oh Mom, she knew something was wrong between us. She didn't know about Karina. I didn't tell her. But she sensed that there was someone else. She asked me, that day in the hospital, the day before her surgery. And I—I didn't say yes. I didn't say no. I took her life away." His voice faded into a whisper. He gripped his mug so tightly that his knuckles paled.

"You didn't take her life away," Elaine said fiercely. "You said nothing that would hurt her. Yes, you made a mistake when you got involved with Karina. But mistakes are made and they're repaired and life goes on." She looked at her son. "Do you love Lauren?"

"God, yes. More than I realized."

"And what about Karina?"

"Karina. She seems like a dream. A fading dream. A fantasy. What we had together was an interlude I might have imagined. When I tried to call her today I couldn't remember her phone number. When I tried to think about her I couldn't remember her face. She seemed unreal. All those years I shared with Lauren are my reality. We were lovers, Lauren and I. For years and years we were each other's world. We were so young when we met that we actually grew up together. And then we were husband and wife and mother and father to our children. How could I have forgotten that moment of first light, her glow when she looked at our babies? I forgot how precious she was to me then, and sitting beside her bed today I realized how precious she is to me now. Our lives are bound up together. All those memories."

"Marriages are like that," Elaine said. "A mountain of memories. Daybreak after daybreak." *And heartbreak after heartbreak until the last and final heartbreak.* The thought overtook her, unbidden.

"Karina called," he said, staring down at the dregs in his teacup. "I spoke to her as I was driving home."

"Oh?"

Elaine remembered Karina reaching for her cell phone as she left the café. She wondered, dispassionately, if she had told Peter about their meeting.

"She was concerned about the documentary. She asked about Lauren, of course, but she was really worried about the production schedule. I told her that I couldn't be involved in it with everything that was going on and I had turned everything over to my assistant. She asked if that meant that I couldn't be involved with her. I didn't answer. I think she began to cry. At least I heard her gasp and then she hung up and I didn't try to call her back. I feel guilty as hell but it was what I had to do." He bit his lips, clasped and unclasped his hands.

"You did the right thing, Peter," Elaine said.

It occurred to her, with relief and sadness, that she too had done the right thing. She had gambled and the stakes had been high. She had risked Peter's future, his family's future. But she had no regrets. That risk, uncalculated as it was, had been well taken. Peter would never know of her meeting with Karina. In that, at least, she and the young Russian woman would be complicit.

They mounted the stairs together, mother and son, holding hands, as though to support each other. He leaned toward her and she felt the weight of his body, the weight of his fear.

"It will be all right." She spoke the reassuring words but her own heart hammered heavily and rapidly and her hands trembled.

fifteen

The phone rang early the next morning. It was Elaine who answered, her heart hammering, her body tensed as though to ward off the impact of the ominous. But it was Herb, who roared his news, his voice elated. Unable to sleep, he had gone to the hospital at first light. Lauren had awakened, bewildered but fully conscious. The neurologist assured him that there had been no impairment. She was asking for Peter, asking about the children. Peter seized the phone atremble with relief and excitement.

"I'm on my way," he told his father-in-law.

He embraced his mother and then he took her hands and, in the remembered celebratory rite of his boyhood, he whirled her about the room.

"Us, too. Us, too."

Renée and Eric, barefoot and in pajamas, still flushed with sleep, burst out of their bedrooms and joined them. They circled the room, sunlight spattering their upturned faces, hands tightly clasped, unwilling to relinquish the soaring excitement of joy reclaimed, of life renewed.

Lauren returned from the hospital at the end of the week and slowly the daily routines were resumed. But Elaine noticed small and subtle changes. Peter was home every night, sometimes arriving late but always in time to see the children before they went to bed, to share a late dinner with his wife. Elaine, who ate with her grandchildren, who relished their talk and laughter, glanced at her son and his wife as they ate in the sunroom and remembered the intimate dinners she and Neil had delighted in. She was no longer overwhelmed with sadness when such memories visited her. Like Lauren, she, too, was a convalescent, nursing herself back from grief.

Lauren curtailed her own schedule. Less driving, fewer manic races down the freeway. Lessons and appointments cancelled. Eric and Renée did not seem to miss the steady round of playdates, did not mind missing music lessons and tutoring sessions. They were, parents and children alike, in a silent agreement, at a new beginning. The pace of their lives was slowed. There was time, each morning, to sip a second cup of coffee, time each evening to watch the moonlight silver the verdant lawn and streak the blue waters of the pool.

Lauren was newly relaxed, newly quiescent, Peter newly

contented. They recognized that they had survived a dangerous time and they worked carefully, quietly, to avoid future hazards.

They spent weekend evenings wandering through Little Tokyo because Peter was considering a documentary on the colorful Los Angeles Japanese community. Elaine imagined them eating sushi in the booth they called their own, their hands now and again touching, their eyes meeting, their togetherness reclaimed.

The days passed into weeks. She herself went to dinner, to concerts and to the opera with Herb. They were comfortable with each other. It pleased her when he lightly stroked her hair, her cheek, when his lips brushed her own. She had not realized how much she had missed the tenderness of touch, a hand upon her own, an admiring gaze across the dinner table.

"Mom, you really like it out here, don't you?" Peter asked. "Why not stay longer?"

"I'm waiting to hear from Lisa," she replied. "There's our trip to Russia, things to take care of in Westchester. I'm really not ready to make any long-range plans. But I'll be here for another month at least. I've promised Renee Evers enough pieces for an exhibit."

"Perhaps you'd think of living here for at least part of the year. You could buy or rent a small studio, sort of a pied-à-terre," Lauren suggested, echoing Sarah's words.

Elaine smiled. How easily her children proposed a scenario for the rest of her life. Did they think that the days of her year could be divided into equal segments, that she could travel with such ease from Los Angeles to Jerusalem, from the east coast to the west, seamlessly adjusting her life to their own?

"We'll see," she said simply, in answer to Lauren's suggestion, closing all further discussion.

Reading the *Los Angeles Times* one morning, Elaine found herself looking at Karina's photograph. The caption read *Karina Mendelowitz Whose Memoir* Russian Odyssey *Will Be Published In The Fall*. The accompanying story described the documentary based on the memoir which was currently in production under the aegis of a British film company.

She passed the newspaper to Peter. He scanned the story and nodded.

"Yes. I arranged the British deal. It was profitable for me and very good for her. Closure of a kind. A relief to both of us."

And to me, Elaine thought as she ripped the page out of the newspaper and carefully shredded it. She would no longer have to feel guilty about Karina who had, after all, achieved exactly what she wanted.

She drove to Renee Evers's studio each day. Renee had become her friend, a woman whose experience matched her own, who was, at once, wise and cynical. Renee had friends and lovers. She dressed with a bohemian flair, applied makeup with an artist's skill, mauve eye shadow, apricot blush. Her hands moved nervously and her laughter came easily. She spoke of weekends in Palm Springs and Malibu.

"It's okay for widows to have a sex life," she told Elaine. "It was our husbands who died, not us." But the laughter that followed was threaded with pain.

Elaine understood Renee's words, her pleasure and her pain. She thought of the warmth she felt at the touch of Herb's hand, at the admiration in his eyes. That sufficed. For the moment. She dared not venture further. She was too new to loss to think or feel otherwise. Work was her anodyne, the mural a milestone marking Neil's life and her own reluctant acceptance of the sad and terrible finality of his death.

She completed two more tiles for the mosaic which was slowly taking shape, the enamel satin smooth and shimmering with color. Neil and his grandchildren. The maple tree in their garden that he had watched with such delight— its branches thick with leaves, then skeletal and snow-laden. Passing seasons, passing lives.

"You miss him very much?" Renee asked when Elaine explained the tiles to her.

The question neither offended nor pained her.

"Yes. I miss him every day." His loss, like his love, had been woven into the fabric of her life.

She did several sets of bookends, alternating in size, then nests of bowls in warm earth colors, tints of amber and gold in each distinctive glaze. She fashioned deep bowls of an aqueous blue and filled them with ceramic lemons and citrons. Renee scheduled a show at her Santa Monica gallery. Herb accompanied her to the opening and stood beside her as she discussed her work with one critic, then another.

Had her stay in California influenced the texture and color of her work? Did she anticipate working on larger projects geared to the Los Angeles sensibility, the more casual Californian lifestyle? Did she plan on opening her own studio in the hills?

Interior design and crafts were important to the California public. Every newspaper and glossy magazine featured articles on new trends in the field. With the exception of Hollywood, Los Angelinos entertained at home and their furnishings, down to the smallest objects that they placed in their kitchens, were important to them. They embraced the culture of personality and it seemed as natural to them to know as much about the artists whose work they purchased as they knew about the movie stars they watched on the screen. They spoke knowledgeably, authoritatively, about the vases and bowls they placed on their low tables, the wind chimes that dangled in their doorways. They recognized the names of ceramicists and weavers, of glass blowers and woodworkers. Elaine knew that her work would not have attracted similar attention in New York.

Herb said as much as they sat across from each other at dinner.

"You could have a wonderful life here, Elaine. You have a constituency in Los Angeles, clients who will look for your work. And you have your family here, Peter and Lauren, Renée and Eric."

Elaine smiled.

"And you, Herb," she said slyly.

"Yes. And me. The two of us can share in our grand-children's lives. We can take them on trips, celebrate holidays with them. I am not asking you for more than that. You are not Gertrude and I am not Neil but together, even living our separate lives but in close touch, we can cancel out each other's loneliness."

He fell silent then, his cheeks flushed, his eyes bright with hope. She thought of how kind he was, how gentle, how deeply he cared for his daughter and how sensitive he had been toward Peter, containing his anger and anxiety. He was a good man, a very good man.

She reached across the table and touched his hand.

"I'm grateful to you, Herb. We will always be friends, very good friends. But I have to figure out my own life. I don't want to be defined by my children, their needs, their concern about me. I have to find my own strength. This is not the time for me to make decisions. There are things I must do, things I must understand."

She paused. She could not tell him that she wanted to understand her children; she wanted to balance the ledger of their resentments and their love, to understand the lives they had chosen and where she herself fit into those lives.

"Lisa called last night," she continued. "We leave for Russia next month and I want to spend a few weeks in my own home, to work in my own studio. Of course I'll come back to L.A. and of course we'll do a great many things together, you and I, Peter and Lauren. Our grandkids."

She thought of Renée and Eric, both born at first light, and felt a surge of hope.

"There will be other visits, Herb. New days dawning for both of us." Her words were a promise, to herself and to the gentle silver-haired man whose blue eyes were flecked with gray.

"I understand," he said softly.

Hand in hand then, they left the restaurant and walked slowly down the Santa Monica boardwalk and watched the gentle waves break against the shore. The evening sun was slowly setting, its waning light now threaded with amber. They paused, watched its steady, inexorable descent, and she lifted her face to his and felt the softness of his lips upon her cheek.

sixteen

The night before her mother's arrival, Dr. Lisa Gordon, exhausted from a long day during which she had traveled from her main office in Rittenhouse Square to two of her subsidiary laboratories along the Philadelphia Main Line, ate a hasty microwaved dinner, careful as always to check the caloric and carb contents, took a long hot shower and slipped into the soft flannel nightgown she favored on the nights when David Green was in a distant city. He called as she wandered through her living room, arranging and rearranging the various gifts her mother had crafted for her over the years.

"I'm fine," she assured him as she centered the turquoise-glazed oblong fruit bowl in which she always kept lemons and limes on the rosewood dining room table. "It was just an incredibly long day. And I guess I'm sort of bracing myself for my mother's visit."

David understood her ambivalence about her mother although he himself was at ease with Elaine, whose work he admired, just as he admired the calm undemanding way in which she had dealt with her husband's death. His own mother had suffered a brief nervous breakdown when his father died and immediately moved to an assisted living facility in Arizona, which caused him both guilt and relief.

"I'm glad you'll be in Philadelphia tomorrow night," Lisa continued, rearranging the gold and scarlet enameled trivets in the vivid autumn colors which had been her mother's gift when she first moved into her spacious apartment. "I think she feels more comfortable with you than she does with me. I know I sound like an ingrate. I'm really relieved that she's traveling to Russia with me."

"I'm glad she'll be with you," David said. "Damn it. It's Russwell. I've been trying to reach him all day. Can you hold on for a second?"

"Sure, I'll hold."

David was still at his office, she knew, juggling phones and e-mails, mauling his way through piles of memos. Congressman Russwell was an important client for whom David was coordinating a conference. Holding the phone she went into her bedroom and stood before the mirror and studied her reflection. Her hair was black like her mother's; but while Elaine's was a mass of dark curls, now tinged with gray, Lisa's was satin-smooth and helmeted her head. She had her father's bright blue eyes and thinness of face and, like him, she was tall and slender, swift of movement and calm of tone. She had memorized the reassuring, comforting cadence of his voice and made it her own. On impulse, she dabbed a drop of perfume behind each ear just as David returned to the phone.

"I've just wasted two drops of Chanel on you," she said softly.

"Will it hold until tomorrow night?" he asked. "Lisa, I'm going to miss you. I wish I was going to Russia with you. Will you be all right?"

The odd wistfulness of his tone surprised her and she hesitated before replying.

"Don't worry. I'll manage," she said at last. "And remember, I guilted my mother into the trip so I won't be alone."

"I'm sure she wants to be with you. It's a chance for the two of you to be together and for her to meet her new granddaughter."

"Genia. Her new granddaughter's name is Genia," she said with deceptive softness.

It was important to her that David speak the name of the dark-eyed little girl she would bring home from Russia, Genia, her daughter, whose shy smile in the photo she had seen in the adoption agency's album, had pierced her heart.

"Right. Genia. Okay, we're set for tomorrow," he said too brusquely and she knew that he was probably studying a file even as he spoke to her.

David seldom did one thing at a time. He was, he had told her when they first met, a master of multitasking and she had archly countered that she could easily match his pace. They had, early on, drawn the battle lines of independence.

"Unless you suddenly get called to conference in Paris or Mexico City," she retorted playfully.

"There's no restaurant in Paris or Mexico City that can compete with Bookbinders," he said, light-heartedness restored. "Hey, see you in my dreams." His signature sign-off, murmured each night they were apart.

"And I'll see you in mine." Her words matched his own and she repeated them even after she heard him click off and knew he was no longer on the line.

Moodily then, she placed the bookends of a mosaic design which her mother had made for her on her end table, setting two unread bestsellers between them. Elaine would be gratified to see her work so prominently displayed and Lisa realized, with some surprise, that it was newly important to her that she please her mother. She had, after all, lost her father whose pleasure and approval had always been dominant in her life.

"Oh, Daddy," she said as she unlocked the bottom drawer of her desk, removed the cloth-covered journal and opened it to a blank page.

She had always kept a diary. As a girl, she had written in it late at night when her twin sister, Sandy, was already asleep, transcribing her deepest thoughts and feelings as she crouched in bed, holding a flashlight over a page that more often than not was worn thin with erasures and moistened by tears. Later, in high school and college and then in medical school, she would waken at first light, reach for her notebook, always hidden beneath her nightgowns, and record her thoughts, her experiences of the previous day and her plans for the day to come.

It was her father, perhaps sensing a need she herself could not define, who had given her that first blank journal and suggested, in his quiet professional tone, that she write in it daily. It would, he had assured her, give her focus.

It had also been her father who had given his twin daughters copies of *The Diary of Anne Frank*. Sandy had read it in silent sadness, her eyes brimming with tears, but Lisa had read it with a shock of recognition.

It had startled her to learn that the young girl, hidden in an Amsterdam attic, had feelings about her parents that closely matched her own. She had found it comforting that Anne, like herself, had adored her father and resented her mother and that she, too, had envied her sister Margot's serenity just as Lisa herself envied Sandy's gentleness. Like Anne, Lisa had written about her feelings and like Anne, her words suffused her with guilt. She read Anne's entries again and again, shamed to compare her own situation with that of the sad-eyed Jewish girl who would die in a Nazi death camp and yet aware of the emotions she shared with her.

Lisa's own earliest memory was of herself as small child trailing after her father as he walked through their garden and then rushing up to him, to grasp his hand, to match her small steps to his own, pausing when he paused, listening earnestly as he spoke. In dream she felt again the light touch of his fingers, heard again the softness of his voice. He plucked a flower and showed it to her, inviting her to share its mystery. "See," he said. "The petals, the pistil, the stamen, all the secrets of the flower's life." She watched him place a golden caterpillar in tall grass, as he motioned her to silence so that they would not disturb a fat honey bee nestled in the heart of a primrose. She listened as he explained how pollen was gathered and new plant life perpetuated. Her heart swelled with pride at all that her father knew. He was a doctor. The secrets of the universe were his to comprehend and decipher. As early as grade school, she had known that she wanted to share his knowledge, to be part of his world. She, too, would study medicine and become a doctor. She had even imagined herself wearing a long white coat and walking beside him down a hospital corridor, father and daughter locked into a professional closeness that excluded the rest of the family, her sister, Sandy, her brothers, Peter and Denis but especially her mother, who so often seemed to exclude her.

It was an exclusion that Lisa accepted, that she tried to understand. Her mother was a creative artist and her work was important to her. Her studio adjoined their house and her children called to her when they arrived home but it was tacitly understood that, except for Sandy, who often worked beside her, they would not invade her workplace. Their meals were effortlessly prepared as Elaine drifted from studio to kitchen, often igniting first her kiln and then her oven. She was an organized and orderly woman who listened with appropriate attention to her children's tales of the school day, refereed their bickering, arranged for creative birthday parties and carefully scheduled medical and dental appointments.

But she hummed and smiled only when she prepared the meals she and Lisa's father would share when he returned home, well past the dinner hour, after his last appointment. There were always patients who could not come during the day and he was an analyst who tried wherever possible to accommodate those who relied on him. Lisa recognized that his late arrival, the privacy of their dinner alone, was an arrangement that suited both her parents.

Her mother's face brightened and her eyes softened when she heard his car pull up to the house. She hurried then to brush her hair, to place flowers on the small table in the alcove where they shared their meals. They sipped their wine, her head inclined toward him as they spoke, their faces radiant with candlelight, wedded lovers, impervious to the interruptions of their children who dashed through the house, shouted from room to room, quarreled briefly, giggled wildly. Now and again, after their dinner, one or the other would enter a child's bedroom to help with a homework assignment, to arbitrate a disagreement, to listen to a joke, a complaint. Caring parents. Involved parents.

But later in the evening they sat in the living room, their eyes closed, their hands touching, as they listened to music. Berlioz, Brahms, Mahler. They did not need words then. They were happily locked into a gated intimacy. Lisa, who often watched them from the head of the stairs, knew herself to be unhappily locked out of their impenetrable closeness.

It was Sandy who spent long hours with their mother in the studio, working on her own drawings, her own designs. She stood before her easel as her mother stood at her potter's wheel and they worked together, clay taking shape, colors taking form. There was no place for Lisa in that work space that smelled of paint and chemicals, of damp clay and Elaine's Madame Rochas toilet water.

But Lisa was pledged to her father and she lay in wait for him at the door of his study on weekend afternoons, clutching her own book which she read, lying across his cushioned window seat as he sat at his desk reading journals, writing up reports, opening and closing his huge reference books. The world of nature was within his intellectual domain and he took delight in sharing it with her on walks through their garden and down their country road.

"What's that, Daddy?" she had asked one day, pointing to a small sculpture that stood on his desk.

"It's a model of the human brain," he replied and moved it closer to her, his long finger traveling across its knobby surface. "A fascinating organism, the human brain. Here is the cerebrum. The cerebellum. The medulla oblongata."

"The cerebrum. The cerebellum. The medulla oblongata," she repeated.

The words were musical and fascinating. They offered her entry into the world of his work, a world that did not interest her sister and brothers, that even her mother did not understand. He was a psychiatrist. He had studied the secrets of what he called "that fascinating organism" and she, too, would study and understand them. She took biology, excelled and excelled again in an advanced placement course in physiology.

"You have a gift for science," her teacher told her. "Have you thought about medical school?"

"Of course," she said without hesitation. "My father's a doctor and that's what I want to be."

Neil Gordon was proud of her aptitude, proud of her achievements, but too often he answered her questions impatiently. Too often he cautioned her to be quiet because he had work to do. Slowly, she came to understand that although he loved her, loved all his children, his all-consuming passion was vested in his work and in his marriage. He and Elaine were inextricably linked, each defining the other. Lisa had recognized that and when they were in college and flirting with an introductory psychology course, she had too flippantly defined their relationship to Sandy.

"Mom and Dad are a cult of two," she had said. "We're important, of course, but they're a world unto themselves, by themselves, for themselves, of themselves."

Sandy had forgotten those words, perhaps banished them from memory when she morphed into Sarah, but Lisa remembered them all too well. In a way, she confided to her diary, that recognition had freed her, thrust her into an early independence, an independence that had sustained her even during her junior year abroad in Rome, those golden months that had ended in such dark misery.

Even now, staring down at the blank page of her journal, in her beautifully appointed apartment, she could not bear to think of that time. She flinched from the memory of pain and betrayal, of a loss that had overwhelmed her then and overwhelmed her still.

She sighed and began to write, growing calmer as she sorted through her thoughts and feelings, acknowledging in careful script her uneasiness about spending such a long period of time with her mother. And yet, she admitted, she was relieved that she was not going to Russia alone. Her mother was a skilled traveler. Organized and savvy. She stared at the adjectives. Her mother was more than that, she knew, much more.

She turned a page and began a new entry, writing about her reasons for adopting Genia, the child of the heart-shaped face and soft eyes whom she had claimed as her own from the moment she saw her photo and watched her on video.

"I want her in my life," she wrote. "I have waited so long for her. I want to love someone who will always and forever belong to me. Oh, I want to be Genia's mother."

She reread her entry then carefully replaced the journal in her desk drawer and locked it. Her father had been right about the diary, as he had been right about all of the advice he had given her. It did provide her with focus and emotional privacy.

Before going to bed she went into the nursery she had

prepared for Genia. She wandered through the cheerful sun-colored room, straightened the flower-sprigged coverlet in the white crib, held a fragrant soft, hooded towel to her cheek. She paused, too, in the doorway of the pleasant room she had prepared for Ellen, the young nanny she had hired. If Ellen did not like the plaid bedspread she would, of course, replace it. She wanted Genia's caregiver to be happy. She wanted all of them to be happy.

Newly calmed, she went to bed and slipped into a dreamless sleep.

Elaine arrived too early at Bookbinders but she was immediately escorted to the table reserved by Dr. Lisa Gordon.

"A lovely woman," the maitre d' said. "A valued client of this restaurant."

"My daughter," she told him proudly.

She hesitated and then ordered a martini.

"Vodka. With both an olive and an onion," she told the waiter. Neil's preferred drink and her own.

She sipped it slowly, glad of this interval of solitude before Lisa and David Green arrived. She had been caught up in a whirlwind of activity since her return from California. The Westchester house had been swarmed with handymen as she arranged for new windows, masonry repairs, the painting of the outside trim. Such arrangements had always been Neil's responsibility. It was unfair, she thought bitterly, suffused with an irrational anger, that he had left her to cope with so much.

"Widow's anger," her friend Serena had said when she described the feeling. "We all go through it. Part of phase one of widowhood."

That transitory anger had dissipated into a sober assessment of her situation. The house was too large for one person; it required too much care and its very size intensified her aloneness and vulnerability. She would have to make a decision about selling it and deciding where she wanted to live. *For the rest of my life.* She thought the words, thrust them aside. She would not think about that now. She had time. She would decide, but not yet.

Serena approved the delay.

"I waited for almost two years after Sam's death before I put the house on the market. The therapist I saw said that I was in synch with what she called 'the widow's timetable.' The shock, the anger, the reconciliation and finally, the acceptance and the reentry. It took me five years to arrive at the reentry," Serena said, draining her second glass of white wine.

"I'm stalled at anger, I'm afraid," Elaine had replied dryly.

She had spent an afternoon at Mimi Armstrong's gallery, carrying with her the completed tiles for the mural. Mimi thought them beautiful, admired the smooth firing of the enamel glaze with professional dispassion.

"It's a wonderful idea, Elaine," she said. Ever the shrewd businesswoman, she added, "A memorial mural is something that other people would want. I could get you a slew of commissions."

"This is for Neil." Elaine's reply had been sharper than

she intended. "I'm not about to go into the memorial mural business. That's not what I plan to do for the rest of my life."

The rest of my life. That phrase again, springing up unbidden. She turned her attention to the work Mimi was showing her, collages by a young artist who was experimenting with mixed materials, intricate small sculptures crafted of blown glass and papier-mâché.

"Interesting," Elaine said. "This would sell well in California."

"According to Renee Evers, you did pretty well yourself. She also said you had a handsome silver-haired gentleman in attendance."

Mimi, long divorced, always on the prowl for a new and preferably brief relationship, shot her a quizzical look.

Elaine laughed.

"My daughter-in-law's widowed father. And yes, he is attractive," she admitted and realized that she did, in fact, miss Herb Glasser, missed his admiring glance, his gentle touch.

"Attractive gentlemen grow rarer as women of independent means grow older," Mimi said caustically.

Elaine shrugged.

"I'll take my chances," she had retorted, her words more flippant than she had intended.

She returned from her visit with Mimi and sat at Neil's desk to study the packet of legal papers Denis had sent. Neil's estate had been settled and, as Denis pointed out, her position was more than comfortable. She was, as Mimi had said, a woman of independent means.

"You might want to think about investments," Denis had suggested gently when he called her.

"I will. After the trip to Russia."

"I hope you'll think about coming out to Santa Fe then. Andrew and I are building a guest cottage. You'd have absolute privacy." He chose his words carefully.

Elaine wondered if Denis, the most sensitive and vulnerable of their children, had been aware of the unease she and Neil had felt when they stayed in the home he and Andrew shared. It was possible, although she and Neil had made a special effort to treat Denis and Andrew with the same quiet acceptance they had offered to Sarah and Moshe, Peter and Lauren, Lisa and David. It was, perhaps, that very effort that they sensed.

"Of course I plan a visit to Santa Fe," she assured him, staring out the window at the maple tree which swayed dangerously in a sudden gust of wind. "We'll talk about it as soon as Lisa and I get back with Genia."

"Genia." He repeated the name slowly.

"Lisa's baby. Your niece." *And my granddaughter. And Neil's. A grandchild he will never know.* Bitterness soured her mouth, tears burned her eyes. "Denis, we'll talk soon. Give Andrew my love."

"I will."

She had hung up then and reached for the photo Lisa had sent her of the Russian child. The camera had captured Genia's wistful smile and the soft dark eyes that seemed to plead for love.

Now, seated in Bookbinders, her drink finished, the

olive tart upon her tongue, she removed the photo from her purse and stared again at the sweet-faced child soon to be welcomed into their family. She replaced it as Lisa and David hurried toward her, their hands linked, their faces wreathed in smiles of welcome.

She embraced Lisa and extended her hand to David. She liked the tall man who had been Lisa's constant companion for more than five years. He was the last in the procession of lovers who had trailed after Lisa through the years, all of them attractive and attentive, all of them gone from her daughter's life within months. She and Neil had learned not to ask about the various young men who disappeared from Lisa's radar with disquieting regularity. But David Green had remained, a caring and affectionate presence who would not, Elaine suspected, easily be dislodged.

He was a divorced father and his son and daughter lived with his ex-wife in a Washington suburb. Craggy-faced, his dark hair spattered with gray, graying eyebrows thick above serious eyes, he had a solidity and a demeanor that inspired confidence. He spoke slowly and carefully, his words always backed with a depth of knowledge and a seriousness of approach. He was a political consultant, advising legislators and government agencies, business executives and international conglomerates, his name occasionally appearing in news stories on critical issues. Based in Washington, he traveled extensively, jetting to Paris or London, to conferences in South America and think-tank meetings in the Middle East. Still, he and Lisa managed to scavenge time together, sometimes in Washington, sometimes in Philadelphia, sometimes in obscure resort areas, a complicated arrangement that appeared to suit them both.

"I have the best of all possible worlds," Lisa claimed. "David and I have a marvelous relationship and we both have absolute freedom. I have my work and David has his. Our lives are not on a collision course."

Actually, Elaine thought, they were remarkably in synch. It was pleasant to be with them in the busy brightly lit restaurant as waiters sailed through the large room balancing huge trays laden with platters of steaming red-shelled lobsters and deep bowls of fragrant golden garlic butter. Young couples leaned toward each other across tables covered with red-and-white checkered cloths and a group of Penn students, assembled at a round table, lifted mugs of foaming beer and toasted the end of exams. The celebrated fish restaurant was an island of urban gaiety, all cares abandoned at its heavy oaken door. Elaine's mood lightened.

"Another drink?" David asked.

"A short one," she said, glancing at Lisa who smiled at her indulgently.

David, a man who was used to giving directives, to taking control of situations, authoritatively ordered for the three of them. They would all have the sole with salads and an extra order of garlic bread. A baked potato for Elaine. She marveled that he remembered her preference but that, of course, was one of his professional talents. He remembered trivia, birthdays, tastes in food and literature, with the same acuity with which he analyzed international events. She thought that he would make a marvelous husband, competent and caring, but she would not dare say as much to Lisa. She had long recognized that an inexplicable emotional barrier existed between her daughter and herself and she would not risk breaching it.

"Give her time," Neil had advised when she spoke of it to him. "She has issues of her own, I'm sure."

Elaine sipped her second drink and looked at her daughter, who seemed so happy, so at ease. Perhaps the time to clear the air between them had finally arrived.

Lisa, wearing an apple-green suit, looked especially beautiful. Her color was high, her closely cut raven-black hair framed her angular face and her eyes glittered with amusement as David described a meeting on Capital Hill at which a ranking diplomat had spilled a Bloody Mary over his light-colored slacks.

"Probably set Intermonetary Fund negotiations back a full year," David said and they laughed as the waiter set their salads down.

Lisa's pager went off before she could lift her fork.

"Damn," she said, glancing at it. "I'll have to make a call. It's a colleague who asked me to read his wife's mammogram. I'll have to give him news he would rather not have. I'll find a quiet corner to talk and be back as soon as I can. You two go ahead."

She hurried across the room and Elaine noticed that several men looked after her as she passed. David, whose gaze followed her own, smiled.

"She's beautiful in a very special way, isn't she?" he said.

"She is," Elaine agreed.

"I'm going to miss her while she's in Russia."

"We'll only be away for a few weeks. But David, if you feel that way, couldn't you have gone with her?" she asked. It was ironic, she thought, that she could speak more easily to her daughter's lover than to her daughter.

He frowned, toyed with a piece of garlic bread, glanced across the room to the corner around which Lisa had disappeared, so that she might speak at a remove from the raucous restaurant sounds of pleasure and quietly tell her colleague of the darkness that lurked within his wife's body.

"I have a lot of commitments just now," he said at last. "I could have managed to juggle them but the truth is that Lisa never asked me to go with her and I didn't want to trespass. We're careful about turf, Lisa and I. Her life. My life. She'll be meeting her daughter for the first time. I guess she wants to be alone with her."

"But I'll be there," Elaine protested.

"Yes. But you're Genia's grandmother. And I—" His voice faltered. He held his large hands up as though despairing of finding the words to describe what role he would play in the life of the small girl asleep now in a distant city.

Elaine was silent. She understood that David Green loved her daughter and she understood too that both Lisa and David stepped carefully around clearly defined parameters, so wary were they of jeopardizing their relationship.

Nothing she could do or say would alter that, not now, perhaps not ever. She remained pensive as Lisa returned to the table, her expression grave.

"It was a really tough conversation," she said. "And I'm not sure I handled it too well. They say that radiologists and pathologists select those specialties because they're reluctant to deal with patients directly. And I know that's true of me. Maybe because I saw how Dad was constantly worried about his patients and I hated the way they intruded on our lives. The midnight phone calls from the near suicides, the emergency consultations on weekend mornings, the psychotics who always seemed to flip out just as we were loading the car for a vacation. I didn't want to deal with any of that, not with tears and not with pain and not with situations that I couldn't control. All I wanted to do was straight radiology. Get the imaging right, keep up with the technology, read the pictures, write the reports. But here I am, telling my friend Max that his wife has a stage-three carcinoma with compromised nodes."

"Lisa, I'm sure you handled it as well as anyone could. Drink some wine. Eat your salad. Let's talk about good things. Journeys out, arrivals home," David said gently.

Elaine looked at him gratefully. How gentle he was, this large man who spoke with such quiet authority, this powerful man who loved her daughter.

Deftly, David steered the conversation to their trip to Russia. He had been to Russia many times and he reminded them to pack heavy clothing.

"You don't understand the word cold until you walk across Red Square on a chilly day," he said. "And make sure that all your documents are in order. The ones for the Russians and the ones for our INS."

"All taken care of," Lisa assured him. "Claire and I went over it, page by page, checking everything off, making sure that I had every damn form in duplicate or triplicate, embossed certificates, apostilled data sheets. The damn dossier must weigh ten pounds, maybe twenty."

"Who is Claire?" Elaine asked, "and what does *apostille* mean?"

"*Apostille* is a kind of notarization. And Claire's the social worker I've been working with at the international adoption agency. She's the one who first showed me the album with Genia's picture. She's great. She set me up with a facilitator in Russia who's important because the Russians can be tough when it comes to adoptions. Really tough," she said worriedly.

"And so are we," Elaine countered grimly. "They'd better not tangle with the Gordon gals."

Lisa smiled and reached across the table and stroked her mother's hand. Elaine folded her fingers around her daughter's soft palm and reflected that it had been a long time since Lisa had touched her with such ease, with such a spontaneity of affection. It might well be, she thought hopefully, that their shared journey might heal the inexplicable breach between them.

David lifted his wineglass.

"To the Gordon girls and to Genia."

"To Genia," they replied and clicked their glasses in a toast to the dark-eyed child who was already part of their lives.

The next morning Elaine and Lisa shopped for baby clothes.

"I have to bring everything Genia might need," Lisa explained. "The orphanages have a strict policy. They will give you the child but the baby's clothing is their property. I would bet that they wouldn't be above sending the kids out naked if the adoptive parents hadn't been told to bring new clothes."

"Or arrange for you to buy their own gorgeous garments," Elaine said dryly. "What size are we looking for?"

"Genia's about two years old. A guess because she was abandoned so they don't have a birth certificate. The Russians don't put babies into the adoption database until they're six months old. Then, of course, it takes time for all the red tape. I would have wanted to adopt Genia sooner but that didn't work out. But from what I've seen on the video she's small for two so maybe we should go for the eighteen-month size," Lisa said, holding up a pink sleeping bag of the softest fleece.

"Sarah always buys her children's clothes a little bit bigger. Easier to dress them and they grow into them. And of course Sarah really knows about things like that," Elaine reminded her.

"Of course. Sarah knows best. She always has, even in her Sandy days," Lisa retorted sharply and immediately regretted her tone.

Her twin had been nothing but supportive and the days when they competed for their mother's approval were long gone. It was stupid of her to resent the sister who was her best friend, who had done so much for her. She would never forget all that Sarah, Sandy then, had done so long ago during that Roman spring.

"What colors?" Elaine asked. She ignored Lisa's comment. Her daughters were grown women, too old for sibling wars.

"She's dark-haired and from what I could tell from the video, olive skinned. She looks a lot like Sarah's Leora."

Lisa remembered visiting Jerusalem when Leora was a baby. Sarah had sat contentedly on her balcony, Leora nestled against her shoulder. The little girl's dark hair had brushed her mother's cheek. Lisa had turned away, fearful that her sister would see the sadness in her eyes and sense the memory and desire that teased her still. She wondered if it was that memory that had drawn her to Genia, that odd resemblance to Leora, or was it the wistful smile that had tugged at her heart? It did not matter. Genia would be hers as surely as Leora was Sarah's. *My daughter, Genia.* The words seemed magical to her.

"I suppose dusty rose, violet, yellow. What do you think?" she asked her mother.

"I've always been partial to little girls in red," Elaine said, holding up a red corduroy dress with matching tights.

"Completely impractical but let's take it," Lisa decided.

Then they plucked up undershirts, pajamas, fleece-lined sleepers, sweaters and jaunty woolen hats with matching scarves. They laughed in delight at the discovery of a soft white blanket across which a flock of lady birds fluttered and Elaine nodded approvingly at the padded royal-blue snowsuit Lisa selected.

"What a lucky baby," the clerk who rang up their purchases said.

"My daughter," Lisa said.

"My granddaughter," Elaine added although the clerk was no longer listening.

She and Lisa smiled at each other, delighting in their new complicity.

They packed that night. Lisa filled a small pink suitcase embossed with a picture of Dora the Explorer with the new baby clothing. The suitcase was a gift from Peter and Lauren. The huge teddy bear which Denis and Andrew had sent and the soft blanket across which Sarah had sewn felt cutouts of smiling red pomegranates and dancing oranges and lemons were already in the high white crib. Genia's new aunts and uncles had been swift to welcome her into their family, their gifts awaiting her arrival.

Lisa groaned as she placed the huge dossier encased in a blue plastic file into her carry-on luggage.

"What's in it?" Elaine asked.

"Everything that the Russian authorities and the American government will need to verify that Genia is not a terrorist. Also my entire identity. My birth certificate, my degrees, the incorporation papers for my labs, financial reports, income tax statements, my fingerprints, letters from ten different people swearing that I'm honest, sober, hardworking. Reports from the social worker on the suitability of my apartment, the size of the nursery. Photographs of the apartment and the nursery. Letters from my nanny's previous employers vouching for her competence. If this dossier disappears, Mom, I cease to exist."

Elaine grimaced.

"All that for a country where the minimum monthly wage is twenty-two dollars," she said. "Russia today is hardly a land of opportunity. I heard a little bit about it from a young Russian woman I met briefly in California. Karina. A former colleague of Peter's."

"Former?" Lisa asked.

"Yes."

"Good."

Elaine looked at her in surprise. Her children clearly knew a great deal more about each other's lives than she had supposed.

Lisa folded the white blanket and pressed it against her cheek.

"Oh, Mom. It's going to be so wonderful to bring Genia home. I imagine her voice, her laugh, just her being. Is it weird to love a baby you've never met?"

"No," Elaine replied. "Expectant mothers love the babies they haven't met. And that's who you are, Lisa. An expectant mother."

Lisa's eyes filled. She sat quietly beside Elaine on a bed covered with their own thick sweaters and the delicate rainbow-colored baby clothing.

"This is a wonderful thing you are doing, Lisa," Elaine

said. "Wonderful and brave. Your father would have been proud of you."

"That was all I ever wanted." Lisa's voice was very soft. "To make him proud."

"He was always proud of you," Elaine said. "We both were."

"I just wanted never to disappoint." Lisa struggled to find the words she should perhaps have spoken all those years ago but still they eluded her.

"You never did," Elaine assured her.

They sat side by side in the gathering darkness, their fingers intertwined, reluctant to shatter their new and surprising closeness.

seventeen

Their Aeroflot plane landed at Moscow's Sheremetyevo Airport in the early hours of the morning. Lisa peered through the window at the stark buildings shrouded in the milky light of a lingering darkness and wondered if the sun would ever break through. She sat very still as they taxied across the badly paved runway until the heavy Boeing 737 lurched, gathered speed and thundered to an abrupt stop.

"Welcome to Moscow," she said dryly to her mother.

Elaine smiled wanly. She had slept fitfully during the long flight, her brief naps disturbed by the grim-faced flight attendant who insisted on thrusting at them trays laden with foods of mysterious origin covered with thick and oily gravies. They ignored the airline meals and instead ate the sandwiches and fruit in the festive white boxes from Zabar's that David had given them.

"Trust me. I've flown Aeroflot often enough to know that you don't want to eat their food," he had said.

"Don't check the bag that holds your dossier," he had cautioned. "It's not unknown for checked baggage to mysteriously disappear between New York and Moscow. Be careful."

"I feel as though I'm going into battle," Lisa had said ruefully.

"In a sense you are." He had smiled but she had heard the warning in his tone and seen the worry in his eyes.

Throughout the flight she had periodically checked her carry-on and as they landed, she opened it yet again and slid her fingers across the smooth surface of the bright blue plastic file case.

"Still there?" Elaine asked, smiling.

"Still there," Lisa replied. "I know you think I'm nuts for being so nervous but, Mom, if I lose the dossier or any part of it I could lose Genia."

"You won't lose the file and you won't lose Genia," Elaine assured her.

She looked worriedly at her daughter. It surprised her still that Lisa, cool, competent Lisa, so committed to her career and her independence, so resistant to marriage and impatient with her sister's pregnancies, had vested so much in this adoption. Genia, known to them only through photos and a brief snatch of videotape, had woven herself into Lisa's life. Elaine could not bear to think of what might happen if the adoption was ambushed, if Genia did not accompany them home to the States. Lisa, she knew, would be devastated and she herself, she acknowledged, would be awash in sadness and disappointment. She thrust the thought aside. Of course everything would proceed without difficulty. Lisa had been so careful, Claire's advice and perusal of each document so explicit and helpful. She smiled reassuringly at her daughter.

"Everything will be all right," she said and wondered how many times through the years she had repeated that maternal mantra to each of her children separately, to all of them together.

Those were the words, she knew, that mothers used to comfort their children, to allay their fears and uncertainties, although clearly, they could not always be true. There were times when things would not be all right, when ill luck would prevail, when an assured happiness would be aborted, when a ringing phone might bring news of disaster and morning brightness would be vanquished by evening shadows. She shrugged, as though to shake off her own dark thoughts, and stared up at the damp grayness of the Russian sky.

They exited the plane slowly, their way blocked by passengers who pushed ahead of them, using their small suitcases and clumsy bundles as battering rams that enabled them to progress an extra inch. A small chubby woman wearing a bulky coat of pale yellow fur bitterly cursed a tall youth who cut ahead of her.

"*Babushka,*" he spat out disparagingly and pushed ahead of yet another passenger.

"Russia," an American man who stood behind them said wearily. "You'll get used to it."

"I doubt that," Elaine replied.

She was grateful that they had arranged for "VIP Light Service" on Claire's advice. They would be met as soon as they left the airplane by Misha, the Russian facilitator employed by the adoption agency. He would hold up a sign with their names and take them immediately to the baggage claim area, avoiding the queue for passport control.

"At least, I hope it's Misha," Claire had added. "We've had very good experience with him."

Lisa had refrained from asking about difficulties with other facilitators. She did not want to hear any Russian adoption story that did not have a happy ending.

They deplaned and she searched the crowd that awaited the arriving passengers. Cardboard signs were frantically waved and she looked past the neatly lettered Cyrillic names and the awkwardly scripted English ones until she saw her own name on a sign held by a heavyset blond man who wore a thickly padded long gray overcoat. She and Elaine rushed toward him.

"I am Dr. Lisa Gordon," she said. "And this is my mother, Elaine Gordon."

"And me, I am Misha," he said and licked a dark fleck of tobacco that clung to his thick yellow moustache.

They followed him as he expertly elbowed his way through the crowd and they waited with him at the carousel which moved with exasperating slowness. They pointed to their suitcases and he heaved them off with ease, smiling at the pink bag embossed with the jaunty picture of Dora the Explorer.

"Your little girl, she will like that bag," he said and Lisa smiled gratefully because he had already granted her motherhood.

He guided them through customs and then to passport control, jovially making small talk with the clerks who flipped through their documents, checked their visas and asked perfunctory questions.

"What is the purpose of your visit to Russia?" asked the stout woman with iron-gray hair to whom their passports and visas had been passed.

"I'm here to adopt a baby," Lisa said.

"And you?" She peered at Elaine through rimless glasses.

"I am—that is I will be—the baby's grandmother," Elaine said.

"Ah." Her voice softened. "I, too, have grandchildren."

She stamped their passports vigorously and waved them on. Misha doffed his cap and trailed after them, pulling their luggage on a rusting trolley up to a small gray Lada that idled curbside. They waited as he deposited the bags in the trunk and nodded at the pleasant-looking young woman who sat behind the wheel of the car.

"Sonia," he said as he opened the rear door for Lisa and Elaine. "She will be your translator and your driver. Her English is very good."

He slid into the seat beside her and she turned to look at them.

"I studied at Massachusetts University for two years,"

Sonia told them as she maneuvered her way through the maze of morning traffic. "I studied American literature. I very much love Henry James. I am happy to be of service to you. Dr. Gordon. Mrs. Gordon."

She pronounced their names carefully and Misha beamed at them.

"Thank you," Lisa said.

She wished she knew more about Henry James. It was important, she thought, that Sonia like her because it was Sonia who would guide her through the minefield of Russian bureaucracy until Genia was safe in her arms, everything settled, the adoption final and irrevocable.

Elaine chatted easily with Sonia and Misha as they drove from the airport to the heart of the city. She admired the Gothic skyscrapers of the Ukrania Hotel and the Foreign Ministry, the wide avenues, the squares that bustled with activity. It was exciting for her to be in their country, she explained because her late husband had been born in Russia.

"My husband's parents spoke to me often of the beauty of their homeland. They came from a village somewhere near Yaroslavl," she confided.

"Yaroslavl is a special place," Sonia said. "It is a river city. It is there that the Volga and Kotorosl rivers meet."

"Yes. They spoke of a journey on the Volga," Elaine recalled.

She did not add that Neil's parents and her own had also spoken of the harsh anti-Semitism they had experienced and the grinding poverty that had spurred their decisions to emigrate. Neil had been very young when they left, perhaps only a year or two older than Genia. It occurred to her that Lisa's daughter would be the second Gordon child to leave Russia for the United States, an irony that Neil would have appreciated.

"But you never came here with your husband?" Misha asked.

"No. He died before we could plan such a journey," Elaine replied.

It surprised her that she could speak of Neil's death, of the forfeit of plans unrealized and journeys never taken, without being pierced by grief. Another mark of recovery, she supposed and wondered at her reluctance to acknowledge the easing of her loss. Did she want to hug her sorrow like those recovering invalids who cling to the symptoms of their illness? Was that, too, a stage of widowhood that Serena's therapist could identify?

"It is sad that you did not visit Yaroslavl with your husband. But perhaps you will visit his village, you and Dr. Gordon. I will be glad to take you there. You have such a long stay in Russia."

"Perhaps," Lisa said.

She estimated that they would spend at least six weeks in Russia, accomplishing in a single visit what most adoptive parents accomplished in two separate journeys. Usually, Claire had explained, the first trip was to choose a child while the second one was designed to cope with the legalities. But Lisa had made her choice the moment she saw Genia's photograph and watched her on the videotape.

Because Genia was an abandoned child no family releases would be required and the adoption would be that much simpler. Still, Lisa's interactions with the child would have to be observed over a period of time, her dossier studied and she would have to attend a court hearing. And of course when that was done the American embassy would have to authorize a visa.

"If there is time," Elaine said, "I should love to visit Yaroslavl."

The thought of visiting the village of Neil's birth excited her. It would be an opportunity to step into his earliest childhood, to walk the streets that had been so familiar to his parents.

Her own parents had harbored few memories of their own village. When they spoke of it at all, it was with a controlled sadness, their legacy to her. She had been conditioned, from earliest childhood, to exercise emotional restraint. She had organized her life, her family's life against the encroachment of chaos. Anger had been repressed, all actions and reactions calculated. But somehow that was changing. She felt herself slowly and mysteriously edging free of that carefully constructed carapace. She marveled still at her outburst at Sarah's seder table, at the daring of her confrontation with Karina. She wondered if Neil would approve or disapprove.

Neil. Tenderly, she turned his name over in her mind, allowed a gentle sorrow to sweep over her and abate, as now she knew it would. She was mastering the lessons of grief. *Neil.* She wondered if it would be possible to locate his childhood home should they indeed have enough leisure to visit Yaroslavl.

"Oh, we'll have time for such a visit." Sonia swerved past the grim façade of the Kiev train station and pulled up in front of the Radisson Hotel. "Time is not in short supply in Russia."

Misha removed their bags.

"We shall come tomorrow morning to take you to the Children's Home Number 31. There you will meet the child, Genia."

"Oh no," Lisa protested. "We want to see her today. Please come back in two hours. We're so anxious to meet Genia."

"It is not a good thing to disrupt the schedule of the Children's Home," Sonia said. "The directress of this home is particular about that and you do not want to anger her. She can cause difficulties."

"There will be no difficulties," Lisa countered swiftly. "Everything is in order. Claire checked everything."

Misha sighed.

"In Russia there are always difficulties. And where there are no difficulties they can be created. A directress who is angered can invent a new law or discover an old one and this directress, Irina Petrovna, is a difficult woman. She makes some adoptions very complicated. Sonia is right. It is best not to anger her. But we will try to arrange a meeting today. We will return at three o'clock which is after the children's naptime and before their dinner. I will call Irina Petrovna and explain how anxious you are to see the child," he said.

"That sounds fine," Elaine agreed although Lisa frowned.

Her daughter, Elaine knew, was not used to having her wishes thwarted. Lisa's staff was obedient, her patients and colleagues deferential. It was difficult for her to understand that in Moscow she was not a distinguished physician vested with authority. She was simply another vulnerable adoptive parent at the mercy of a woman known to be difficult and perhaps arbitrary.

Misha and Sonia drove off and Elaine and Lisa followed the bellhop to the registration desk. Lisa looked at the restaurants and high-end shops that lined the ostentatious lobby. Hotel guests milled about, hurried past the casino and into the health club, speaking too loudly in a mélange of languages.

"I wonder why David insisted that we stay at the Radisson," she said with some annoyance. "It can't be for its character."

"He told me that it has excellent security and that seems to be true." Elaine pointed to the armed guards posted at the entrance. "David worries about you, Lisa."

"I know," Lisa said, smiling. "He worries about everything. About his clients. His pro bono projects. About his own kids, his son, Kenny, his daughter, June, and the impact the divorce had on them. He worries about being away from them so much."

"And now he'll worry about Genia."

"I suppose," Lisa replied, her words tinged with apprehension.

She was worried, Elaine knew, about the effect that the

adoption would have on her relationship with David. She would no longer be a free agent, able to dash down to visit him in Washington at a moment's notice, to join him on a Caribbean jaunt or at a weekend conference.

"He's a wonderful man, a caring man," Elaine said.

"Thanks, Mom."

Lisa smiled at her, grateful for the words she had not spoken.

Elaine handed their passports and reservation forms to the clerk who looked at them sharply, studied their photographs and nodded slowly. Nothing in Russia, Elaine realized, was taken for granted. Not a hotel reservation and not the appropriate hour to visit a Children's Home.

"Actually, I don't want him to worry about Genia. She'll be my daughter, my responsibility. It's one thing for David to send box lunches from Zabar's and arrange for a secure hotel. But for him to worry about yet another child, my child, would be to raise the ante too high. We're good together, David and I. I wouldn't want to endanger that," Lisa added. "We'll work everything out."

"I'm sure you will," Elaine said, surprised by her own certainty.

The clerk gave them their room key and returned their documents and again they followed the bellhop through the thickly carpeted corridor to the elevator and then to a room so ornately furnished that it embarrassed them.

"Are you sure we're still in Russia?" Elaine asked dryly.

She went to the window and saw that their room overlooked the Kiev Railroad Station. A homeless family squatted at the entrance, their belongings packed into over-flowing shopping bags. Their small son thrust his ragged cap at passersby who averted their eyes and hurried on. An old woman wrapped in a tattered shawl ferreted through a trash can and a man, still clutching a half-empty vodka bottle vomited into the street.

"Yes. We are indeed in Russia," she said and drew the drapes.

They ate a quick lunch and precisely at three o'clock Misha and Sonia returned and once again Elaine and Lisa sat in the rear seat of the Lada. Lisa held the video camera that Claire had suggested she take with her and Elaine carried a shopping bag that contained the red corduroy dress and matching tights for Genia and small gifts for the caregivers. Claire had advised them to take disposable cameras, small bottles of toilet water, brightly colored silk neckerchiefs.

"But don't give anything to the directress," she had cautioned. "She might construe it as a bribe and report it to the court. If she's helpful, you can always send her something when the adoption is finalized. Or you can make a gift to the Home."

Lisa doubted that they would be sending a gift to the "difficult" Irina Petrovna. The very name already filled her with trepidation. She turned her attention to the passing scene and listened as Sonia pointed out the sights.

"Red Square," she said. "And just beyond you can see St. Basil's."

They glimpsed the cathedral's swirling domes before the Lada once again lurched forward. They passed the city center and drove past rows of huge apartment buildings constructed of gray concrete blocks scattered across a barren expanse. A few frail, sparsely leafed trees shivered in the wind. Groups of pale children wandered through the courtyards ignoring the steel slides and the rusting jungle gyms. The women who shuffled down the streets, bent by the weight of their heavy plastic shopping baskets, were sallow-skinned, the kerchiefs that they wrapped too tightly about their heads faded and frayed. Elaine, for whom color was as essential as breath itself, cringed and turned away.

"Grim," Lisa said.

"Grim and gray," she agreed.

At last Sonia pulled into a driveway and drove slowly up a long unpaved road. Children wearing identical olive drab snowsuits, dark green woolen hats pulled low over their foreheads, walked single file down the path and looked impassively at the Lada. They did not smile, they did not wave and they moved forward obediently when the red-faced woman who trailed after them shouted a command.

Sonia shook her head.

"Poor things," she said. "Those are the unfortunate ones. They are too old now. No one will adopt them."

"What will happen to them?" Lisa asked.

"They will stay here until they are sixteen, perhaps a bit longer and then they must leave."

"But where do they go?" Elaine asked insistently.

She looked back and saw that one girl still stood on the road, looking wistfully back at their slowly moving car. Abruptly, the child turned and walked on, limping because one foot was an inch shorter than the other. A crippled orphan who would never find a home. Elaine's throat constricted and her eyes burned.

"Who can tell what will happen to them?" Misha shrugged. "Our streets are filled with young people who have no homes. They become thieves, prostitutes. They drink. They take drugs. And, I, I do not blame them. I pity them."

"Do you have children, Misha?" Lisa asked.

"One son. He is at school. A very good school. We can care for only one child, his mother and I. We want to be able to afford to educate him well, to give him everything we did not have."

Elaine thought of her parents, of Neil's parents. They, too, had opted to have only one child. There would have been no time in their frantic hardworking lives, no room in their tiny apartments, for another child who would have to be provided with everything that they themselves had been denied.

"I have a daughter," Sonia said. "A daughter who lives in America. She is an American. Born in Massachusetts."

Lisa's heart turned.

"I'm sorry, Sonia. You must miss her."

"Don't be sorry. She will have a good life, my Tanya. It is her life that is important."

She drove on, her face expressionless although Misha

frowned darkly and spoke harshly to her in Russian. She stared straight ahead and did not reply.

They stopped at last in front of a large stone building. Sonia parked as Misha pressed a buzzer and spoke into an intercom. The door swung open and a heavyset woman, her graying coarse hair twisted into a bun, stared at them.

Misha spoke rapidly, gesturing to Lisa and then to Elaine. The woman frowned but she smiled slightly, revealing two gold teeth, when Sonia joined them. Sonia spoke softly, cajolingly and Misha stepped away. Clearly, he knew that Sonia would have rapport with this woman who was unused to men, who lived in a world of children and their female caregivers.

Lisa heard Sonia say *Dawkta Gordon* and caught the word *Americanski*. She continued adding a spate of words that ended with *Genia, baibee, rebyonok*.

"Ah." The woman's pale face brightened. "Genia," she repeated, as though all was suddenly clear to her, and she motioned them to follow her.

They walked down a long windowless hallway that smelled of carbolic soap and boiled cabbage. The house, despite its impressive exterior, was in a state of disrepair, the paint peeling from ochre-colored walls, the linoleum floor spotless but worn, sheets of grimy plastic covering broken windowpanes. An odd rhythmic bleating sounded from behind closed doors and Lisa realized that the sound was a muted chorus of crying babies.

But the room into which they were beckoned was painted a gleaming white and brightly-colored nursery rhyme characters were stenciled across the walls. Dolls and stuffed animals lined the shelves and picture books were neatly arrayed on a low table. The toys and books were pristine and carefully arranged. Elaine remembered the gay but shabby toys in Ruth's Jerusalem day-care center and she wondered if the Russian orphans were ever permitted to cuddle the stuffed animals or allowed to turn the pages of the brightly jacketed books.

The woman motioned them toward a leather sofa, smiled her thin gold-toothed smile and left. Elaine and Lisa sat side by side, their apprehension growing with each passing minute. Sonia and Misha went to the window and stared out at the bleak play area where a faded blue plastic swing dangled from a single rope and a sagging jungle gym cast its shadow across the sere earth.

At last the door opened and a young woman, wearing a pale green coverall, a snood covering her hair, entered, carrying a small dark-haired child. Lisa gripped her mother's hand and together they moved forward. The caregiver turned and they saw Genia's elfin face, her rosebud of a mouth, her large long-lashed hazel eyes flecked with amber, her hair a cluster of damp dark curls. Lisa's heart stopped. Impetuously, she touched the child's cheek, tenderly stroked the satin-smooth olive skin and felt the heat of a single tear upon her hand. Genia wept soundlessly, her small body rigid, her hands clutching the strap of her caregiver's coverall.

Lisa's face froze, her eyes clouded with disappointment. She looked helplessly at her mother and Elaine, in turn, approached and smiled at the child.

"Krassavitsa," she said, summoning the word from the depths of memory, hearing again her mother's voice all those years ago when she braided her hair. *"Oom-nitsa,"* she murmured soothingly. "Beautiful little one. Darling child."

Wide-eyed and puzzled, Genia looked at Elaine who repeated the words of endearment. The weeping ceased. Elaine held out her arms and wordlessly, the caregiver handed her the child. Elaine carried her to the window and Lisa stood beside her mother and the daughter she had traveled so far to claim. She reached up and twirled a dark curl about her finger.

"Krassavitsa," she murmured soothingly, copying her mother's intonation. "Sweetness. Little beauty."

Genia turned toward her and Elaine placed the unprotesting child in her arms. Misha lifted the video camera and filmed them as they stood together in a circlet of waning sunlight.

Suddenly the door opened. A tall stern-looking woman, her black dress offset by a necklace of gemstones, stared at them, her frown lines creasing her high pale forehead. She spoke harshly to the young caregiver who cringed and, too swiftly, almost roughly, took Genia from Lisa's arms. Lisa moved forward to protest but Elaine placed a restraining hand on her daughter's shoulder. This was a situation for Misha and Sonia to deal with, she knew instinctively.

Misha was already smiling, his voice conciliatory as he offered an explanation. He smiled obsequiously, motioned to Lisa and Elaine, repeated their names and flipped open a folder of documents.

The woman turned to them, inclined her head.

"I am Irina Petrovna," she said. "The directress of Children's Home Number Thirty-One."

"And I am Dr. Lisa Gordon," Lisa said. "And this is my mother, Elaine Gordon. We are here, of course, to meet Genia and to arrange for her adoption. But you must know that."

Irina Petrovna shrugged and spoke rapidly in Russian to Sonia and Misha. Genia began to cry and the young caretaker cradled her in a futile effort at comfort. The child cried harder. Lisa was very pale, her lips set in a thin line of anger.

Misha spoke again, his tone even more unctuous, a man who made his living reasoning with the unreasonable. Elaine and Lisa looked questioningly at Sonia whose translation was hesitant and softly spoken.

"The directress is annoyed that she was not informed of your visit. Misha explained that he had tried to phone her but she was out and we chose an hour that we hoped would not interfere with the baby's mealtime or her nap but still she is angry."

"Tell her that I, too, apologize but I was eager to meet my daughter," Lisa said.

Again there was a rapid exchange in Russian. Irina Petrovna twirled her necklace, studied Lisa's high black leather boots, her matching shoulder bag. She was a woman with an acute eye for fashion, Elaine realized. She noted that the directress's own dress was of a soft wool and well tailored. It was, she supposed, an irrelevant observation but she filed it away.

Again Misha spoke pleadingly. Another rush of words followed by a brief nod of assent.

"You must go now," Sonia reported. "But you may return tomorrow morning. At nine o'clock. Misha has explained that you want to take Genia to the American Medical Center for a checkup. This Irina Petrovna will permit although she says their doctor at the Home is very experienced and she does not see why you want another examination."

"Tell her that I am sure the doctor here at the Home is excellent but we are following the advice of our adoption agency and, as she should know, the requirement of the American embassy," Lisa said. "And ask her if I may dress Genia in these new clothes I have brought for her from America."

Again Sonia spoke to the directress who glanced at the small garments, gave a curt reply and stalked out of the room, nodding cursorily in their direction.

"She says that in the Home Genia must wear the clothing of the Home," Sonia explained unhappily. "Tomorrow she may wear the clothes you brought for her because it is forbidden to take anything that is the property of the government out of this building."

"I suppose if we hadn't brought something for her to wear, Genia would have to leave naked," Lisa said angrily. She looked at Genia who had not stopped crying.

The young caregiver hesitated, then gave her the baby. Immediately, Genia was quiet.

"You see, Lisa," Elaine said gently. "She knows who you are. She can feel your love."

Lisa smiled and pressed her cheek against the baby's soft dark hair.

Elaine reached into her bag and offered the young caregiver a disposable camera, a small bottle of toilet water and a gaily patterned silk neckerchief. The young woman blushed, put the camera and the toilet water into her pockets and slid the neckerchief into her sleeve. She spoke softly to Sonia.

"She thanks you," the translator said. "She wants you to know that her name is Alla. She was once a child in this Home and she knows how much it means to hug the babies and play with them. She takes very good care of Genia who is her favorite charge. She tells me that everyone here has a special love for Genia. She must take her now or Irina Petrovna will be angry."

Lisa nodded, pressed her lips to Genia's cheek and surrendered her to Alla who glanced nervously at the door.

"Thank you," Elaine said and Alla hurried out, holding Genia close. They stood in the doorway and watched her disappear down the corridor. Slowly then, they followed Sonia and Misha out of Children's Home Number Thirty-One.

"I hate Irina Petrovna," Lisa said grimly as the Lada carried them back to the Radisson.

Misha murmured something to Sonia.

"Misha says that you should not be frightened of her. Everything will be all right," Sonia reported.

"Of course everything will be all right." Elaine covered Lisa's hand with her own as she repeated the reassuring words she only half believed.

★ ★ ★

They returned the next day and Alla brought Genia to them in the waiting room. The child did not cry as Lisa gently peeled off her flimsy faded pajama and frayed undershirt. She unknotted the rag used as a diaper and replaced it with a disposable one and dressed her in a soft white onesie and the red corduroy dress and matching tights. Alla touched the fabric, smiled and whispered in Russian to Sonia who smiled as she translated.

"Alla says that such a fabric is made for a princess and now Genia looks like a princess," she said.

They bundled the baby into the royal-blue snowsuit and Lisa carried her out to the car, walking swiftly as though fearful that Irina Petrovna might appear at any moment and stop them.

"No, she cannot do that," Sonia assured her when she voiced her anxiety. "It is Russian law that she must allow you to take the baby to a clinic of your choice."

There was no wait at the American Medical Center. The smiling receptionist told them that there had been a call from the American embassy alerting them to Lisa's arrival.

"David's influence," Lisa said. "Reaching from afar. He's tracking us." She spoke lightly but her face was bright with pleasure.

"It's nice to be taken care of, isn't it?" Elaine asked, smiling.

"I wouldn't know," Lisa replied too quickly. "Being taken care of hasn't really been part of my life."

Elaine stared at her, shocked and bewildered by the implication of her daughter's words. She and Neil had taken very good care of their children. They had sought out the best summer camps, the best after-school programs, every talent explored and developed. Lisa's fierce independence had been self-imposed. She had chosen to share little about her life with them and they, in turn had respected her privacy.

She bridled at the unfairness of Lisa's words but she remained silent. This was not a time for emotional archaeology, for airing grievances of the past. This was a time to concentrate on Genia, on the building of a future. She lifted the video camera. Lisa wanted a visual record of their first days together, a record she would one day share with her daughter.

The young American doctor weighed Genia who whimpered as she was eased out of her pretty dress.

"Don't worry. You'll wear it again," Lisa told her and the child seemed reassured by the words she did not understand.

"Not too underweight," the doctor reported. "Perhaps by just a few pounds. The children from Home Thirty-One eat pretty well. I'll say that much for them."

He measured Genia on a paper sheet stretched out on the examining table, then listened to her heart, her lungs. She wiggled mischievously away when he pressed his fingers against her joints.

"Whoa. We're not in a race," he said and laughed as he caught her and tickled her playfully.

She smiled back.

"She's very responsive, Dr. Gordon. That's unusual for a child from an orphanage. Most of them have trouble relating at all. In fact there are some adoptions that I try to discourage because I can see real trouble down the road. The kids have been deprived of affection for so long that something inside of them twists up or freezes. But this little girl here—no problems. She's going to make you very happy. Someone must have made her happy."

"There's a young caregiver at the home who seems to have a special liking for Genia. She's played with her and shown her some affection. That might have made the difference," Lisa said.

"That would do it," the doctor agreed. "A little cuddling during the first few months of a child's life is tremendously important. You were lucky in that."

Lisa nodded. She remembered how Genia had clung to Alla. She would have to ask Sonia how she might express her appreciation to the sad-eyed young caregiver whose entire life had been spent in the grim confines of the Home.

The doctor touched Genia's neck lightly and she laughed gleefully.

"I don't think I've ever heard an orphanage child laugh before," he said and whipped a lollipop out of the pocket of his white coat. He held it out to Genia.

She stared at it but made no move to take it.

"And I don't think she's ever seen a lollipop before," Elaine said as she peeled the cellophane wrap off the sweet and held it to Genia's lips. The child smiled with delight as she tasted the green sweetness and she reached up, clenched the stick and eagerly licked the candy.

The doctor studied the records that had been sent to him and filled out the form which the United States embassy required in order to issue a visa for Genia.

"She's a healthy little girl," he said as Lisa struggled to dress Genia, who refused to relinquish her lollipop. "No fetal alcohol syndrome, no hint of maternal drug use, no HIV. That's what we look for in Russian orphans. Strangely, the kids in Genia's age group from that particular home are pretty healthy. A lot of them were simply abandoned when their parents died during the flu epidemic two years ago. There was no one left to care for them. But they don't present with any in-utero symptoms. I don't foresee any physical problems for your gal."

"Thank you. Doctor, I'm a radiologist and I have some machines that are really adequate but not state of the art. Would you be interested?" Lisa asked. "I could arrange to have them shipped here."

"The clinic would be grateful. We have only one functioning X-ray machine."

"I'll speak to a friend about the best way to arrange it," Lisa said.

They shook hands, Elaine flashed the doctor a grateful smile and they hurried out to the Lada where Sonia waited patiently.

"I'm sorry it took so long, Sonia," Lisa said apologetically.

"No problem. I write a letter to my daughter in America." She snapped her pen closed and started the car.

"When will you see your daughter again, Sonia?" Elaine asked hesitantly.

"When I have enough money to return to America. Her father is American. We were not married. Many difficulties. He had a wife who would not give a divorce so we could not marry. I had a student visa and I had to leave when it expired. But Tanya, my daughter, she was born in America so she is a citizen. When I could not renew my visa and had to return to Russia I would not take Tanya with me. How would we live? Where would we live? I sleep on a sofa in my parents' apartment but in America Tanya lives in a house with her father's cousin. A big house. She has good food, good clothing, her own room. Good schools. Everything that you will give to your daughter, your Genia, my Tanya has. The people she lives with are good people. They send me letters, pictures. I write to her. I send her photographs. On her birthday I call her." She braked at a light and reached into her oversize worn purse. "Here. I show you a picture of my Tanya."

She held out the picture of a smiling girl, her hair, like Sonia's, copper colored. She wore a UMass sweatshirt and a Boston Red Sox baseball cap was perched jauntily on her head.

"But you must miss her terribly," Elaine said. It occurred to her that Sonia had not mentioned that man who could not get a divorce, Tanya's father. He seemed oddly incidental to her story.

"Of course I miss her. She is my heart," Sonia said. "But I did what was best for my Tanya. That is what a mother must do."

She drove more slowly as they merged into traffic, her gaze fixed on the road but Elaine saw her reflection in the rearview mirror, saw the misery that contorted her face.

"Of course. That is what a mother must do," she agreed as Lisa cuddled Genia.

The little girl drifted into sleep and she did not awaken when they arrived at the Home. Lisa carried her inside and placed her in Alla's arms. As they left they passed the directress who walked rapidly by, barely acknowledging them.

"Bitch," Lisa muttered as they hurried out of the building.

"Do not worry," Sonia said. "It is best that we avoid Irina Petrovna."

"If we can," Elaine added apprehensively.

"She doesn't frighten me." Lisa's tone was defiant but she clasped and unclasped her fingers throughout the ride back to the hotel.

eighteen

They returned to the Children's Home the next day, Misha having arranged their schedule with Irina Petrovna. It was necessary, in order to satisfy the requirements of the Russian courts, that Lisa's interaction with Genia be observed over a reasonable period of time. Claire had explained that to Lisa and seated in Claire's airy sun-filled Philadelphia office, surrounded by photos of healthy smiling children, all of them inscribed by grateful and satisfied adoptive parents, it seemed an acceptable requirement. Those children were Claire's adoption success stories and the happy mothers and fathers who had signed them had, of course, submitted to those mandatory observations. It was less acceptable in Moscow when it became clear that Lisa's time with Genia would be monitored by

Irina Petrovna who sat in judgment, armed with a notebook and a pen. Her presence on the very first day was an irritant swiftly dispelled by Genia's smile of delight when she saw Lisa.

"You see, the child begins to know your daughter and be more relaxed with her," Sonia told Elaine.

From across the room, Irina Petrovna, stylishly dressed in a pale blue wool suit, lifted a reproving finger to her lips and made a notation in her notebook. Ignoring her presence, Lisa rolled a soft cloth ball to Genia and clapped when the child rolled it back to her. The time passed pleasantly as Lisa improvised one gentle game after another and Sonia and Elaine watched quietly. With Genia seated on her lap, Lisa turned the pages of *Goodnight Moon*. She softly read the words that the child did not understand but to which she responded with a sweet babble. Irina Petrovna moved her chair closer, her gaze stern and unflinching.

When Alla appeared to reclaim Genia, they rose to leave but Irina indicated that Sonia should remain in the room. Elaine and Lisa looked nervously at each other but they followed Alla out.

"Bye bye, Genia," Elaine said and blew the child a kiss. They laughed as Alla held the child's finger to her lips.

"Bye bye, Genia," Lisa called and waved.

Genia waved back and then buried her head shyly against Alla's shoulder.

They waited for Sonia on the steps of the Home but when the translator joined them, her face was furrowed with worry.

"What did she say to you?" Elaine asked.

"She wants to observe Dr. Gordon when she is alone with Genia. She does not want you or me in the room. And that is not good," Sonia replied worriedly.

"Why not?" Elaine asked.

"Irina may say things that are not true. If there are no other witnesses she may perhaps claim that Dr. Gordon hit the child or that she did not behave properly with her. Misha and I worked with one adoptive family last year and Irina asked that only the father be with the little boy during her observation. Then in the court she said that this man, who was such a nice man, such a good man, opened the boy's trouser and touched his penis. It was a lie but the judge believed her. Of course he would take the word of a Russian official against that of an American. He would not approve the adoption and that man and his wife could not adopt any child in all of Russia. We cannot let that happen to you. We must ask Misha what to do." Sonia pursed her lips.

"But Misha was not able to intervene on behalf of that other family, was he?" Elaine asked.

"No. He could not help those poor people," Sonia admitted sorrowfully.

"Mom, what are we going to do?" Lisa was very pale. She did not discount Sonia's warning. She had felt Irina Petrovna's hostility from the moment of their first meeting. "Should I call Claire?"

"Claire's in Philadelphia. But I'm right here." Elaine's tone was decisive. "Wait here for me. I'm going to speak to Madame Directress right now."

"But you will need me to interpret," Sonia protested.

"Oh, I think she will understand what I have to say. She did speak some English to us," Elaine assured her as she knocked at the door.

She stalked past the woman who opened it and walked straight into Irina Petrovna's office.

The directress frowned and rose from her desk chair, her hand threateningly raised, her finger pointed to the door. Elaine noted that her fingernails were long and painted with a scarlet polish that matched her lipstick, too thickly applied.

"I am here to tell you that I will be with my daughter during every observation session and our translator will also remain in the room," she said.

Irina Petrovna flushed angrily.

"You will leave this office," she commanded sharply. "I do not understand what you say in your English."

"Oh, I think you understand well enough," Elaine retorted. "I want you to know that if you deny me the right to be with my daughter I will go directly to the American ambassador and register a complaint. I will also complain formally to your Ministry of Education. I do not think such complaints are taken lightly in Russia. Nor should they be. Do we understand each other?"

There was no reply.

"I will return with my daughter tomorrow. And with our translator. *Dosvedanya,* Irina Petrovna."

The directress nodded. The slight inclination of her head was a surrender of sorts although her lips were pressed together, sealing an anger which would not be easily assuaged.

Trembling herself, Elaine left the building.

"Mom, what happened?" Lisa asked anxiously as they hurried to the car.

"I simply told our friend that Sonia and I will be with you at every session."

"And she agreed?"

"So it seems."

"How did you manage that?"

"Your father's modus vivendi. Act authoritatively and authority will be assumed. I think they teach that in Psychoanalysis 101."

Lisa smiled.

"That's right. I remember Dad saying that the only authority he had with his patients was the authority he assumed for himself."

"He said that more than once," Elaine reminded her. "But I never thought to practice it at all, certainly not in a Moscow Children's Home."

"Thanks for practicing it on that bitch, Mom. Dad would have been proud."

"Actually, I think he would have been surprised," Elaine agreed. She, after all, had surprised herself.

Bonded by shared memories, they sat quietly in the rear of the Lada as Sonia drove too quickly past the huge government apartment complexes.

Irina Petrovna came to their next session and glared at Elaine and Sonia, but raised no objection. She watched as Lisa showed Genia the toys they had brought with them from America, the pop-up board books and the yellow wooden ducklings that could be pulled along with a bright blue string. Genia stood unsteadily on her spindly legs and imitated Lisa's movements. She took one step, then two, then three, clapped her hands at her own progress and then turned and clapped approvingly for the obedient ducks. Lisa built a tower of soft cloth blocks and Genia knocked it down and chortled with delight as Lisa built it yet again.

Elaine sat beside Lisa and Genia on the floor, opened her sketchbook and drew a picture of a house and a garden. Her house. Her garden. She drew the tree that shaded the yard, the tree all her children and grandchildren had climbed.

"Pretty?" she asked liltingly and Genia nodded although she did not understand the question. What she understood was the love in Elaine's voice.

So absorbed were they in Genia, that they forgot the presence of Irina who sat erect in a high-backed chair and made copious notes. Occasionally Sonia spoke to her in Russian, translating Lisa's affectionate murmurs, Elaine's replications of the picture that flowed from the brightly colored markers onto the pages of her sketch pad. The directress listened without interest, adjusted her scarf, toyed with a brooch.

They repeated the games and the drawings each day and when they left they smothered Genia with kisses. At the end of the week, Genia pressed her lips against Lisa's cheek and jeweled it with a moist flutter.

"I love you," Lisa said as she held the child close.

"Ya loo-blue tibya," Sonia interjected softly. "That is how we say 'I love you' in Russian."

"Ya loo-blue tibya," Lisa whispered to Genia and the child's face lit up with joy.

"Mom, I love Genia so much that my heart breaks each time I see her," Lisa confided that evening as they sat over their shish kebab dinner in a Georgian restaurant.

Elaine glanced disapprovingly at the flocked red wallpaper and the chandeliers in which half the bulbs were dead, and turned to her daughter.

"You're wonderful with her," she said.

"You sound surprised."

"I suppose I am," she admitted. "I never thought you were that interested in children. You seemed irritated each time Sarah announced she was pregnant."

"It never occurred to you that I might be jealous of those pregnancies?" Lisa asked quietly.

"Jealous? Why would you be jealous?" Lisa's reply surprised her. "You could have married any number of times. You could have had a child of your own. You could have had a child even if you chose not to marry. You still can. Your biological clock is still ticking. You could give Genia a sister or a brother." She smiled encouragingly.

"No, Mom. Actually I can't have a child of my own. Not then. Not now. Not ever," Lisa said, her eyes downcast, her voice heavy with sadness.

Elaine set her knife and fork down and looked at her daughter.

"Why not?" she asked quietly.

Lisa looked at her, crumbled a bit of bread and toyed with the crumbs, staring down at them while she spoke in a voice so soft that Elaine had to strain to hear her.

"You remember my junior year in Italy?"

"Of course I remember. You wrote us the most wonderful letters. You loved Rome, your courses, those wonderful trips to Tuscany. Your father and I read your letters aloud."

"I had a boyfriend that year," Lisa reminded her.

"Yes. Of course. Bert. I remember him. He was in your class at Penn. A tall lanky boy. From California, I think. And you liked him a lot. I remember now."

"I loved him," Lisa corrected her.

Elaine took a sip of wine.

"What happened, Lisa?" she asked. "What happened between you and Bert?"

"You're sure you want to know? You're sure you're ready for this?"

"I'm sure."

Lisa took a deep breath and when she spoke her voice was husky and the words came slowly, as though wrested from a bedrock of painful memory.

"We were together. Together in Rome, lovers in Rome. Young and free and so happy just to be with each other, to play house, to study together and then go to the market and fill our baskets with vegetables and then go back to our student apartment near the Spanish Steps and cook crazy silly meals."

Lisa paused. She would not tell her mother how she and tall lanky Bert had often cooked naked, laughing at their own daring as they stirred thick sauces while the sun poured through the windows ribbing their bodies with rays of gold.

"Yes, there were those trips to Tuscany," she continued. "And weekends when we camped out or stayed in cheap *pensiones* pretending we were a honeymoon couple which I surely thought we would be one day. And then—" Her voice faltered, her eyes clouded. She lifted the carafe of wine, filled her glass but did not drink from it.

"And then I found out that I was pregnant. Carelessness. Stupidity. My fault, I suppose but I didn't think, at first, that we even had to think about whose fault it was, because I was so happy about it. What was wrong with my being pregnant? We loved each other. We both had supportive families. All that had happened, I thought, was that our timetable had accelerated. We'd get married sooner rather than later. I'd have the baby and somehow I'd work out medical school. I could organize my life. After all, I'd watched you organize yours. I walked on air, those first two months. I had a secret. My own secret. I'd never had such a wonderful secret before. I was a twin and twins don't have secrets from each other and lovers can only keep secrets for so long. So I hugged that secret to myself. I didn't tell Bert. I thought that I'd surprise him and share it with him on his birthday. We were going to celebrate it in our favorite trattoria."

Lisa closed her eyes, remembering that dimly lit restaurant, candles in straw-encased Chianti bottles burning on each table. She struggled to remember what she had worn that night but could only recall that Bert had bought her a bunch of violets and the waiter had placed them in a small vase and set it on the table next to the candle.

"How old was he on that birthday?" Elaine asked.

Lisa smiled wistfully.

"Twenty-one. I realize now that the news that your girl-friend is pregnant is not a terrific twenty-first birthday present. But back then I was naive enough to think that he'd see everything from my perspective, that he'd be as happy as I was."

"And he wasn't?"

"That would be an understatement. He totally freaked out. He was furious, accusing me of tricking him. He said terrible things. It was as if I had never known him, never slept beside him in a field full of sunflowers, never walked across the Ponte Vecchio with him. I didn't recognize him. He knocked over the candle, the flowers he had bought me fell to the floor and he stormed out of the trattoria. He didn't come back to our apartment that night."

"What did you do?" Elaine asked calmly although an unfamiliar weakness swept over her. That distant memory, an old and bitter memory for Lisa, was a fresh sorrow for her.

"What could I do? I waited. He came back to the apartment the next morning. He was miserable. He cried. He apologized. He got angry, accusative and then he cried again. He said that he didn't know what he wanted but he definitely knew what he didn't want. He didn't want to be a husband and a father at twenty-one. And I saw that he couldn't be. He would have to be a man to be a husband and a father and he wasn't a man. He was a boy. A scared, bewildered boy. I went to class. Then I went to the movies. I sat in that dark theater near the Piazza Navona and I cried and cried. Then I went back to the apartment and Bert was gone. He'd taken his books, his clothes, even the frying pan that we had bought together from an iron monger in the old market. That's what I couldn't forgive, that he took that frying pan. But he left me an envelope with five one-hundred-dollar bills and the name of a clinic. *A really good clinic,* he wrote, although he didn't even sign his name." She shook her head as though still bewildered by that wounding omission.

"And then?"

"And then I called Sandy in Jerusalem. She flew to Rome and we went to that really good clinic together and Sandy held my hand while they scraped my wonderful secret out of my womb. It was all sterile, that clinic, and the very good doctor administered a local anesthesia so I didn't have too much pain. But that night I hemorrhaged and Sandy and I were scared to death. She called an ambulance. They told me at the American Hospital that the doctor at the very good clinic had made a slight error. He had perforated my womb. I would be fine but I would never carry a child again. Never," she whispered as though to cushion the terrible finality of the word.

"We never knew. Why didn't you tell us?" Elaine's voice broke.

"I don't know, Mom. Sandy and I talked about it. Sandy thought that we should tell you. But I just couldn't. You and Dad were so content, so wrapped up in each other, so happy with your lives, so glad that we all seemed to be doing so well. I didn't want to shatter that happiness, that contentment. I didn't want to be an intruder, breaking into the brightness of your life, darkening it with my problems, my mistakes. And I didn't want to disappoint Daddy. He'd always been so proud of me. I didn't want to lose that pride."

"You wouldn't have," Elaine assured her but her own mood grew heavier.

Of course, it would have been Neil's reaction that concerned Lisa all those years ago and even now, it was of Neil she spoke. The parent of choice, the parent to be emulated. The thought shamed her and swiftly, she banished it. She would not allow herself to be jealous of her dead husband, to begrudge her daughter her preference.

"But I never lost the memory of that sweet secret, the knowledge that I hugged to myself for those brief weeks of my pregnancy," Lisa continued. "A life was growing within me. I would be a mother. And then my baby was gone and I listened to that very kind Italian doctor tell me that I could never become pregnant again. But still, I wanted to be a mother and I wanted it more with each passing year. So I began to think about adoption and when it became clear to me that I was so well established professionally that I could manage my career and life as a single mother, I made inquiries and I was referred to the adoption agency where I met Claire. I remember the day that I sat in her office and she showed me an album of photos of Russian children who might be available for adoption and I saw Genia's picture. I stared at it and I thought 'that's what a daughter of mine would look like— that dark-haired child with her heart-shaped face.' She could have been my never-born baby. That night I dreamed of Genia, I saw her as a baby, sheltered deep within my body, playing within the soft pinkness of my womb, and I woke up smiling. I called Claire and asked her to begin the process. I kept thinking, 'I have another secret, another sweet and wonderful secret and I don't have to share this secret with anyone and no one can endanger it. I am going to be a mother.'"

"And you'll be a wonderful mother," Elaine said firmly.

She gripped her daughter's hand, grateful to her for the sad truth she had revealed to her, even after the passing of so many years, grateful too that the barrier of silence between them had, at last, been destroyed.

"Lisa, what happened to Bert?" she asked and struggled to recall what he had looked like. A nice smile, she remembered, but a weak mouth. And, as it turned out, a flawed character.

Lisa smiled grimly.

"He transferred to a university in California and went to medical school out there. I met him at a conference a couple of years ago. He was divorced and had two kids or maybe three. Forget about lanky. He had a potbelly and was balding. He sort of hit on me in an embarrassed and embarrassing way. I did have a drink with him and he apologized for Rome and I told him that he didn't need to apologize, that actually he had taught me a lot."

"Oh?" Elaine frowned. "That was carrying forgiveness a bit far."

"That's true, Mom. He taught me to be self-protective, self-reliant, to never give my trust lightly. Because of Bert I came to recognize that nothing is permanent and most relationships are, at best, tenuous."

Elaine sighed. She understood now why so many lovers had drifted in and out of her daughter's life, why Lisa had resisted long-term commitments and pursued financial and professional success, always insisting on her own inalienable independence.

"And David. What about David?" she asked. "How much does he know?"

"He knows that I can't have children, which doesn't impact on him. He never asked why. He's not the kind of man who would ask such a question. He has his own children. He's supportive of the adoption and he's never intimated that it would cause any problems for us. He's happy with our relationship as it is and so am I. We fit into each other's lives. And yes, I think that we love each other. At least I love him and I think he loves me. All of which is good."

"Yes. It is good. He's a remarkable man," Elaine said.

"Then why do you sound so sad, Mom?" Lisa asked. "I'm exactly where I want to be."

Elaine sighed. "Are you?" she asked.

"I think so," Lisa said but a hint of uncertainty had crept into her voice. "Mom, things have worked out for me. Please don't be upset."

"I just wish I had known the truth about your life sooner. I wish you had called me from Rome or at least shared what had happened to you when you came home. I could sense the change in you, the distance you put between us but your father and I didn't want to invade your privacy. We were wrong. I was wrong. We should have asked more questions, insisted on your trust, your confidence. We could have helped you."

"No. You were right, you were both right to keep your distance, to give me space. I wasn't ready to tell you. Not then. Not for a long time afterward. Actually, not until now, not until this time we've had together, just the two of us. From the very beginning of this trip I felt that we were getting closer and closer, that we could talk to each other in a new way. Maybe it was because I had you all to myself for the very first time and we had the time to understand each other, to be a team. The Gordon gals, mother and daughter, doing battle in Moscow. I saw you here as I'd never seen you before. When you dashed in to corner Irina Petrovna I felt so proud to be your daughter, so lucky that you were there to protect me. My Wonder Woman mom. I understood then that there was nothing you wouldn't do for me and nothing that I wouldn't do for you." Lisa spoke very slowly, each word chosen with care.

"But that is what it is to be a mother, to be a father," Elaine replied. "That is what it will be like for you and your Genia. There will be nothing that you would not do for her and nothing that she would refuse you."

"Ah, Genia." Lisa whispered the name and she closed her eyes, imagining the child of her dream sheltered within her body, safe in her heart, her own wondrous secret to be treasured and protected.

Arm in arm then, they walked back to the hotel.

Their days in Moscow assumed a routine that was at once gratifying and grindingly monotonous. Because Misha estimated that it would be at least six weeks until a court date could be arranged they moved out of their room at the Radisson into a small suite. Elaine wandered through the Izmailovsky flea market and returned with brightly colored cushions of a Georgian weave which she tossed across the beds. She arranged the wooden bowls decorated in the *khokhloma* style, bright oils painted on gold and black backgrounds which she discovered in the State Historical Museum gift shop, across the surface of an improvised worktable. She studied the colors and the designs, sketched the patterns and thought of how she might translate them into shapes and glazes when she returned to her studio. She spent hours during the long evenings, drawing and discarding ideas for additional tiles for the mural, a theme that would reflect Neil's earliest life, the brief years of his Russian childhood. She realized, regretfully, that she knew too little about them to grasp a meaningful visual image. Perhaps a visit to Yaroslavl would ignite an idea.

Lisa also spent the evenings answering the faxes she received from her labs, placing calls to colleagues to clarify readings. David's itinerary was taped to her rented fax machine. It exhausted Elaine to simply glance at his hectic schedule. Two days in Paris, an afternoon meeting in London, a weekend back in Washington and then a long stay in Helsinki to address an international finance conference. As competent and organized as Lisa, he had included phone numbers and addresses for each location. He called every night and Elaine smiled to hear her daughter's voice, so cool and businesslike when she conferred with her office, soften as she told him about her day, as she enthused over her sessions with Genia. Each conversation ended with Lisa's lilting reminder to her lover, "See me in your dreams."

And then one evening the phone rang and it was Moshe calling from Jerusalem. He and Sarah were the happy parents of a new son. A healthy baby boy who would be named for Sarah's father.

"We will call him Noam," he said, ignoring the interdiction against revealing an infant boy's name until the day of his circumcision.

Denis called from New Mexico. He was concerned about Lisa, concerned about the length of their stay in Russia.

"It's routine," Elaine assured him.

"I've spoken to colleagues. The Russian courts can be pretty unpredictable," he warned.

"Lisa's had very good advice. I don't think we'll have any difficulty."

"I hope not. And Mom, when you get back, I hope you'll come out to Santa Fe. You know we've built this new guesthouse cum studio. You'll have a place to work and absolute privacy."

Elaine understood that he was staking his claim to her time and she heard in his voice the petulant complaint of the small boy he had been, the last-born child who somehow always felt cheated. She did not have world enough or time for him. She had visited his brother, his sisters. He would have his turn. She wondered again if he stressed the new privacy that would be hers because he had sensed the unease she and Neil had felt during their visit to New Mexico, when they stayed in the guest room that adjoined the room he and Andrew shared. It was an unease they had not acknowledged, not even to each other. It would have obviated their claim of unconditional acceptance.

"Of course I'm planning a trip to Santa Fe," she said. "I saw that wonderful montage of Andrew's photos in *Art News*." She would have her son know that she was proud of him, proud of the achievements of his partner.

"His work is great, isn't it? And he's great. In fact, Mom, we're great together." She wondered if she imagined the slight defiance in his tone. "Well, enjoy Moscow," he added more gently.

"We're trying."

And they were trying. She and Lisa spent the afternoons wandering through the city, occasionally with Sonia, but more often on their own. They explored different neigh-borhoods, rummaged through the stands of the sidewalk vendors. Elaine found lengths of fabric embellished with folkloric imprints which she sent to Sarah and Lauren and, on impulse, she bought two pairs of amber cuff links and sent them to Denis and Andrew, pausing to wonder, after the package had been mailed, if they ever wore shirts with French cuffs. It occurred to her that she knew very little about her youngest son and the life that he had built for himself.

They walked down the cobbled streets of the Arbat and watched street artists dash off charcoal portraits as violin-ists hopefully played sentimental Moldavian love songs. At a corner kiosk Lisa bought her first set of nesting dolls. She found hand-carved Georgian toys and brightly colored nesting dolls at Detsky Mir, the huge children's store. Back at the hotel, she displayed her purchases in a colorful parade across the bureau.

"I want Genia to have a sense of the country where she was born," she said. "Russian toys. Russian crafts. I'm going to take a course in Russian cooking."

"That's important," Elaine agreed. "My parents only passed on their sad memories. They had nothing else."

She paused, recalling the pall of sadness that had en-shrouded the small apartment of her childhood. She had worked hard to be the good girl, the quiescent daughter who spared them further pain. She and Neil, who had also felt himself held hostage to his parents' sadness, had deter-mined that they would live differently, that they would give their own children the latitude to live their lives free of parental expectations. A determination that had backfired, she thought bitterly as she toyed with a set of nesting dolls, running her fingers across their brightly lacquered surfaces.

"Your father always regretted that his parents had brought so few things with them when they emigrated to America," she continued, regretful now to have begun this conversation. "Some photos, your grandmother's brass candlesticks, a silver cup. That was all they had to remind them of their life in Yaroslavl. That and your grandmother's wonderful blini and perogen. She taught me how to make them and I'll give you the recipes."

"We should go to Yaroslavl," Lisa said.

"As soon as we have a court date, we'll try to arrange something," Elaine promised.

She turned back to the letter she was writing, a reply to Herb Glasser who had written to ask about her journey, adding that he had met Renee Evers at a party and she had told him that she was eager to commission additional ceramic pieces. *Lamp bases appear to have replaced bookends as the crying need of Southern California decorators,* he wrote wryly. He added that Peter and Lauren were taking the children to Hawaii but he had declined to join them. *I will be alone,* he wrote, pointedly underlining the word. *I hope you feel sorry for me.* She, in turn, ignored the underlined word and his playful plea and wrote back in reply that she was grateful for Renee's interest but she had had no time to think of new ceramics. Events in Moscow were too interesting, too absorbing.

Each day they visited the Children's Home and each day Genia grew more responsive. Lisa played with her, read books to her and Elaine brought her a sketch pad and markers and drew pictures for her. Animals, flowers, a smiling sun, a crescent moon. The child watched with great concentration and after a few days she took the marker from Elaine and made a few tentative scrawls of her own. From her seat in the corner, Irina Petrovna clucked disapprovingly and barked a harsh command which Sonia translated.

"She does not want Genia to touch the marker because she will get her clothing dirty," Sonia said regretfully.

Elaine looked at Genia's faded blue pajama, the fabric frayed and worn, the sleeves ragged.

"Tell her that if that beautiful garment gets dirty I'll replace it," she said.

"Please," Sonia said quietly. "Do not anger her."

Gently then, she herself took the marker out of Genia's hand.

"Why should we be afraid of that woman?" Lisa grumbled as they drove back to the hotel. "Our documents are in order. She can't have anything negative to report from her so-called observations."

"It is best not to anger her," Sonia repeated enigmatically.

And then, as though to appease them, she suggested that they spend the following morning at Red Square.

"Tomorrow is a Saturday and you know that Irina Petrovna schedules visits only in the afternoons on weekends. I will take you to Red Square, to the Kremlin."

"That's all right, Sonia," Elaine said. "You take the morning off. Lisa and I will manage on our own."

She had a sudden urge to simply be a tourist in Moscow, exploring the city as a visitor, forgetting for a few hours the stress of the adoption and Sonia's kind but ubiquitous monitoring.

They did feel a new sense of freedom as they climbed the slight incline that led to Red Square and the multicolored onion-shaped domes of St. Basil's Cathedral came slowly into view. They entered the huge building and Elaine, who had delighted in the exotic exterior, was disappointed by the dark antechambers, the brick walls decorated with faded flower frescoes, the chapels stark and forbidding. She was relieved when they emerged into the bright sunlight of an unseasonably warm morning. They strolled on with the luxurious aimlessness of visitors to an unfamiliar city, unbound by a set schedule, lingering now in one square, now in another.

They turned onto a narrow cobblestoned street and noticed a white stone Byzantine-style building, its frontage supported by a series of Greek columns. Small groups of people made their way up the high steps, now and again glancing furtively over their shoulders. The men, most of them middle-aged or elderly, wore dark suits and hats and their wives, huddled in oversize coats, had covered their hair with faded felt berets.

Elaine and Lisa drew closer and read the plaque that marked the entry. They were standing in front of the Choral Synagogue. They looked at each other in surprise and wordlessly, in tacit agreement, they entered. They followed a young mother, who held the hands of her two small daughters, up to the women's gallery, which overhung the huge dimly lit sanctuary on three sides. Looking down they saw that only a few rows in the cavernous room were occupied. The chanted prayers drifted toward them in a sad and wistful chorus.

The other women looked at them curiously and smiled in tentative welcome. The young mother offered them a prayer book to share, the pages yellowed with age, the leather binding frayed and discolored.

Elaine looked down at the altar, illuminated by electric light and flanked by two tablets representing the ten commandments inscribed in Hebrew and in Cyrillic. There was also a large plaque containing the words of the Kaddish, the mourner's prayer, in Hebrew.

She wondered if Neil's parents had ever come to this synagogue, if Neil himself, as a toddler had climbed up to the women's gallery with his mother. She and Lisa stood as the rabbi intoned the Kaddish and repeated the prayer in hushed tones. It was fitting, she thought, that they invoke Neil's memory in this city, not far from the village of his birth.

When the service ended, they followed the other worshippers to a small anteroom where a single bottle of wine and two small braided Sabbath loaves had been placed on a table covered with a snow-white, much-mended cloth. The rabbi welcomed them and they were surrounded by eager questioners. Where were they from? Ah—New

York. Ah—Philadelphia. Everyone had relatives in New York. One elderly woman had a daughter and grandchildren in Philadelphia. She held out a scrap of paper with her daughter's address and beamed when Lisa told her that it was a good neighborhood.

"Why did you come to Moscow?" the young mother asked. Her own family, she told them in stilted English, was awaiting visas for Israel.

"I came to adopt a baby," Lisa explained. "A wonderful little girl."

"From which Children's Home?" she asked.

"Number Thirty-One."

There was a sudden silence, an exchange of glances and then the rabbi spoke.

"We came to know of that home," he said. "There was a flu epidemic, perhaps two years ago. Several children from Jewish families were orphaned in that epidemic and the youngest of them were placed in Children's Home Thirty-One. We made an effort to remove them to a Jewish home but we had no success. The directress could not be persuaded to release them. They were lost to us."

Lisa and Elaine looked at each other, a single thought in both their minds. It was possible that Genia was one of those children, an infant abandoned by the death of her parents rather than a foundling as she had been described in the database, which, after all, had not been specific. That she might be Jewish was an odd coincidence but not an improbable one.

"My baby's name is Genia," Lisa said.

They shook their heads. The name was unfamiliar to them.

When Sonia picked them up that afternoon, they told her of their morning adventure.

The translator looked at them gravely.

"Do not speak of your visit to the synagogue when Irina Petrovna is in the room," she said warningly.

They asked no questions. The implication of her words was clear.

nineteen

At the beginning of their fourth week in Moscow, Lisa commented worriedly that Misha seemed to have forgotten them. They had come to rely on Sonia who was apologetic on his behalf. Her excuses for his behavior did not surprise them. Misha, after all, was her employer whose steady assignments brought her closer to the sum of money necessary for her journey back to America. Sonia explained that he was a sought-after facilitator, that he made arrangements for many clients and that much of his work involved dealing with officials, checking documents, obtaining signatures on one or another of the myriad forms required for the completion of an adoption.

"Misha understands how to work with these officials,"

Sonia had said suggestively and Elaine had flashed Lisa a conspiratorial look.

What Misha understood, they assumed, was who could be bribed and how much of a bribe was necessary to expedite the adoption process. Bribery, Lisa supposed, was the "miscellaneous" category on the expense statement Claire had shown her. She had not questioned it when she wrote the check to the agency in Philadelphia although the size of the amount had surprised her.

They were relieved then, when Misha arrived with Sonia one morning, his face flushed with pleasure. Triumphantly he waved an oversize official-looking envelope.

"A court date has been arranged. It is sooner than we anticipated. We have been very fortunate. Here I have the confirmation. You are to appear before Judge Timashkov in one week. In this also we are fortunate. He is a good man. Is that not true, Sonia?"

"He is a very fair man," Sonia agreed. "I have often worked in his courtroom. He is guided by the law and only by the law."

"That is very good news, Misha," Lisa said. "We were wondering when we would next hear from you."

"I have been busy," he said. "Very busy. Many couples have arrived. Some from America, some from South Africa, some from Australia. Not all of them are so well organized as you, *Dawkta* Gordon. They do not have such complete dossiers. I must help them as I helped you."

Lisa nodded. Misha had indeed carefully examined her

dossier, checking each form, each letter, ticking them off against his own tattered list. He had taken the report from the American Medical Center and made several photocopies of it, inserting them into the bulky blue file. He had insisted that Lisa obtain a letter from a relative who would act as Genia's guardian in the event of Lisa's death, frowning when Lisa suggested Sarah.

"No. It must be someone in the United States. The judge will say that Israel is not a safe country."

He had rejected Elaine because she was too old and Denis because he was single.

"In Russia the family is very important. The judge will want a family—a mother, a father."

Lisa had felt a vague uneasiness. Claire had assured her that she had arranged several adoptions for single parents but still Misha's words were unsettling. They had decided at last on Peter who had faxed an affidavit of agreement which Misha had copied and added to the dossier.

"I know how busy you are, Misha," Lisa said. "But please arrange some time for me before the hearing. I want to know the procedure and be prepared for any questions I might be asked."

"Yes. Of course. I will explain to you exactly what will happen in the courtroom. But you have no need to worry. Your Genia was an abandoned child so there is no need for release from her family. Who knows who they are? So that is one big problem that you do not have. Do not be concerned. Misha has been the facilitator of many adoptions. Yes, Sonia?"

"Misha is an excellent facilitator," Sonia agreed. "But now we must go to the Home. We do not want to anger Irina."

Lisa grimaced. Misha darted out of the Lada and hurried into the hotel where, in all probability, another anxious adoptive parent waited for him.

That morning Elaine sat beside Genia and Lisa on the floor, her drawing pad open, her colored pencils neatly arranged. She drew a picture of her own home, a young woman with a child in her arms standing in the doorway, the garden crowded with flowers. Genia stared at the picture and Elaine pointed to Lisa, then to the woman in the drawing.

"Mama," she said.

She pointed to the drawing of the child and then to Genia.

"Genia. Genia and Mama."

Genia looked puzzled and then, as though a new understanding had broken through, she smiled, her heart-shaped face newly radiant. She touched the drawing and reached up to touch Lisa's face.

"Mama?" The word was a question, the touch a caress. Lisa nodded.

"Mama." The question had vanished, the smile remained.

Lisa's eyes filled and Elaine put her hand on her daughter's shoulder. Sonia nodded approvingly but across the room, Irina Petrovna shifted in her seat and jabbed angrily at her notebook.

They ignored her. Elaine added other drawings, creating

a panel. Lisa handing the child a doll. Toys. A ball. An airplane. Genia looked puzzled. She fluttered her arms but realized that the child had never seen an airplane. She drew a bird instead.

"Tweet," Genia chortled happily. "Tweet, tweet."

Elaine and Lisa clapped their hands and then Genia clapped for herself.

"She's wonderful, isn't she?" Lisa said happily, as they drove back to the Radisson.

"Wonderful," Elaine and Sonia agreed in unison.

"Oh, Mom, can you believe it? In a week's time she'll be mine. In a week we'll be on our way home to America."

Elaine nodded but she did not answer. She was the daughter of a woman who had hugged all good news close, fearful that any premature proclamation could tempt the evil eye. A stupid superstition, she knew, but she trembled at the thought that Lisa's optimism might be premature.

"We'll be together always, Genia and I," Lisa said dreamily.

"It will be wonderful for me to have a granddaughter nearby," Elaine reflected. "Only a two-hour drive away. I hop into my car and claim a kiss, a hug. A blessing when I think of the flights to Los Angeles and Tel Aviv to see my other grandchildren."

"Mom, why don't you think about moving to Philadelphia or at least to a nearby suburb?" Lisa asked hesitantly. "You don't want to spend the rest of your life rattling around that big house, so far from all of us."

"Actually, Lisa, I don't know what I want to do," Elaine replied. "I don't want to stay in the house. I know that much. But I'm finding it hard to decide where I want to live for the rest of my life."

She stared out the car window. They were passing a housing project and as they stopped for a light a Russian grandmother wearing the traditional babushka crossed the street. She held the hands of laughing twin boys and smiled benevolently at them. Elaine had no doubt that she was a woman who knew exactly what she wanted to do for the rest of her life and where she would live. She leaned back, grateful to Lisa for not pursuing the question to which she had no answer.

Misha and Sonia came to the hotel the evening before the court hearing and reviewed the questions that were usually posed to adoptive parents by the judge and the prosecutor.

"Prosecutor?" Lisa asked in bewilderment.

"In Russia the prosecutor means the attorney who acts on behalf of the government," Sonia explained. "No need to be frightened by the word."

"They will ask about your life, your profession, why you are adopting in Russia rather than the United States," Misha continued. "There may be a question about why you do not have a biological child of your own and another about the religion in which you will raise the child. What else will they ask?" He consulted his tattered notebook. "Some more questions. What will you tell Genia about her

Russian heritage? Does your family approve of the adoption? What are your child care arrangements? This will be an important question for you because you will be a single mother, a working mother."

"I'll explain that I've hired a live-in nanny. I even brought a picture of Ellen and the letters of reference her former employers wrote. And photographs of her room in my home and Genia's nursery. Claire suggested that I do that," Lisa assured him.

"Ah, Claire. She thinks of everything," Misha said admiringly. "Yes. I remember that those photographs and letters are in your dossier. And that the judge will have them before him. Refer to them but keep your answers very brief. And if the judge or the prosecutor asks one question after another wait until Sonia has translated all the questions. We are fortunate that we have permission for Sonia to act as translator. Sometimes we have the court translator and their English is not as good as Sonia's. You see, *Dawkta* Gordon, we are well prepared for this hearing. No need to worry."

"I do see. And I'm grateful," Lisa said.

It rained the morning of the hearing, a doleful drizzle that was impervious to Sonia's windshield wipers. She cursed briefly and pressed the accelerator, indifferent to the lack of visibility.

"We don't want to be late," she muttered.

Sonia's irritability and the weather darkened Elaine's mood. She was relieved, however, to see that Lisa remained light-hearted. David had phoned early that morning from

Helsinki to wish her luck and his call had energized her. She had dressed carefully for the hearing, following Claire's advice. A dark suit, a tailored white shirt, sensible shoes. She wore scant makeup, carefully applied, and she had brushed her helmet of dark hair into an obsidian gleam.

"Do I look like a mother?" she asked Elaine playfully.

"You look like a beautiful woman," Elaine had replied. "And you will be a beautiful mother."

"Oh, Mom, that's what David said. That's exactly what he said," Lisa responded happily. "Nothing can go wrong now."

"Of course nothing will go wrong," Elaine agreed.

She herself wore the turquoise-colored skirt she had bought in Santa Monica and she stroked the fabric, taking tactile comfort from its softness even as she wondered why she was in need of that comfort. Everything was in order. They were in great shape.

They arrived at the courthouse, a stately neoclassic building, its facade adorned with the bronze busts of stern-looking men, jurists and lawmakers of a distant era, Elaine supposed. The metal was unpolished and scratched, marred by graffiti in elegant Cyrillic scrawls. They climbed the steps to the main portico, which was supported by square black pillars. The interior contained no vestige of former elegance. They walked down a dimly lit corridor, the walls bare, the paint flaking, and entered a courtroom which was surprisingly small and austere. Its windows were narrow and droplets of rain slithered down dirt-encrusted panes and formed small puddles on the pockmarked granite sills.

The court stenographer, a heavyset woman, her iron-gray hair tightly twisted into a bun, sat at a small table and fiddled with an ancient stenotype machine, now and again interrupting her efforts to sneeze into a thin white handkerchief tucked into the sleeve of her dark dress. A chubby, pleasant-looking man, wearing a gray suit shiny with age, sat in the front row intently studying the sheaf of papers he balanced unsteadily on his lap.

"He is a representative of the Department of Education," Misha whispered to Lisa. "He was charged with reading through your dossier to determine if there is any reason why his department should not support the adoption. We can rely on him to support it. He does not want to waste another morning in court if you should appeal his denial."

Sonia took a seat beside Lisa. She nodded to a pale young woman in a dark woolen dress who hurried to take her place. Wispy hair framed her thin expressionless face. Her eyes were narrow, her lips pursed shut.

"Who is she?" Elaine asked Sonia.

"The prosecutor. She may ask some questions. The judge will ask other questions," Sonia explained. "She is not the most pleasant woman but do not be concerned about her."

"If you say so," Elaine said but her heart sank when the door opened and Irina Petrovna, resplendent in a purple knit dress, swept in and took a seat beside the prosecutor. The two women spoke briefly, their heads bent close.

Lisa glanced worriedly at Misha who shrugged his shoulders dismissively.

"Not to worry," he said. "It is not unusual for the directress to appear at an adoption proceeding."

Lisa nodded and stared straight ahead, fixing her eyes on the raised dais in front of a huge judicial bench that contained three large chairs. A copy of her dossier was placed in front of the center chair where the judge would sit. A sudden silence fell across the room as the door opened. Everyone stood as Judge Timashkov, a stooped gray-haired man, his judicial robe frayed at the sleeves and rusted at the yoke, entered. They all inclined their heads deferentially and the elderly stenographer blew her nose very loudly. The judge flashed her an avuncular smile and sat, motioning the others to do the same.

He opened the dossier and turned the pages slowly and then sat back as though satisfied. He nodded and the carefully choreographed hearing proceeded with an almost rhythmic slowness. Elaine loosened her scarf and tried to avoid looking at Irina Petrovna who was, she knew, staring hard at her.

The portly representative of the Department of Education gave a brief report, his tone noncommittal.

"He says that his department has studied all your documents and it supports the adoption," Sonia whispered to Lisa. "You see. There is nothing to worry about."

Lisa breathed more easily. She rose when her name was called and stood before the judge. The judge spoke softly, slowly and Sonia translated softly, slowly.

Lisa's hands trembled and her heart beat too fast, but her voice was calm as she gave her name and informed the court that she was a physician.

"The judge asks why you have come to Russia to adopt a baby," Sonia said.

"Please tell him that my father was born in Russia and Russian culture was always part of my life. I want to share my life with a child born in my father's homeland. Also I have friends who have adopted Russian children and their experiences have been excellent," Lisa replied.

The judge listened to the answer and nodded approvingly. He asked another question which Sonia translated in turn.

"What will you teach your child about her Russian heritage?" Sonia asked.

"I have been collecting things during my stay in Russia that will help me show Genia how rich and colorful Russian culture is. I have bought picture books of Russian cities and the countryside, collections of Russian fairy tales and nesting dolls as well as other Russian toys. I hope that she will learn the language of her native land. When she is older we will return to Russia together on more than one visit," Lisa said.

The prosecutor rose. She fired off a question in rapid Russian. Sonia shrugged.

"The prosecutor takes note of the fact that you are a physician with a large practice. How will the child be cared for if you are always so busy and not at home with her?"

"I have arranged for a very competent nanny who will live with us so that she will be available at all times. I believe the judge and the prosecutor will find references to her in the dossier."

The judge rummaged through the papers and smiled when he came upon the relevant documents. He spoke brusquely to the prosecutor, glanced at his watch, and shook his finger at her but she shrugged and asked yet another question.

"She wants to know in what religion you will raise the child," Sonia said.

"I am Jewish. Genia will be Jewish," Lisa replied.

Another question. Almost impatiently, Sonia translated.

"Does your family approve of this adoption?"

Lisa smiled.

"They are enthusiastic about it. In fact, my mother traveled to Moscow with me." She pointed to Elaine who nodded vigorously.

The prosecutor sat down but Irina Petrovna rose and turned to the judge, speaking rapidly. Sonia frowned. Misha clasped and unclasped his hands, his face furrowed in anger.

Lisa willed herself to calm as she and Sonia returned to their seats.

"What is Irina saying, Sonia?" she asked nervously.

"She says that she observed your sessions with Genia and they went well but she is opposed to this adoption because you are a single mother. There is a regulation in the rules of the Children's Home Thirty-One that says that adoptions by single parents are to be discouraged and can only be permitted with the agreement of the directress. The judge is trying to persuade her to permit the adoption. See, how he argues with her."

Lisa nodded. The judge was in fact pulling pages out of the dossier and waving them at Irina Petrovna. His voice rose in anger. The directress remained calm, her face frozen into a mask of obstinacy. She spoke to the prosecutor who, in turn, rose and addressed the judge.

"What's happening?" Lisa asked anxiously.

"The judge is angry because he feels that you will provide this child with a wonderful life. Irina Petrovna will not be persuaded. Irina asked the prosecutor if she was not acting within her rights according to Russian law and the prosecutor agrees. She has told the judge that legally, he is bound to deny the adoption," Sonia said, her voice heavy with defeat.

Lisa felt a weight descend upon her heart. She leaned forward, her face flushed, her eyes wide with disbelief. Elaine gripped her daughter's ice-cold hand, her own breath coming in stertorous gasps. This couldn't be happening. They couldn't lose Genia. Not now. Not ever.

Misha sprang to his feet. He spoke reasonably, cajolingly. The judge lifted his hands and shook his head. His gesture was one of defeat. He turned to the prosecutor who shrugged. He uttered his words of judgment slowly and reluctantly.

"The judge explains that according to the law of this precinct, he cannot grant the adoption over the objection of the directress. However, he is allowing a ten-day period during which this decision may be appealed and perhaps reversed," Sonia said.

"On what grounds?" Elaine asked.

"The directress may change her mind. There have been cases where a situation has changed," Sonia said unhappily. "Perhaps your situation will change."

Elaine nodded. They were grasping at straws, she acknowledged but at least there were straws to be grasped.

The judge rose, murmured a few words and left the room, carrying the dossier with him. Lisa sat very still as though paralyzed by grief and Elaine stroked her daughter's hand. Irina glanced at them as she left, her thin lips twisted into a grimace of triumph. She murmured a few words to Sonia as she brushed past her.

"What did she say?" Elaine asked.

"She said to tell you that she thinks your skirt is very beautiful," Sonia replied bitterly.

"What I don't understand," Lisa said, "is why she opposed the adoption. Claire told me that she's arranged adoptions for single parents without difficulty. Misha, have you acted as a facilitator for other adoptions by single parents from Children's Home Thirty-One?"

"Yes," Misha said.

"And they proceeded without difficulty?"

"Yes."

"Then what was our problem? Simply an antipathy to us?"

Misha and Sonia looked at each other. Sonia murmured something to him. Misha hesitated briefly and nodded.

"You remember that I told you about a family for whom

Irina created difficulty, even lying about the man's behavior with the child?" Sonia asked.

Lisa nodded.

"That family was also Jewish. That is why I advised you not to tell her that you went to the synagogue," she said. "Irina could not deny that adoption on the basis of religion because that would be against Russian law and so she invented that false accusation against that man. In your case, she had to find some obscure regulation."

"Anti-Semitic bitch that she is," Misha said harshly.

"Come. Let us have some lunch, some wine and I will take you back to the hotel," Sonia said.

"But I can still see Genia, can't I?" Lisa asked.

"Yes. You still have ten days." Misha spoke hesitantly. "But perhaps it would be easier for you, for her, to cut your ties to the child now."

He looked pleadingly at Elaine but she shook her head.

"We cannot decide anything now," she said firmly. "We need time to think. To plan. Damn it. I'm not going to let that woman win."

"I want to see Genia now," Lisa said quietly. "Mom, please understand. I want to be alone with her just now."

"I understand," Elaine said. She would not intrude upon her daughter; she understood her need to sit quietly with the child she had taken into her heart.

Sonia drove Lisa to the Home and by tacit agreement drove Elaine back to the hotel. There would be no recourse to the false comfort of wine and food in the face of a loss they could not bring themselves to discuss.

"Perhaps Misha will think of something," Sonia said.

"Perhaps."

Their voices were devoid of hope.

Back in her room, Elaine stood at the window and stared at the street below. The rain had stopped but the sky remained dark and overcast. She looked down at the travelers hurrying in and out of the railroad station and her gaze focused on a couple who stood beneath the gray corniced entry, locked in an embrace. The young woman wore a jaunty red beret and she stood on her toes so that she could look into her tall lover's eyes. He, in turn, smiled down at her and kissed her forehead in a tender pledge of affection and support. Elaine thought of David Green whose eyes softened when he looked at Lisa, who called her each evening, his gentle voice laced with concern and caring.

Perhaps your situation will change, Sonia had said.

Elaine seized upon the remembered words, spurred to action.

"I will make it change," she said aloud.

She turned away from the window and went to the phone. She looked down at David's itinerary and dialed the number in Helsinki where he was scheduled to be that day. She had thought to leave a message but she gasped with relief when David himself answered the phone.

"Elaine, is everything all right?"

She heard the anxiety in his voice and, willing herself to speak calmly, she told him about the hearing, told him that the adoption had been denied because Lisa was unmarried.

"But there is a ten-day appeal period?" he asked. "Is that what the judge said?"

"There is."

"How is Lisa?"

"Her heart is breaking."

He sighed.

"We won't need ten days," he said. "I'll be in Moscow tomorrow. I just need a few hours to cancel my meetings, reschedule things."

"Oh, David." Dizzied with gratitude, she sank into a chair. "Was I right to call you?"

She anticipated her daughter's anger. She knew that she had overstepped an invisible boundary, that her interference might never be forgiven, that the new and precious closeness between her and Lisa might be irrevocably shattered. Lisa would not have called David. Of that Elaine was certain. She would have felt that such a call would place undue pressure on him, would violate her independence and threaten the fragile parameters she and David had erected around their relationship. And perhaps, conditioned as she was to betrayal, she might have feared David's response.

"You were absolutely right to call me," David assured her. "Don't say anything to Lisa and don't worry. I'll arrange everything. It will be all right. I promise you. You did what you had to do. For all our sakes. Thank you, Elaine."

She hung up then and went back to the window. She was still staring down at the windswept street when Lisa returned. They embraced then, offering each other the solace of sorrow shared. Elaine dared not tell her daughter that her own heart soared with hope. David was right. She had done what she had to do. Just as her mother had called Neil all those years ago, so she had called David. Like her mother before her, she had acted to protect her daughter, to protect Genia, to salvage all their dreams.

It was Lisa who answered the knock at the door the next morning. David stood there, a bouquet of yellow roses in one hand and a small white box in the other. His craggy face was wreathed in a smile.

"I hear that you are in urgent need of a husband," he said and opened his arms wide.

Wordlessly, Lisa stepped into them and lifted her face so that his lips brushed her cheeks, wet with tears and radiant with joy.

Elaine turned away, weak with relief. Her risk had been well taken.

twenty

Lisa and David were married three days later in the American Embassy. Misha and Sonia stood beside Elaine, watched the brief ceremony and signed the registry as witnesses.

Misha then sped over to the courthouse to present a copy of the certificate of marriage to the judge's clerk.

"There will be no difficulty," he said happily. "The judge wants to grant this adoption. Irina Petrovna's objection will be dismissed and the judge will issue the decree of adoption. I myself will wait at the courthouse until I have it in my hand."

He was right. Two hours later he and Sonia returned, aglow with triumph. He waved the manila envelope excitedly and embraced Lisa.

"When can we get Genia?" she asked anxiously.

"Now," he said. "This very day. This very hour. Genia is your daughter. Let us go to the Home and claim her."

Hurriedly Elaine and Lisa raced to their room. Lisa packed clothing and diapers for Genia and Elaine placed her turquoise skirt into a carrier bag. Lisa looked at her curiously but said nothing.

"What about Alla?" Elaine asked.

"I have an envelope for her," Lisa replied. "Sonia spoke with her. She wants to study nursing, pediatric nursing. I've given her enough money to complete the course."

"That's very generous of you, Lisa," Elaine said. "She'll be grateful."

"No, Mom. It was Alla who was generous. She gave Genia affection. She taught her how to love and laugh. I'll be forever grateful to her. And I'm giving Sonia a gift as well. I want her to be reunited with her daughter. She has helped us and I want to help her."

Elaine looked at her and thought of Neil. How proud he would have been of this daughter, of her kindness, her competence, her capacity for love.

It was Misha who rang the doorbell at the Children's Home, pressing it again and again, perhaps to announce that he no longer came as a supplicant but as a claimant. Irina Petrovna herself opened the door, her face flushed with anger. She stared at Misha.

"What do you want?" she asked harshly.

"It is not what I want. I am here on behalf of my client."

He pointed at Lisa and David who were slowly climbing the steps with Elaine following behind them.

"My client *Dawkta* Lisa Gordon has come to take her daughter, the child known as Genia, home with her," Misha said.

Irina laughed. "You may recall that the judge denied the adoption," she said.

"But that has been reversed." Misha opened the envelope and showed her the Decree of Adoption. "Your objection is no longer valid. My client has married."

The directress stared at him in disbelief. She took the decree from him and read it. All color drained from her face. She motioned them inside and they followed her into the familiar playroom.

"I will tell Alla to bring the child to you. See that you leave all her garments here," she said harshly.

She turned and would have left but Elaine called out to her.

"Irina Petrovna, I have something for you."

She took the turquoise-colored skirt from the bag and held it out. She turned to Sonia.

"Tell her that she admired this skirt and I want her to have it," she said.

Sonia frowned as she translated Elaine's words.

The directress shook her head but even as she did so she reached out and touched the gauzy fabric, sliding it between her fingers. Elaine had not been wrong. She was indeed a woman who loved clothing, an addict of color and fashion.

"Tell her that the skirt is an expression of gratitude for the care she gave to Genia. I want her to be reminded of our family when she wears it. It is in no way a bribe. Only a gift," Elaine told Sonia.

Irina listened impatiently to Sonia, glanced briefly at Elaine and then, as though bestowing a favor, she took the skirt, tucked it beneath her arm and left the room.

"And what was that about?" Lisa asked her mother.

"It was vengeance of a kind. I forced her into accepting a gift from us which, for her, I think, is a kind of humiliation. She knows that I recognize her weakness. That skirt will be a reminder of that recognition and of our generosity. She is a woman who knows that it is dangerous to accept generosity from an enemy, especially after a defeat," Elaine replied.

David smiled at her.

"It's especially dangerous to underestimate you, Elaine," he said. "I've got myself a great wife and a formidable mother-in-law."

They all laughed then and were still laughing when Alla entered the room carrying Genia. The child cooed with delight when she saw Lisa.

"Mamamamama," she babbled excitedly as Lisa took her into her arms.

Lisa smiled and pointed to David.

"Dadadadada," she said in turn but Genia clung to her. David grinned.

"Don't worry," he said. "She'll have plenty of time to learn to love me. I love her already. We have a beautiful daughter, Lisa mine."

He held his finger out and magically, Genia grasped it, stared at him from the sheltering cove of Lisa's embrace, and smiled shyly, tentatively.

Swiftly then, Lisa dressed Genia in her new clothes, zipped her into the royal-blue snowsuit and handed the frayed and soiled garments she had removed to Alla. Tears filled the caregiver's pale eyes and she bent to kiss Genia one last time.

Lisa opened her bag and removed an envelope which she slipped into the pocket of Alla's coverall. She turned to Sonia to whom she had given a similar envelope when they left the hotel.

"Tell her how grateful we are. Tell her that the money I give her means she can leave this place and study to be a nurse. We will always remember her."

Slowly, softly, Sonia translated Lisa's words. Alla's shoulders quivered as she grasped Lisa's hand and pressed it to her lips.

"*Spaseebo,*" she said through racking sobs. "*Spaseebo. Spaseebo.*"

"She thanks you," Sonia said, her own voice breaking. "She thanks you again and again. As do I."

Alla ran from the room, leaving behind her the small mound of rags that Lisa had peeled off Genia's delicate body. It was Elaine who picked up the faded pajama, the ragged undershirt, the soiled diaper, the unmatched socks. She folded each item carefully and left them on a low table.

They left then, slamming the door behind them and walking down the high stone steps for the last time. They did not look back as Sonia put the Lada into gear and drove back to the city. Halfway there Genia fell asleep, cradled in Lisa's arms.

During the mandatory ten-day period, as they waited for Genia's passport, birth certificate and U.S. visa to be issued, they traveled to Yaroslavl. Sonia took pride in showing them the dramatic riverfront where the Volga and Kotorosl waters merged. They visited the Church of Elijah the Prophet and followed the semicircular path of the town's former earthen ramparts. But when Sonia, at Elaine's request, asked towns-people where the synagogue had been and where the Jews had lived, they shrugged their shoulders and averted their eyes. They asked the questions at last of a sweet-faced elderly monk who guided them through the Monastery of the Transfiguration of the Savior. He looked at them sadly.

"All gone," he said. "The synagogue burned. The houses destroyed."

"And the people?" Sonia persisted. "The Jews?"

"No more Jews in Yaroslavl." He shook his head wearily.

They walked slowly back to their hotel, David carrying Genia along the stone paved roadways as once Neil's long-dead parents must have carried the son they would bring to safety in America. Elaine stared up at the watchtower on the Volga embankment and thought that Neil, as a toddler, might have played on its narrow shingle beach. Her gentle mother-in-law, who loved skyscapes as she herself did, might have looked up at the canopy of clouds that drifted lazily from river to river.

That night back in the hotel, she took out her sketch pad and, with pen and India ink, drew the next two tiles of the mural. A mother and father, burdened with suitcases, their child perched on the man's shoulders, followed the path that led from the Volga to precincts beyond the city. The second drawing was of a tall man walking beside a slender woman who carried a laughing little girl, her dark hair awash with river mist, following the exact same path. Elaine looked at the drawings with satisfaction. How serendipitously family history had repeated itself. Neil's parents with Neil. David and Lisa with Genia. Impulsively, she drew ribs of sunlight along the paths in both sketches. Yes, those drawings could easily be etched onto tiles. She thought about using different shapes, different sizes. She sprayed the drawings with fixative and left them on her bedside table to dry.

She was eager now to return to the quiet of her studio, to work with stylus and glaze. She would visually preserve Neil's vanished childhood, now come full circle in this city of his birth where Lisa, in an adjoining room, sang a lullaby to the granddaughter he had never known.

The day before they left Moscow, they returned to the Choral Synagogue on Arkhipov Street. A marriage canopy was erected in the rabbi's tiny study and Lisa and David stood beneath it, David's voice vibrant with love and joy as he intoned the ancient pledge. "Behold you are consecrated unto me according to the laws of Moses and of Israel."

Elaine held Genia in her arms and the small group of

worshippers, so hastily assembled, admired the dark-haired baby.

"She is from Children's Home Thirty-One?" the young mother whom Lisa recalled from the Sabbath service asked.

"She is."

The young woman's eyes filled with tears. She kissed Genia's hand and turned to Lisa.

"May she have a good life, this precious child of yours, of ours," she said gravely. "May you raise her to a life of study, of good deeds and her own joy beneath the marriage canopy."

"Thank you," Lisa said. *"Spaseebo."*

"Shalom. Mazal tov."

"Shalom, shalom. Mazal tov, mazal tov."

The sweet wishes became a muted chorus as the others added their voices to hers and so it was with farewell benedictions of peace and luck they left Moscow at last.

Seated on the plane beside David, looking down at the soft white clouds tossed by the winds that carried them westward, Lisa opened her cloth-covered journal.

I am happy, she wrote. *Happier than I ever thought I could be. And my mother, for the first time since my father's death, seems to be happy as well.*

She looked at David, then glanced across the aisle at Elaine who cradled the sleeping Genia in her arms, a smile playing on her lips.

twenty-one

Denis Gordon was not surprised to find the house empty
when he returned from his law office in Santa Fe. Andrew,
he knew, was probably still in the darkroom, working at
breakneck speed to develop the film he had shot in Alaska
on assignment for *The National Geographic*. He wanted to
send the magazine the commissioned prints and select the
photos for a projected exhibit. Always disciplined about
his work schedule, Andrew did not want to leave for their
annual trip to Jamaica without finishing the project on
hand. Denis sighed. He would have to tell Andrew that
the pressure was off. He could work at a more leisurely
pace. Their Jamaica visit would have to be delayed until
Denis himself returned from his unexpected business trip
to New York. Of course, Andrew would be disappointed

and Denis hated to disappoint Andrew, but he had no choice. A surprise settlement had been offered in the securities case which had engaged him for months, and his presence at the negotiating conference was mandatory. He had thought of asking for a continuance but immediately decided against it. His client, a powerful venture capitalist, was a mainstay of his practice and the New York appearance meant that he would earn enough billable hours to offset the donation he and Andrew had made to the new AIDS clinic.

He went out to the studio but the red light on the darkroom door glowed warningly.

"I'm home," he called out.

"I need another half hour."

Andrew's voice was muffled. He was in all probability bent over trays of chemicals, concentrating on obtaining the exact solution necessary for each contact sheet. There were photographers who sent their film to laboratories for processing but Andrew had always insisted on doing his darkroom work himself.

"I like to be in control of the project from beginning to end," he had explained to Denis who understood that meant the actual composition of a particular photograph to the final darkroom steps of the developer, the stop and the fix. Andrew had worked too long and too hard to build his reputation. He would not chance it on relying on someone else's technical skills. In that, Denis thought wryly, he was very much like his ceramicist mother. Elaine mixed all her own glazes, supervised her own firing, although other successful potters and ceramicists often turned such work over to assistants.

Back in the house Denis sifted through the mail. There was an enthusiastic letter from Lisa and she had enclosed a photograph of herself, David and Genia. Lisa, always the most restrained of the Gordon siblings, was newly effusive. She wrote in superlatives, happily underlining each adjective. Genia was *marvelous, delightful, responsive.* She and David were *deliriously happy.* And when, she demanded, was Denis coming east to meet his new niece?

Denis smiled. The unplanned business trip to New York had its positive aspects. His sister would be surprised and his mother pleased at his arrival. There would be time, during this visit, to speak with Elaine yet again about her plans for the future.

He had spoken to her several times since her return from Russia and although she had emphasized how much she had enjoyed the journey, how meaningful it had been for her to watch Lisa and Genia together and to witness Lisa's marriage, he had heard the fatigue in her voice. Yes, she was tired, she admitted, and she had had a brief bout with the flu but she was recovered and back at work in her studio. She was focused on completing new tiles for the memorial mural which, she said, had morphed into a mosaic, a new concept in enamel craft work.

"Mom sounded really tired," Denis had observed to his sister Sarah when she called from Jerusalem. Her new baby, the child she and Moshe had called Noam, choosing their father's Hebrew name, was two months old and Sarah often called when she was nursing.

"I'm really tired also," Sarah had responded laughingly. "Actually a good tiredness. But seriously, Denis, you have to remember that Mom's not a young woman. She's getting older, she can't do everything she used to do. She simply doesn't have that kind of energy. You can understand that, can't you?"

"Of course," Denis had agreed but the truth was that while he understood it, he had difficulty accepting it. He had always perceived his mother to be a woman of extraordinary strength. He could not remember her ever being ill or displaying any weakness. Both his parents had always seemed to him to be indomitable, energizing each other, invigorated by their enthusiasm for their work.

Always, Elaine had spent long hours in her studio, sometimes returning to continue her work at night if she was particularly involved in a project. His father maintained both his clinic hours at the hospital and his private practice, taught and wrote for psychoanalytic journals, never complaining of the demands on his time. Fatigue was foreign to both of them. Denis as the youngest child, the only child at home after his sisters and brother left for college, was the beneficiary of their gentle and generous attention, their boundless energy. Elaine cooked his favorite foods, bought tickets for shows he would particularly enjoy, worried over his too-frequent colds, his penchant for solitude. His father hiked trails with him, bought books that he thought Denis would enjoy, taking the trouble to read them himself so that he and Denis could discuss them. It pleased both Elaine and Neil that Denis shared their love for music, that he could spend winter evenings sprawled on the rug between their two chairs listening to the string quartets they favored.

It was Andrew who had pointed out, years later, that perhaps his parents made these extra efforts because they sensed his vulnerability and they understood that he was not quite like their other children, that his withdrawal from his contemporaries was self-imposed and rooted in a haunting sadness that he could not yet explain.

Denis had shrugged off his partner's explanation. It was irrelevant. What mattered was his perception of their strength, his knowledge that he could rely on a mother and father of unique energy and unique power. He had thought them immortal, at a remove from the shadow of death. He recalled how, in grade school, the mother of one of his classmates had died and the class had signed a sympathy card. Denis had gripped the pen tightly as he signed his name and thought, *My parents are never going to die, they will live forever.*

Perhaps that was why he had been so shaken by his father's death, so overwhelmed by its suddenness. He had choked down his feelings of betrayal and disbelief but for weeks after the funeral his nights had been wracked by dreams of loss.

"It can't be," he had said over and over again to Andrew. "I still can't fathom it. My father was so healthy, so strong. He had so much to live for."

"People die," Andrew had replied. "Strong people, healthy people. Weak people, sick people. Straights and gays. Death is part of life, Denis."

He spoke slowly but his voice was edged with impatience. Andrew, after all, had watched a younger brother and an older sister die before he had reached his thirteenth birthday. Their lives had been claimed by the malnutrition and disease that poverty is heir to. Death had haunted his childhood, informed his adolescence. He had watched funeral corteges wind their way through the narrow streets of his Jamaican village and throughout his boyhood he had worn his one white shirt to the funerals of friends and cousins, relatives and neighbors. He had wondered bitterly if his mother kept it always so starched and ironed in anticipation of yet another inexplicable passing, another burial.

His mother's lesson had been well learned. Now he and Denis hung their dark suits, newly dry-cleaned after each funeral, in an easily accessible closet, in readiness for loss that followed loss as AIDS claimed the lives of one friend and then another. They had worn those suits to Neil Gordon's funeral, partners in grief as they were partners in life. Andrew had waited patiently for Denis to assimilate his father's death, offering him the comfort of words and the solace of silence.

Slowly Denis had emerged from the miasma of sorrow, had seen to the legal aftermath, the intricacies of his father's will, the accounting of his mother's assets. He gathered letters testamentary, filed papers, totaled columns of figures and tried to imagine how she would live the rest of her life, the wife become a widow, the mother of widely scattered adult children who would now live alone in the large house that had once overflowed with love and laughter.

Sarah attributed their mother's fatigue, her bout with the flu, to age but he knew that his father's death had sapped Elaine's strength, diluted her energy. He worried over the toll her trips to Jerusalem, to Los Angeles, to Russia, had taken and he knew that his worry was tinged with resentment. When would she visit him, when would it be his turn? He wanted his mother to spend time at his home, to understand his life, to consider how it might be merged with her own.

When he called her in the evening and heard the phone ringing in that large home, he imagined her seated alone opposite his father's empty chair and sadness suffused him. He felt himself charged with new responsibility. The burden had shifted. The child had become the parent. He now worried over the mother who had, for so many years, worried over him. He sought to banish the loneliness of her widowhood as she had sought to banish the despair that had darkened his boyhood.

He reread Lisa's letter and dashed an e-mail off to her, telling her the dates of his visit to New York, then changed into shorts and a T-shirt, set the radio to the University of New Mexico station, which was featuring an Odetta songfest, and began to prepare dinner. Andrew's favorite, chicken enchiladas with a vegetarian chili. As always, cooking relaxed him. He chopped vegetables vigorously and tossed them into the sizzling olive oil. By the time Andrew came into the kitchen, the room was redolent with the fragrance of garlic and onion and awhirl with the throbbing guitar that accompanied Odetta's deep and soulful voice.

"Smells great," Andrew said, dipping a spoon into the skillet and tasting the chili sauce. "And tastes great also. Are we having an anniversary or something that I've forgotten?"

He draped an arm over Denis's shoulder and grinned. Denis turned. He was moved, as always, by Andrew's subtle beauty, startled anew each evening and morning by his parter's fine features and lithe grace. They had been together for more than a decade, yet he was still overwhelmed by the knowledge that this lean, golden-skinned man, so soft of voice and gentle of gesture, had chosen him as a life companion.

"No anniversary. Go change. You stink of chemicals. I'll mix us some margaritas."

"We're not running tonight?" Andrew asked in surprise.

It had become their habit to run at first dusk along a path that wound its way through the foothills of the Sangre de Cristo mountains, looking up now and again as the descending sun painted the sky a gold-tinged vibrant pink that deepened slowly into the majestic purple arcs that preceded the star-studded desert darkness. They ran with swiftness and ease, occasionally increasing their pace for the sheer joy of the effort, the sweat glistening on their bodies an affirmation of the strength they so carefully and determinedly cultivated. As illness had decimated their small community, they defiantly pledged themselves to a regimen of health and exercise, of survival and endurance.

Andrew looked at his friend but asked no questions. Denis would explain the break in their routine over dinner. He showered quickly, changed into chinos and selected a freshly ironed shirt. Even after all the years of success, he still experienced a thrill of wonderment when he opened his closet and saw the serried rows of slacks and varicolored shirts, the drawers laden with clean underwear and socks, his shoes always polished and neatly aligned.

He had grown up wearing faded hand-me-downs, ragged pants and tattered shirts scavenged from older cousins or plucked from the barrels of used clothing in his mother's church, his feet more often than not bare or squeezed into shoes that did not fit. The very first photograph he had of himself, the candid action shot Gordon Cummings had taken in the marketplace of Ochos Rios, so long ago, showed him sprinting away from his mother's papaya stand. An oversize T-shirt tented his skinny body, his legs were stick-thin, his arms thrust out like delicate wings, his lips parted in a mischievous laugh as he glanced over his shoulder, never breaking pace.

Gordon Cummings, the photographer, was a legend in the village. The soft-spoken Brit was said to be a famous man and there were those who thought that he had even been knighted by the Queen. The village doctor, who subscribed to British and American magazines, had found his photo essays on their glossy pages. It thrilled the islanders that this famous man and his wife spent the winter months in Jamaica. It saddened them when he arrived alone one year and told his housekeeper that his wife had died. A wreath of dried flowers and a small bottle of rum had been placed at his door, sympathy offerings in the island tradition.

"Jamaican Boy Running," Gordon had titled that action shot of Andrew and he had sought Andrew out when it won a prize in a London exhibit and given him a copy of the gallery catalog and a box of chocolates.

"See, I've made you famous," the white-bearded photographer told sixteen-year-old Andrew.

Neither the fame nor the chocolates had interested Andrew. But the catalog intrigued him and he turned its pages, studying the photographs as though he would engrave them upon his memory. It was the art of photography, the magic of the camera's eye that enticed him, that drew him to Gordon Cummings's hilltop home day after day.

He would sidle up to the house in the late afternoon and stare through the windows at the framed photographs on the whitewashed walls, the portraits of famous world leaders and ordinary people, the scenes of battlefields and those of pastoral landscapes. There were pictures of foaming waves taken from the decks of sailing ships and a singular shot of a huge saguaro cactus standing vigil in a vast desert expanse. Andrew wondered how the photographer knew how to aim his camera so that he might capture the softness of shadow as it fell across the golden sand. Then one afternoon, as he stood on an upturned milk crate and strained to see a high-hanging nightscape, the door opened. Startled, Andrew fell off the crate. Gordon Cummings laughed, held out a glass of lemonade and invited the boy inside.

He explained his work, spoke of his travels. Andrew asked questions, turned the pages of albums. His interest pleased the lonely widower. He invited Andrew back, paid him small sums for doing chores and going on errands and then, step by step, he introduced him to the routines of the darkroom. Gradually, he became Andrew's mentor. He took the boy with him on field trips, gave him a small box camera of his own and taught him the secrets of lights and angles, of perspective and distance. When he left the island for his annual trip to London, it was Andrew who held the keys to the house and with the keys came permission to use the darkroom, to read the books, to hone his craft because it was clear to both of them that Andrew would one day follow in Gordon Cummings's footsteps.

When Andrew graduated from the island high school, there was a scholarship arranged for him at the Royal Academy of Photography in London. Gordon had carried a portfolio of his protégé's work to the registrar and established a fund for Andrew's upkeep during his studies. Andrew excelled. Gordon Cummings attended his student exhibit at the Academy, watched him graduate and glowed with approval. Six months later, the famous photographer was dead of a heart attack, his island home willed to Andrew Caruthers.

Andrew was no longer a ragged Jamaican boy, a barefoot

sprinter. He had become a lithe and talented London art photographer who ran fashion shoots even as a student and garnered awards at graduation as well as a fellowship to the Yale School of Fine Arts in New Haven. And it was in the cafeteria at Yale, one wintry evening, that he set his dinner tray down opposite a tall gray-eyed law student, whose tangle of dark curls was badly in need of cutting. They smiled at each other, the tentative smiles of shy and careful young men, and softly said their names. *Andrew. Denis.* They looked through the large glass windows at the slowly falling snow, left the cafeteria together and stepped without hesitation into their shared future, their lives melded, fear and loneliness forever vanquished.

Andrew shrugged into a denim jacket against the chill of the desert evening and hurried downstairs. The Odetta selections were over and a program of violin music had taken its place. Denis's favorite, the Bruch violin concerto, wafted through the room and Denis came toward him balancing a tray of margaritas, salt crystals aglitter on the rim of each glass.

Andrew took his glass and smiled at his partner.

"Why do I have the feeling that this drink and your dinner is a way of softening me up for some sort of unpleasantness?" he asked.

Denis blushed.

"Probably because it is," he said. "You're a mind reader, Andrew."

"No. Yours is the only mind I read."

Andrew grinned.

"So what's the bad news?" he asked.

"We're going to have to jettison the trip to Jamaica for a couple of months. A settlement's been offered in the Stevenson case and I have to be in New York to represent him at the final negotiations. It will take a week at least, which means that all my cases here will be backed up. I'll need time when I get back. I know you're disappointed and I'm pretty disappointed myself but I had no choice," Denis said, disliking the defensive tone that had crept into his voice.

Andrew swirled his drink.

"Not to worry, Denis. I can use the time to do some studies of the cliff ruins in Rito de Los Frijoles Canyon. *Travel and Leisure Magazine* has been after me for a spread and I can use the photos for the opening exhibit at the gallery." Andrew spoke soothingly, as always setting aside his own feelings to calm Denis. "And another thing," he continued. "This will be a good time to see your mother. I know you've been worried about her. You'll have some time to talk to her, maybe to convince her to come out to New Mexico, to spend some time with us and see how we live. That's what you want, isn't it?"

"Yes," Denis agreed. "That's what I want. I want her to know you better, to understand us both, to appreciate the life that we've built here. When she and my father visited, they breezed in and out, said all the right things the way they always said all the right things. I want more than that. I want her to see us as we are. I want her acceptance. I want her to be able to say 'Andrew and Denis' with the same ease that she says 'Sarah and Moshe,' 'Peter and Lauren,' 'Lisa and David.'"

"And what if you don't get that acceptance?" Andrew asked gravely.

"I'll deal with it. But I don't think that's going to happen. My mother is a pretty spectacular dame."

"I know that," Andrew said.

He had always liked Elaine Gordon, admired her work as he knew, with the artist's instinct, that she admired his. They were bonded, too, by their love for Denis, each recognizing his extraordinary tenderness, his extraordinary vulnerability. All this he knew, although he had never spent as much as an hour alone with her.

"And don't obsess about Jamaica," he added. "My island's not going anywhere anytime soon."

Denis smiled.

"We'll plan another trip after her visit. If, in fact, she decides to visit us."

"She will. She's making the rounds, toting up her options. You're next," Andrew said and wondered how he could be so certain.

They ate dinner on the patio and watched the glinting stars slowly emerge and sail into place across the sheltering sky. Denis remembered then how his mother and father had often stood in the garden of the Westchester house, their eyes raised to the starlit sky as they murmured the melodic names of the constellations. *Cassiopeia. Perseus. Andromeda. Cepheus.* He wondered if his mother now stood vigil alone and his heart turned at the thought of her aloneness. Andrew was right. The trip to New York would serve a double purpose. He yearned to comfort her, to persuade her to visit his home, to recognize Andrew's uniqueness and the tenderness of their bond. He wanted her to think of how she might perhaps share their lives. He looked gratefully at his partner who had, as always, put words to the yearnings that haunted him.

twenty-two

He remembered Andrew's words as he sat opposite his mother in the familiar Westchester living room later that week. He had driven north from the city after grueling days of meetings and negotiations but the case had been settled to his client's satisfaction. He had even managed to squeeze in a meeting with a local Realtor, a kindly woman who clutched her calculator to her ample cashmere-covered bosom as she told him that his mother's house had appreciated greatly.

"One week, two weeks on the market and it'll be snatched up," she had said and her words had depressed rather than elated him. When the house was sold his childhood, too, would be snatched up. Sadness and fatigue blanched the color from his face and caused his shoulders to sag.

Elaine looked at him worriedly and lifted a hand to his brow, the almost forgotten maternal gesture of concern.

"You look exhausted," she said. "Are you sure you're all right?"

"I'm fine, Mom. I'm always exhausted after shepherding through a deal like this. A lot of *i*'s to be dotted, a lot of *t*'s to be crossed. But I'm pretty resilient. When I feel that way in New Mexico after a tough day, Andrew and I go running, I take a shower and I'm fine," he assured her.

She sipped her drink, tried to visualize Denis sprinting through the desert, remembered that he and Neil had often run together on weekends—tall, lean father and tall, lean son in graceful pace disappearing down their rural road. *Neil.* Her husband's name lilted through her thoughts and came to rest upon her heart.

"I guess I don't really have a clear picture of your life there," she acknowledged.

"Which is why it would be great if you came out to New Mexico," Andrew responded quickly. "And I don't mean for a quick weekend. I mean a real visit, a real span of time. The kind of time you spent in Jerusalem and California, the kind of time you spent with Lisa in Russia. Enough time for you to see how we live, Andrew and myself, to understand us. It would mean a lot to us."

He spoke calmly but Elaine recognized a brittle anger in his tone. He was determined to have his turn, to lay claim to the same attention she had given to his brother and his sisters. He wanted to be included in the circle of her concerns, his life to be given equal weight on the scales of her affection.

She did not reply but poured him a glass of wine. He held it in his hand as he wandered through the large room, his eyes resting now on the paintings, now on the books and finally on the framed family photographs that lined the mantel. He stood before the wedding portrait of Sarah and Moshe in Jerusalem, of Peter and Lauren in California, the enlargement of the black-and-white snapshot Elaine had taken of Lisa and David in Moscow outside the Choral Synagogue minutes after their marriage. Austere mahogany frames encased the sepia wedding photographs of his two sets of grandparents, transported across the ocean, removed from their cluttered inner-city apartments to this place of pride in Westchester. He stared at his own face on the day of his graduation from law school. Andrew had taken that picture, developed and framed it and presented it to Elaine and Neil along with a photograph of Denis and himself laughing, their heads turned skyward, their arms about each other's waists. Elaine had never placed the photograph of Andrew and himself on the mantel and the omission pained him. It gave the lie to his parents' oft-repeated claims that they were comfortable with his homosexuality, that they accepted Andrew as they had accepted their other in-law children.

He understood that they had long been ambivalent about his orientation. That ambivalence explained the swiftness of their visits, the odd uneasy silences that had overtaken them as they sat together at the dinner table, he and Andrew, his mother and father, searching desperately for a topic that would affirm the normalcy of a shared family meal that, in their eyes, was hardly normal. He had once heard his mother speak of Andrew on the phone to her friend, Serena.

"He's a very attractive, very talented young man of color," she had said and the control in her voice had angered Denis. He wanted his mother to see Andrew as he himself saw him, as the caring, insightful, tenderhearted man whom he loved. An "attractive, talented young man of color" was an abstraction, a dismissal of a kind of Andrew, the full-blooded sensitive man who wakened beside him each morning.

Elaine watched her youngest son, her baby, the child whose vulnerability had always touched her heart, over whom she had worried during long sleepless nights, study the family photographs. She saw the sadness on his face and went to stand beside him.

"Of course I'll come to New Mexico," she said. "It will be good for the two of us to have some time together."

"The three of us," he corrected. He would not allow Andrew to be excluded.

"Of course. The three of us." She blushed, aware of her blunder. "I had always intended to do just that," she continued. "I just want to finish working on the tiles I designed in Russia. When I've fired them and set them in place on the mural I'll book my tickets."

"Look, bring your stuff with you—your etching tools, your brushes, your pads and drawing pencils. You can work in Andrew's studio and we have a couple of friends with kilns."

"We'll see," she said evasively. "Do you want to see the mural? It's still a work in progress but I'd like to know what you think." Her own suggestion surprised her. She seldom showed her unfinished work to anyone.

"No," he replied firmly. "I want to be surprised."

She nodded, although she did not understand his reluctance.

Lisa, David and Genia visited the next day and Denis immediately fell in love with his niece. He crawled across the carpet on all fours with a giggling Genia perched on his back, hoisted her onto his shoulders and dashed through the garden with her, now and again lowering his head so that she might pluck leaves from low-hanging branches.

"He's wonderful with her," Lisa said, watching her brother.

"He's always been wonderful with children," Elaine agreed. "That's why it's so painful that…" Her voice trailed off as she remembered Neil's words the night Denis had told them that he was gay.

No little Denises, he had said, as he and Elaine sat in the gathering darkness, shivering in their sadness although the early evening air was unseasonably warm.

"Mom, he's happy. He and Andrew are great together," Lisa said. "That's what important. He's happy."

"Yes. Of course," she agreed as he loped toward them, Genia happily threading her harvest of young green leaves through his curling dark hair.

And Denis did look happy as he met her plane at the Albuquerque airport two weeks later and hurried toward her, relieving her of the paint-encrusted wooden work kit she clutched too tightly.

"So you decided to bring your tools with you after all," he said excitedly. "That's great. Andrew set up a drafting table for you in the guesthouse. You'll have total privacy whenever you want it."

Elaine smiled up at her son. His gray eyes were mica-bright and the pallor she had noticed during his visit to New York was gone. There was a ruddy glow to his skin, gained he told her, during a hike deep into the desert that he and Andrew had taken over the weekend. He lifted her suitcases with muscular grace and tossed them into the trunk of his car. He had come to the airport straight from the courtroom and he loosened the collar of his white shirt, removed his tie and jacket and rolled his sleeves up, impatient to feel the touch of sunlight on his arms. She marveled at how at ease he was in this landscape, at how comfortable he seemed to be in his own skin. He was at home in this territory, beneath the cloudless skies saturated with golden sunlight. He and Andrew had found each other during a cold New Haven winter but they had found the life that they both loved in the desert city surrounded by snow-covered mountain peaks, a city that offered them both privacy and an accepting community.

As they drove north to Santa Fe, following the Turquoise Trail, Denis pointed out the delicate blossoms that had begun to sprout on the cactus plants that lined the road, advised her to look westward so that she might see the gentle rise of Cochiti Pueblo. The air grew fragrant with the scent of piñon smoke and he smiled.

"Now you know we're getting close to Santa Fe," he said. "We're a city of fireplaces. Andrew and I have planted a windbreak of piñons. We have a fire in the living room every night and fuel it with the pine nuts. Music, wine and a low-burning fire in the hearth—nothing like it."

"I know," she said sadly and he remembered, too late, that that, after all, had been the pattern of all the winters of his parents' marriage—wine, music and the low-burning flames that they watched each winter evening, seated in their armchairs, their books open on their laps, cocooned in the firelight, cradled in their love.

"Sorry, Mom," he murmured, cursing himself for his thoughtlessness in evoking memories that were surely painful to her.

"Don't be. I'm glad, Denis, that you and Andrew have what we had—your father and I."

He reached out and touched her hand lightly, grateful that she recognized that what he and Andrew felt for each other was not unlike the loving tenderness she and his father had known.

They drove through the city and he concentrated on maneuvering the car through the ancient narrow streets, past the brown adobe houses whose patios were rimmed with swaying hollyhocks. Towering cottonwood trees cast patches of shade across multi-colored slabs of slate. Stalled in traffic outside the Fonda Hotel, Denis waved and smiled at a man who called his name, at a woman who waved to him. A toothless old Navajo hurried up to the car, his dark sun-wrinkled face wreathed in a smile, his wife trailing behind him.

"Señor Gordon, we thank you for what you did for us."

"Nada," Denis said. "Nothing. I was glad to help."

"For us it was everything," the old man said.

His wife came forward and offered him a garland of red chili peppers and a bouquet of sunflowers which Denis passed to Elaine.

"Mia madre," he said. "My mother. *Gracias.*"

"You must be proud, Señora, to have such a good man for a son," the aged woman said.

"I am," Elaine agreed as the traffic eased and Denis moved the car forward.

"What was that about?" she asked.

"A land dispute. Some developer wanted to evict his family and others from his tribe from the home they've lived in for years and I went to court pro bono and got them a restraining order. It was nothing." He honked his horn lightly to warn a group of schoolchildren to hurry across the road.

"Apparently to them it was everything," Elaine said and thought, for a fleeting irrational moment, that she must tell Neil about their son's kindness. The car lurched forward and she was catapulted back into reality. *Neil is dead,* she told herself severely and buried her head in the bouquet of sunflowers so that Denis would not see the tears that burned her eyes.

They left the city limits and drove eastward toward the Sangre de Cristo mountains and the gentle incline where Denis and Andrew had built their pueblo-style adobe home amid a grove of aspen and cottonwood trees.

Andrew, wearing a collarless white shirt and soft white slacks, waited for them on the flagstone patio and Elaine was moved as always by the sheer beauty of his finely chiseled features and the golden hue of his skin. It surprised her that for the first time she felt no discomfort as her son kissed his partner and when Andrew turned to her she held her hand out and, almost instinctively, he pressed it to his cheek.

"Welcome to our home, Elaine," he said and took the chili garland and sunflowers from her as Denis carried her suitcase into the guesthouse.

They had dinner that night in the spacious dining room, its walls pearl-finished, its hardwood floors covered with brightly colored Navajo rugs, the ceiling beamed with vigas and latillas and a gentle fire burning in the kiva fireplace. Over the grilled corn tortilla and lime soup, which Andrew had prepared, Denis discussed their plans for the early part of her visit. Both he and Andrew had taken several days off so that they could take short day trips with her.

"You never really saw New Mexico," Denis said. "Before."

The word hung heavily between them. *Before. Before* death changed our lives. *Before* you were alone, *before* when you were as uneasy with us as we were with you. *Before.*

He looked down but Elaine nodded.

"You're right," she agreed. "I never really saw New Mexico. Your father's patient schedule was so demanding that we could never stay long enough."

"Of course," Andrew said smoothly. He knew the truth but he accepted her excuse with grace.

They decided then that they would drive to Los Alamos the next day. And because the journey west had exhausted her, Denis took her to her room in the guesthouse. She was touched to see that like Lisa and Peter, Denis had placed ceramics of her own design in the room, objects she had created to mark his passage to new experiences. There were the earth-colored bookends she had made him when he went away to college, the deep aqua bowl in which he had kept fruit during his years at law school. It occurred to her that although she had brought each of her other children a gift of her own design when they bought their own homes, she had never crafted a gift for this house that Denis and Andrew had built together. It was an omission that shamed her even as she kissed her son good-night.

twenty-three

They drove west to Los Alamos the next morning, turning at the Pojoaque junction to reach the small town spread over the rainbow-hued narrow mesas of the Pajarito Plateau. Elaine reached for her sketchbook and her colored pencils, trying to capture the varied desert colors, the rise of the Jemez mountains and the graceful incline of the Rio Grande valley. She pondered how she could translate the different subtle pastel tones into defining glazes. As they approached the city she stared out at the charred earth and the skeletal trees, lonely survivors amidst the blackened stumps and parched shrubbery that had once covered a forest floor.

"What happened here?" she asked.

"A forest fire back in 2000," Andrew replied. "They

evacuated the town and acres and acres burned. Nature getting its own back, some said, providing its own destruction. The Indians thought it was some sort of retribution for the Manhattan Project research and the explosion of that first atomic bomb in their desert. They reasoned that the gods must have been angry to see that blinding cloud of light covering their peaceful plateau so they sent their own arrows of fire to remind the crazy gringo scientists of their power. I'm not an Indian but it sounds plausible enough to me."

Elaine wondered at the bitterness in his voice. Denis, who was driving, took one hand off the wheel and reached over to touch his partner's arm, a gesture of comfort for a pain she did not understand.

They stopped briefly at the Los Alamos National Laboratory and then continued on to the Bradbury Science Museum. Elaine stood between the two young men as they wandered from display to display, pausing to read the letter Albert Einstein had written in 1939 to President Roosevelt advocating research into uranium which could possibly become a useful source of energy.

"Just think of how the course of history might have been different if Hitler had not been so intent on exterminating Jews," she said. "Einstein would have remained in Austria and Germany might have developed the atomic bomb before we did."

"We?" Andrew asked dryly.

"The Allies. The United States," she replied, mystified by the sudden anger of his tone.

They walked on, passing through the Defense Gallery, staring at the 5-ton Little Boy bomb replicating the bomb dropped on Hiroshima. Elaine shivered.

"I remember when the war ended," she said. "Both endings. VE Day, VJ Day. Victory over Europe. Victory over Japan."

She had been a small girl, bewildered by her parents' tears on VE Day, their joy on VJ Day. She had danced with them on the broad Brooklyn street, blocked off for the celebration, beer flowing, trays piled high with food, a neighborhood band playing and American flags waved by laughing children. The war was over, the fighting and the killing done with. There would be no more gold stars hanging in curtained windows, hearts would not sink at the sight of a Western Union messenger ringing a doorbell. The concentration camps had been liberated, the memorial candles for the nameless dead had flickered out. Neil had told her how his mother had fainted on VE Day, how his father had spent hours on the phone talking to representatives of the Hebrew Immigrant Aid Society, spelling the name of his town over and over. "Yaroslavl. Y A R O S L A V L. Did any Jews from Yaroslavl survive the war?" Holding Genia in her arms she had learned the answer to his question decades later, from the sweet-faced elderly monk who had so sadly said, "There are no more Jews in Yaroslavl."

They left Los Alamos and drove to the nearby White Rock Overlook in Bandalier where they shared the picnic lunch Denis had packed, looking down at the wondrous panorama of the river valley, undulating its way toward Santa Fe.

"It's so peaceful here," she said, lifting her face toward the sun.

"Yes. It's a relief to get away from Los Alamos, from everything it stands for," Andrew replied, tossing a crust of bread to a chipmunk who scurried by.

"You mean the Manhattan Project, the atomic bomb?" Elaine asked.

"The Hiroshima bomb. The Nagasaki bomb. The ongoing development of nuclear weapons," he said.

"You don't believe that we should have dropped the bomb?" she asked.

"I wish it had never happened."

"But it brought the war to an end. If the bomb had not been dropped hundreds of thousands of Allied soldiers would have died," she protested but even as she spoke, she reminded herself that Denis and Andrew had been born decades after World War II. The war had not impacted on their lives. For them, those terrible years were a historical abstraction. The morality of the A-bomb decision was a question to be debated in cafés and dorm rooms, in seminars and auditoriums. They had the luxury of hindsight, of cool analysis and cooler judgment while her generation had lived in the very cauldron of terror.

"Why wasn't it dropped on Europe?" Andrew asked.

The question startled her.

"What Andrew means," Denis said slowly, "is that the

bomb was dropped on Japan because there were fewer qualms about a genocide against people of color."

"You can understand why that would anger me," Andrew said. "Considering my own ethnicity."

"I can understand that," she said, struggling to offer him an answer that would satisfy. "There was, of course, a great deal of discussion of that during my own university days. I think the general agreement was that the war in Europe had ended before the Manhattan Project detonated its first bomb in this very desert. I don't think that the skin color of the people of Hiroshima contributed to the decision to drop the bomb. And, with all due respect, Andrew, I don't think it was genocide. Jews of my generation understand exactly what genocide was."

Again she heard the monk's sorrowful voice.

"There are no more Jews in Yaroslavl." Nor were there any more Jews in the Polish villages where her own parents had been born or in the cities of Germany and the small towns of Hungary and Rumania, Czechoslovakia and Yugoslavia that had once been home to Sarah's Jerusalem neighbors.

"All right. Genocide is the wrong word," Andrew said. "But don't you agree that skin color must have played some role in the decision, that people of color, Asians, African-Americans, Caribes like myself, were a more comfortable choice for the powers that be?"

She hesitated and as she carefully weighed her words, Denis spoke, his tone, like Neil's, calm and thoughtful. Like his father he was a cautious dispenser of hard-earned insights.

"If Andrew and I were living in Hitler's Europe we would be doubly vulnerable. He because of his skin color, I because of my religion and both of us because of our homosexuality."

He put his arm about his partner's shoulder and pulled him close as though to protect him from the very vulnerability of which he spoke. This too they shared, these two sensitive and handsome young men, bonded by love, shadowed by fear.

Elaine looked at him. Only once before had Denis used the word *homosexual*—the night he had come home from Yale and told them what they had long suspected. She and Neil had listened quietly and had assured him that night of their total acceptance, of their respect for his honesty, their unstinting support, and, when he had left, closing the door softly behind him, Neil had wept and she had sat immobile with her hands in her lap, fearful that if she moved her heart would shatter into tear-shaped shards of sorrow.

But now, seated on the high mesa beneath a Ponderosa pine, she looked at her son and his chosen partner with a new perception, a clearer understanding. They had spoken, for the first time, the three of them, with a groping honesty, daring to disagree, daring to speak the truth. She puzzled over what had happened to alter the dynamic. Perhaps it was because she was alone and could focus entirely on Denis and Andrew. She no longer had to defer to Neil, gauge her words to his reactions. It was not a demand that Neil had ever made but rather one that she had thrust upon herself. And then again, it was possible that her conversations with her other children over the past several months had stripped the veneer from her own self-satisfied portrait of their family's past and revealed truths she had not recognized. It did not matter. What truly mattered was that they had, the three of them, arrived at a new place, achieved a new understanding.

She rested one hand on her son's arm, the other on Andrew's palm, drawing them closer to her so that, as the evening sun slowly faded, they sat together in a circlet of vanishing radiance.

They spoke very little as they climbed down the overlook and they drove back to Santa Fe cocooned in a comfortable and companionable silence.

Back at the house she worked for several hours in the studio, grateful to Andrew for so accurately lighting the drawing table. She drew a man and boy running down a shaded road—Neil and Denis—father and son—her sketch reflecting the fluidity of their movements, their shared grace. Her second drawing was of two young men holding hands and a man and woman, their own fingers intertwined, staring up at a star-spangled sky. Denis and Andrew, herself and Neil. It would be difficult to etch the stars onto the tile, she knew, but she would manage, perhaps using a microstylus. She had learned over these past months that she could manage many things.

It was Denis's suggestion that they spend a few days in Taos. "Andrew has a couple of photographs on exhibit at the

Taos Institute of the Arts and we want to see how they've been mounted to get some idea of how to best position his work in our gallery," he said over dinner after their return from Los Alamos.

"Your gallery?" she asked in surprise.

"Well, not ours exactly. Andrew and I formed a committee to raise money for a small clinic—an outpatient treatment center for AIDS victims and a walk-in for anyone without insurance. We added a small gallery which we hope will be a money-maker for the clinic. A percentage of anything sold will be invested for operating expenses. It's taken us a while but we've got it up and we're planning an official opening in a couple of weeks. Wine and cheese in the hospital lounge and an opening exhibit in the gallery. Andrew's contributed some photographs and I'm hanging some pen and ink sketches—the first work like that I've done since high school." He smiled ruefully. "Amateur stuff," he added.

"Damn good work," Andrew protested.

"I'm sure it is," Elaine said. She had all but forgotten that Denis had shown a talent for life drawing, had even accompanied Sarah to studio classes, and then, inexplicably and abruptly, had abandoned all such efforts, not even bothering to take his drawing pens and chalks with him when he left for college.

"Too busy," he had said then.

"Too frightened," she realized now. Too intimidated by the nude models, too confused by his own yearnings.

Her heart ached for all the pain her son had endured until

he had the courage to reveal the essence of his being to others and lay claim to his own life. Why had she not recognized the conflict that raged within him? And why had Neil, the trained psychoanalyst, been blind to his own son's agony? A brief irrational anger swept over her and swiftly subsided into a quiet abiding sorrow. She and Neil had not seen what they did not want to see. The answer was that simple.

"Where is this clinic?" she asked.

"Actually not far from here. A short walk along the mountain trail. Do you want to see it?"

She nodded.

They walked then along the narrow trail, shaded by aspens and cottonwood trees, Andrew and Denis clasping each other's hands, their footfalls silent upon the soft leaf-strewn earth. The clinic was a small white building, its straight lines and flat roof not unlike those of pueblo dwellings. The domed wide-windowed gallery was artfully constructed of *tierra blanca* adobe, the natural white adobe mud, across which evening shadows danced but which would take on an alabaster glow in the pale light of dawn.

"It's a lovely building," she said. "You should be proud."

"Phil's design. He's a good friend of ours, whose partner, Mel, died of AIDS. He really got the project going," Andrew said. "He arranged for a lot of the funding. Mel had a hard time getting treatment at the municipal hospitals and Phil didn't want that to happen to anyone else. And neither do we."

"I'd like to meet Phil," Elaine murmured. "He sounds like a remarkable man."

"You will. When we get back from Taos. He's a regular at Friday night services."

"Friday night services?" She did not mask the surprise in her voice.

"You'll see," Denis said and flashed her the grin that had charmed her all the days of his boyhood. "Hey, Mom, you didn't think I'd forgotten my bar mitzvah, did you?"

He laughed and Andrew chortled. Elaine, too, laughed and their mingled chorus of spontaneous jollity echoed down the tree-lined mountain trail.

On impulse she called Herb Glasser that evening, remembering that Peter and Lauren had taken the children skiing and he would be alone. She smiled to hear the pleasure in his voice and breathlessly, she told him about Andrew and Denis, about their trip to Los Alamos, their planned visit to Taos and about the snow-white clinic that stood alone on a mountain trail.

"New Mexico sounds wonderful. And it's not very far from Los Angeles," he said.

She heard the longing in his voice and understood that he was waiting for an invitation to join her or perhaps he thought that she might tell him that she planned to return to California. She remained silent, staring at herself in the mirror opposite the phone, pulling her fingers through the thick tangle of dark curls increasingly threaded with silver, practicing a smile that he could not see.

"I want you to be happy, Elaine," he said at last.

"I know."

How kind he was, this lonely man who was grandfather to her own grandchildren. She had been wrong to call him, wrong to incite a false and selfish intimacy. She acknowledged that she had wanted to hear his exclamation of delight when he heard her voice, the delight that reassured her that she was still a desirable woman, that her sensuality had survived Neil's death. She wondered if she was being unfaithful to Neil and smiled bitterly at the thought. Infidelity was the province of the living and Neil, her wonderful, beloved Neil, was dead.

"Good night, Herb," she said softly.

"Good night, Elaine."

She went out to the patio of the guesthouse and stared out at the bedroom that her son and Andrew shared. A small bedside lamp beamed through their wide window. She imagined them lying side by side in that room, painted a shade of blue that Andrew had told her was considered the color of good fortune in Jamaica. She was suffused with gratitude that they had found each other, that they were not alone. All her children then had reached safe harbors of love and intimacy. Perhaps, she and Neil had been skillful navigators after all.

"Neil."

Weighted by memory and desire, she spoke his name into the velvet darkness.

They set out for Taos early in the morning and made the drive northward as the sun slowly, almost reluctantly it seemed to her, rose in the cloudless cerulean sky. Elaine had heard of the beauty of Taos but she was unprepared for the sheer majesty of its aspect as they ascended through the Rio Grande Canyon rimmed by huge igneous rock cliffs on to the plateau. The sudden clarity of light seemed to purify and illuminate the colors of earth and sky and every leaf quivered with a vibrant verdancy. There was a sweet quietude, as though the peaceful small villages had succumbed to an enchanted sleep, sheltered by the tall blue mountains that shielded them from the turmoil of the modern world.

Denis stopped the car and Andrew took his camera and shot the panoramic view from several angles, now crouching, now mounting a small promontory, aiming his lens westward and then eastward.

"I must have tried to capture this view dozens of times," he said as he got back into the car. "But I just can't get it. I know what I want but it escapes me."

"I know exactly what you mean," she said, thinking of all the drawings she had discarded, of all the graceful shapes she had visualized in her mind's eye that had remained unrealized in the clay beneath her hands. Neil had spoken of a patient, a poet, who had complained that words whirled through his mind in delicate sequence but fled, like butterflies in flight, when he touched pen to paper.

"I think my mother understands you better than I do, Andrew," Denis said laughingly.

"That's good," Andrew responded. "It's time that I had a mother who understood me."

Elaine glanced at him. Andrew seldom spoke of his childhood, of the parents and siblings he had left behind in Ochos Rios, although she knew that he sent them money on a regular basis and he and Denis visited them each year during their vacations at the house Gordon Cummings had left him. Those visits, Denis had complained, were often awkward, laced with sudden silences.

"They don't understand him," Denis had said bitterly. "He lives in a different world."

"Of course he does."

Andrew was received deferentially in galleries throughout the States and Europe, he moved easily, indifferently among the famous and the affluent while his family remained mired in the poverty of the small Jamaican town, struggling against heat and hurricane. They were island dwellers who did not dream of what lay beyond their sea.

She had not added that children, inevitably, live in a world different from the one their parents had known. It had taken her long enough to understand that each generation, in turn, traveled through different emotional terrains, settled in alien landscapes, in distant states, in distant lands. The life she and Neil built in Westchester was at a far remove from Yaroslavl, where Neil had been born and the small Polish village from which her own parents had emigrated. Their comfortable suburban world bore no resemblance to the immigrant struggles of their parents. Her children's choices, their opportunities to make such choices, were at a variance with anything that either she or Neil had known. Neither Andrew, nor her sons and daughters, had abandoned their families. They had simply veered off in different directions, each of them choosing a road less traveled. The poet's words came flooding back in memory. *And that has made all the difference.* All the difference to them and now, at this turning point, all the difference to her.

She smiled and concentrated on the Taos scene as they passed through the Plaza and down the winding lanes lined with traditional adobe homes. They arrived at the bed-and-breakfast Denis and Andrew favored, which was, in fact, a small colony of charming casitas, run by Lily and Sean, a smiling rotund Irish couple who exuberantly embraced their guests.

"You're going to love Taos," Lily promised as she showed Elaine to her casita.

"I love it already," Elaine said, looking around her room with its kiva fireplace and knotty pine-paneled walls, the bed covered with a spread of Navajo weave. The Mexican tiles on the floor were bright islands of color. She took note of the various shades. She wondered if she could duplicate the Aztec red and the sapphire blue in a glaze for the small section of her mural that she hoped would capture the ambience of New Mexico.

She stood at the large window that faced the Taos mountains and overlooked the garden which was a riot of varicolored tulips and pansies, interspersed with gentle blue blossoms of flax. She smiled to see the hummingbirds that flitted through the chamisa bushes, briefly perching on a fragile branch before flying off to yet another arm of greenery.

All tension left her, all sadness, for the moment, was as-similated. She had arrived at a place of healing, an anneal-ing landscape. She could see herself working for long periods in this peaceful artists' town, now looking up at the majestic peaks of the Rocky Mountains, now looking down at the deep incline of the Rio Grande Gorge. She understood that Denis had an ulterior motive in taking her on this journey to Taos. He had wanted her to be inspired by this radiant vista, to lay claim to its dramatic colors and the wondrous shapes of its cliffs and mountains, its plateaus and vales. He was, in fact, extending an invitation of a kind, reminding her that her options were not limited, that she might find a creative home in a landscape of such rare and urgent beauty.

They spent the rest of that day at Taos Pueblo and she stared in wonderment at the two large buildings, rooms shaped of adobe mud and artfully piled one atop the other, in a pyramid of cubicles that assumed the shape of the Taos Mountain toward the northeast. It startled Denis that the one hundred residents of the Indian community managed without running water or electricity. Andrew, however, was unmoved.

"I grew up in a house without running water and elec-tricity," he said dismissively. "And my parents have only had it for the past five years."

"My parents also grew up without running water and electricity. My mother often told me how frightened she was when she first heard a toilet flush," Elaine recalled.

"We have that much in common." Andrew flashed her a grin and she smiled back.

"Oh, we have much more than that in common," she assured him as Denis, walking between them, linked arms with them and nodded.

"Of course you do," he agreed. "You're both artists and you both love me."

"Don't be so sure," Andrew teased and ran off, with Denis in playful pursuit.

A group of Indians watched the two dark-haired young men race downhill through ribs of sunlight. At the bottom of the hill, their snow-white T-shirts sweat-drenched, their faces damp, they embraced and laughed up at Elaine. She looked hard at them and closed her eyes as though she would commit to memory that burnished moment of their shared happiness.

As their days in Taos passed, her feelings for the town intensified. She wakened early and relished eating a solitary breakfast on the Plaza while she watched the town slowly come to life. Shops were opened, galleries were unshuttered, delivery vans moved slowly down the winding roads. She looked up at the morning sky and inhaled the scent of the dry sweet air. It surprised her that eating alone no longer saddened her, that solitude had ceased to be painful.

They spent a day driving the enchanted circle, through Red River, Eagle Nest and Angel Fire, charmed by the old Hispanic villages of Arroyo Honda and Questa, stunned by the beauty of Moreno Valley and the surrounding majestic mountain peaks. It was clear to her that her son and Andrew loved this expansive landscape because it was here that the glory of nature triumphed over trivial human aspirations and prejudices.

She went with them to the Art Museum where a small exhibit of Andrew's photographs had been mounted. She marveled at the tenderness with which he had photo-graphed the barefoot Indian children of Taos Pueblo.

"He really caught them, didn't he?" the sad-looking gaunt man standing beside her said as she studied a collage of por-traits, the lined and wrinkled faces of the older Indians a stark contrast to the bright eyes and smooth skins of the children. Andrew's camera had captured the impact of the passing years on youth and innocence, the assault of life on face and figure.

"They are," she agreed, "sad and wonderful." As she spoke Andrew and Denis approached.

"Phil, we didn't know you were in Taos," Andrew said excitedly, draping his arm over the man's shoulder. "I see you've already met Denis's mother, or have you? In any case Phil London, this is Elaine Gordon. Denis and I wanted her to see Taos. Can you have dinner with us? We can talk about the exhibits for the opening of the gallery."

"Sorry. I just came up for a couple of hours to deliver some new paintings to the gallery. It's the first time I've been out of the city since Mel…" Phil London's face twisted in a paroxysm of sudden grief and his voice trailed off.

Elaine felt a surge of sympathy. She recognized the symptoms of raw sorrow, the devastation of a loss not yet assimilated.

"I have to get back to my studio," he continued, struggling for composure. "You guys decide on your own about the exhibit. I appreciate it, I really do. And I saw your drawings, Denis. They're good, really good. You should think about giving up the law."

Denis shrugged.

"I don't think that's a real option," he said. "But thanks. We'll see you at services Friday night?"

"I hope so. It was good to meet you, Elaine."

He held his hand out to her, his paint-scarred fingers thin as stalks, blue veins rising from the translucent pallor of his slender wrists.

Her heart called out to him.

I know, she wanted to say. *I know what it is to lose a lover. I know what it is to watch a life ended, to walk alone through empty rooms. But it will get better, the sadness will lift.* Her own sadness was slowly dissipating. Slowly, very slowly, she was restored to herself.

She said nothing and watched him disappear through the shadowed archway into the glaring sunlight.

Only then did she turn inquiringly to Denis.

"He's a wonderful painter," he said. "And a wonderful man. His partner Mel Abrams, who was a sculptor, died a couple of months ago. He was a good friend of ours and the gallery at the clinic is dedicated to Mel. Phil is just lost without him. I can understand that."

He reached for Andrew's hand, lowered his head. Elaine saw that Andrew's eyes were closed, his narrow-featured face frozen into a mask of grief and fear.

"I don't know what I would do if I ever lost Andrew," Denis said.

His words came in a whisper, and Elaine looking down at their clasped hands, remembered that Neil had died with his hand resting on her own.

"People survive," she said. "You would learn to go on. The morning sun comes up. The evening sun goes down."

She turned again to Andrew's collage and stood for a very long time staring up at a photograph of an elderly couple seated beneath a piñon tree, their life-worn skin dappled by the low-hanging leaves.

On their last afternoon in Taos, while Denis and Andrew met with an artist who was contributing a large painting to the clinic gallery, she wandered through galleries, leisurely wending her way through the Navajo exhibits in historic homes and in adobe houses. She bought turquoise jewelry for Sarah and Leora, and a necklace for Ruth's daughter Michal who was marrying her Gideon in a few weeks' time.

"What will come first—my baby or Michal's wedding?" Sarah had written. "And you will miss them both."

Elaine had discerned the teasing accusation in her daughter's words and carefully placed the letter in the bottom of her work box.

At yet another gallery she bought filigreed silver earrings for Lauren and Lisa and sets of kachina dolls for Renée and Genia.

"Would you like to see some ceramics?" the proprietor

asked her. "I have some interesting new work. And please take my card. I'm Jane Cunningham and this is my gallery."

"It's a beautiful gallery," Elaine said and she followed Jane Cunningham to a far corner of the huge room. There, on a pale wooden shelf, were the golden glazed bookends and a slender vase of silver-stippled purple she herself had crafted for Renee Evers in California.

"Elaine Gordon's work," the gallery owner said proudly. "I managed to buy just these two pieces from a gallery in L.A. Do you like them?"

Elaine smiled.

"Actually," she said, "I'm Elaine Gordon."

Jane Cunningham flushed with astonishment and pleasure.

"Fantastic," she said, "I love your pieces. Are you working in Taos now? Would you have any work to show me?"

"I'm just here on a visit," Elaine explained. "My son lives in Santa Fe and I'm staying with him for a few weeks. It's not a working vacation but I've fallen in love with the land-scape—the blending of colors, the rock formations. It's a haven of inspiration for a ceramicist."

"Then you should really think about working here. Taos is a great place to live. There's terrific studio space, access to cutting-edge kilns. And a ready market. Really. Here. Please take my card. Think about it and get in touch. I'll help in any way I can. It's a privilege to have met you, Elaine Gordon."

A customer approached her and she hurried off.

Elaine studied her card and placed it carefully in her wallet. Yes, she thought, as she left the gallery and continued her walk down Paseo de Pueblo Sur, Taos would be a wonderful town in which to live and work. She glanced at her watch. She was late. Denis and Andrew would be waiting for her and the thought of their loving impatience filled her with pleasure.

twenty-four

They returned to Santa Fe and Denis and Andrew were immediately caught up in their demanding work schedules. As the days of her visit drifted into weeks, they established a comfortable routine. They shared cooking and food shopping, adjusted their schedules to accommodate each other. Occasionally, on a Sunday morning, Andrew went to church. Always, on Friday evenings, a Sabbath service was held on their patio. Each evening Denis and Andrew went running and once a week they went to Vanessie's piano bar. Elaine was often awake when they returned home and she smiled to hear them humming snatches of Gershwin or softly singing a Billy Joel ballad.

Each evening Elaine walked alone up the mountain path and once a week she and Denis had lunch together in town. She was grateful for those hours of ease because she knew that her son had little time to spare.

He left for his office or for a courtroom appearance early each morning. His caseload was heavy, his work varied. He represented large commercial interests but he also was an advocate for native Americans. He had a reputation among the Pueblo, Navajo and Apache tribes for fairness and they turned to him to resolve threatening legal issues.

Elaine waited in his reception area one afternoon, seated opposite two Navajo men, each of them clutching a worn envelope crammed with documents. She watched as Denis escorted three well-dressed corporate executives out of his conference room, smiled apologetically at her and invited the Navajo men to enter.

"I'm sorry you had to wait, Mom," he said, when they at last sat over lunch in the garden café he favored. "But these meetings were important. A technological company wants to set up an information technology center in Santa Fe and they have their eye on some land owned by the Navajo. They want me to represent them."

"But you do so much work with the Navajo. Won't that be a conflict of interest?" Elaine asked.

"I've made it a merging of interest, actually. I've gotten them to agree to set up a training program for the Navajo and in return the tribe will lease the land to them. A good balance. Their fee offsets my pro bono work for the tribe."

She smiled, proud of his competence, of his sense of justice. Neil's legacy, clinic work balanced with private practice.

"A good balance for me," he had said more than once and his words had not been lost on Denis who spoke them now without self-consciousness.

"Your father would be proud of you," she said to Denis. "He would be proud of all of you. As I am."

She reached across the table, took her son's hand in his own and felt the answering pressure of his touch.

"I hope Andrew won't be home too late tonight," Denis said. "He's really involved in this project."

Andrew had been commissioned to do a series of photographs for a brochure being prepared by the New Mexico Tourist Bureau. He was often away, scouting out new locations, taking action shots and now and again gently encouraging a shopkeeper or a school child to pose for a candid portrait.

"I want people to see this state as it is," he said as he explained the assignment to Elaine and showed her his contact sheets. "The faces of the people, the mountains and the plateaus, the majesty of it all. That's what Gordon Cummings did for Jamaica."

He glanced at the action photo of himself as a skinny, barefoot boy that Gordon had taken all those years ago in the Ochos Rios marketplace. Denis had framed it and hung it above their kiva fireplace. "But damn it, although I can see what I want in my mind's eye I simply can't get it on film. I think I have it and then the developed film proves me wrong," he continued.

"I know just how you feel," she commiserated.

She herself was spending long hours at the drawing

board, executing and discarding design after design for the mural until finally deciding on those that captured the elusive visual image that chronicled Neil's relationship with Denis. *Father and son reading beside a fire. Father and son hiking a mountain path. She and Neil separated by a shadow from Denis and Neil, although the four of them stood in a circlet of sunlight.*

The shadow, she realized, as she wire-brushed it onto the yielding clay, symbolized their shared inability to honestly confront the truth of Denis's life in all its joy and in all its pain. They had, instead, protected each other, sealed themselves into a false acquiescence rather than the loving, wholehearted acceptance of their last-born child that now invigorated her.

Denis had never questioned them but she knew that he had of course sensed their evasiveness, and although they had heard the pain in his voice and seen the hurt in his eyes they had said nothing, not to each other and not to him. But the tiles in her mural would not dissimulate. Neil would have wanted the visual chronicle of his life, of their family's life, to be honest. He would have approved of that delicate shadow that did not, after all, cancel out the pool of light in which they stood.

She etched each concept onto her carefully crafted tiles, and brought them to the ceramic studio where she had rented space. She mixed her glazes, waited breathlessly as each small piece was fired, the enamel baked to the precise shining gloss she hoped for. Sometimes it worked, sometimes it didn't, and she willed herself to surmount disappointment and begin again.

She went with Andrew on a day trip to Santa Clara
where he took photograph after photograph of the beautiful Black Mesa. It was there that she bought a beautiful
carafe crafted of the unique black-on-black pottery of the
region. The potter wrapped it in newspapers and Elaine
put the awkward bundle in her newly purchased straw
basket as she and Andrew walked back to their car.
Suddenly two muscular motorcyclists, steel staples glinting
on their black leather vests, one of them with a shaven head
and the other with greasy blond hair falling to his shoulders, swerved down the narrow street, barely avoiding two
barefoot Indian children. The blond cyclist careened so
close to Elaine that the basket was knocked from her hand.

"Hey, watch where you're going," Andrew called angrily
and they veered back toward him, their revved motors
racketing in staccato bursts.

"You watch where you're going and what you're doing,
Sambo. Faggot," the bald cyclist shouted and they rode off
in a cloud of dust, shaking their fists threateningly, their
harsh laughter mingling with the frightened sobs of the
children.

"Bastards, homophobic bastards," Andrew muttered as
he picked up the basket.

Elaine turned to the frightened children.

"Please," she said. "Don't cry."

She wiped their tears and walked them over to a kiosk
where she bought each of them a chocolate bar. Only
when they were in the car on their way back to Santa Fe
did she look into the basket. The carafe was not broken

but all her pleasure in it was gone. Her heart beat rapidly and she looked at Andrew who drove too quickly, his fine-featured face a mask of misery.

"Who were they?" she asked.

"Homophobic hatemongers," he said. "We have our own lunatic fringe in Santa Fe. They're not worth worrying about. But please, Elaine, don't tell Denis about it."

She nodded. She would be complicit with her son's partner. She could not protect Denis from danger but she could shield him from fear.

She left the house that evening, as she always did, at the twilight hour. She would not allow that brush with ugliness in Santa Clara to deter her from the walk she took most evenings. She wanted to banish the memory of the motor-cyclists, to submerge herself in silence and beauty. How naive she had been to observe only the peace of the life Denis and Andrew shared and never to recognize the lurking danger. She had not wanted to recognize their vulnerability just as she had not wanted to acknowledge the very real danger that confronted Sarah's family in Israel. Now, at last, she confronted both the danger and the vulnerability.

She followed the narrow trail that led to the clinic, now stooping to pluck up an oddly shaped stone or a slender cottonwood twig, now glancing up at the slowly darkening sky across which a crescent of moon floated while glittering constellations, reluctant actors on that vast celestial stage, slowly appeared. Slowly, with the onset of evening, the tensions of the day eased.

Denis and Andrew had seldom joined her on those nocturnal strolls. They sensed her need for solitude, for the precious privacy of melancholy, and she was grateful for their tacit understanding. There was so much she had to think about. She walked slowly, her steps weighted by decisions untaken and as she neared the clinic, a flock of wild geese scissored their way southward through the cobalt-colored sky. She stared up at them, startled by their beauty, their symmetry, their certainty of destination, their purposeful infallible radar. She herself was still without direction or anchor.

When she returned from her walk, Andrew suggested that Denis show her the drawings he planned to exhibit at the gallery opening. He hesitated briefly and then spread the contents of his worn black leather portfolio across the table. She studied her son's work and admired the fluency and tenderness with which he captured moments of intimacy. She stared for a long time at a drawing of two men reading before a blazing fire and thought of her own etching of Andrew and Denis in the garden. Her heart turned at his rendition of a bearded man seated at the bedside of an emaciated invalid. Phil and Mel, she guessed and swiftly shifted her gaze to the drawing of a quartet of men and women, prayer books in hand, eyes lifted skyward, candles blazing on a simple wooden table.

She marveled at how subtly Denis had captured the mood of the Friday night services held each week on his patio, the coming together of men and women who forged their own Sabbath celebration, reading and singing from the prayer book of their own compilation. They sang the hymn that welcomed the day of rest, the same hymn Moshe intoned each Friday evening as Sarah stood beside him in their Jerusalem home, and they swayed to a chant taught to them by a Navajo shaman. At one service Elaine had listened to a slender blond woman dressed in white play a haunting Cabbalistic tune on her flute and at another she had watched two graceful young men dance toward each other, their hands clapping in rhythmic devotion. And at the conclusion of each service she had stood with sad-eyed Phil and together they had intoned the *Kaddish*. Her husband, Neil, and Phil's partner, Mel, were remembered and mourned in this small congregation gathered beneath a canopy of stars. She had wondered briefly if Sarah and Moshe would sanction that prayer offered in such an unorthodox setting and decided that probably they would and the thought comforted her. She was glad that Denis had included that tender pen-and-ink drawing of the four worshippers among the work he planned to exhibit.

The largest and most complex drawing, the only one executed in charcoal, was of a family gathered around a table. Her own family, Elaine realized and she recognized herself in Denis's fluid drawing of the woman seated at one end of the table, her mass of unruly dark curls so closely threaded with silver, her large long-lashed eyes darkened with grief. He had sketched her holding a ladle suspended over an oval-shaped tureen that she herself had made. Neil's seat, at the head of the table, was empty. Easily she picked out Sarah and Lisa seated side by side, Peter holding a decanter and, at a slight remove, Denis himself, with the family yet subtly apart from them.

As in her own etching, barely perceptible charcoal strokes, scant and gentle brushings, darkened the space between each seat, wispy shadows of secret hurts and resentments separating each from the other. But those shadows, so tenderly drawn (just as she had moved her own stylus with a controlled lightness of touch) did not negate the togetherness of the family, newly bereft and newly aware of their need for each other.

Denis had caught the mood of that dinner she had prepared with such manic energy, the meal they had shared after the seven days of mourning. She remembered how she had concentrated on her cooking, welcoming the fragrance of the roasting meat. Her face had been flushed as she carried the meal to the table, the hot food that would do battle with the chill of death and fill the void of irrevocable loss.

She saw that in his drawing all the bowls on the table were empty. Denis had held his charcoal stick aloft and refrained from filling them. He understood his siblings' needs, their sense of deprivation that matched his own. He had sketched them as they awaited her maternal distribution of nurturing and nourishment. And they awaited it still, all these months later.

She stared down at the drawing, and thought of her sons and daughters, remembering the children they had been, thinking of the adults they had become. Sarah and Lisa,

Peter and Denis. Their names and faces, the homes they had built, the lives they had invited her into, danced through her mind; their love filled her heart. She thought to speak but words eluded her.

"You don't like the drawings?" Denis asked and she realized that her long silence had unnerved him.

"But I like them very much," she protested. "I'll help you mat them."

He smiled in relief and Andrew nodded, the comforting I-told-you-so shake of the head lovers offer each other.

They worked together on the mats over the next several days and Elaine built simple frames of pale wood. A week before the opening they brought them to the gallery and hung them on the whitewashed wall across from Andrew's black-framed serial photographs of the trees of New Mexico.

"They offset each other wonderfully," Elaine said.

"As well they should."

Andrew took Denis's hand and they looked at each other, proud of their work, content in their love.

The next day Elaine returned to Taos and visited Jane Cunningham's gallery. She was relieved to see that both the golden glazed bookends and the slender vase she had crafted so carefully were still on display. She smiled at Jane who hurried to her side.

"Don't think that there hasn't been interest, lots of interest, in those pieces," Jane assured her. "But I've held on to them. Partly because I think they'll appreciate and partly because I just love having them here."

Elaine smiled.

"I'm flattered," she said. "But Jane, if you'll let me buy them from you, I promise to let you have some other pieces that I think you'll like as well or even better. I'm working with new colors, desert hues. Perfect for your gallery. I should have them ready in a few weeks but I need these pieces now. I want to exhibit them next week at the opening of the gallery that will be part of a clinic that my son and his friends have underwritten."

Reluctantly then, Jane Cunningham packed up the vase and the bookends.

"I'll be waiting for your new work," she said, as Elaine left. "I told you that New Mexico would work its magic on you."

"And it has," Elaine agreed.

She drove swiftly back to Santa Fe. She had arranged to meet Denis at his office for a late lunch. "Our weekly date," Denis called it teasingly, always reserving a table at a small garden restaurant where they watched varicolored hummingbirds flutter through blazing flowerbeds as they waited for their meal and spoke softly, trading memories, making plans. The past and the future melded as they sat in the sunlit garden, Denis now recalling a hike he had taken with Neil, then speaking of a reunion. "All of us," he had said. "Moshe and Sarah, Peter and Lauren, all the kids, Lisa and David and Genia, you and me and Andrew."

"Where?" she had asked.

"It doesn't matter. Here. Jerusalem. California. New York. As long as we're all together. Dad would have liked that."

"Yes. He would have."

Elaine marveled at how effortlessly they spoke of Neil, his name, the memory of his likes and dislikes, falling from their lips with gentle ease. Time was doing its work.

She had thought, during the drive from Taos, that she would speak to Denis during lunch about her decision to leave New Mexico after the opening of the clinic and the gallery. The tiles she had worked on were fired, the enamel baked to a subtle glow that would easily complement those she had completed in Jerusalem and Encino and those she had designed during her stay in Moscow. It was time to unite them into a single cohesive unit, into the mural she had envisioned. Neil's life, Neil's legacy, an enduring visual memorial, ready to be installed.

She would complete the ceramics she had promised to Jane Cunningham and then she would return east and assemble the tiles in her own studio. She imagined the texture of the tiles against her fingers, the scent of the wood she planned to use for the frame, the sapphire color of the ink she would use for the last remaining tile, the micography she would practice and perfect. She wondered if she should share her idea for that micography with Denis as she mounted the stairway to his office. Suddenly she heard a door slam and the sound of running steps. Instinctively, she thrust herself back against the wall, barely avoiding the man who hurtled past her, his narrow face contorted in a mask of fury, his rasping voice spewing epithets of hatred down the narrow passage.

"Faggot. Faggot Jew! Ambulance chaser! Bastard."

She smelled his bilious breath and, with sinking heart, recognized both his words and the harshness of their utterance. His greasy blond hair, caught up in a ponytail, whipped across his black leather jacket. He was the same cyclist who had sideswiped past her in Santa Clara, who had hurled abuse at Andrew.

Breathless and frightened, she remained perfectly still until he ran from the building, leaving the door open so that she heard the roar of his motorcycle as he drove away.

"Mom, Mom, are you there? Are you all right?"

Denis, his brow furrowed, rushed toward her.

"I'm fine," she assured him as they went into his office. "But what was that about?"

"The guy's an idiot. A retard. He got involved in an accident and he wanted me to represent him. I refused. Not my kind of case and not my kind of client. I was ready to refer him to someone who does that kind of work when he got abusive. I threatened to call the cops and he bolted out of here. I guess you know the rest." Denis shook his head, shrugged into his jacket. "Let's go. He's not going to ruin our lunch."

"Of course not," she agreed, struggling to keep her voice light but knowing that their lunch was already ruined.

"And please don't tell Andrew what you heard," he added.

"I won't," she agreed and realized that she had promised as much to Andrew.

She wondered how many secrets they could keep from

each other, Denis protecting Andrew, Andrew protecting Denis, before those protective silences darkened into a lingering shadow. Her own life, and Neil's, too, she realized now, had been shadowed by the words their children left unsaid, the feelings they left unshared. Their joy and involvement had been diminished because their sons and daughters had protected them from their own sorrows. They had feared to shatter the self-contained tranquility of a parental marriage so tightly woven that it left no room for interstices. That fear had imploded, destroying ease and honesty. They could have helped. They would have wanted to help.

Elaine thought of Lisa bleeding in a Roman clinic, of Sarah wandering rootless through the streets of Jerusalem, of Peter in desperate search of intimacy, of Denis who had refrained from speaking of his deepest yearnings. Their revelations had been late in coming but she was grateful that they had come at all. And she was grateful, too, that her own role had shifted, that she had accepted the challenge of their needs, abandoned all passivity. Her words and actions impacted on their lives. They were, all of them, in a new time, at a new place.

She looked at her son and thought to warn him of the dangers of concealment but she remained silent. There were lessons that could not be taught. Denis, who understood the subtlety of a charcoal brush stroke, the beauty of scudding clouds and gentle touch, would acquire that knowledge in his own time.

She took his arm and together they walked through the

brilliant sunlit streets to the small garden restaurant where they sat beneath a network of vigas, the long beams garlanded with wreaths of crimson chili peppers. Their lunch was not ruined. They sipped their margaritas, dipped tortillas warm from the oven into earthenware bowls of guacamole, and spoke, without constraint, of Neil, of the music that he had loved, of his wry humor that had so often ignited their family's laughter, trading memories, sharing love.

"Neil."

"Dad."

Their glasses clinked in tender toast as a flame-colored oriole perched patiently on the low-hanging branch of a pepper tree, took wing and soared through the cloudless sky.

twenty-five

That night Elaine carried the bookends and the vase up the mountain trail. She had already decided to position them on a low shelf just beneath Denis's drawings and she paused beside an overgrowth of wild roses, thinking that the pale pink blossoms would add just the right color. She climbed a small boulder to reach a spray of flowers and turning slightly, she caught sight of the clinic. Her heart stopped.

Tongues of golden flame licked at the darkened windows and clouds of smoke soared skyward. The gallery area was on fire.

She whipped out her cell phone and breathlessly punched in 911. She shouted into the phone, heard the strange rasping of her voice, her terror fraying each word.

"Fire! At the clinic on Jones Trail. Fire!"

She heard her words repeated and repeated yet again as emergency services were alerted.

"Jones Trail! Just kilometers from the new clinic."

The dispatcher's voice was calm, controlled.

"I've got that, ma'am. Trucks are on their way. Stay away from the flames, ma'am. That wood is full of dry piñon and cottonwood. Go back, far back."

But she tossed her phone away and sprinted forward, her own package discarded on a fallen log. The paintings and sculptures for the opening exhibit had not yet been installed but Denis's drawings and Andrew's photographs hung on the pristine walls. There were negatives for the photographs but if the drawings were burned they were forever lost. She would not let that happen. She could not let that happen. She ran without regard for trail or path, her breath coming in harsh gasps. She felt the wind whip across her face, heard the brittle chorus of trembling branches and then the sudden roar of a powerful engine. She pressed herself against a tree as a motorcycle careened past her, two men riding in tandem, wildly shouting into the night. A beer bottle was tossed against a tree. She recognized their voices, recognized the lank blond hair of the cyclist who swerved crazily and accelerated, his wheels scattering stones and branches in harsh cacophony.

She rushed on, ignoring the encroaching heat. She followed the oddly melodic sound of slowly shattering glass, her face damp with sweat and tears, her arms and legs scratched by thorns and nettles, until at last she reached the building.

The door, always so carefully locked, was ajar, and she plunged into that flame-lit darkness and struggled toward the farthest wall of the gallery, her way lit by fingers of fire. Frantically, she unhooked the drawings, ignoring the wire that sliced into her fingers, hugging them to her body. One, two, three, four. Yes, she had them all. She bolted through the door into a night that was suddenly alive with the lights that blazed from the fire truck, the shrilling of sirens and the blaring of voices.

"Over here! There's a water point!"

"Aim the damn hose to the left!"

Luminous whips of water flogged the flames and she thrust herself out of their path, her throat aching, her breath coming in painful gasps.

"Hey, there's a woman. Someone help her."

Booted feet ran toward her and a man in a rubber coat eased the framed drawings from her grasp. Strong hands carried her away from the heat and laid her gently on the ground. She looked up and saw Denis and Andrew kneeling beside her. Denis's face was pale and Andrew's eyes were wet with tears.

"Mom, what were you thinking?"

"Your drawings. I had to save your drawings," she said.

"Damn my drawings. You could have been killed."

He lifted her to her feet then and with Andrew holding one arm and Denis the other, they walked very slowly down the trail, rutted now by the vicious impact of the motorcycle tracks. They paused to retrieve the small carton that contained her own ceramics, wondrously intact, their glazes shining into the night.

"I wanted to display them at the gallery opening," Elaine explained, sliding her fingers across the golden surface of the bookends, so carefully fired to a radiant smoothness.

"If there is an opening," Andrew said wearily. "Those bastards did a pretty good job on us."

"There will be an opening." Denis's voice was resolute. "They're not going to win."

The timbre of his voice, his calm certainty, were his father's legacy. Elaine leaned heavily against her son, taking comfort from his strength and his support, as she looked up at the starlit sky. She was widowed but she was not bereft. She held precious memory close, thrilled to the sound of a remembered cadence in Denis's voice, moved by the agate blue of her husband's eyes in a grandchild's gentle gaze. She understood that grief diminished but love endured.

There was an opening, held on schedule in a building bathed in softly filtered light. The fire had been brought under control so quickly that the damage was minimal. Windows had been replaced and crews of volunteers had whitewashed the stucco walls, erasing all traces of smoke. A team of Navajo carpenters had arrived without notice and installed new beams, laid a slate patio. Andrew worked through the night developing a new set of prints and his photographs and Denis's drawings were carefully repositioned, Elaine's ceramics were placed just as she had envisioned them, a spray of pink wild roses offsetting the purple of the slender silver-flecked vase. Because the evening was cool, a small fire burned in the kiva fireplace, dancing flames that warmed and did not destroy.

The room was crowded with friends and well-wishers. A group of Native American weavers presented Denis with a rug of desert hues, the sage green of cacti, the ochre of sand, the sapphire blue of a cloudless sky and the vivid Aztec red. He and Andrew spread it across the floor of the gallery and two small girls removed their shoes and danced from color to color as their father played his guitar. The guests looked at them, looked at the paintings and photographs, at the handicrafts set on low tables, sipped their wine and smiled happily. Small red dots began to appear on object after object, indicating that they had been sold.

Elaine, regal in a dress of black wool offset by a heavy copper necklace of Pueblo design, her dark hair braided into a single long plait, wandered through the room, smiling at her son's friends, greeting acquaintances, answering questions about her own work. Jane Cunningham, who had come from Taos with two other gallery owners, paused to congratulate her and to remind her of her promise.

"I haven't forgotten," Elaine assured her. "The new pieces will be ready and delivered to your gallery before I leave Santa Fe."

Her own words surprised her. Her decision had come

unbidden but she knew with instinctive certainty that it was time for her to return east, to take up the life she had left behind and to plan for a future that would be hers alone.

"Great," Jane Cunningham said. "And remember. My offer still stands."

"I'll remember," Elaine promised as Jane drifted across the room to speak with Phil London who, for the first time since Elaine's initial meeting with him in Taos, seemed relieved of his burden of grief and loss. It might well be, she thought, that this clinic, dedicated to the memory of the man who had been his companion for so long, validated a life so sadly and painfully ended. Elaine closed her eyes and thought of her mural, the mosaic of memory she would soon set in place tile by tile. She envisioned its completion and thought of how she might word the plaque that described it so that his name would endure and the gift of his life might be forever remembered.

"Elaine." A man's voice, soft and tentative, a man's hand gentle upon her shoulder.

Startled, she opened her eyes and turned. Herb Glasser smiled down at her, took her hand and bent to kiss her cheek.

"Surprised?" he asked.

"Astonished."

"As I told you on the phone," he said, "New Mexico is not all that far from California. Peter told me about the gallery opening. He and Lauren planned to fly out here just for the evening to surprise Denis and Andrew. So I thought that I'd tag along and surprise you."

"Well, you succeeded," she said and wondered if he had noticed how the color had rushed to her cheeks and how she trembled ever so slightly at the touch of his hand.

Her sons rushed toward her, Lauren and Andrew trailing behind them, smiling to see the two brothers and their mother embrace, their faces bright with joy, their voices light with laughter, all lingering shadows swept away.

Later that evening, after Andrew and Denis and Lauren and Peter had left for dinner in the city, she and Herb sat on the patio. They stared up at the starlit sky.

"Cassiopeia," he said softly. "Perseus. Andromeda. Cepheus."

She smiled.

"Neil, my husband. He, too, loved looking at the stars, repeating the names of the constellations."

"We have a lot in common then. Your Neil and myself."

"You do."

She lifted her hand to his face, touched the softness of his lips, the creping skin of his cheeks, the thickness of his silvered eyebrows. He moved closer to her, lifted her thick braid, slid it across his neck, allowed it to fall gently onto her breast as his lips brushed her mouth, as their arms entwined and their hearts beat in arrhythmic unison.

"Elaine." Her name upon his lips was a plea.

Gently, slowly, she pulled away.

"Herb."

His name, so sadly whispered, fell softly into the star-spangled darkness.

"I understand," he said although he was not clear on what it was he understood. He wanted only to ease her unspoken sadness, to accept whatever tenderness she might offer him.

"Soon," she said, and from that single word he took hope and was content to remain on the patio, her hand encased in his as, mysteriously, a light rain began to fall.

One week later, she packed three modular bowls in the unique blues and pinks of a desert sunset and delivered them to Jane Cunningham's Taos gallery. The bookends and the vase remained in Denis and Andrew's living room, house gifts long delayed. They each kissed her as she set them in place. The next day they drove her to Albuquerque and, as she boarded the plane, she turned and waved to them. They stood side by side, Andrew's arm draped protectively over Denis's shoulder. She had photographed them in just that pose on the day of their visit to Los Alamos. Andrew had developed that film and given her an enlarged print. She would have it framed in silver, she decided, and thought that she would position it amid the wedding pictures of her other children. Almost at once she changed her mind. She would place it on the bookshelf next to the fading sepia wedding portraits of her parents and Neil's, each stamped with the imprint of vanished studios in a land and a life abandoned.

twenty-six

Elaine arrived home from Santa Fe as winter slowly surrendered its frigid edge and the early winds of spring rattled the still sere branches of the slender maple just beyond the wide window of her studio. She glanced up at the tree as she worked, noting the hesitant sprouting of the bright green leaves, still curled into their protective furls. She watched them each morning, marveling at how they grew day by day until at last, she looked up from the completed etching of the very last tile of the mosaic and saw that they were in full foliage, casting a long shadow across the lawn. Neil had planted that tree on the day her studio was completed, and she had captured it with her stylus, carefully mingling emerald and sap green for its tentative leafage. She smiled and slid the tile into the oven. It would be the crown of the mosaic, combining as it did Neil's optimism and his legacy. He had bought a sapling but he had envisioned a tree. He had wanted her to look out at its beauty as she worked at her drawing table and so he had planted it within easy view. He had wanted his children and grandchildren to run and laugh in its shade. He had set it into the ground with great tenderness and she had watched his hands mold the earth that blanketed its roots. Neil's hands, so slender and graceful at work in the garden, Neil's hand so slender and graceful, resting in her own, as he died his too-swift death.

She sat quietly, adrift in memory, until the timer rang and she opened the oven door and slid the tile onto the flat wooden spatula. She had not erred. The glaze shimmered, the verdant leaves seemed to waft in a gentle wind. The mosaic was complete. All that remained was the grouting. *Tomorrow,* she thought. She could begin the grouting tomorrow but now there were calls to be made. To Sarah in Israel. To Peter in California. To Lisa in Philadelphia. To Denis in New Mexico. It was important that they all be together when she told them of her decision.

She calculated the time differences. She would call Sarah in the morning. But later that evening she would call Peter and Denis. She could reach Lisa at once and that, perhaps would be the easiest call to make. Lisa would ask discreet questions, perhaps make discreet suggestions. She was half prepared for Elaine's choice but then, Elaine thought, "I'm only half prepared for it myself."

She thought of her children's reactions and braced

herself for their questions, their resistance to her request that they all assemble in Westchester for the unveiling of the mosaic. There would be excuses, protests. Their children's schedules, the pressure of their work, logistic difficulties. She anticipated their objections, summoned her own gentle arguments and sat down at the phone, a gin-and-tonic in hand, although the glass remained full as she spoke to Lisa. She did not take even a sip when she spoke first to Denis and then to Peter. In the morning, after her conversation with Sarah, she carried it into the kitchen and poured it into the sink before returning to her studio to begin the grouting, still surprised by her children's swift quiescence, the unanimity of their response. They had agreed at once to the date she had set, to the tentative ceremony she proposed.

"Of course we want to be there when you unveil that mosaic," each of them had said in turn. "June is fine," they each assured her. School would be over, summer not yet begun. It gave them enough time to arrange their schedules, to make plans. No problem.

She sighed in relief. Her apprehension had been premature. She had, she observed to herself ruefully as she mixed the grout, once more misjudged her sons and daughters. She had learned a great deal since Neil's death but clearly not enough.

The brothers and sisters talked to each other, placing their calls late in the evening when children were sleeping. They spoke in the cadences of their shared childhoods,

their voices confident and then uncertain, briefly strident
with half-remembered rivalries and then gentler as they
realized that all sibling competitions were over. They were
grown men and women. Their father was dead and their
mother, they each knew, was about to tell them how she
intended to live out the rest of her life.

"She changed so much this year," Lisa said to Sarah,
glancing at the clock.

It was twilight in Israel where her Sarah was nursing
Noam. She smiled down at her son, delighting anew in his
name…*Noam* meant pleasantness. The name had suited
their father, as it surely would suit his grandson.

It was morning in Philadelphia where Genia sat on Lisa's
lap and toyed with the phone cord while David shaved.
Always the happy intimacy of such moments startled her
and always she thought of how she owed them to her
mother. What if Elaine had not called David? The thought
caused her to shiver.

"No," Sarah disagreed. "I don't think she changed. I
think she became who she always was."

Lisa puzzled over her sister's words, pressed her cheek to
Genia's head, inhaled the sweetness of her daughter's newly
washed hair.

"What do you think she's decided?" Sarah asked.

"What do you think?"

They were on familiar turf now, playing the odds, offering each other alternatives but never relinquishing their
claims, their familiar girlhood jousting effortlessly resumed.

"She worked so well while she was staying with us,"

Sarah said. "And she enjoyed the children and the land-scape so much. I think she found a kind of peace here. It wouldn't surprise me if she decided to settle in Jerusalem."

"Can you see her accepting your kind of orthodoxy?" Lisa's voice was harsher than she intended.

"She wouldn't live in our community, of course," Sarah admitted. She did not tell her sister of Elaine's outburst at the seder table, of her own recognition that the beliefs she and Moshe shared would be forever alien to her mother. But now, at last, they understood each other, understood and acknowledged even that which they could not accept.

"But nearby, perhaps. Nearby. People live on many different levels in Israel." Her voice trailed off into a wistfulness that both saddened and irritated Lisa.

"Actually, I have the feeling she might opt for somewhere not too far from Philadelphia, close to us and close enough to New York so that she could pop over to the museums, to Mimi's gallery, to have lunch with Serena. She has a special bond with Genia," Lisa said carefully.

"As she does with Leora," Sarah retorted. "Uh-oh, we're doing it again," she said. "Playing who does Mommy love best?"

"Yes, we are, aren't we?" Lisa agreed and the sisters laughed, ease restored, doubts still unresolved.

Denis and Peter talked, the long-legged brothers restlessly roaming their homes as they spoke, shifting their cell phones from ear to ear, Denis filling a wineglass, Peter activating and then deactivating his e-mail.

"Mom loved New Mexico," Denis said. "She fit in so easily with the artist community here. And the climate's terrific for her."

"You know she and Lauren really bonded during her stay here," Peter countered. "And Lauren thinks she kind of has something going with Herb—you know, Lauren's dad."

Denis was silent for a moment.

"Yeah. I remember. He came to the gallery opening in Santa Fe. A great guy."

"They're good together," Peter said. "Not that anyone could ever replace Dad for her. But you know—they share the same grandchildren—"

"You win on that score. Andrew and I have no children to use as bargaining chips." Denis's voice was caustic.

"Hey, Denis—I didn't mean anything by that."

"I know. Sorry. I'm too sensitive."

Regret in one tone, resentment in the other. An uneasy hang-up and a quick call back.

"Look, whatever she decides, we'll be happy for her," Denis said. "The way she's happy for us—whatever we decide."

"Maybe she hasn't decided anything at all." But Peter's voice was doubtful and Denis remained silent.

Of course, their mother had come to a decision. A letter from her real estate broker lay on his desk. A fair price had been set for the house and there was considerable interest in the property.

The brothers talked to their sisters. The sisters to their

husbands. Denis talked to Andrew. Their speculations intensified. They asked cautious questions, knowing that
there were no answers to be had.

Sarah dreamed of her childhood in their sprawling home
and awakened weeping because the garden was stripped
bare of all flowers, her mother's herb beds disintegrated
into dust. The children of strangers slept in the room she
and Lisa had shared, a man and a woman whom she did
not recognize sat in her parents' chairs at either side of the
fireplace.

Lisa made dinner for David, preparing a cassoulet her
mother had always cooked only for their father but when
Genia wakened, she carried the child into the dining room
and Genia sat on her lap as they ate. She would not replicate those intimate dinners her parents had shared. She
thought of the candles that had flickered gently on a table
set for two, of the scent of new-cut flowers in the pale blue
bowl her mother had crafted.

"Too many memories in that house," she told David.

"Memories move with you," David replied gently. "Especially the good ones."

Peter and Lauren invited Herb Glasser to join them on
their trip to New York. A calculated invitation which did
not surprise him.

"Actually, I've thought about it but I want to run it past
Elaine," he said.

A day later he told them that Elaine had thought it was an
excellent idea and Peter and Lauren glanced at each other and
nodded, pleased that their hesitant complicity had prevailed.

Denis spoke to Andrew about the hikes he and his father had taken on wintry days and of how they had returned home to the welcoming warmth of the softly lit living room where a low fire blazed and his mother sat listening to music. What would happen to those two chairs that faced each other when the house was sold? he wondered and Andrew smiled indulgently.

"Perhaps we'll inherit them, you and I," he teased.

"I want those chairs," he said and the solemnity of his own tone surprised him.

By early June the work on the mosaic was completed. It would be installed in the portico of the new hospice wing of the hospital and Elaine accompanied Jack Newnham there one afternoon. They stood in silence, inhaling the aroma of the early blooming lilacs in the small Japanese garden that rimmed the newly constructed annex. She saw that sunlight sprayed the wall, bathing it in a gossamer radiance. If the mosaic was properly angled, those rays would burnish her enamel tiles and dance across the subtle glazes.

"We're planning to put a stone bench just opposite the mosaic," Jack said. "We'd like visitors to take a few minutes to sit there and study it, to understand it."

She nodded. She had, since the idea seized her and throughout the long months of working on it, seen her mosaic as a tribute to life, to Neil's life, a visual message of continuity. Perhaps it would bring comfort to those heart-sick visitors to the dying to know that lives were remembered, that vanished days were treasured, that families survived sorrow and loss and emerged into new seasons of joy and togetherness. She thought with pleasure of the circular tile she had fashioned with a microstylus for the center of the mosaic—Neil's grandchildren gathered in a circle, the older children surrounding Noam and Genia, the grandson and granddaughter welcomed to the family after his death.

"Thank you for giving me such a meaningful location for the memorial mural," Elaine told Jack Newnham. "He loved this hospital. He loved being a doctor."

"We miss him, you know," he said softly. "We miss you, too."

"But I'm here," she reminded him gently and took his hand in her own. "And, in a way, so is Neil."

Days later, she supervised the workmen who carefully cemented the mosaic into place. She herself affixed the small bronze plaque, its simple calligraphy of her own hand, its message lifted from her heart. *In Memory of Neil Gordon: Healer of Souls. Beloved Husband. Cherished Father and Grandfather. The Bonds of Love Are Stronger Than Death.*

She hurried home then. Her family would be arriving within a few days. There were arrangements to be made, borrowed futons and camp beds to be set up in the finished basement where the older children would sleep. Her grandchildren, the cousins plucked from their Jerusalem and California homes thrust into sharing and thus, she hoped, into friendship. She anticipated their awkwardness with each other. She prayed for their laughter. A neighbor lent her a crib for Noam and a trundle bed for Genia was set up in David and Lisa's room. Lisa had suggested that her family could go to a neighboring hotel but Elaine had been insistent that everyone stay in the house.

"It's important to me," she had said and they had not argued.

She drove back and forth to the artisan bakery, the organic farm, the butcher, the supermarket. For the first time in a year and half her refrigerator and freezer would be fully stocked. She looked with pleasure at the overflowing shelves and with even greater pleasure she began to cook, juggling her oversize pots, her huge casserole dishes, her food processor whirring as both her ovens slowly warmed and the fragrance of a spice-infused, simmering soup wafted through the room. She thought, wistfully, but without real regret, that she had always loved this kitchen.

And then her children arrived, family by family drifting in throughout the day. The tensions of their journeys, the apprehensiveness they had shared over the weeks, melted in the joy of their reunion. Sisters and brothers embraced. Peter threw his arms about Andrew's shoulders. Lisa cuddled Noam and when Genia, bewildered by the sudden rush of talk and laughter, burst into tears, Moshe wiped her eyes and spoke to her with great gentleness. Elaine showed Herb Glasser who had, after all, insisted upon staying at a hotel, around the house. He lingered in her studio and quickly left Neil's study. When they returned to the living room he carefully avoided Neil's chair but sat beside Lauren on the sofa.

Elaine rushed about, offering drinks, setting out platters of sandwiches, huge **bowls of** salad.

"The big dinner, the real dinner, will be tomorrow evening," she told them. "After."

After. The word hung heavily in the air. *After* the dedication of the mosaic. *After* she had told them of her decision.

They asked no questions. Tomorrow would come soon enough. For now, they were safe in the home of their childhood, all of them together, bonded by memory and their shared history. They smiled as the older children played the board games that had been theirs. There were still two deeds missing from the Monopoly game and they laughed at the substitute cards their father had fashioned. Colonel Mustard had vanished from the Clue box during a quarrel on a wintry afternoon and Elaine had crafted a new game piece, a twisted yellow bit of ceramic. They tried to remember the quarrel. Someone had cheated but they could not remember who.

"Denis," Andrew guessed. "Now and then he cheats at Scrabble."

"Only at desperate moments," Denis rejoined and they all laughed.

Elaine, seated in the kitchen opposite Herb Glasser, delighted in the sound of their laughter and then, almost immediately was seized by a spasm of sadness that caused her hands to tremble, her eyes to fill.

Herb refilled her coffee cup.

"It comes and goes," he said softly. "You think you are fine, that you are reconciled and then suddenly it hits you."

She nodded, grateful for his gentle recognition of her pain. He was a man who understood loss, a man who grieved still for a beloved wife, who dreamed still of a cherished son whose boyhood had ended in death.

"I am fine," she said. "I am reconciled. Most of the time."

"Most of the time is pretty good. It took me a long time to get to 'most of the time.' But you should get some rest. Tomorrow will be a difficult day."

"And tomorrow evening even more difficult."

Together, they rose from the table. Briefly, he placed his hands on her shoulders. She lifted her face to his and briefly, gently, his lips brushed hers and his fingers threaded their way through the tangled thickness of her silver-spattered hair.

She remained in the kitchen as he said goodbye.

"Drive carefully, Dad," she heard Peter say and it occurred to her that Peter had never called Lauren's father "Dad" while Neil was alive.

"Don't worry," Herb replied. "I don't want you kids worrying about me."

Elaine smiled. Neil would have liked Herb Glasser.

It had been Jack Newnham's suggestion that the dedication ceremony be held in the late afternoon.

"There will be people who want to come after their shifts are over," he had explained. "Hospital staff. Nurses. Other doctors."

Reluctantly, she had agreed. Initially she had wanted to invite only family and close friends, but Neil had belonged to a community of colleagues, men and women who had worked with him for many years. They had shared his hopes and ideas and they, too, felt his loss. She had supposed that some few of them would scavenge time from their busy schedules for the brief ceremony but she was unprepared for the small crowd that awaited them when they arrived at the hospital.

"So many people," she murmured to Lisa.

"A lot of people loved Dad," Lisa said softly.

"Let me fix your scarf."

Deftly Sarah adjusted the folds of the long paisley scarf that draped her mother's simple black dress and Lisa tucked a vagrant silver tendril into one of the tortoiseshell combs that held Elaine's thick hair back from her face. Elaine smiled. How swiftly adult daughters assumed maternal gestures, offered affection with touch and tone, roles reversed. It would be easy, she thought, to spend the rest of her life submitting to their ministrations.

"Elaine."

Lizzie Simmons, Neil's longtime secretary, embraced her.

"Lizzie. How wonderful of you to come."

"How could I not have come?" Lizzie asked and rejoined the small group of nurses, some still wearing the soothing pale green uniforms that Neil had introduced to the psychiatric floor. "Color counts," he had said. He was, after all, an artist's husband.

As though by tacit agreement, Neil's family assembled on the left, his children's hands linked, his older grandchildren smiling shyly, struggling against the impulse to dash

across the lawn of the Japanese garden and lift their faces
to the gentle spring wind. His colleagues gathered on the
right in uneasy groupings, their faces solemn, their voices
low, their smiles of greeting hesitant. Friends from the
neighborhood and the synagogue drifted in. The rabbi
who had officiated at Neil's funeral stood alone and briefly
Elaine wondered if she should have asked him to speak and
was immediately glad that she had not. This was not, after
all, a memorial service. This was a celebration of Neil's life.

Serena and Mimi Armstrong arrived together, both of
them wearing dresses of lemon-yellow linen, a coincidence which caused Elaine to smile in spite of herself.
They stood beside the two grave-eyed men and the three
women, one young, the other two middle-aged, who
averted their eyes from her glance. She did not recognize
them but she knew, intuitively, that they had been Neil's
patients, men and women whose confidences he had kept,
who had felt his kindness, benefited from his wisdom and
had come to honor his memory. She smiled at them and
they nodded, a silent mutuality of recognition.

At last Jack Newnham approached her, offered her his
arm and they walked to wall of the portico where a gauze-
like veil had been draped over the mosaic. Leora and
Renée, wearing identical white dresses and pink sandals,
trailed after them, each holding a pink carnation. They
smiled shyly. Neil's granddaughters from afar who would
long remember his gentle affection and an afternoon saturated with sunlight and memories.

Jack spoke briefly.

"Neil Gordon was our friend and our colleague," he said. "In life his presence was felt in so many areas of this hospital where he initiated a cutting-edge program of psychiatric intervention. He left us a remarkable legacy of compassion and kindness. And now Elaine, his wife, with her wisdom and talent, insures that his presence in these precincts of healing will endure. She has gifted us with a visual tribute to Dr. Neil Gordon's wonderful and useful life."

He nodded to Leora and Renée and the two small girls stepped forward and pulled lightly at the gauze veil which fluttered to the ground. The enamels sparkled in the sun's brightness, their polished surfaces aglow, each tender design bathed in radiance. There was an almost communal intake of breath as the assembled group leaned forward, struggling for a better view. They nodded, touched each other's hands, dabbed at their eyes.

Leora and Renée placed their flowers at the base of the mosaic.

Elaine bent to kiss her granddaughters and watched as they walked into the outstretched arms of their mothers. Then she began to speak, her voice trembling at first and slowly gathering strength.

"I think all of you know that Neil's death, coming as it did with such suddenness, was a shock for me and for our children. Eighteen months have passed since he died in this very hospital and in the Jewish tradition the number eighteen means *chai*, life. I have spent these last eighteen months traveling, spending time with my children—our children." Swiftly, she corrected herself and continued, "Revisiting vanished days, gleaning a new understanding of our shared past, new hope for our shared future. I thought about the many seasons of Neil's life and the legacy he left us. Each tile of this mosaic reflects such a season. There are the days of his earliest childhood in Russia where our granddaughter Genia was born and where our daughter Lisa married her David. There is the skyscape of Jerusalem where he rejoiced with Sarah and Moshe and their children, the rolling hills of California and the expanse of the New Mexico desert where he hiked with his sons, with Peter, and Lauren, his wife, with Denis and Andrew, his partner. I tried to capture, in form and in color, the serenity of the home we shared, the grace of the tree he planted in our garden, the calm of his consulting room. Above all I wanted to emphasize the sweetness and generosity of the life he lived. It was a life interrupted but it will be remembered always by the children and grandchildren he nurtured, by all who knew him and felt the blessings of his hands, the tenderness of his heart, the wisdom of his mind. Neil is gone from us but his message endures and his memory will be for a blessing. For all of us."

Her voice broke and she turned to look at the mural, at the sun-burnished work of her hands, the testament of her love. Peter and Denis, Lisa and Sarah, their hands linked, ascended the small platform and stood beside her. Their voices soft, their eyes moist, they intoned the Kaddish. Elaine herself remained silent until the final amen had been murmured. And then she found her own voice.

"L'Chaim," she said. "To life."

"*L'Chaim*. To life."

The gentle chorus resonated through the garden as the evening sun slowly descended and pastel-tinged clouds floated across the sky.

They gathered again around the large dining room table, set for this meal with the snow-white linen cloth always reserved for holiday meals, the crystal glasses sparkling, the silverware polished to a high gleam. Renée and Leora marveled at the pale blue dinner plates patterned with whimsical butterflies of Elaine's own design.

"They look like party plates," Renée enthused. "My friend had butterfly plates at her party. Are we having a party, Grandma?"

"Renée," Lauren said warningly but Elaine smiled.

"I suppose in a way we are. We're having a celebration. A celebration of all of us being together."

They relaxed then, the melancholy of the afternoon slowly lifting, as they savored the golden chicken soup, wiped up the children's spills, hurried in and out of the kitchen to help Elaine bring out the platters piled high with the favored foods of their childhood, chickens roasted to a crisp, brisket cloaked in mushroom and onions, potato and zucchini puddings. They ate fast and talked fast, each dish summoning up a memory.

"Remember how Dad made us draw lots for the drumstick at Thanksgiving?"

"Remember that holiday dinner when Sarah dropped the platter with the brisket?"

"It wasn't Sarah. It was Lisa," Denis recalled.

"It couldn't have been me. I never helped," Lisa retorted.

They laughed, carried empty dishes in the kitchen, refilled salad plates. Herb circled the table refilling water glasses. Eric spilled his juice, cried in embarrassment and was consoled by Lauren and Peter, the soothing cadences of their voices perfectly matched. Andrew took pictures, moving swiftly to capture Moshe cutting Renée's meat, Lisa cuddling Noam, Denis fashioning his napkin into an airplane causing Yuval, Ephraim and Leah to break out in wild laughter.

"Babies," Leora said contemptuously to Renée. The two older girls had formed a swift alliance. Already Renée had implored her mother to allow her to visit her cousin in Jerusalem and Lauren and Peter had glanced at each other and smiled, with the patience born of their new and magical togetherness.

Elaine, flushed with pleasure, stared down the long table, as though memorizing the bright faces of her grandchildren, mentally recording her children's laughter, their ease with her and with each other. She caught Herb Glasser's eye, registered his approving nod, his reassuring smile. She nodded back, smiled back, carried in the cakes, chocolate for Lisa and Sarah, apple for Peter and Denis, frosted cupcakes for the children, childhood preferences remembered and satisfied. Only then did she suggest that the children play in the garden.

"The swings are up. There are balls. Battered but still bouncing."

They scurried out, eager to race through the dying light of the long bewildering day, to play with the toys that had belonged to their parents, to toss the faded balls high into the branches of the tree and watch them bounce onto the hard leaf-shadowed earth.

Elaine refilled their coffee cups and her own, although she did not lift it to her lips. They were silent, the quiet of the room an expectant void that they waited patiently for her to fill.

"Mom, please." Denis spoke for all of them, his voice gentle, yet insistent.

"Yes. Of course." She took a single sip of the coffee, felt its bitterness upon her tongue. She had neglected to sweeten it. "I wanted you all to be together when I told you what I've decided. This will be the last time that we will all be together in this house, this home. I'm selling it to a wonderful young family, a doctor and his wife who have two young children. He worked with your father at the hospital. He and his wife, who is pregnant with their third child, love the house, love its history, or what they see as its history—by that I think they mean our family. The wife is a painter. I think the studio clinched it for them."

She looked at her children, saw how Moshe moved closer to Sarah, David to Lisa, how Lauren put her hand protectively on Peter's arm and how Andrew shifted position so that his shoulder brushed against Denis's. Gestures of reassurance against the impact of her words, reminders to the brothers and sisters that they were safe, their lives intact, sheltered by love, even as this house, the fortress of their childhood, was forfeit. Noam, who had been asleep in Sarah's arms, wakened then and cried softly. It seemed only natural that Herb take the baby from her and calm him while walking back and forth with a measured pace.

"I don't think any of you are surprised by this decision," she said softly and one by one they nodded in assent.

"I think each of us assumed as much," Peter affirmed, speaking for all of them. "None of us liked the idea of your living here alone. We worried. It's sad, of course. We've all loved this house just as you and Dad did but you're doing the right thing."

Again they nodded. They were in agreement. Their mother's decision had been inevitable. They looked at each other, each of them recalling her visits to their homes, her transient incursions into their lives, the truths that had been revealed, the hurts too long held secret exposed and healed. They had felt her yearning, recognized her strength, and matched it with their own.

"How is she? How does she seem?" they had asked each other, speaking from Jerusalem and Los Angeles, Santa Fe and Moscow, never acknowledging that they really meant "What has she decided? Who has hit the jackpot in the lottery of maternal affection?" Would the haunting question of childhood ever be resolved? "Mirror, mirror on the wall, who is the best loved child of us all?" Ruefully they acknowledged that it should no longer matter. And yet it lingered teasingly.

It was Sarah who asked the question, speaking so softly that they strained to hear her.

"But where will you live, Mom?"

They clasped and unclasped their hands, sat more erect, their eyes fixed on their mother's face.

"There's a community almost at the northern border of the county. A development really, but quite a beautiful one. It's not a retirement village. I wouldn't want that. I'm hardly ready to retire. Younger families live there but there are many residents who are my age, a bit younger perhaps, a bit older perhaps, but everyone active and quite friendly. I visited several times. Alone and with Serena. She's considering a smaller unit there but I've already closed on a town house. I think you'll all love it. Three bedrooms and a large den so there's plenty of room for visitors—overnight or long term. There are lots of windows so the light is wonderful, and a big kitchen." Her voice gathered strength, grew vibrant with a new excitement. "I have some terrific ideas about how to furnish it. Lots of blues in the living room. Cream-colored drapes perhaps."

Her enthusiasm dazed them. They tried to imagine her in an unfamiliar room, in a home that would belong only to her, looking out at a landscape she had not shared with their father.

"You closed on it? Alone?"

Denis, the lawyer, skilled at closings, aware of the perils of real estate deals, was astonished.

"With a lawyer, of course." She flashed him a reassuring smile. "Reputable. Referred by the Realtor, vetted by an attorney at the hospital. It just had to be done quickly. Someone else was interested in the house."

"But your work. Where will you work?" Sarah asked.

"Ah—there's a huge studio in the development. Fully fitted. Worktables, potter's wheels, kilns. I'll move the oven for my enamels there. I've been asked to teach workshops and I'm going to try it."

"It sounds wonderful." Lisa spoke with an approving firmness. "But just how rural is the development?"

They cringed at the word but Elaine smiled.

"Rural enough but close to major highways. And thus to airports," she replied teasingly.

"Convenient for both the boarding of planes and the meeting of them," Herb Glasser said.

They turned. They had all but forgotten his presence in the room, all but forgotten his odd and undefined role in their mother's life. They turned and smiled at Lauren's grave-eyed father, the tall man, slightly stooped now, his iron-gray hair tousled by Noam's small hands. They acknowledged finally what they had each supposed might be the case. Herb Glasser would be their mother's sometime companion. They would await each other at terminals and they would, perhaps board planes together. Lauren rose and went to stand beside her father, to kiss him on the cheek, to smile as he placed his large hand on her head.

"Good for you, Mom. You did it."

Sarah's softly spoken words encompassed all their thoughts. They had each wanted to lay claim to their mother but they recognized, with admiration and gratitude, that she had reclaimed her own life. She had, through the long months since their father's death, urged them each toward difficult choices and now her own choice has been made. Their disappointment was assuaged. Their pleasure was palpable.

Moshe lifted his water glass.

"*L'Chaim,* Elaine. To your new life."

For the second time that day, the word was repeated in a soft and melodic chorus.

"*L'Chaim.*"

Elaine smiled and gently took Noam from Herb. She walked with him to the large picture window and looked out at the garden where her grandchildren dashed after a large red ball. She remembered the sunswept afternoons when she and Neil had stood together at this very window and watched their own children at play. She cuddled Noam, the child named for Neil, her Jerusalem-born grandson whose name meant pleasantness. She looked into his eyes, deep-set and agate-blue—Neil's eyes.

"Noam," she whispered. "Neil. My Noam. My Neil."

Tears she had not anticipated streaked her cheeks. Denis came to stand beside her.

"Are you all right, Mom?" he asked.

"I'm fine," she said. "Just fine."

She held Noam closer and realized that she spoke the truth.

About the Author

Gloria Goldreich is the critically acclaimed author of several national bestselling novels, including *Walking Home, Dinner with Anna Karenina* and *Leah's Journey,* which won the National Jewish Book Award for Fiction. Her stories have also appeared in numerous magazines, such as *McCall's, Redbook, Ms.* and *Ladies' Home Journal.* Gloria and her family live in Tuckahoe, New York.

Award-winning author
Gloria Goldreich

*"And the worst of it is, you understand,
that I can't leave him:
there are the children, and I am bound.
Yet I can't live with him..."*

The words from *Anna Karenina* resonate with the women who have gathered over good food and wine for their first book club meeting of the year. These six very different women are not quite friends, not quite strangers, but bonded by their love of literature, they share a deep understanding of one another—or so they think.

"In lyrical prose, Goldreich offers a sad yet hopeful tale of a woman whose personal tragedy ultimately yields to greater self-awareness and deeper happiness."
—*Booklist* on *Walking Home*

DINNER WITH ANNA KARENINA

*Available the first
week of October 2008
wherever books are sold!*

www.MIRABooks.com